LESBIAN HUSTLER'S

CHAUNCEY

BALBOA.
PRESS
A DIVISION OF HAY HOUSE

Balboa Press books may be ordered through booksellers or by contacting:

Balboa Press
A Division of Hay House
1663 Liberty Drive
Bloomington, IN 47403
www.balboapress.com
1 (877) 407-4847

Printed in the United States of America.

ISBN: 978-1-4525-9818-5 (sc)
ISBN: 978-1-4525-9819-2 (e)

Balboa Press rev. date: 12/16/2014

A BIG SHOUT OUT TO ALL MY PEEPS

FOR MY MOMMY MARYJANE FOWLKES. SHE PASSED AWAY SEPTEMBER 18, 1970. I MISS YOU VERY MUCH. TIME HAS NOTHING ON MISSING YOU AND WISHING YOU WERE HERE TO SHARE MY JOURNEY I AM DEDICATING THIS BOOK TO YOU FIRST. YOUR ALWAYS IN MY HEART..

FOR MY OLDEST BROTHER TERRANCE MCMICHAEL (SILKY-TEE) WHO HAS ALSO PASSED AWAY OCTOBER 9, 1995. I LOVE YOU.

I WANT TO THANK MY DAD CLYDE MCMICHAEL (POPPA THE STOPPA) FOR BEING THERE THE BEST WAY HE KNEW HOW.

I LOVE YOU DEARLY MY SISTERS BRENDA MAYO, VASEAH AND YVONNE (SMILEY) MCMICHAEL AND MY BROTHER RONNIE MCMICHAEL. MY NIECES AND NEPHEWS. YOU ALL ARE VERY MUCH LOVED BY ME. GOD BLESS YOU ALL.

TO THE TWO MOST WONDERFUL PEOPLE WHO HAVE HELPED ME THROUGH THICK AND THIN WITH THIS BOOK. I COULD NOT HAVE DONE THIS WITHOUT THEM. I AM SO GRATEFUL TO THEM. MY BEST FRIEND IN THE WHOLE WIDE WORLD, LOUISE PITCHER AND MS. SHELLEY BEHRMANN.

ALSO... A WONDERFUL SHOUT OUT TO INCARCERATED FRIENDS AND OFFICERS. YOU ALL KNOW WHO YOU ARE...

PROLOGUE

THE SUMMER OF 2010

ME AND MY GIRLS, THE Lesbian Crew ("TLC"). We're all straight up gay girls from the womb. Niggas couldn't understand us at all because none of 'em could comprehend our preferences. They tried to break on us and voicefu1ly beat our pussies. There are three of us and trust and believe we ride and die together protecting each other to the fullest no matter what, whether or not one of us is right or wrong.

The coldest bitch is Vah. She is 24, Africa-American and Cuban, with sweet looking chocolate skin, hazel eyes and dreads halfway down her back; she's 5'2", 34B and fly as hell.

She is like a slithering snake, just because you are not a part of TLC, which is tattooed on each of their necks.

Jaia is Dominican and German. She's sexy, flirtatious and into dildos; she will dildo your asshole to death. Jaia's all about the Benjamin's. She has light brown eyes and is 32 - 24-36 and, like the Connnodores song, a Brickhouse.

Aunya is 21, Asian and Puerto-Rican and is always fully loaded, smoking weed and looking to fuck a bitch in a minute to show a bitch what her hand ca1ls for, for fucking with her. She has light brown eyes looks like a man with 360 wave haircut that'll make a bitch seasick. Females flock to her.

We all decided it was time to get out of corny ass Washington Heights and start a hustle by any means necessary. We needed a new scenery and decided Albany would be the place. We heard a coupla niggas from the block mention how they work and were making money quick and easy. So fo sho our motto on our journey to get rich was "Get Rich, Get Paid, Fuck'em Hard and Kill' em in the Process."

CHAPTER ONE

WE ARRIVED IN ALBANY ALL packed with what we needed to start our hustle; we had three kilos of pure cocaine. We were paranoid like a motherfucker driving with Aunya smoking her weed and music blasting; hoping no got dam State Trooper pulled us over. Plus Jaia had taken the cocaine from her uncle Tito.

Vah kept saying, “We'll just blast the motherfucker. We got shit to do and I'm a motherfuckin' assassin, bitches. True story. We gonna make our money. All heads gotta go fo sho You feel me bitches? I'm hot and ready to blow. Now, we need a jump off to kick shit in this town. Let's get to thinking bitches.”

No sooner did we try to devise a plan and we saw homeboy in a black Denali with 22” chrome rims. He was profiling with a Kool-Aid smile for attention. Little did the motherfucker know we needed to use his dumb ass. He was waving his hand saying, “Yo, Shorty, let me holla at ya.” We all pointed at ourselves thinking' *this nigga got to be kidding.'* We debated on who would reel in this nigga.

Jaia agreed with a real quickness and said, “Let me holla. With my looks he'll tell his mannna's bank account number. I will fuck his head up in his Denali. Trust me bitches, it's time to get paid. Watch me bitches. I got money on my mind and a nigga ain't one of ‘ern.”

Jaia says to him “Hey Cutie Man, what's your name and does it ring bells anywhere I should know?”

“Yeah Shorty, my name rings bells, chimes, alarm clocks and any other bells you can think of. Ma Bell sell love. My name is Da-Stev. What's yours, Ma?

“My name is Jaia and these are my right hand, left hand bitches I ride with *2417,* Vah and Aunya. We just got into town looking to rest our heads in peace for the night. Do you know where there's a motel, hotel where we can chill without the rah-rah in it, Da-Stev?”

"Sure Shorty," said Da-Stev.

"Yo, Da-Stev, my name is Jaia, not Shorty, so let's get that covered. I ain't one of your hood rats on crack, OK nigga? Now get us to our destination, Da-Steve," said Jaia.

"Okay Jaia check this. There is a Hampton Inn over on Wolf Road and it's one bill and change a night. It's quiet and you'll sleep in peace. Follow me Ladies." *Whoa, those bitches ridin' lovely and they look pa-pow.* True Story, Da-Stev said to himself.

TLC, sportin' a bright red Range Rover, followed Da-Stev to the Hampton Inn. They registered and received their room key pass on the fifth floor. Aunya and Vah shared a room and Jaia had her own plans for reeling Da-Stev in for the night. As everyone settled in, Da-Steve waited patiently in the lobby of the hotel. Da-Stev had plans to be with Jaia. His dick got hard thinking of how he was going to sex Jaia with the tip of his dick. He was 8" long and new that all females like a long, hard, stiff dick. His dick grew another two inches just thinking about dogging a bitch out, like Jaia. He felt his dick lashing out something terrible, so he had to have her, most definitely.

Jaia's room was next door to Vah's and Aunya's. They knew she had plans and were cracking up at the shit she had in store for Da-Stev.

ah said, "I can see that motherfucker cummin' and crying."

"Yeah, and hollering for jaia," Aunya added.

They hollered, laughing their asses off. Meanwhile, Jaia went to the lobby and asked DaStev if he'd like to come to her room. He obliged. They took the elevator to the fifth floor. DaStev's dick was so hard that it was about to bust at the tip. He started poppin' some ole macho shit like he was a real big time Willie Bo Bo character.

He said, "Yeah, a lot of shorties be trying to holla at a nigga. I ain't feelin', em, ya feel me Jaia? It can be about you and me, Boo. Ya feel me? I find you very sexy and attractive, in which you'd do a nigga summin' good on his arm and ridin' shotgun in my Denali *2417* Jaia, all at my expense. Holla back at a nigga. How about that, Jaia?"

Alright, Da-Stev, I'll holla when we're in the room where it's comfortable to conversate, OK?"

As soon as they reached the room, Da-Stev started feelin' himself like he was in total control sexing Jaia. Jaia was like "Hold the fuck nigga. First of all, you ain't put no dime in this motherfucking pot to be rolling up in here in my room, like you been up in this pussy, Boy! This is my domain and I'm controlling this whole fucking scenery, Boyee."

Da-Stev got heated at her words. He said, "So, bitch, what you think? I'm up in this here room to sleep? Hell, nah, I want some of that pussy, Ma."

"Nigga, please. Listen Da-Stev, I need some infonnation about getting' my hustle on.

So, can you give me some locations of the people to interact with on this hustling tip?"

"Yea, Ma. What's in it for me other than when 1 decide to give you some of this big dick, Ma. Ok, check it Jaia, I'll run you over to a couple a spots on the block and hook you up with sum peeps so you can see how shit rolls from the top. Then I'll run you over to Clinton Ave. and Lexington Ave., over by the police station and the courthouse. So, basically if you fuck around in that bitch ass area, it's like go directly to jail, Ok?" Da-Stev continued, "Over on Swan Street, there's this chick called Smiley. She is a bad bitch. She had Swan Street sewed up for years. Her right hand man is Brickman. That motherfucker is fucking huge and the nigga's hard body in anything Smiley demands. He'll kiss the tip of her stiletto heel. True story, Ma. Nigga will die for Smiley."

Jaia thought to herself, *It's time to go, pronto! Kille'm dead."*

Da-Stev was scheming on Jaia's pussy at the same time, although he knew he'd have to take her, Vah, and Aunya around Swan Street before he got any sexing from Jaia. He told Jaia he would pick them up in the morning and stated to Jaia, "Ma, it's all good with me and you, right? Go for your jump off fo sho."

"Yeah nigga," Jaia said, "love you Daddy straight like that." Jaia thought, *"Dead in your ass, BoBo.*

* * *

The following morning we all got our gear and shit together for another busy day. Jaia had given Vah and Aunya the run down on the bullshit. Da-Steve relayed to her what was going on, on Swan Street, Da-Stev arrived at the hotel at IO:OOam. and had the receptionist page Jaia.

He said, "Y'all ladies ready to roll for the cause of getting paid?" They replied, "Sho ya right my nig. Let's do this. First we gotta get your grub on and then it's all good in the hood."

They all ended up at IHOP on Wolf Road. Everybody ate until their bellies were full as they had a full day ahead. Who would think of eating later?

As they exited IHOP, Aunya saw this cutie and hollered at her. "Yo, Ma, are you straight or can I get a date?" The female replied "What's your name Love?"

"Aunya."

"Mine is Coco, Boo and if ya wanna halla, here's my cellie, Aunya."

"Whoa, you're fine as hell girl. Where you rest, Love"

"Right now I'm over at the Hampton Inn, Aunya." Aunya continued, "I just got into Albany yesterday with my homegirls. This is Vah and Jaia. Everyone this is Coco. Oh, and this is Da-Stev. Right now we gotta make some moves Ma, so I'll hit you up later, OK? Maybe we can make something happen for sure Boo, cause I do wanna get with you. Holla back. One. Here's my cell number."

Vah and Jaia were all up in Aunya's grill.

They stated, "Dam Aunya, you a thirsty bitch. Just cause she looks good don't mean she's any good."

Aunya replied, "Fuck ya hoes. This is my rap sheet bitches, don't hate. Y' all bitches know ya sure can participate. Hatin' Hoes." They all laughed in unison.

Da-Stev said, "What the fuck just happened? Are you on some ole freaky Jason shit, Aunya? I got some ole freak ass bitches that'll suck your clit off, Boo."

"Yo nigga, we ain't here for your info on her shit. Mind your motherfuckin' business. True that." Jaia said. "Now let's get the real shit poppin ASAP, MOTHERFUCKA"

TLC followed Da-Stev in their fly ass Range Rover. They headed for Swan Street, Low and behold, Ms Smiley and her nigga Brickman were holding down the block. We pulled up behind Da-Stev and all eyes were on the new chicks on the block. Da-Stev made his rounds to his homies Kevin, De-La, Preston-n-Sam. All were playing Ce-Low.

"See how low ya monies go," one of them hollered. Then there was this stank ass hoe named Adrianne; Da-Stev used to fuck her in the mouth. She seen TLC get out of the Range Rover. She was all fucked up with a crummy ass attitude, but Vah caught the vision and stepped to it with a quickness.

"Bitch, yo eyes see summin, ya heard so break off hoe. These sights are not for your eyes. Recognize bitch," stated Vah.

Adrianne responded "Where y'all bluebell hoes stepping to on this block? Ain't enough room for no hoes that git cold."

Vah stated, "Bitch the only hoe gittin' cold is your Raggety Ann-hair-weaving-sour lookin' -ass bitch. So what's good hoe? Step to your business. Come see me if you're sure you're shit is proper bitch."

Vah had the box cutter ready and a razor in her mouth. She thought if this bitch even mumbles one more word, even if it's the word "he" or "it", I'ma commence to slicing or scratching her face with my razor, fo sho Instead, Aunya jumped and cold cocked and knocked that bitch out. Face first she hit the ground. Motherfuckers looked like "What the fuck just happened?" Jaia yelled, "That's my bitch. That's what I'm talking about. She laid that stank ass out like alight."

"Yo, shit is banging," shouted Auyna, "that bitch is still dreaming. Let her lay so she can wake up to this foot in her ass."

Niggas on the block were like, "Who the fuck are they?" Da-Stev was like, "These are my peeps and they're on the come up."

Ms. Smiley agreed and stated, "All transactions are final."

From what just happened, Ms. Smiley thought, *"wow these bitches got heart and are all about getting paid. Their game is tight and just between them. I'ma need them for some death warrant shit. I like 'em and they are cruel. That girl Aunya knocked Adrianne to fuck out.*

Homegirl put her foot in that ass in broad fuckin 'daylight on motherfuckin' Swan Street. That's the fuck it."

Ms. Smiley then said, "Ladies, it's my pleasure to introduce myself personally. I'm Ms. Smiley. Call me Smiley. I think we need to discuss business."

"After that introduction to Swan Street, y'all bitches is off the chain," said Da-Stev. Da-Stev introduced Vah, Jaia and Aunya to Smiley and Brickman. Fuck everybody else on the block for now. He took 'em straight to the Top Dawg!

* * *

Uncle Muff stated, "I just met her sitting here getting my drink on. We started conversating about rap artists and shit. I like Fifty-Cent, she likes Three Six Mafia." Jaia said with a smart ass remark, "So what's the fuckin' point?"

Vah said, "Yo, bitch, what the fuck has gotten into your ass? If ya ass is a little tipsy bitch, then maybe I outta take ya ass home." She said, "Nah. I want Unc to take me, when I decide to leave. A'ight, Vah? 1f she'd like, it's okay."

Uncle Muff said, "It's almost that time for me anyway."

Vah, "Don't let Jaia be rushing you and shit. Me and this bitch. came here on a. whim, Unc. Plus, I'ma finish my shit, ya bullshitting. Yo, come on y'all, let's dance, shake our asses for a minute. Ya feel me. Hey!" They were all dancing to Whitney Houston, "It's My Pride." They were doin their thang.

Amy's dancin' with Vah, Jaia with Unc. She started pressing up against Unc all seductively, letting her know she's feeling her. Unc knew since the day they were all at the mall. She was also catching feelings for Jaia, but she felt that it would somehow intervene with the business relationship. Although she bit her fingers thinking, *'this bitch is gorgeous and tempting. Aw fuck, J'aia tap that twat fo sho She do not have to go far for good lovin', cause I'ma put it on her lovely. Yeah, she dam sure got the right motherfuckin one. I just have to set that being family thought shit aside. I want some of that. I hope her pussy is as good as she looks, cause I'ma tear that ass up.'*

Jaia'swhispering all in Unc's ear, "Ya know I'm feeling you a'ight, with your fine. Ass self, boo. I'm sort of attracted to your style. It's very suave, ya know, nice toned body. Your arms are very muscular, strong enough to hold me at bay, babe. Huh!" "Sho, ya right," Unc responded with a proud smile, then she said "Listen, Jaia, I'm not tryin to rush into any sexual activities with ya ma, so soon, but if ya ready and you're sure, we can make it happen rna, with the utmost pleasure to be enjoyed, boo. Ya feel me? I want you to feel me literally, ma. You know you got my clitoris thumping,. love."

Jaia said to Unc, "I'm all wet inside, waiting for you to take this pussy, so it can feel the tenderness of your tongue, boo. My juices are waiting to be tasted, Unc. 'You ready for Jaia's punanny, Unc?" She laughed so seductively.

Vah, Jaia and Aunya became familiar with the drug-infested area of Albany. Their names started gettin' clout in the hoods with the help of Ms. Smiley. Their shit was poppin' like gum with big bubbles of champagne to comfort their hustling flow. All was good in the hood after being on the set for a good month. The TLC decided to try and get some workers over on Morton Avenue in the courtyard. Vah had hooked up with this girl named Uncle Muff. The bitch was straight up sick in the fuckin' head. Vah asked her why they call her Uncle Muff. She entailed that it ain't none of her fucking business and she don't give a fuck why they call her Vah. Crazy ass nut. One thing Vah could say about Uncle Muff was she loved herself some alcohol. She'd drink anything with no shame to her game. She'd drink until the bitch got comatose. When she was in her intoxicating mode, fucking with her was like an all night war.

Then her stupid ass would get tired and she'd conk the fuck out and it would be the fuck over, for sho Vah kinda really took a liking to Uncle Muff because she handles her shit proper. Also the fact that she is straight up gay. No bullshit. Everything about Uncle Muff was sexy. She was full-figured with light brown eyes, caramel complexion, toned body and muscular. When Uncle Muff was partying, she'd dance all night. One thing fo sho is she loves having fun, sober or drunk. She is a versatile bitch. The money was being made and everything was coming so fast over the courtyard. Uncle muff was handling shit like a Commander in Chief. That's when she took full and total control.

She put on one of her peeps, a so-called Lt. Amadeus. He definitely wasn't anything to play with. Especially when it came to getting his paper. Fucking with Uncle Muff was a no-no. She was his Number One Love. Although she was gay, Amadeus always figured he'd be the first nigga to bust her cherry. He despised Vah just thinking she has a thing for Uncle Muff. Every time they were trying to handle business you could feel the bad vibe in the air. Uncle Muff began getting tired of Amadeus' antics when Vah was present because she did not like Vah in that manner at all. It was all about the paper, so sooner or later she was going to have to get rid of Amadeus. He was fucking up her bread and butter and acting like he was fucking her. On the strength of Vah, Uncle Muff really did not want the motherfucker terminated. He's a good hustler, but at the same time he's fucking up her shine. She likes to glitter without having to think of a bitch or a man wanting to crowd her space. It infuriates her mood being around him. Seriously.

Jaia was waiting in the basement patiently. She heard them enter the door upstairs, walking to the basement and coming down the steps. She could hear Black bragging about the damage he intended to do to her. He was saying how she was going to beg him to be her Daddy.

He *said* she'd have his dick in her mouth while he's pulling her hair and screaming for her life to be put on hold for another chance and she'll leave Albany or die instantly. Kevin and De-La agreed as if they were all in it to the end. When he reached the bottom of the *stairs* he saw Jaia sitting there all pretty and calm.

"I've been waiting for your arrival Black," Jaia stated calmly.

In an instant De-La put his 9mm to Black's head to shoot this sucker ass chump. He'd been got, let along being set up by one of his bosses' clientele. Her main money maker tied that cheap trick up to the chair after stripping him of his gear. "Take what ya want. He won't be needing his attire anymore. Trust me. After this treatment, we won't hear from good ole boy for sum time. He'll be too humiliated and embarrassed to show his mug on the streets again," stated Jaia. He was naked and Jaia had an extension cord and dipped it in a bucket of water. She then started beating him in his chest and his legs while his feet were on broken glass. Kevin took out a hammer and began hammering nails through his feet. Jaia was yelling in his ear, "Ah-ha boy.

You had plans for a bitch like me huh? What now son? I can't hear you. You're screaming like summin' you said I'd be doing. Well, motherfucker, I want you to beg like a crack head for a crumb. Sucker ass nigga." She hauled off and slapped the bejesus out of his ass. She was really starting to get violently hyped. She said, "Lay that bastard on his stomach."

All of a sudden two faggots came in looking like football players.

Jaia said, "OK guys, do what you do and cum all in him and fuck his mouth."

Preston had slapped so much Vaseline up in Black's ass and spread his ass cheeks so everyone could see how tight it was. And boy, it was tight, tight. Preston then started with his tip entering Black" ass.

Black begged and pleaded, "Please Jaia, we ain't got to go out like this, Ma. Please. Oh no, please."

Preston kept putting the pressure to his ass with his dick.

Jaia said, "Hold up. Let me do a lil' surnmin' summin'."

She told Preston to hold Black's ass cheeks apart. Then she took her shoe, an expensive Prada stiletto and rammed the heel in his ass.

So all went well and Vah was happy camper. It had been about three months the TLC has been in Albany and everything is alright on the front.

Jaia called Aunya over to S. Main where she took the liberty of finding a nice four bedroom flat. They all had their own privacy and a guest room for company. It was their stash house in a very discreet neighborhood. No one knew about it except he TLC. Money was coming out of the fucking woodwork. The clientele was starting to really pick up as far as Albany, NY. I mean shit was trippin' with nothin' but weight galore. Jaia, Vah and Aunya each made their transport trips one time a week copping from Ms. Smiley. They started flowing in money, especially with Vah's shit in the courtyard.

* * *

Jaia started her flow over by First and Judson. Boy, this bitch loved the rah-rah scenery. She had it locked the fuck up. Niggas were hating on this bitch because she had it cheap and it was good. It was the best shit niggas had in a while. They had to respect her game. Although one nigga wanted her fucked, raped and brake her down, knowing she was a straight up lesbian. His name was Black. He'd been doing his thing for years, so he felt like this bitch came and stepped on his man hood. As a result, he tried to set J aia up with these niggas from Swan Street. He didn't know she knew he paid the niggas $10,000 a piece. He wanted them to kidnap and blindfold her so he could have his pleasure of plunging his piece of dick in her hard to bust her shit. Oops! Nothing happening. Once the guys were paid off, Kevin and Le-La reported it to the one and only Ms. Smiley, she cellied Jaia's and relayed the set-up.

"Ooh shit," Jaia responded, "thanks Smiley. Now you know a bitch gotta live and do what she gotta do. I kinda felt funny around that nigga, so he wants me fucked and raped. OK Smiley, tell Kevin and De-La to tell that pussy ass bitch Black they have me captured and on Lexington in the basement, tied and blindfolded. They'll know where the spot is. Yo tell 'em to see Black though. Holla back one."

"Now it's an open start boys. Phew! That was a thrill. Fucker," stated Jaia.

Fonso said, "C' momma, let me show you how easy my pecan stick can cream ya insides.

Oooh, oooh, oooh."

Black continued to scream in agony. Fonso pumped away on his ass like he'd ride a bull. Soon he began to bust a nut! Then Preston came with a twelve inch dildo with a sandpaper wrapped around it. He shoved it right in his ass like he was plunging a toilet. Blood was oozing out of Black's ass.

Fonso said, "Let's make him suck sum dick."

Black said, "Kill me motherfucker. Ain't nobody getting their dick sucked."

Jaia said, "Well, I guess you'd like to eat some fresh pussy, huh?"

"If that's what you want Ma. Come let me show you the feeling of some real good pussy eating." Black said. Jaia then told Black to crawl to her sweet candy pussy. Black did as he was told as Jaia made an attempt to pull her pants down. She hit Black in the head with a hammer. Bam. Black hollered.

Jaia said, "Take this piece of shit and spread his ass out in the middle of the street on Lexington Avenue, between Orange and Clinton. That's where all the so-called ballers and players he rolls with be. Also, shoot his ass up with some heroin. This way he'll nod on his sorry ass. Then kill 'em after everybody on the block gets a good view of the new black ass, Black."

Yo, the whole block looked back at Black in the middle of Lexington Avenue. All the drug dealers, crack-heads, boosters, and DVD sellers. Everyone was stunned. "Oh shit, look at that nigga Black. Oh Dawg, my nig Black. Who'd he do dirty to deserve his asshole scraped the fuck out," this dude Sam stated.

Munchie, who is one of Black's skeezer's, came over to look at his closer. She spit on his ass and said, "You bitch ass, no fucking dick, bastard. I see you finally got yours. You fucking prick! Ha, ha, ha," she laughed, "you down and finished bitch."

BANG, BANG. She shoot him dead in the head and kept it moving right along, as everyone else did once the show was over.

"That's sad," one senior citizen said as she passed by through the block.

CHAPTER TWO

Meanwhile, Jaia, Kevin and De-La were telling Smiley word for word what was done on the block Smiley said, "See these cats come up and can easily be put down, fucking with the hustle.

Bet that. Sooner or later you git got or got git. Either way something always coming at you. It's up to you to handling yours, like ya crazy ass just did."

Jaia said, "I fee! ya Boo-boo. It's all good in the hood. Now let's get back to business like we know we should. All ears hustle in the street. Keep me posted, fam. I'm out."

TLC met back at the stash house. Everyone agreed to start putting money aside to open up a legitimate business. A gay club; lesbians wall to wall.

Aunya said, "Well, Coco mentioned this hot club in Cohoes called Big C's. So let's check out the scenery there and get an idea of who's who in the club. So are we ridin' tonite to spread some of these partying ways, ladies? Let's have fun, relax and enjoy the bitches, honies and hoes getting' our freak on. Oh, I'll be freakin' with Coco, and hopefully, all night long until the break of dawn."

They all started getting ready to decide what they were going to wear. Yah's attire consisted of navy blue tank top and a pair of Docker's with a Calvin Klein belt and fresh new Timberlands. She figured she'd be leisurely for a night instead oflooking thuggish. Aunya wore sky blue Sean John sweat suit and a pair of Tupac Macavelli sneakers. Jaia had to wear something to attract attention. That's what she thrives on, gracefully. Her attire consisted of Apple Bottom Jeans, Baby Phat pair of stilettos and a white wife beater. Her body was so toned and luscious.

They all began their night of hanging out at Big C's. As they arrived, Coco showed them to the door. There was a twenty dollar cover charge. The woman at the door mentioned to them about Happy Hour. They arrived at 11 :30pm and the music was pumpin'.

Vah said, "This shit is kosher, yo."

"Dam sure is," Jaia responded, "Aunya's flying off at the hinges at the wall to wall lesbians. She's in heaven. She's mesmerized something terrible."

"Everybody in the club git typsy," said Jaia.

"When shit is on I gotta dance" said Vah. "They playing my song, 'The Steppin' Song" by R. Kelly."

Everybody followed in movement to the music on the dance floor upstairs. Coco ordered the drinks.

Aunya said, "I *also* want a bottle of Crista1."

The bartender, Chauncey, looked and said, "Hi, I'm the owner and it's a pleasure to serve you. I hope you have a wonderful night. I'll have one of my waiters bring your Cristal and drinks upstairs to you, beiug you have expensive taste. Ms...? I am sorry, I did not get your name."

"My name is Coco," Coco replied. "Very nice to meet you. OK, I am going to enjoy the sights of this cozy club. Later."

As Coco went upstairs to join everyone, she bumped into this real stocky aggressive butch. They both said at the time, "Oh, excuse me, I'm very sorry."

Coco said, "Sorry Miss."

The woman looked at Coco. Her thoughts were *'dam baby, what are you working with, Ma? She is a gorgeous bitch. I gotta get with that somehow, someway.'*

So she went up to Coco and said, "Hi. My name is Free-Free. May I buy you a drink Ms. Lady and possibly have a dance with ya before the night is out? Dam, am I asking for too much? Stop me, please."

"No, you're not Free-Free. The night is still young. I can't help it if I look that dam good. Anyway girl, I am with some associates over by the bar, love. If you'd like I can introduce you to them. That's if you're okay with it Free-Free. Come on, Ma." They made their way across the dance floor to where, Jaia, Vah and Aunya were.

"Yo, Coco, who that be with you" Aunya shouted because the music was so loud.

"Everyone, this is Free-Free," said Coco.

All were introduced. So far the night was fun and enjoyable.

"Oh shit, they're playing my motherfucking jam. To the window, to the wall until sweat runs down my balls, all you bitches crawL"

"Ahh, skeet, skeet, skeet, skeet, ahh skeet, skeet, skeet, skeet, skeet, skeet," Everyone said in unison. The night turned out to be a blast. Everyone was twisted, feeling good.

Aunya said to Coco, "Do you wanna chill with me tonight at the crib, Baby?" Coco said, "Nah, I'm good. I'ma let Free-Free drive me home, Boo. Well everyone it's a beautiful night ladies, but I got to go. I got a 9-5 and it's 3:45am. A couple of winks then I'm off to live the plain Jane life once more."

"Ahh, Coco," Jaia said, "It's a bummer. Well, next time we can hang until the break: of dawn kid. It's a pleasure girl and thanks for showing us out here to the only lesbian joint. It's really nice girl Hope to see ya soon, Coco. Later."

Free-Free said her goodnights to all. She asked Coco if she was ready and Coco responded, "Yes," and they were outtie. Aunya was feeling some type of way with Coco leaving with Free-Free because they all came together.

Why would she be so disrespectful, Aunya thought. 0 well, fuck that skeezer, she does not know what she is missing out on and just to think I kinda felt a little summin' snmmin' for her.

Vah was talking to this Italian chick all night and dancing. Her name was Laurie. She had jet black hair, cute shape, funny as hell, and by looking at her she was all into Vah, seriously. Dam, you would have thought they came in this motherfucker together. Laurie was just rambling on about how she loved Vah's dreads.

"So, Vah, you got a partner," she asked.

"No, and I'm not really in the market for anyone. I just came out to have fun and check out the club. So far it's cool and I've met a pretty stud muffin as yourself. I kinda took a liking to you, Laurie. So let me get your number Babe, and I'll call you throughout the week to hook up, okay," said Vah.

Jaia was talking to this hard-body looking female. She looked like Birdman the Rapper, trying to put her rap down to Jaia. She was telling her how she drives a school bus for a living and how she's been doing it for ten years.... She had just broke up with her girl about three months ago.

Jaia asked, "By the way Boo, what the hell is ya name, Baby?"

"It's a common name. Cream," she said. "I am sorry I did not introduce myself. That's rude. I've been rambling on as if I've known. You quite a while. I apologize. What's your name?"

"Jaia. Well it's all good when you're having a nice time. Things just happen so dam naturally, Cream." I enjoy listening to you, Babe. So, are you from this area, Cream?"

"Nah. I am in Watervilet on Broadway. It's a nice quiet area. I'm a settled individual. I work, come home and enjoy my clubs and meeting people. So Jaia, how old are you, Ma Jaia said, "Twenty-four. Why you ask me my age, girl? Do I look old or something, Cream?"

"Nah, Ma You look to be about eighteen years of age. I don't want to get busted for child bait. Ya know what I mean? Ha, Ha, Ha," Cream chuckled.

"Cream, you full of shit. You been in my grill all night like I am what you been waiting for Sweetie. Am I? Just answer yes or no without going into details. See, I'm straight up to the point, Cream. It's been a beautiful, fun night. I am all danced out and talked out, so I'm gonna get my homegirls together. We're outtie like Gotti," said Jaia.

As they were heading out of tbe club, the owner approached them and asked, "Did you ladies enjoy yourselves?"

Vah said, "Yes, we did Ms. I didn't get your name."

"I'm Chauncey. I am the owner of Mr. Big C's, ladies."

Aunya said, "Dam Gina, this place is really a hot joint. Thanks for the good time."

Chauncey handed Jaia, Vah and Aunya her business card and said, "Just in case you ladies would like to have a little special event or party in my establishment, please feel free to call, OK? Goodnight ladies."

Vah ended up driving back home while Jaia and Aunya slept. By tbe time they reached home it was 4:15 am.

"Alright," Vah shouted, "Get up bitches, we're home and next time one of you hoes are chaperoning my black ass. Get up, get tbe fuck out and lock the doors. I'll meet you bitches upstairs."

Vah was a little pissed. She really wanted to spend some time witb Laurie, but with Jaia's and Auyna's tipsiness, she couldn't risk anything happening to them trying to drive home.

So, she did the honors. She loved her crew. They were her only family for life. Do or die to the end together; these are my only one loves.

Everyone slept until 10 : lOam. Bitches are tired.

* * *

Aunya's cell phone started ringing; she looked at the caller ID, it was Coco. She answered, "Yo holla. Good morning, Coco. By the way, what are you calling me for you disrespectful bitch!" Coco hung up. She was heated not knowing what the fuck this dam thugett bitch is referring to. She thought she'd wait until she got off work and address the situation personally.

"Who the fuck she talking to like that anyway. Wanna be fucking man. Oooh, this bitch got me uptight. I can't wait to confront her showboating ass, even if she is fine,"

Coco thought, "My little episode kinda stung her feelings. She feeling summin' for me. Ha, gotcha hoe."

Coco's game plan was a cinch. Now she needed for Aunya and her to really get wit it as in a couple. She thought, "Dam right, I gits mine anyway I can. She's ballin' too. Bitch is getting paid," referring to Aunya. "I'ma give Baby girl all the pussy she can eat and then some of my sweet tasty nipple. She definitely gonna get stuck and fucked depending on her game status. Aunya got it goin' on...."

Meanwhile, Vah' s daydreamin about Laurie, thinking she is a little stud muffin and arrogant. *"I guess I am going to have to teach Miss Itty Bitty the nitty gritty my way. She 'll definitely jump on my wagon for sure. J'ma holla at ole' girl and set up some sort of date for this evening. It's time for me to get some sexual healing. Marvin Gaye ain't wrong and I ain't mad at him."*

Unbelievable for Jaia. She started thinking about the female Cream, from the club.

I should holla at ole girl on the real wit her mannish looks. She seems kinda calm, but all that shit can be a fuckin' front until she get with a bitch and pull some ole Mandingo shit on a motherfucker. Probably even if I let her lick my clit!; shit, I might let a dam beast loose, being I'm so fine! Ha, ha, hal I'ma conceited hoe. Nah. I'm not gonna fuck wit her on that tip. I might have to kill that Birdman looking butch. Jaia thought she seemed so humble and sweet, as she gave serious thought 'bout Cream. She felt her pussy getting wet and wondered why this bitch was making her feel summin'. She looked at herself in the mirror and said to herself, "OH, HELL, NO!"

Well, TLC decided it was time to get paid in full. They'd relaxed enough for one day.

Money is on the brain. They were going to do pick-Ups from the spots today, they all decided.

TLC all hopped in the Range Rover on their journey for the day to see what lies ahead.

Vah stopped over at Morton to see what's been going on with Uncle Muff-n-Amadeus. Uncle Muff saw Vah and her homegirls pulling up to the curb and shouted, "Holla at a girl, bitch! Booya...."

With a forty ounce of Old English Beer and a half-pint of Vodka sticking out of her back pocket, she said, "What is it Vah? I had hoped you'd stop by. Oh, don't worry money is good; all fucking good with a little extra."

Vah stated, "How'd that come about Uncle Muff?"

Uncle Muff answered, "Well, my homeboy Amadeus is dead. The nigga was ballin' with our shit over on Elizabeth Street. He had a good amount of clientele working with some whities in weight and I just happened to overhear a conversation in the hood. The nigga was bragging about how he got on the hustle wit these durnb ass females called the TLC and how he was cutting the cocaine with a five, more cuts selling to them. Fucking cracker's making two times more than what we've been selling them for. I had my boy Boone rattle his crib. He found $75,000 in the back of his speaker. I had no idea this nigga would fuck me royally. He was supposed to be my one man Army Lt. Ya feel me, Vah?"

"I had his greedy ass knocked the fuck off for fucking ever," Uncle Muff continued, "Anybody in my stable will definitely be proper, not disrespecting my bread and butter or peeps, Vah. That's for real. I appreciate you puttin' me on and seeing me through. I'm always gonna be there for ya, Vah, no matter what. That's just where my heart is; at your disposal, always.

One Love." After Uncle Muff explained Amadeus' episode to Vah, she responded.

She said, "Check it. I want you to meet the real dynasty behind your bread and butter, Uncle Muff. Come over to the truck. J aia and Aunya, this is my bitch of all trades in the game, Uncle Muff."

"Yo, you handling shit," Aunya said.

"Hell, yeah taking down for the count for the money. Ya feel me?" Ha, ha, ha. They all laughed.

"Uncle Muff; you a funny motherfucking Bi-atch. Yo, Vah, I'm feeling Uncle Muff," Jaia said, "I like her style. She is for real all the way.

Vah said, "Well Uncle Muff, I'ma leave you to handle yours as far as another worker, but In the meantime, be safe, you crazy bitch. Holla back! Oh, listen Uncle Muff, maybe one weekend we'll hang at this gay spot in Cohoes I checked out over the weekend. Ok? Everything is on me." Vah jumped back into the truck.

Jaia said, "Let's stop by my spot next. It's time to get paid. So what the fuck you bitches wanna do once we've all picked up our paper, hoes. We should all make a day of splurging on us together for a change."

"Yo," Aunya said, "To the mall ballin' players. Booya. After we stop by our crib, I need to share suummin' with you hoes. It's official ladies. I'm opening a spot in the Lark and Orange Street area with Ms. Smiley's help. Shit is going to be off the chain with them young ass niggas over there."

Vah said, "We really gonna have to take some heads off, boo, fo sho I am ready to eliminate them fools anyway." Aunya said, "It's all damage control. Now we are going for it all. Them motherfuckers status ain't shit in the hustle. Come on hoes, let's get our troops on the streets, bitches.

"Yea, that's what I'm talkin' 'bout," Vah said. "I'll use that extra $75,000 for some gats. Jaia call Smiley for some connections to blow shit out the frame. Seriously. We're getting ready to put some work in play."

"Well alright," Jaia yelled.

* * *

Coco's cell was vibrating. She looked at the ID; it was Aunya.

"Yo, what's up Coco? I'm referring to the episode last night you pulled by steppin' off with that chic Free-Free. Her taking your ass home was definitely disrespectful. I do not give a fuck how the fuck you try to explain that shit. It wasn't proper. Meet me at the IHOP. One Love."

Coco was waiting at the IHOP on Wolf Road where they first met. She's wondering about Aunya's attitude. It's kinda' fizzled, Coco thought.

Aunya pulled up to the IHOP where Coco was waiting and started blasting her fucking ass out of the frame; calling her all kinds of bitches, sluts and cunts. She told her she was trying to play with her feelings. Aunya was fuckin' furious with her and Coco couldn't get a word in edgewise.

Aunya stated, "Let me say this, yo, you came up in the club with me and my peeps, then you gonna leave with some scaly ass bitch with a name like Free-Free. Maybe she got some of that pussy for Free-Free. See, I'da paid ya if I knew that's what the dealie was, yo. Coco, you tried to play me in front of my dawgs, knowin' I'm feeling you, Ma. Now whatever type of game you sitting on bitch, get off it hoe. I am not the herb, ya heard.

Coco replied, "Bitch, now let me speak. Shut the fuck up, you wanna be a thugget bitch?

I ain't one of those motherfucking hood rat bitches you think go for this and that. Bitch, don't get it twisted by a long shot. Your so-called big ballin' ass kept every other bitch in da club up in your grill, buying 'em drinks, keeping them smiling and grinning until you had lock jaw for the night. Then you gonna ask me some 'ole crazy shit about coming home with ya Jay-Z wanna be motherfucking ass, you ain't ask me to dance with your fake ass feelings, not one time, bitch.

So who disrespected who in front your clowning ass peeps?" Aunya responded, "Yo, Coco, watch your slick ass mouth taking about my dawgs. Say some 'ole bullshit, flshit, out ya fuckin' grill again. Go ahead, so I can break ya got dam jaw right here bitch. Come on. You thinkin' I'm a joke to be played with. I will body slam your sorry ass all over this shitty ass parking lot. Try me!"

Aunya hauled off and slapped the holy shit outta Coco. Coco grabbed her face and looked at Aunya.

Coco said, "Bitch, have you lost your fuckin' mind, hoe? What the fuck is wrong wit you, bitch?"

As Aunya continued to yell and shout at Coco, Coco punched her in the mouth full blast.

The fight is on in the IHOP parking lot. People started staring and a bunch of onlookers came over to where they were throwing blows at each other. One white man tried to step in between them but thought twice and gave it up. He said, "Them black bitches done gone crazy."

Aunya kicked him in his ass and then she pulled out a razor and sliced Coco's face.

"Oh shit," one of the onlookers shouted, "she's been cut and she's bleeding. Call the police. 911. We need an ambulance quick. She's bleeding bad."

As Coco stood stunned, feeling the blood ooze from her face, she started screaming.

"Oh my god my fucking face. This bitch cut my face. NOOO! I'ma kill you bitch. I'ma get ya ass, Aunya. I swear to god, hoe. When I get my ass from the hospital, I'm gunnin' for ya bitch. Don't let me catch you in da hood where ya'll be slinging ya drugs, bitch. Your motherfucking ass is a done deal, yo."

The cops arrived. Aunya went to the crib, but thought not to stay long. She knew Coco knew where she lived. She called Jaia on her cell phone.

Jaia answered, "What's up peeps?"

Aunya then explained the situation with her and Coco to her and that the po-po were looking for her and one of them needed to get the truck.

"Where are you?"

"At the crib."

Jaia says, "Come over to First and Judson and I'll relieve you of the truck. It's in Vah's name, so we gotta get her on the cellie and pull her coat on what's going on."

Jaia dials Vah's cellie and Vah picks up, "What's up peeps?" Jaia explains the situation.

Vah says "Say no more, I'm on it. Where Aunya at?"

"Right here," states Jaia.

No sooner does Jaia hang up with Vah than the po-po pulls up with the white man in the back seat; the one Aunya kicked in the ass during the fight. He's pointing her out to the officer.

The two cops get out of their car and walk over toward Jaia and Aunya by the truck.

The officer says, "Excuse me ladies. Do one of you go by the name of Aunya?"

Aunya steps to the officer and says, "Yeah, that's me man."

He then cuffs and tells her she is under arrest for assault with a deadly weapon, assault in the third degree and assault in the first degree.

Aunya thought, *'Dam, the third charge is for kicking the cracker right in his ass. Boy, I fucked up. I might as well handle this shit and let my peeps get a lawyer to handle the' formalities. I really fucked up and brought attention to my dawgs over some skank ass bitch that I haven't even hit the skins with. Dam, I fucked up!'*

As the officer handcuffed her, he read her Miranda rights fucking with and put her in the car.

Everyone on First and Judson chanted slurs, "Po-po pussy, arresting a woman. Punk ass cops."

The officer responded, "Shut up or you'll be next for loitering, or better yet, interfering with an arrest. Get the fuck away from the car, you fucking morons. Go get an education on how to spell the word cocaine that you distribute, killing your own neighborhood."

The next hour Vah and Jaia were at the Albany Police Courthouse on Morton Avenue.

They were hoping Aunya would get to see the judge being it was a Saturday afternoon.

"The shit is absurd. Is Coco in the hospital?" Vah asked Jaia.

Jaia replied, "Yes, with 37 stitches in her face. That dumb ass Aunya cut her with a box cutter."

"What was she thinking?" asked Vah.

"Vah, I do not know what the fuck got into her and why she would jeopardize everything we've accomplished in the hustle by bringing attention to the po-po. All over a bitch she ain't even fucked, or kissed, or ate her punanny. I can't believe this shit. Over a bitch. Aunya actually caught some type of feeling for Coco, especially when she left the club with that aggressive named Free-Free. I bet that's what all this bullshit is about, I guarantee ya."

Jaia continued, "Oh wait, Vah. Aunya said Coco called me and you clown ass bitches, she set her straight with stitches."

Vah replied, "That's my motherfucking nig! Hell yeah. But Jaia, you know she is going to do some time, ya know. We need a good lawyer."

Jaia said, "Don't worry, I'm on it boo."

Jaia cellied Smiley and explained what happened with her dawg Aunya.

Smiley replied, "I'm on it babe. Let me go. I gotta make some calls to some serious peeps, OK? Holla back. One."

CHAPTER THREE

VAH AND JAIA WENT TO the spots and gathered all the workers of Aunya's crew and explained the situation. She told everyone, *"All* systems still a go. Work 'til ya asses drop," she was on a rampage, "anyone of you motherfuckers fuck up from here, it's a wrap. Ain't no more shots, no credit, no shit."

One of Aunya's troop stepped up and said, "Who the fuck we report to from now on?"
"Yo, check this Shorty. Anyway, 'lil nigga what's your fuckin' name?" Jaia said.

"Nubian, Ma," he said.

"Well, being that you had the balls to step to a question, I'ma make you the Lt. In charge.

How old are ya lil nigga?"

"I'm nineteen year old."

"Cool," Jaia said. "Well, you punk ass Motherfuckers heard the drill Now get the fuck to work. Yo, Nubian, hold up. Let me holla at ya, Baby Bro. Listen, I need a trooper. True story. Someone who ain't afraid of dying or to pull the trigger. Ya feel me, Nubian? Especially since my dawg, Aunya's gonna be tied up for a while. I want shit handled smooth. Understand? And you do not Nubia, "l, report to no one, but me and Vah. Is that shit understood?"

Eye to eye Jaia stared at Nubian. He thought, *'This bitch is a straight up for real killer. I better stay on her good side fa sho'* Yah said, "Come on Jaia, enough said. Let these troops do what they gettin' paid to do with no fuck-ups. Let's be out, hoe."

Ms. Smiley called Vah and said, "Yo, peeps, I got that connect for the gats babe. When do y'all wauna set up a meet? Make it real soon. Shit is hot. There's too much going on right now. Oh yeah, I also got the lawyer, Mr. Hassan Tlyer. He's good. I told him to save all the details for you guys to hear. He gave me his number where you can contact him and get the ball rolling for Aunya to get bail Oh, he also said the judge will hear her case Monday morning at 9:00am, so the weekend is dead. You can't even see her fam, ya feel me?

Well, I gotta be out. I got things to do and peeps to see. Are y'all satisfied wit the information I've related? Don't forget the connect. What time do ya'll wanna do the dirt wit these gats? I'ma be present and make sure shit is right, ya heard? Tall gain' through a 'iiI summin'. I wanna help and lend a hand as much as possible. All jokes aside, my money gats to keep moving, ya feel me? No pun intended. So y'all got other shit going or what? Ladies, let's go do this. No more wasting time."

Jaia and Vah followed Smiley in her cream colored Lexus. They headed up Lark Street to Clinton Avenue to get on the highway. When passing the Palace Theatre, the marquee read "Patti LaBelle Performing Live."

Jaia was yelling all excited, "Oh shit that's my girl. I'm comin' to see ya Patti. Bet that." They followed Ms. Smiley, wondering where they were headed, being that Vah and Jaia are not familiar with the Upstate area.

Jaia asks Vah, "What do you think Aunya is facing as far as time?"

Vah was like, "She really fucked up over a bitch she didn't even know. She is too darn short-tempered."

"Ya know Vah, she stood up for us dawg. Coco was ragging on our crew, ya heard?"

"Well, sometimes Jaia, in this game a word ain't shit if a bitch ain't in our crew. Dam it, we're on a come up. She should have used her fucking brains, not think with her pussy over a bitch. She is feelin' Coco like candy; sweet on her. How the hell that happen from just conversation? She needs to slow her clit down from thurnpin' like a man's dick. Ya feel me?

Aunya caused us unnecessary attention. Believe you me -- this isn't over as far as Coco is concerned - not by a long shot, Jaia. We are gonna have a real big problem if we don't think fast Jaia," Vah declared and continued, "so let's put our heads on brainstorm."

In unison Vah and Jaia said, "Coco gotta go, ya heard."

Ms. Smiley flashed her lights to let them know she was turning off onto the Selkirk exit.

They drove another ten minutes and were at their destination. Ms. Smiley's right-hand man, Brickman, stepped to Vah and Jaia in their Range Rover, opened the door for them and said, "Ladies, this way please."

Everyone followed until they reached a log cabin, looking homely house, out of beautiful wood. A white woman opened the door and introduced herself as Natalie. As everyone entered, they said their names. Natalie says, "OK. Let's get down to business and keep it simple. We do not have all season. What are you ladies looking for as far as holding shit down? Let the haters feel your wrath, 'cuz I got some shit for a mutha-fucka, ya feel me?" Everyone laughed at Natalie.

Jaia said, "This bitch is ridda die."

Vah said, "She better be with all these good ass lookin' pretty fuckin guns she got in this place. If not, she better off being a dead bitch."

Natalie stated, "I know that's right. It's all good though. Now to the business at hand.

What ya want?"

Jaia responded, "Listen, we got $40,000. What can you furnish us with? We're goin' all out to keep on the come up with our peeps in the street. Ya know what I mean? Keep it sweet Natalie, ya feel me?"

Natalie says, "OK, let's see. I'll give ya five AK-15's, six 9mm's, four 38's, six scope rifles, two double-barrels and all the ammunition you need. If you keep cummin' back, I'll also give ya ladies three boxes of shells for every gun you buy; plus I'll throw in three 25's for you ladies to keep under your skirts. You do wear skirts, don't you? Us ladies gotta get our props too."

Jaia says, "Good lookin', Nat. Nice doin' business with you."

Ms. Smiley says to Vah and Jaia, "Yo, what about me? I can't get no gun to root-n-toot too or what?" "Here," Jaia said, "Take one of these here 25 automatics, they're for ladies anyway.

Alright, let's bounce! Time to drop it like it's hot, bitches."

Natalie was thinking to herself fthat Jaia is one wicked bitch not to be fucked with, but she likes her style. She looks familiar to some peoples I've done business with. I'll figure it out.

Right now, I gotta get paid.

Everyone was back on the highway toward Albany, while Brickman was driving, he mentioned to Ms. Smiley, "Did you see the way Natalie was eyeballing Jaia? It was like she knew her or she was trying to figure her out."

"Yeah, I caught the whole scenery, Brickman. I think I better start doing some background shit on these bitches 'cause they coming up hard and ya know Brickman, they're fuckin' dangerous hoes, but I like their style and they operate and maneuver their game in the hustle. Although they're moving fast, let's see how long they will last on the scene with Aunya getting ready to do some time. Her lawyer, Mr. Hassan Tlyer said she's looking at least three years. She did fuck up royally. By that I mean bringing attention to her crew, ya feel me, definitely with po-po because of a bitch named Coco." They both laughed.

Vah and Jaia beeped to Ms. Smiley once they exited in Albany to tell her they were parting ways. Once they arrived at the crib on N. Main Street, they took the guns inside and began deciding who gets what on Aunya's crew over on L & 0, where they put in their work.

Jaia called Nubian and he picked up, "holla at ya boy!"

"Nubian, this is Jaia. Yo, we packin' heavy, dude, so I'm gonna drop by the spot, hit ya off with some gats and you distribute them to your troops. Ya feel me?"

Nubian responded, "I got you, rna. It's all good in the hood, Jaia. I just wanna let you know with no disrespect, ma. On the real, but keep it real. I'd rather stay a trooper for ya, you're a raw gangster, ma. Ride or die for life and that's real. Ya feel me? I'm that real gangster nigga honoring ya Boo, so, I'm gonna keep it gangsta, ma, fo sho, ya heard. You can depend on Nubian to be by the beautiful- Queen of Gangster."

Jaia thought, "What is this Iil nigga on, some ole Egyptian shit. I am Dominican and German; I think like Castro and Hitler when it comes to taking over. He has no idea." She said aloud, "Well, Nubian, I dig your rap, sway, play, my nig, but we got work to do, so let's roll."

So Nubian called his troops cellie's. He had a call coming in on his cellie so he flipped it open. It was Lil Kill, one of his workers.

"Holla at a nigga, dude," Lil Kill said. ''I'm callin' to check to see if you'd come pick up this paper. We makin' a killin' over here. Also, try to re-up Nuby. Ya feel me? I'm over on Lark and Clinton, bro, in front of the laundromat."

Nubian said, "Lil Kill, come over to L & O. I got a lil summin' for you that I think a nigga will make your hustle a stronger one."

That had Lil Kill puzzled like a motherfucker. He started walking up Lark Street toward Orange and as he turned on to Orange, hesaw Nubian talkin' to this fly ass Dominican female. He couldn't keep his mouth closed. He thought it was Nubian's shawty. As he got closer she was rockin' the baddest stilettos he'd ever seen. Her toes looked like perfect ones, (he had a fetish for feet).

Nubian was yelling his name. "Lil Kill, snap out of whatever fuckin' type of trance your ass is in, bitch ass nigga. I know you're not undressing our boss, motherfucker, and I haven't given you the intro yet. Yo, what is your fuckin' problem Lil *Kill?* We can straighten that shit out right now, dawg, fo sho."

Lil Kill said, "Nah man, I'm good. Sorry boss. I didn't mean to dis you or nothing. It's just I gotta keep it real. You are a fine ass down chick" Nubian says, "Meet Jaia, Lil Kill. She's dropping us off sum gats man. That shit's a'ight yo, ya heard?"

Jaia told Nubian that she has to prepare herself for the preliminary hearing for Auyna tomorrow morning at nine o'clock.

She stated, "I'm headin' to the crib. I've had a busy weekend, so I need some rest, a couple of hours. Ya feel me Nubian? One, I'm out. If you need me, only you have the cellie.

Am I right? None of those other birds do, do they Nubian? That's a no-no for now, until I give you the right of way on who's trustworthy without them thinking with their dicks. Know what I mean. Later."

As Jaia pulled off, Nubian thought, *'Dam that* is *a hellified bitch, but there* is *somethin' that doesn't click with her. She seems gay but she* is *as femme as I see 'em. She's gorgeous and she doesn't act at all like she ain't feelin' a nigga.'*

Nubian's dick started to get hard, so he held it and squeezed the tip thinking, *"Dam, I want some of dat pussy. That* is *some sure enough dangerous pussy. I'll probably have to kill her* if *she lets me fuck her, fa shoo* Then he thought again, *'I'd have to rough house that bitch and take the pussy then kill her. Yeah, that's more like real gangster thinking.'* He smiled to himself.

Meanwhile, Vah sat in the Ranger Rover thinking about that bitch Laurie, and that she needed to really release some sexually frustrated cum and she would do right about now. So she dialed Laurie's home phone number. She picked up on the second ring.

Vah said, "Hello, is Laurie home?'

Laurie responded, "This is she."

"This is Vah. I met you that night at Big G's in Cohoes. I have dreads."

Laurie thought, *'Oh yeah, that pretty chocolate black bitch. Oh my gosh! She actually called me. Oh my god!! I'm blessed.'*

So Laurie says, "Yes, how are you, Vah and what do lowe for this wonderful surprise a call from you? It's nice to hear from you. You know I thought about you cause I never forget about a nice lookin' female such as yourself."

Vah said, "Well, I decided to calL I kinda wauna see you, rna. If you have some minutes in your schedule."

Laurie said, "Oh that is such a great idea. If you'd like to stop over to my crib, I'll gladly give you my address or we can go out to eat or something. Whichever you prefer is fine with me."

Laurie thought, *'I want this bitch to fuck the shit out of me. She looks like she knows how to put it on a motherfucking bitch and that bitch [think is gorgeous and so dam pretty. [can git with her.'*

Vah told Laurie she'd be over, but she was going at the pizza shop first -- JG's on Lark Street. Vah asked if she'd like somethin' to eat and Laurie responded, "Yes, a sub and a large Diet Coke."

Vah thought, *'Whoa it's 'FUCKIN'time. [wonder ifshe has a strap on. Knowing her, she's so dam freaky, I bet she does. Dam this shit is gonna be on and poppin '. [need some fucking head and she is the chosen one for tonight. Oh yeah.'*

In the meantime, Jaia's ready to go home and rest, retire for the night. She tells Vah to drop her off.

Vah replies, "I'll just make my rounds, OK, to officially do some spot checking for the night, Jaia, then I'll check with you later, OK? Oh, so everything is a'ight with Aunya's peeps.

Yo, listen Jaia, tomorrow is her court date at 9:00am sharp. We'll be there dawg. Yo, we holdin' her down by law Jaia, in there and on the streets. We got this, sho e-nuffbitch. I'ma make sure her account is to the fullest at all times, Jaia. Keep her on point, ya know, definitely on her troops and her spots.

Vah continued, "to be honest with ya Jaia, the L & 0 spots are nothin' but trouble because of the gang cliques, ya know and it'll be all out wars time. We're still on our come up and Aunya with this Coco shit brought this shit on her motherfucking self, I believe we should just move her troops to another spot area, ya know. For some reason, I feel some sort of fishy shit going in her area, ya feel me? So let's think about this, a'ight. But one thing for sure, Coco has to git got J aia. That is my word on everything I love. We gonna let her live, fo sho, but not too long, Jaia. You know I love Aunya, I do not care how hardheaded that bitch is. I owe her, because of her loyalty, ya feel me, to us dawg. This is just the way I feel, personally."

Vah dropped Jaia off at home. They gave each other sums dap. Booya.

Jaia said, "Get with you tomorrow at court. Be there, Vah."

So Jaia couldn't wait to relax and get some sleep, she thought. Instead, she started thinking about how much time Aunya would get and what is going on with her dawg mentally.

It really started to hit Jaia that she'd really miss her dawg. She started gettin' all mushy for Aunya. She loved her just as much as Vah. She also thought about the situation as far as Coco. She thought that it's time to move out of the Main Street apartment and leave it as a place of business for now, as far as having some fun. She was thinking of a nice place over a Sand Creek Road in Colonie. It'll be closer to the county jail to visit Aunya. She thought she'd get a jeep of her own cause her spots were making money; so after court she'll handle hers.

CHAPTER FOUR

VAH'S ON HER WAY TO Laurie's for a night of pleasure, for her sexual appetite and activity.

She had everything she needed for the both of 'em from JG's Pizza Shop.

She stops at 70 Columbia Street where Laurie said she lived and rang the doorbell.

Laurie came down the stairs in a wife beater and some sweatpants smiling from ear to ear. She was thinking of how she was going to please Vah in any way possible to keep her. She'd lick the pretty black ass if need be. Laurie intended on going all out tonight to please Vah.

Vah entered her apartment amazed at how Laurie kept her place. She's kind of a slob, Vah thought, so now I know how to treat this bitch; like the pure fuckin' white trashy ass bitch she is. No wonder the bitch stays lookin' desperate. Nobody wants a nasty bitch. Oh yeah, this is gonna be one hell of a night.

* * *

Aunya laid in her holding cell beating herself up about how she could have avoided the shit with Coco and knew she had let her emotions and her anger get the best of her. *'Oh well, she thought, it's a done deal. I gotta handle mine now. State time. A fuckin' one to three, that's what I feel the outcome* is *going to be '. Well, I go to court tomorrow and I know my dawgs are going to be there, holding me down with a lawyer. Dam, I fucked up, cause we're just on the come up with the hustling. I know both Vah and Jaia are pissed at how I handled shit, but what the fuck - what's done is done."*

Aunya kinda felt stupid in all reality, so she started planning her state time. She was nervous at the fact it's her first state bid she'll be doing. Then again, she thought, *'it ain't nothing but a whole bunch of bitches from the streets in a fuckin 'village. Pussy village, here I come.'* She had to laugh at the shit her dam self. Plus, she knew her dawgs would be doing her bid with her. Then she started thinking of how she should get a hustle on during her stay in jail.

Then she thought 'NAH!'

Aunya remembered their motto when they first began their come up: "Get Money, Get Paid, Fuck'em Hard." She loved Vah and Jaia. She said she is gonna do her time and make her dawgs proud of her. She felt obligated in a family-orientated way with them. She looked up to them as the big sisters she never had. She was the only girl with two brothers, who used to sexually abuse her. She had to fight them off all of the time. One night when she was thirteen years old, her older brother Don came into her room and jumped on her. He held her mouth with his hand over it and tried to rape her. She had a box cutter under her pillow and got to it as he put his hand over her mouth, while his other hand was tearing at her panties. He then put his body in between her legs so he could stick his dick up in her pussy. He was panting like a dog.

Don kept telling her in her ear, "You say anything Aunya and I'll kill you."

She responded "Not if I kill your slimy no good fucking, raping ass first. You piece of fuckin shit molesting incest sick motherfucker." She then slit his throat with no regret.

Aunya just laid there at the thought of the real shit she just went through. There was blood everywhere; all over her face and body. She was in shock. Then she thought, *'It's finally over. This scumbag will never be able to luck no bitch again in his life.'*

From that incident, Aunya was put in a group home and from there, a diagnostic center for teenagers. BCW had really scuffled her around. Her mom had died and her father was in jail already for murder, facing fifty years. Her brothers were left to raise her. *'Yeah right,' Aunya thought, 'so they can have homemade pussy to come home to.'* She ended that shit. Since that happened her other brother stayed as far away from Aunya as he could. She had thought about getting revenge on his ass too; his name was Choi-Choi. She felt that the streets taught her to survive. In return, it was the result of a fucked up life. *'Oh well,' Aunya thought, 'thank god I met my two dawgs when I did.'*

I was hanging in Washington Square Park, listening to my walkman when I met Vah and Jaia. I'll never forget, I was seventeen years old. They came and sat next to me on the bench I was sitting on. I was looking all depressed wondering where I was going to live. I had run away from the diagnostic center after three fucking years of torture with the male counselors trying to get at me and the females hatin' all the time. I was just trying to live from one incident to the fuckin' next. I've had it with all that institutional shit. Vah and Jaia looked over at me sitting next to them on the bench.

Jaia says, "Yo son, you alright?"

Aunya responded with an attitude, "No, I'm not."

Vah says, "So, what's good? You can break bread with us. We cool, son. My name is Vah and this here is my dawg, Jaia. We're as one since we were in junior high school. We're from Washington Heights, 181st Street. Ya feel me? What is your name?"

"Aunya," she replied.

Vah says, "What kind of fuckin' name is that?"

"I don't know," Aunya says, "My moms died, so 1 never got the chance to discuss the meaning of my name. Is that okay with you?" Jaia said, "She is a smart mouth bitch, Vah, but she is going through somethin' serious.

She seems kinda lost, ya heard?"

"Shut up Jaia," Vah told her, "Can't you see she is fucked up in the head. 1 know that look. I've had it plenty of times; she is hurting. Come on Jaia, let her hang with us, alright.

Let's offer her some of our weed and some brew. Let's all just chill."

"Yo Aunya, yo come hang with us nigga," called Vah and Jaia.

Aunya's thoughts to back in the days of reminiscing with her dawgs were memories of wonderful times they shared. Times she will miss being in jail. *'The time they sentence me to) I'ill fly by as long as I keep myself busy. I am twenty-one years old and do not have a GED, so that is something I will accomplish to make Vah and Jaia proud of me. I'll do shit correct. Well enough of daydreaming and shit. I need to get my ass to sleep for court tomorrow.'*

"Hey maitre'd," yelled Aunya, "Kiss my ass, bitch. 1 am outta here tomorrow bitch, ya heard. How 'bout that missy."

* * *

Back on the block at Vah's spots, Uncle Muff was handling shit. She had it airtight. The fiends were out on a Sunday night like it was Friday, Saturday night. Money comin' right until this one fiend approached Uncle Muff and asked for a $50 click.

She said, "Hold up, let me check with my dawg cause I'm not holding," as she signaled for her boy Boone. "Yo, son, you holdin' a $50 click?"

Boone said, "Yeah."

Uncle Muff said, "Serve this fiend proper and a little extra summin. Make sure they keep coming back. Ya feel me, Boone? You know tomorrow is Aunya's court day, nigga.

She'll probably get served at 1 to 3. If so, I wanna know who is running her spot on L & 0." Boone said, "They should let me roll over up in there and get shit poppin' cause that's my kind of scene. All the thugs and shit, always ready to pop off or be on some do or die DMX shit.

I'll put a bullet straight through those gangster wanna be young motherfuckers heads in a minute.

Ya heard, Uncle Muff?"

"I am no clown ass joke. Everything is fo sho when it comes to the hustle on the streets.

Ya feel me. I'm dying for mine and that includes you Uncle Muff. We are the fire power behind this game. So, do you think you can put in a word for ya boy to Vah and Jaia about Aunya's spots?"

She reached out to Boone for some dap. "I will my nig. Defuinitely. One love."

Uncle Muff and Boone were chilling and all of a sudden po-po was chasing some white dude up on Morton Avenue toward Lincoln Park. That white boy was doing about sixty miles an hour, with a big brown bag in hand, flying down the block. Then he threw the bag right toward us. We weren't sure if the cop had seen him so we sat tight; then the cop flew right past us. We waited until they both ran into the park as dark as that motherfucker is. The cop stopped quick at the corner of Eagle and Morton. Then the other cops started driving all through the park with their sirens on looking for the white guy. That motherfucker was long gone. The cop that was chasing him came over to us and asked if we saw the guy throw anything.

We said, 'No."

"What, are we suppose to look out for y'all asses as good citizens or somethin'." Boone said.

They both started laughing. The cop was furious and made a smart remark to Boone.

"Oh, so you wanna be a smart ass on a Sunday night. If I wasn't on my way to clockin' out nigga, I'd haul your ass in, and this dyke looking bitch for loitering."

They both stared at the cop, so then he walked over to the cop car and said to the officer, "Those two over there claim they didn't see shit. You know they saw something. The lying pieces of shit."

The other officer said, "Well, let's get going, we're not getting any information here." Then they drove away.

Both Boone and Uncle Muff got up from the steps and went to retrieve the brown bag. They looked inside and it was filled with bundles of heroin.

"Oh shit!" they both said in unison.

"Yo, Boone, we are on the come up nigga. This is us man. If that white dude even thinks of coming back for this shit, he's dead, I'll tell ya. Dead as a door knob. True that. All the bundles amount to 200 bags. Yo Boone, that's $25.00 a bag. That's close to at least 50Gs, motherfucker. Dam, we hit the mutha-load dude."

"Listen up I am a loyal bitch to my dawgs, Vah and Jaia. "because of them, I am where I am, Ya know. So check it Boone, I'ma put them on to this piece of information. Ya feel me, son. Also, Boone, by being loyal, maybe they'll grant you your props in holding down L&O shit. Ya know what I mean? So, it's on you Boone."

He said, "I'm in like Flynn, girl. We'll let 'em know after court. The courthouse is right down the street and we'll catch' em coming out and find out about Aunya's situation. You know they are going to put her shit over in county court fo sho, Uncle Muff. But for now, my bitch, let's go get us some 40's and celebrate our new come up with the motherfucking Heroin.

Yo, you know we gotta keep our eyes open for that sleazy ass cop. I got a funny feelin' there's more to this shit, by him chasing that white dude. He seems as though he could be a dirty mutha-fucker. There's a lot of dope in that bag, yo. For some reason I feel he knew that shit, Uncle Muff. Also, it's a lot of money to be handling on a Sunday night in the hood. Ya feel me?"

Monday morning Jaia and Vah got up at 7:00 a.m. to get ready to face the music, as far as Aunya's court case. They both were feeling it this morning as far as not seeing her for a while after they ship her ass from county to upstate. They appeared at court with her lawyer Mr Hassan Tlyer. They thought better than to have some of their crews in the courtroom. Coco showed up with the female she meet in the club. That's how all this fucked up shit started in the first place.

* * *

The court officer brought Aunya out of the holding pen. She was so happy to see Vah and Jaia that she started to yell their names, but then thought it better not to. Then she saw Coco with the bandages on her face and stared at her with hatred, once she saw who she brought with her to the court; she gave her a look of death. Coco turned her head to talk to Free-Free and told her that bitch is going to pay lovely. Just by her ass goin' to jail is satisfaction for me. She stuck her finger up at Aunya then whispered, "Fuck you, Bi-atch," and smiled.

The judge came out and said, "All rise."

Aunya's case was first. He went through the hearing quickly and then transferred her case to the County Courthouse. The lawyer was ecstatic. He really did not get one word in on Aunya's behalf. See, because The Honorable Judge Danzy despised violence on his streets, period. His son had been killed by an initiation of some gang member with a box cutter. They slit his throat and sliced his face twenty-seven times, so obviously he had a thing about box cutters. He looked over at Aunya and said, "Young lady, I hope this is a lesson you learn from and refrain from violence by working on your anger by the time you're back on the streets."

Coco yelled out, "Yea, hang that drug dealin' bitch."

Everyone in the court room looked with amazement at this crazy bitch and started making remarks such as "Sit your snitchin' ass down bitch." "That's why you have stitches, hoe."

Judge Danzy yelled, "Quiet in the court room."

Court officers were yelling to the people standing. "Sit down now."

The court officers escorted Aunya back to the holding cell until the Albany County Jail.

COs came to take her to the county jail until her next court date in Albany County court.

As they exited the Police Court, Boone and Uncle Muff motioned for Vah and Jaia to come up to the spot. Jaia said for Uncle Muff to hit her cellie because she'd only accept emergencies from her cellie.

Although she knew that anything Uncle Muff had to tell her was always some jewels.

That is why she was definitely material for her and her dawgs to step in for Anyna until she finished her bid.

She thought to herself, *'dam, I really like that bitch Uncle Muff. She kinda reminds me of Aunya with the pissy fucking attitude but the bitch is not the herb. She* is *like a fucking bomb.'*

There was a Yukon Denali honking the hom for Vah's and Jaia's attention. They were wondering who the fuck it was until Da-Stev stuck his head out.

He yelled, "Yo, fam, it's me love, Da-Stev. A-ight, you forgot about a niggar, huh. I stopped by to see what is the delio, ya heard, with Aunya. Ms Smiley wants to know, too. She said she'd been here. Its better she didn't, ya heard? So, she sends her regards, fam. I want to holla at ya about a 'lil sunrmin' summin'. Ai-ght. Listen, there's this po-po and he tried to bag this white kid last night that was suppose to deliver him some heroin, two hundred bundles, right up the block here. The dude reneged, ya heard. He took off running and what was said to me is one of the peeps, in your crew over on Morton Ave., is involved. Her name is Uncle Muff. She hangs out with this scrap mutha-fucker named Boone. Well, the white boy threw the bag with the shit toward them when he was being chased by po-po."

"Now ladies, he ain't the type of dirty motherfucker to be fucked with. Me, I personally know because he's my contact inside. Ya heard? So, the bottom line is he wants his shit and not one bag missing outta a bundle. Ya feel me? I explained to him, I'd let you know what the handle is on this situation so shit wouldn't get hectic in your area. You know? There is enough money to be made for everyone."

"Once a nig gets the greedies, all hell breaks loose. If they do not give po-po back his shit, the whole fuckin' Morton Ave. will be locked down. The court will be filled, ya feel me, Jaia and Yah? Yo, whisper in your peeps ears cause that cat Boone, he ain't nothin' but a problem waiting to happen. He is desperate for a come up by any means possible. I just do not want nothing to happen to the fam. Take the info and holla back. You got my cellie number, if there is anything you need. Don't be shy to ask, cause I don't like a motherfucker that begs, at all. Well, it's nice to see y'all. I'm out to do my usual, running game-on-game. Jaia thought as soon as Da-Stev left, that is what Uncle Muff wanna holla at me about.

Then her cellie vibrated. She knew it was her, so she told her they'd all meet up at the McDonald's on Madison and Pearl in fifteen minutes.

"I am there," replied Uncle Muff. "One out."

* * *

Jaia and Vah started toward the car so they could head over to McDonald's. When they entered, Uncle Muff was already there waiting with this big ass grin on her face, as if it was her birthday or some shit. In the meantime, Vah went to the register to order hers and Jaia's breakfast; a number two for Jaia and a breakfast special for herself and Uncle Muff. She knew Uncle Muff needed some breakfast 'cause the bitch was ready to get her fucking drink on. It's only right if the bitch puts something in her stomach, as she waited for her orders, she thought of how Laurie had sucked and licked her pussy all night. She busted about five nuts. The Italian stud had some good tongue and some hellified head. She was gettin' wet, thinkin' of the feeling of cumin, all over again. That nasty thirsty bitch. I had a funny feeling she was a freak, fo sho When she let me put four fingers to penetrate her pussy's insides, she was hollerin', wantin' more. She was telling me not to stop and that she wanted to cum forever and she called me her daddy. I was very demanding, saying, "Bitch, you love this, right? Tell me how far you want my fingers to go. Open your legs wide, hoe. Open them now, bitch. You like this shit, slut. I was drilling a hole in this bitch's pussy, for sho The sick shit about is that she loved it. I was kinda surprised 'cause I've always wanted a bitch to take whatever sexual activities I had in store for their ass. I'll be dam if she ain't the one. I got some plans for this hoe. She will be stuck like a chuck for a fuck.

The cashier called Vah for her order. She kept saying, "Miss, your order's ready." V ah snapped out of her trance with a smile and looked at the cashier.

She said, "Oh, sorry ma'am. Keep the change from the twenty dollar bilL"

She then headed over to the table and they all began to eat their breakfast. In between chews, Jaia asked, "Yo, where's yo boy Boone?"

"He's taking care of some stuff," Uncle Muff replied.

Jaia responded, "What kind of stuff? Keep it gully, yo, 'cause it's what I think it is, the motherfucker is on his own. Uncle Muff. Check it out. I got word on the white dude the po-po the other night and shit is dangerous, yo. I'm tellin' you, yo, yo! The po-po is dirty. The white dude was makin' a drop to po-po and he decided to fly with po-po 's shit. So dead the thought of slingin' his shit right now, cause you family. One of my peeps is connected to that po-po, ya heard? It's in Boone's hands, let him have the problem. Ya feel me? I know that's your boy, but he's desperate and hungry and we're not lettin' you be a part of that. Is that understood,

Uncle Muff? No more said. E-nuff of your man's problems."

"The reason I wanted to holla at ya dawgs, is about Aunya's spot over on L&O. What's good wit dat y'all? I know her crew Nubian and 'em are holdin' shit down. Boone had asked me to put in a word on that for him, but all is a no go, cuz he just fucked up royally." Jaia thought about ifshe put Boone over there on L&O with Nubian and them at the same time po-po would want his shit. It would start an all out war with getting rid of the pissy ass gangs. They'll retaliate against the po-po thinking they're trying to take over their turf. They know this po-po is crooked like a motherfucker. So all hell would break loose. I gotta get Nubian outta there along with Lil Kill. She had to remove them from L&O some kind of way or have them paired together to make pick-ups.

Jaia snapped out of her shit and said, "Maybe having Boone work L&O isn't a bad idea after all. See, I got a strategy as far as getting them bad-ass gang bangers out of the way. Let me fill you in, bitches."

Vah went ballistic. "Bitch, you sure this will work? Now ya gotta know in the process a whole lotta Motherfuckers gonna get laid to rest or knocked, ya feel me? If you're game for the fame, I feel the same, dawgs."

Jaia stressed to Uncle Muff that she is one of them now for sure and for her to get some troops, so she can have her own spots and hang with her and Jaia, getting to know the contacts too.

In the meantime, Boone is out on Clinton and Swan Street trying to get rid of some of the heroin. He thought about not informing his home-girl, Uncle Muff. He wondered if she had spoken to Jaia and Vah about him handling L&O and had doubts that she did. His cellie began ringing.

He picked up and said, "Yo, talk to me."

"Hey, what's up my nigga," said Uncle Muff. "The shit is official, on and poppin', son.

Yo, you got that L&O dude."

"What?" Boone yelled.

"Ya heard me right. So do what ya gotta do, mutha-fucker. It's all yours. Yo, you still got that shit from the other night, right?"

"Yeah," Boone said.

"She says you're on your own with that Boone, so that's on you okay? Uncle Muff went on, "I'm in wit my dawgs now. I pick up the cash. Ya feel me, Boone, so I will be checkin' on ya, crazy ass nigga. And, listen son, please do right by me. I gave Jaia and Vah good props about ya, so make me look good dude, a-ight? One love, out!"

They listened to Uncle Muffs conversation with Boone. All had wicked smiles and said, "let's go celebrate."

Then Jaia says to Uncle Muff, "Yo, you're gonna have to change your fashion, ma, if you hangin' with the dawgs. Bitch, you a real ass hustler now, so we make some moves to the mall to dress out your dyke ass in some linen and shit. We'll see when we get there or better yet, we'll make a trip to New York City and hit Fifth Avenue."

"Yo, now that's the move, what ya think, huh? Am I ballin' or what? Yo, Vah, I was thinkin' about getting' me a nice navy blue Navigator with some twenty-two inch rims, stereo surround sound and leather interior like a pinkest. Yeah, so how about we start spending some of this money we been stacking for a change for the past months, a-ight? So, bitches, off we go up toward Central Avenue to the car dealers."

"Boy, there's a bunch of 'em on this fuckin' avenue," Jaia said. Then her cellie ring tone went on and the song was Alicia Keyes, "Falling."

She answered, "Holla at ya girl."

Ms. Smiley was like, "Whoa, you feelin' it girl. It's a good thang. What are ya up to Jaia? We need to talk about investing now, cause you can't keep dirty monies laying around your crib or stashed in the car. I wanna show you the real hustling in the game. Ya feel me? I want to introduce you and ya dawgs to some important peoples, like bankers and shit. Also, some real estate investors. You know, make your money work for you through the nice people who do not get their hands bloodied up. Ya know what I mean? So, how fast can you get to me? Better yet, let's do this bright and early tomorrow morning. Meet me in front of Key Bank on State Street at 9:30 a.m. sharp. Dress to impress, boo. Ya feel me? One. Holla back. Out."

CHAPTER FIVE

YO, CHECK THIS OUT FAM. That was Ms. Smiley. She just called to let us know that it's time we start to invest this dirty money we're makin' and let the bank boys who keep their hands clean, clean it up, ya heard? We can live comfortable and not have the feds and tax evaders fuckin' with us. Ladies, we are about to become some rich motherfucking, lesbian girls. Niggas on the block gonna come with their cock at us and sweet bitches gonna flock to us.

Booya-ya! Heyee! That shit sounds ripe, so let's go do this. Git the hooptie," stated Jaia.

They were all so anxious after Jaia's speech. Vah was fillin' in Uncle Muff on things she needed to know as far as their peoples. Vah kept saying, "Do you understand, Unc, and do you know what I mean?"

Uncle Muff came out to Vah with, "Yo, I like when you just said Unc, that's cute plus it cut my name short. I'm diggin' that for real. Long as you do not say Unc-a-Donk. No time ever, we a-ight, ya feel me? Now lead the way to Jaia's new ride." All started laughing.

Back in Selkirk, the white chick that sold them guns just happened to remember when she might have known or seen Jaia before. It was in a picture with a drug lord; a Dominican guy named Manuel Acosta. She had met him at a rifle convention give by the NRA. They met up later to discuss some business down in Florida at one of his penthouses. She knew that when he thought he was getting' some of her Ms. 45's pussy and that's where she thought she had seen Jaia's picture. She was shocked as all hell, wondering why the fuck Jaia is selling dam drugs.

Her father distributes all over the US plus he owns stock in computer software. He owns banks in the Dominican Republic. This fucking guy is made of money.

'What the hell is going on, 'she thought, 'I'll keep a close eye on Jaia and any shit jumps off with any fucking thing that she is involved in, motherfuckers gotta go. I got the bitches back - her and her dawgs. I will not inform her of that or her father Manuel. I'll just be her

babysitter because the streets have ears, so I'm not gonna miss shit. I'm always listening.' Natalie sat on the bed and said to the guy in the room, "Hey come lick this pussy nicely, it's calling you man. Hey man," she yelled. As soon as the guy got close and stuck his tongue out to lick her whole pussy, she smashed his face right into it.

She said, "Suck it like it's a lollipop. I wanna hear you slurp it like juice, so I cau fuck your face as ifit's the roaring sixties. Do it, baby, yeah just like that, oooooh, that's good. Oh it is so good. Baby, suck it slow, please suck it slow. Now lick it four times nice and slow.

Mmmm, oh, suck it like that, slurp it, kiss it. Ahhh, do it baby. I wanna cum all in your face and you drink my cum like you're sipping a straw, baby. How does it taste? Tell me, it's yours.

Tell me you want me to fuck your face."

She had his head so far imbedded in her pussy that nigga could not breathe. At the same time she started trying to shove his fucking head inside her pussy; she was screaming aud hollering. Then he got up. His name was Charles. He smacked her on her ass aud turned her over. His dick is nine inches and she kept saying, "Daddy, you wanna give me sum dat or you want me. to be good and wait?"

With his baritone voice, he said, "Let me just play with your pussy with the tip for a minute." Natalie said, "Yo, Charles, you better stick your motherfuckin' dick, nigga, up in this wet ass pussy, right the fuck now. No bullshit. Stop frontin' bitch and act like you know. Ya feel me? Now get to fuckin' bumping, pumping all up in this here, ooooh, ooooh, oooh, ooooh, don't stop for one, got dam, oooh, oooh, oh shit for one. Oh my, my, my come on, take this pussy.

Take it. Take it. I said, "TAKE IT"

She's getting ready to blow to kingdom cum. Yes, yes, yes, oooh, ooooh, ooh, yes.

I'mmmmm Cummmmmin, Cu-Cu, Curnmin. Whew, Baby that shit is the fucking shit. Whew.... I see you just tryin' to let me know you taking this pussy. Huh! Or you just were claiming it for now. It's alright cause this dick has one helluva charge in it," she said. smiling satisfied. Back at the police station, the po-po that Da-Stev refers to as his contact. His name is Detective Reese of homicide. He sat at his desk wondering about his bundles of heroin and thinking something has to be done soon to that mother fucking white prick Danny is white too, but when you're fuckin' around in the hood slinging shit, all the dudes aud mammas become some type of my nig, nigga. It depends on who you are aud how you use it, cause some dudes in the hood will beat the shit out of you. Shit, I'm lucky I am the law and a dirty one at that. Them motherfuckers on the street know my wrath getting back to busting a coupla these boys off the block. I know that Boone character knows that Clinton is where you get rid of dope. He should have his black ass over there somewhere. He'll catch up to him. Da-Stev had already put him on to Jaia, Vah and Unc, so he had to put his plan into play quick before Boone sold all his shit and started flashing like sum big Willie Bo Bo on the come up. He's shutting him down just as soon as he gets info from Da-Stev as to where Jaia and them will be putting him on the block.

This stupid ass fuck really thinks he's actually gonna sell crack and heroin. *My* fucking heroin on L&O. This bitch ass niggar is in for a real shabang.

* * *

Vah, Jaia and Unc were feeling their oats. Once they pulled Into the Stuyvesant *Mall,* they shopped like crazy for Unc. She had gotten some linen suits in nice pastel colors and h Nine West dress shoes. She looked very casual at times, when she did pick her up. She didn't feel it was important to get all jiggy, as she would say. However, or Vah and Jaia, she'd make herself look presentable when it came to handling business with her new found family. She also gotta lotta women's briefs from Victoria Secrets, with the paisley design on' em. They felt silky on her ass, so she knew the boxers were history, but not her Joe Boxers.

Then they drove to the outlets for some sporty shit like velour sweat suits. They all got the same colors but different styles. Jaia's was the skin tight sexy suit. Vah and Unc looked at her and in unison said, "Dam, bitch!"

Unc said, "Who you wearin' that scuba suit for? It looks like it'll choke the shit outta your body, girl."

Vah laughed her ass off. Unc looked at Jaia with lust in her eyes and right there Jaia caught it. She though, *'Dam, Unc, do look like she can handle a bitch right and she sure can slurp on my jreezy anytime. I'ma have to git at her when Vah ain't around. She* is *kinda cute.'*

Vah had bought herself some nice Timbs, some LRG shorts and some Air Jordans. The shit runs up to $250 a pair. She was satisfied though.

Vah noticed the attraction going on between Jaia and Unc and started smiling, thinking they look cute together, "Although business and pleasure do not mix with bitches. They put to much drama in shit, so I'll just sit back and watch their episodes. This shit is going to be hilarious," She laughed. Road.

They all had enough of shopping so they decided to stop at the Red Lobster over on Wolf Dnc yelled, "yeah, it'll be my treat, a-ight?"

"Cool," Jaia said, "Let's go and eat up a motherfuckin' storm, my dawgs."

While they were eating Jaia asked Unc if she drives.

She stated, "yeah, the last time I checked. I stole this nice black Honda and had it for a month, until I took this bitch to an appointment at DSS and parked in a no parking zone. I went inside, came back out and they were towing the shit. I watched them as I came out with this friend of mine. I kept on walking, saying "Dam, that a smooth Iil booga." They were all laughing their asses off at the patron's looking, smirking their faces.

We paid 'em no mind continuing our conversations. We had a nice pleasant time at Red Lobster. Afterward, we headed toward Albany, riding down Sand Creek Road; at the same time Jaia was house hunting. They she spotted a nice Iil brick brown one with a "For Sale" sign and jotted down the address of the house.

Boone had everything on lock over at L&O, so he thought. Little did he know Detective Reese was watching every one of the transactions he made. The so called thug in his ass with that cocky ass ego. Detective Reese was pissed the fuck off about his shit. He knew he needed an angle to come at Boone, for sure. He wanted to kill him on the spot cause the cocky bastard knew too much. He had seen Boone with the dude he was chasing that night for his shit, earlier in the day. They must have been discussing that night. They had to be. The dude kept throwing his hands up in the air saying to Boone, "Yeah man, it's you I threw the bag toward. You were sitting with this dyke ass bitch on the stoop. Ah, come on man, I'm not stupid or fucking cracked out, man. That package did not belong to me. There is going to be some real big problems in don't get it back, dude. Some consequences are surely to happen. Sum body gonna pay, suffer, or plain just fuckin' get knocked off. Simple as that."

"So what the fuck is good, man. Are you gonna give me the shit that doesn't belong to you, or what?"

Boone exploded on the white dude so fucking loud that it turned heads in the distance. "Listen you piece of fucking white infested motherfucking crack pipe looking piece of shit. If you do not step outta my space in a minute, son. I'm tellin' you right now white boy, you're gonna be one hurt motherfucker. Ya feel me? Serious son. Go kick some rock. Scat like a rat bitch ass. You ain't getting' shit, a-ight."

So one of Boone's lookouts came over and asked if everything was cool.

"Yeah."

The white dude said to Boone, "By the way that package belongs to a dirty cop. The one chasing me that night. So I guess what goes around comes around. Ya see we both are on the run fo sho, ya heard? My name is Danny, by the way. So don't say I didn't warn ya black ass motherfucker. I'm outta here."

Detective Reese sat in his black sedan with tinted windows, with some binoculars checking out Danny's and Boone's conversation. He knew they were discussing his honky-tonk ass. He has to get on his grind and handle this shit in a lawful way. He needed to do Da-Stev a favor for the TLC crew. He wondered what the fuck is a got dam TLC. Some ole shit to help them bitches get rid of their drugs, so the hood would know he thought he had plans for Danny's scheming ass. He's gotta die. Lil back stabbing fucker. I'll fix his fucking ass.

As he watched Danny walk away from Boone, he said, "That motherfucking crack-head bastard didn't even try to retrieve my fucking drugs. Scary fuckin' punk. I do not believe that cocksucker, fucking creep. Yeah, I'ma kill that motherfucker right the fuck now."

He drove toward Lark Street keeping a close eye on Boone, while Danny walked toward Clinton Ave., and sped toward Swan Street to cut Danny off. Danny was fucking shocked as hell, ready to run back the way he carne from.

"Oh no you don't." Reese said, "You son of a bitch. Don't fuckin' move."

Danny froze at the sight of a 38 special pointed right at his dead.

Danny said, "What the fuck, you gonna kill me right here? I tried to get your package back. That black motherfucker wouldn't give it, up ya know."

Detective Reese said, "I saw the whole fucking conversation. You piece of prick. You're a fucking sissy ass low life motherfucker. Get in the fucking car. First let me handcuff your ass, so that people's watching will know I am making an arrest. You fucking smuck. Then I can beat the shit outta you, kid. First, for having me chase you for my fucking shit. Yeah, buddy, your ass is mine, boy."

* * *

Aunya made it to Albany County Jail, went through medical and then they escorted her up to her cell. She got so pissed when she looked at the bitches in there. She was disgusted.

One bitch said, "Yo, son, what you in for?"

She screamed on the bitch. "Yo, I am not here to make any fucking friends, so don't none of y'all motherfucking hoes, crack-heads, crackers or dope fiends make any attempt to holla at a bitch. Ya feel me? I am not the one, so don't get it twisted bitches or ask about it cause I'm about it. I'ma show you better than I can tell ya. Test the waters, bitches."

The CO yelled to her. "Yo, new jack, shut the fuck up, ya heard that? Better yet, lay the fuck down and rest up for court, so they can send your ass upstate. Then we'll see how much you'll be riffing, new jack ass." She smiled.

Aunya started making her bed wondering how are her dawgs, knowing shit was on and poppin'. By now she should be receiving some mail and monies for commissary.

CHAPTER SIX

SO THEN THE OFFICER SAID, 'Rec."

Aunya was like, "What the fuck is a fucking rec?"

The girl next to her said, "We go outside to the yard and play some ball or just chill out on the grass or on the bench. Everybody and their mother is from the hood except these white collar crime bitches, ya heard?"

Aunya said, "Well, let me see what the fuck is up and listen to the streets talk from these hood rat bitches." Then Aunya thought to herself *'I wonder if I'll hear anything about my dawgs, 'cuz them bitches are reckless.'*

Her neighbor introduced herself as Lisa. She started talking about why she's locked up, volunteering information.

"Dam girl, do you take a fuckin' breather? Shit, you going non-stop, rna. I don't even know ya."

So she kept on and talked over Aunya and asked her what her name was. "Yo, what is ya name, Miss Fucking-Arrogant-Ass-Bitch?"

"Bitch, you definitely got issues callin' me out my name. I don't even wanna start getting' up in your grill too soon, bitch. So, I'ma just ignore your trifling ass. I'll holla at ya another time, bitch. A-ight, ya feel, me."

Lisa was walking around the yard getting her exercise on talking to herself saying "Who does this dyke ass bitch things she's spazzin' on? Oh, she got the right one, for sure. I'ma git at her, especially after she cut my girl Coco in the face. She knows this is the streets behind bars; yeah, she gotta get got, fo sho."

The female CO yelled, "Aunya Mirayes, go to medical," and she proceeded to direct her to medical As she walked through the halls she started feeling the fact that her ass is really doing time. *'It's kinda scary,' she thought, 'but it's not all that it's fabricated to be, like seen on TV.'*

She entered the medical doors into a bull pen cell with three other female inmates. She sat down and felt them hard, staring at her, so she stared back and all eyes turned around. After Aunya received the physician's assistance check up, she headed back to her celL She was walking down the hall when this male inmate was coming toward her on the other side of the halL He started staring her ass down. He then made a remark, seeing her whole presence, that she's a dyke, "Hey girl, you need sum this dick to get you right, Ma?" She looked at him and said, "You pissy looking piece of shit. Hold ya dick for yo mamma. How 'bout that. You know what it is, bitch ass nigga."

The officer yelled, "Shut the fuck up you two. You know I can write both your asses you. You're not to say a dam thing to each other, in any hallway or the jail period. So keep it movin' both of you, before I write your asses tickets. Now, have a nice day."

Aunya was heated, but she knew she had to humble herself with the COs. She'd seen that these motherfuckers look like black hating crackers. She has to remember where she's at, in Albany not New York City. So she went back to the yard from medical, walking and thinking how she overheard the nurse and a CO talking about a female inmate having a crack stem all broke up in her vagina.

The nurse herself boldly said, "I ain't goin' up in no dam inmate's pussy to get jack. They're gonna have to run her ass over to the GYN at the hospital to remove the pieces of glass from her vagina. That shit is off the chain."

Then the male officer stated with so-called humor, "imagine sticking my penis in her vagina and try to fuck her brains out and my dick comes out all cut the fuck up. That would be some shit," they both started laughing. Aunya could not get over their conversation.

As she sat on the bench, Lisa approached her, sat down next to her and began talking to her, said ""You know the streets are always listening as well in jail, girl" Lisa was a pretty girL She had a Halle Berry short hair-do, thick eyebrows and carmel looking skin with light brown eyes. Her breasts were full, nice round ass, nice pearly whites, with one front tooth missing. Aunya said, "So, what the fuck ya heard or tryin' to spit out, yo? Or are you trying to find out? I'ma let you find out, you keep fuckin' trying to holla at a bitch. I ain't feeling you, ya feel me. I don't want to either bitch, and listen, let this be the last time Lisa, or do you want to get to thumpin' right now? Whenever ya ready, bitch, cause trust me it won't be me hurt and fucked up, boo. I know that for a fact, so you better calculate before it's too late. I'm tellin' you, I am not the one Lisa. I don't care what you got up your sleeve or what your plan is, but I guarantee you - I am better! That's a promise bitch." Lisa yelled, "A-ight Aunya, you're gonna feel my wrath bitch and when you do, you gonna think the devil is trying to set ya dyke ass on fire. Ya eating pussy from the ass up bitch? Another thang, ya fuckin' warma be homeboy. I'ma show you how a woman can kick another woman's ass, so ya better bring out all your manly strength boy."

Another female was trying to warn them that the CO was watching them go at it and looked like he would soon be coming over to them. So Aunya got up from the bench and started walking around the yard. The CO yelled, "Rec over."

All the inmates headed inside to their cells. As Lisa started up the stairwell, this female named Dolly came out of nowhere and cold knocked the bejesus outta Lisa's jaw. Everyone heard the shit crack like two drip drops of a faucet.

Dolly was saying, "Yeah bitch, remember, tramp over on Clinton and Lex. Yeah, I'm that bitch ya caught out there wit ya Iil hood rat hoes. Y'all jumped me for my shit. Ya thought I'd forgot. Nah, bitch. Brooklyn bitches keep it raw, Ma."

Then Dolly threw Lisa to the floor and stomped the shit outta her ass.

As Aunya caught the ass whipping being laid on Lisa's ass, she said to Lisa, "Oops! That is one ass kickin'. You sure you want some of me, boo? Oops. I didn't think so bitch. You got your ass almost knocked the fuck out." She laughed so much her stomach started hurting.

She told Lisa, "Ya fake ass, warma be thug-get. Get your ass tore the fuck out of its frame." Lisa was all fucked up bleeding from her mouth, all scraped up and bruised. All the inmates stepped over her ass going up the stairs. They were mumbling, snickering, and some all hyped up at how Dolly came at Lisa with a surprise punch to her jaw. That shit was on and poppin'. One inmate kept saying that afterwards the CO came to assist, but everyone dispersed. Lisa laid on the floor in pain and all she said was, "That bitch ass Dolly, she snuck me. I'ma git that hoe fo sho."

The CO asked her if she could move or if anything was broken. She said, barely moving her mouth, "I think my jaw is broken." He escorted her over to medical.

Dolly needed to relax. She was hyped like a motherfucker. All she wanted was her git back. She made it happen, too, with a wicked smile on her face.

Aunya was in her cell cracking the fuck up at how Lisa got her ass whipped. The fucked up shit is she slipped and forgot who she had jacked on the streets. That's a no-no, especially coming to jail. Ya never know.

She thought to herself, *I gotta give Dolly her props, though, Everybody was so hyped off that shit in the stairwell, even the females that weren't there. They heard about it though. Even Lisa did not snitch about who kicked her ass; that's a good thing. Aunya and the other inmates kept saying that shit was off the motherfucking chain. She wailed Lisa's ass out fo sho'*

* * *

Meanwhile, Detective Reese had Danny in an abandoned building on Swan Street and Orange. He had handcuffed him to a radiator, no clothes on at all, beating his back with a barb wire piece. Danny's hollering as loud as he could, sounding light-headed as if he'd faint any minute. The Detective Reese took out a box cutter and started carving gang signs in his chest, so the police would think it's related to the gang bangers selling drugs in the hood. Then, he himself can begin eliminating them from the block, along with Boone. Danny's crying voice sounded like music to Detective Reese's ears. He really got excited off the pain he inflicted.

He put on some latex gloves and said to Danny, "Here's the good part of the torturing."

He put potatoe chips and some cheese on Danny and left Danny for dead, with a trail of chips and shit, so the rats would go directly to this body and eat the shit right the fuck off with cheese.

Danny laid there in horror. He screamed so much that he'd lost his voice. He couldn't be heard anyway as the rats started scurrying to the smell of the chips and cheese. They went toward Danny and were all over his body. There wasn't anything he could do being cuffed to the radiator. They began crawling on him, tasting the blood that dripped from his wounds. They were eating at his dick ferociously. He wished the cop would have just shot him in the head and gotten it over with. He watched in pain and horror as his dick was getting eaten up by the rodents. He squirmed and kicked, but to no avail; nothing could be done. He started the crack twitching shit looking like he had the disease Tourette's, but in pain.

The following day, Jaia, Unc and Vah had to meet Ms. Smiley down by the Key Bank to see their real estate investors and accountant to legitimize their monies. All three of 'em were dressed to impress, fo sho Yah said to Jaia, "Remember when we first came up here to get our shine on dawgs. It's been three years now and we've done the dam thang so far, huh? I miss Aunya, but we got her share. She'll be proud of us bitches when she hits the streets in another eighteen months. Once we enter those doors to clean up our shit - it's to the motherfuckin' top, boo. Ya feel me, Unc and Jaia?"

Ms. Smiley was proud of her hustlers and that they were doing their fucking thing. Better yet, all of 'em females and young, on the come up. She's glad cause they kinda remind her of herself when she started living in Albany, which she was a little younger than them. She was fourteen years old, her mom was a dope fiend name Sheila, when she had her. Her dad a bum ass so called pimp. That is how she entered this world; her life was living fucking hell. Her uncles and their friends use to give her quarters to touch their dicks, at the age of five. Then she graduated to sucking dick at seven. Then at age nine, a neighbor saw her sitting on the stoop with blood dripping through her jeans. She was crying hysterically saying, "They put it in me.

Their dick, they put it in me."

She called the police and they investigated and Children's Services took her from her house. She had no other relatives who wanted her except her uncle and dad, who fucked her royally that day. She ended up in foster care until she was twelve then she started running away, figuring out ways to get money. She met an old ass man named Boogie who used to collect bottles and cans. The homeless looking old man took her under his wing and he taught her everything she knew about surviving in the streets. He even showed her where she could sleep in abandon buildings and showed her where he stayed. She was shocked at the shit this homeless man had in his crib. He had everything he needed including lights and gas. Although the building he entered was all boarded up, he entered through the backyard. The people on the block knew old man Boogie stayed there. Since he was not a nuisance, they never complained to the authorities about him. He was kind and always said hi and gave the kids some money for ice cream and candy. He had been living in the building for so many years that no one paid him any mind.

He called her Smiley and she stayed with Boogie at his abandoned building. She felt safe with him, so he'd take her with him on his bottle and cans run. They both would call it getting free money. One day, after coming home from hanging in the streets, Smiley came back to get old man Boogie so they could do their bottles and cans run. He was dead and she was devastated. The person she would come to love as a parent had died on her. She asked God -why? Why me? Why can't I have a nice life too, like I see other kids have with their parents? Smiley, at a young age, had already seen people die especially being around her nodding ass mother. So death didn't faze her. It was the relationship she and old man Boogie had acquired in the one year she had known him. She started thinking about what she was going to do now. She thought, *'Boogie had to have a stash cause she had never seen him go to the bank.'* She began searching and under his bed she found cash. Her eyes almost popped out of her head. She had close to twenty-five thousand dollars.

"Oh, shit," she kept saying, "old man Boogie was stashing his life savings."

Smiley was only eighteen and she figured she'd have him a tombstone made. She and the others in the neighborhood showed up at his funeral. Now, she had decided she needed to move on. Staying in an abandoned building would have been too lonely for her without Boogie. In the process of hanging in the streets, she had always seen guys hustling, selling weed, dope and cocaine. She needed to invest the money and keep it flowing.

Since that time in her life it has been up hill for Smiley, who is now Ms. Smiley - H.B.I.C. (Head Bitch In Charge) of all the drug infested areas in the streets of the capital of New York - Albany. She had to smile at her endeavors maintaining her status all these years. That is why she is so into showing Jaia, Vah, and Unc the way to get their dirty ass drug money legit.

Now everyone is at the bank. The accountant is explaining all the procedures to them, especially how much money they can bring to the bank at a time to put in ofshore accounts. Also, the whole nine yards of investing and asking them if there is any type of business they wanted to own, the accountant, Ms. Louise Pitcher, asked.

Vah said, "I've always wanted a laundermat, where you can be served twenty-four seven." "That's a wonderful idea. It shall be done right away," stated Ms. Pitcher. They began thinking of locations and Ms. Pitcher assured them that she'd handle all the necessary paperwork. She told them all she needed was their signatures, depending on who would be conducting the business. They all were satisfied with everything and thanked Ms. Smiley by offering to take her to lunch. She declined by saying she had some things to take care of and she'd give them a rain check on it.

* * *

It was Aunya's day to go upstate to Bedford Hills, She was nervous as all hell. The Co's called her ass early.

"Inmate Mirayes, it's time to go. The only thing you can take with you is a Bible. That's it." She had her Bible, with all her information. Jaia's and Vah's addresses and phone numbers, where they could be reached. As soon as she hit Betty's House, that's what they called Bedford Hills Correctional Facility, she'd contact them.

She arrived mid-afternoon. The Sheriffs Department escorted her. She had to wait for them to call her name before the Albany County Sheriff s could leave, then she'd officially be state's property. She got through all the screening and shit; there were all kinds of tests concerning her health. The CO's that were attending to her were nasty to her, she thought she better keep her mouth shut. They gave her, her DIN number and where she would be housed for the next two weeks. She made it to the back buildings and when she arrived the shit hit the fan.

The bitches were all loud in the big ass room they called the rec room. They were playing cards, Scrabble, talking about the streets and what they wore, what niggas they were rolling with in the hood, how they were getting money and who they conned. Next thing you know bitches started arguing about some fucking rollie (cigarette).

One female named Freda said, "Bitch, I had my fuckin' rollie right here hoe, by my cards and you stood over here for a minute and after you left bitch, my shit left. So you either cough up my shit or get your ass whipped, bitch. Step in the bathroom ya bald-headed-on-the-sides motherfuckin' -biatch. I'ma get mine, ya street dirt tramp. I know one thing, ya better get my motherfuckin' rollie or the got dam CO's are gonna be picking your unconscious ass of the floor."

She grabbed that bitch, started pounding her face out and said, "I told ya Munchie to go get my shit. You didn't have to go out like that. All you had to do was ask. No hoe, you decided to be slick and on top of everything that shit was disrespectful, Munchie. Bitch, I'm going to lock, so it doesn't even matter, hoe. Your ass is done."

She commenced to really fucking Munchie up badly. The CO's came swarming into the dorm.

They said, "Get the fuck back now, unless y'all wanna go to keyblock. Go to your fucking cubes. It's lock-in, on a lock down."

Aunya couldn't believe this shit. *'Oh man, this shit is crazy,'* she thought to herself. *'Dam, ['rna really gonna have to watch my back. These hoes are treacherous up in here. Oh, how the COs threw Freda on the floor on her face to restrain her. I know she'll be in pain for a couple of days. Dam, they didn't have to do the bitch like that. Oh well, welcome to jail.'* Aunya stayed put after the incident in her cube, until all the bullshit calmed down. Right across from her there was a cutie. A nice pretty Hawaiian or Asian looking chick with jet black hair, chingey looking eyes that were sort of light brown and looked full of lust, and some perky tits. The bitch looked hot. Aunya stared at this luscious bitch for a minute.

Aunya then asked her, "Yo, what up. What's your name, yo?"

The female said, "Fran."

"Mine's Aunya. Yo, ma, is it crazy like this all the time?"

Fran responded, "It gets worse Aunya, but as long as you stay to yourself, your time will be easy. Don't get me wrong. Bitches will try you, boo."

"Yo, Fran, where's the phone at? I gotta call my peeps."

She showed Aunya where the phone booth was. Everyone was looking at Fran taking Aunya toward the phone, showing her how to use it.

Fran said, "Yeah yo, you official in my eyes, boo. I wanna get to know you better, if it's okay with you, Boo."

Aunya looked at her like she lost her fuckin' mind. *'Dam this bitch is fast. I gotta definitely watch out for sho; she's up to something. She's not that fine to be all up in mine.'* She thought to herself.

So Aunya said, "Excuse me, while I'm on the phone." The bitch must have took me for a sho nuff sucker or sununin'. I gotta tap this bitch's brains and let her know who she is fucking wit, quick. She seem to got plans, but me personally, *"It's time to let a hoe know all about the kid,"* she laughed.

Jaia's phone rang and the operator came on, "a collect call form inmate Aunya Mirayes." Jaia's reaction was, "Put the bitch tbrough."

She had to listen to the recording, then she heard Aunya's voice; she was so dam excited. "Yo, my bitch, oh man I miss you Aunya. I love ya dawg. Yo bitch, I been waitin' for your call, motherfucka. What took so long man? Oh shit, Aunya, what's good nig?"

Aunya said, "Yo, you know I need some gear, especially some sneakers. The whole shabang, boo. Yo, where Vah at? I got my own hoes now, nigga." They laughed.

That's good dawg. Yo Aunya, shit is good bitch. When we travel to visit, we'll fill ya head wit sum good shit. Gee. We truly bangin', yo," Jaia said, "oh, I am meeting Yah later, so I'ma holla at her so we all can talk together on the phone, dawg. When you call nigga a-ight."

Aunya's like, "Man, I can't wait until you bitches come see a mouthafucka, ya heard. I love you two. Y'all fam for life in my heart. Ya feel me dawg. It's all good, Jaia. Well, I'm outti until later gator. One." She knew in her heart her dawgs were there by law. That's how they've always been - down with each other for life.

CHAPTER SEVEN

DA-STEV HAD CALLED JAIA TO let her know the plan concerning Boone is going into full effect, as he speaks.

He told Jaia, "When Detective Reese goes about his elimination and shit, it's some git back. So, get ready to handle your end, fo shoo Money is in the makin', Babe. As far as the other fools on the block sellin', he's straight getting rid of these dumb ass so-called gangsters. He's the motherfuckin' mob alone. Just got a badge to do his dirt. Check that shit out, Jaia. He also wanna get in good on the profits being made because of the mayhem shit. He's about to put it down on L&O. I'ma bet you that."

He had bagged this white kid, Danny, who'd been doing dirt for him, but the kid tried a skid bid on him. So, he fed his ass to the fuckin' rats. Can you believe that shit, glued cheese to the guy's fuckin' dick. Ouch! That made my dick feel kinda sore. Excuse my language, Jaia.

My bad. But that shit is sick, ya know. But a dude's gotta do what he gotta do, plus he's dam sure helping our pockets. Dam, skippy. That's my boy, yo. It's all good to have a dirty motherfuckin' DT in your realm, especially wit the shit we do, ya know."

Jaia said, 'I feel you Da-Stev'. OK, boo. I just wanted to holla at a beautiful sistah such as yourself Iam, a-ight. I'm out. One." Vah and Jaia went over to Jaia's new crib, checking out the mahogany wood stained floor from the entrance to her dining room. It was nice and cozy. Jaia had told Vah that Aunya had called. We gotta go and visit this weekend. She is expecting us."

"1 miss her, too," Jaia said. "She'll be calling tonight and is anxious to speak to you. Oh, and the operator sounds like some robotic bitch, saying 1 have a collect call, then she says the fucking facility. Fuck all that shit, just put my dawg through. Ya know what I mean? All that dam yapping, even from a recording. Isn't that some correctional facility crap?"

Jaia continued, "So Vah, listen up. 1 got the call from Da-Stev. Detective Reese is getting ready to eliminate our 'Iil gangbanging, lowlife hustlers, along wit Boone. Yeah dawg, Aunya's spot is gonna blow up on the come up while she's doing her time. Her hustling game is gittin' money and still doing jail time. I cannot wait to see her."

Vah said, "Now you know she will be representing this hardened criminal act when she sees us. That stubborn bitch. But, she's gonna be alright, cuz we defmitely got her whole bid. Yo we gotta put a "G" in her account, dawg. She is not gonna want for nothing; send her whatever she wants. The bitch is probably in her glory with all that pussy around her ass. I hope she just is careful wit all the diseases bitches carry, ya know Jaia. It's her first time ever being in jail, let alone state time.

Vah said, "She'll be just fine. She knows how to put the "H" on her chest. She is a stone cold trooper, bitch. Believe that. Aunya has a temper; she's nobody's fool or fuckin' joke. Do not under estimate the Iil bitch, Jaia. That's why we all hit it off. We have to strive to be driven into a determination of empowerment. We are all each other's strength. Ya feel me, dawg?" L&O is busy as hell. Boone is trying to get every lick that comes through the block wanting crack or heroin, cutting off gang bangers. As customers approach for sum shit, this one kid named T.J. kept staring at Boone like, *'Nigga you keep cock blocking my sales, bitch.'* So Boone stared back like, *'Come on punk try your fuckin' luck.'* Then he decided to kinda like tease T.J.

"Yo, lil nigga, why haven't you been try'na git sum this cheddar, boy?"

T.J. stepped back and told Boone, "Nigga, I think you best to raise the fuck back or up. Whichever you choose, homie, bitch ass, corny ass nigga, ya heard."

T.J. had his hand on his gat the whole time. Within minutes all the other gang bangers, about ten of them, stepped to where T.J. and Boone stood.

"Everything a-ight T.J." one of them said, "cause we sure can make shit happen, son. Ya feel me?"

All the while Detective Reese was sitting in his sedan, over on Lark Street, with his binoculars, watching. He started smiling to himself saying, "Yeah boys, get this motherfucker on and poppin'. Gives me a good reason to get y' all imbeciles off my streets, so I can get paid from my three new investors, three the hard way. Whoa, they'll definitely hit me offlovely. It's show time on L&O."

He saw all the Iil dudes surrounding Boone. Then he said he was going to remember every last one of 'em. So, when he decided to do his clean street sweep with his entourage of the State Troopers and Sheriff s Department; they'll actually help do his dirty work and not have any idea about it. He already did his paperwork to authorize his shit. So, it was a go.

T.J. explained, "This mothafucka keeps blocking my money, yo. I ain't tryn'a feel this shit. He's askin' for a serious beatdown."

Boone said, "Yo, money. I don't think so. This here is public property, homes. I do not see no sign or no street signs that say this street is a gang banging street or avenue, nigga. You need to have yo black ass in school try'na spell 'street,' ya lil bitch. We all can make money nigga. Stop fuckin' whinin'. If you can't handle a grown man's game in the hustle, then go play jump rope or summin', a'ight."

All of a sudden these two cars crashed head on; a black SUV and a Nissan. The dude in the SUV jumped out from the driver's side yelling at the other guy, "Yo, you are a fuckin' moron. Didn't you see the stop sign, bitch?"

The other guy replied, "It's too far off from the comer, man."

They went back and forth at each other. The next thing you know a shot was fired and all hell broke loose on the L&O comer. So, T.J and his boys started ducking and dodging the bullets and jumped behind some cars. Some ran in the store on the comer. Then Boone took out his gat, a 9mm and started shooting toward where T.J. was running and caught him in the back of his head. T.J.'s body flicked like a lighter and fell to the ground hard. Boone said, "Yeah, one whining motherfucker gone." And he was out. Detective Reese, with a big ass grin, watched the whole episode go down and decided that is how he'd get Boone's ass, but on the down low.

The two guys involved in the car accident were huddled together in the basement of a house on Lark Street. They told each other, "Fuck the information needed for insurance." Then they went their own separate ways.

Police and an ambulance were on the scene ten minutes later; everyone scattered. One police officer started asking the people, who were standing around the commotion, questions. No one wanted to explain shit. This one lady who always sits on her stoop saw the whole incident, as she does with everything that goes on, on L&O. She told them that the guys who had the car accident fled once the shooting stopped.

She said, "They got the fuck out of dodge and took the fuck off." She also stated she didn't know who fired the first shot.

All of a sudden, one of TJ.'s friend spotted his body in between a parked car and the curb, slumped face down.

"Oh shit, my nigga T.J. is dead." He started yelling, getting all teary eyed and furious began screaming, "Who the fuck did this? Yo, that ass is dead. Dead! Yo, T.J., I'ma get 'em.

That's my word son, on everything I love."

The police officer told him, "Come on now, you're gonna have to let the paramedics do their job, son. Step back, please." Everybody's talking about the death of T.J. and why did that happen and how it happened so fast. Some people saw when the guy, who was T.J.'s homeboy, fired the first shot in the air.

Then everything went crazy. No one said anything. No one liked the snitching game. That's a no-no in the hood and everyone understood that, that is the law. There is a penalty for that shit for real. The penalty is suffering being a snitch and everybody knows it, or death.

* * *

The morning Jaia and Vah got up to see Aunya at Bedford Hills Correctional Facility they both were really so excited. They smoked a blunt, riding on the highway in Jaia's new navy blue Navigator with a pink interior. It had a helluva system, with the TV's in the head rests for back seat riders. Vah gave her girl sum dap. They both where hyped about seeing their dawg. They went shopping the day before and picked her up some uptown's, two pairs, some women's style briefs, T-shirts, white and colorful ones with pockets to match her sweats and a watch. They did the dam thing for a dawg. They also got her a food package, a nice Figaro chain with a cross and gold hoop earrings. They were both saying that Aunya is gonna be straight, not like she doesn't have monies for commissary, plus she knows they stay busy, so the trips are not going to be long.

"She has another year, yo. Yeah and you know," Vah said, "I'ma hook that bitch up with sum gear. Ya feel me, J aia."

Next thing ya know they're pulling into Bedford's parking lot and went through the process.

They called Aunya for her visit. She was shouting, "Oh shit, my dawgs are here!" When she was so excited the female, Fran said, "Have a nice VI baby." Aunya looked like, *'Where did all this baby shit come from? Hmmm?'* As Aunya made her way into the visiting room she spotted her dawgs. Jaia had on some fly ass shit, looking all sexy. Vah looked as cool as ever with her two hundred dollar kicks.

They both looked straight up money. She headed toward them and they all started hugging and kissing. All started crying, happy tears, for the time they missed among each other.

The CO's were staring at them.

One male officer said "Dam, they are dime piece and more, especially Jaia," he thought, "she is so fucking gorgeous."

He said, "Hell, I can dam sure have a menage-A-trois with both them ladies."

His co-worker said, "Hell, they can spank me and beat my dick with their tongue. I don't give a flyin' fuck. Gimmie sum dat. Ya heard."

The aggressive female CO's were checking out Jaia and Vah hard and knew they were straight up lesbians getting' paid. However, they were representing doing the dam thang with class. They smiled hoping they can git their numbers from Aunya.

Vah, Jaia and Aunya felt good about seeing each other. They all laughed, reminisced, and played cards. Aunya ate popcorn. The bought a whole bunch of junk out of the vending machine. Aunya was shocked to see so much shit at their table.

Jaia stated, "So we don't have to get up for shit. Our time is precious, dawg. Oh yea, we put a "G" in your account, a'ight. Now let's make sum jailhouse jokes."

Vah came right out and asked Aunya if she felt Coco should be got or what.

She said, "Nah dawg, cause it was my foolishness of not thinking and also bringing attention to us. It would be reckless to do so dawg. Then we'd be under surveillance, fa sho Let it go. It's a lil thang, but she'll remember me for the rest of her life. She'll have something to tell her grandkids and so forth. Know what I mean? We got better things to focus on. Yo, I'm getting' into weight lifting. Bitch gonna be toned upon release, my nig. Another twelve months and I'm ghost. Ya feel me, Vah?"

Jaia explained how things were being done as far as keeping their monies legit. Also, about Uncle Muff, being on the trio. Aunya looked a little startled until they both spoke very highly o f Unc. She found out how Vah cut her name short. Aunya was surprised at how much they've accomplished and shit is on and poppin' with her dawgs."

Their visit had come to an end. All three were so sad that it had to end but knew it had to. Before they departed, Vah mentioned to Aunya that if she calls and gets the answering machine it's because she's out takin' care of business; it's not that she don't love her. "Never that, dawg." Vah said, "Ya feel me, Aunya? For life we all we got as one. A family. Booya-. Remember, hold that shit, bitch."

They all laughed and said their goodbyes and gave each other hugs and kisses. "Peace out. One," Aunya said.

She got back to her cube with all her shit and the bitches were checking her out as she put her shit away. She was kinda surprised to see two cartons of Newport 100's. She was touched. Her dawgs did her right.

Ms. Smiley called Vah on her cellie as they headed back to Albany. She wanted them to know of an incident concerning her boy Brickman. She truly needed their advice, fo sho This shit is serious. She told her she did not want to go into details over the phone and to meet her at the bar and grill on Madison and Swan Streets.

She hung up and Vah explained to Jaia what was up. Then, they continued talking about their visit with Aunya and how much they enjoyed seeing her and how good she looked. Ms. Thang gonna be kinda diesel when she hits home. They both snickered.

As they came off the highway, Yah and Jaia went straight to the bar and grill. They entered and saw Ms. Smiley at the far end of the bar; they all went to a table. Ms Smiley had a drink already and she told the bartender that Jaia's and Yah's drinking tab is on her; Hennessey for Yah, Cognac for Jaia, no chasers.

Ms. Smiley started telling them about how Brickman smoking crack has affected her business. Also, he stole some shit from the stash house. Only him and her knew of this place over on Dove and Park Avenue. Now two of them knew. She said he had been looking drained and shit, tired looking. Days before, some guy had come to the car asking him about what happened after he left the females house they were getting high with. He promised them he'd get back in touch with some more shit for them to get mgh with. He thought Ms. Smiley wasn't listening to his conversation she was in the back seat handling some business, so he told his associates. "Not now."

Ms. Smiley declared. "The bottom line is this, ladies. He's got to go. Pronto! I need your assistance on this. They were all in all this shit together. Ya feel me?" They said in unison, "Let's do this ladies," and toasted to it. "Drink up," she said, "drinks are on me."

They discussed how they were going to plan on killing Brickman. Ms. Smiley stated, "He loves to get his dick sucked. I'd love to catch him in that situation." She decided to give him a call.

He answered, "Yo, what's up? Holla at yo boy."

She told him. He lit a stem. She could hear it sizzling through the phone. She played it offby saying, "Brickman, I gotta get wit ya, a'ight."

He replied, "Right now I'm banging Shawty out, if ya know what I mean."

She said, "A-ight, I'll holla at ya later, man."

Brickman was geeked out like a motherfucker wit this nice looking female named Mamie, but Shawty's what he called her. She was deep-throating his dick to where you could see his dick print on the sides of her face; then she gargled his balls in her mouth.

He kept saying to her, "Come baby, suck me good. Daddy need to cum." She thought, *'Dam you stupid motherfucker. As long as you keep hitting the stem, you'll stay hard and it 'Il be harder for you to bust a nut, asshole.'* He kept trying to push the tip in so hard. he said. He wanted to come in her now. The crack he was smoking has the motherfucker bugging sexually. On top of everything, it wasn't his supply.

His dick was so hard and stiff, he had to look at it himself. He told Mamie, "Let me fuck you from behind, bitch." He slapped her ass as he stroked her. Bam! The door was kicked in. He went to grab for his gat, but it was to late. Jaia had the jump on his ass quick.

Ms. Smiley came in too. She said, "Motherfucker, you smokin' crack bastard. How long did you think bitch, before you knew I'd find out that you're fucking getting high off my shit motherfucker; plus you're stealing shit from me, Brickman. I don't understand dude. We like family. You couldn't come to me and let me know you have a problem instead of it escalating to you not being trusted. That's what hurts the most, Brickman."

"Yo Vah, git that bitch. Tie her ass up now." Jaia had the gun still pointing at his head. The Ms. Smiley's face just looked furious. She said, Nigga you stole from me. Well, this is what happens when a motherfucker I care about wanna get high and fuck wit my supply."

She had a hot pot of water on the stove to boil with some grits.

She said, "Yeah, you always talking about how you love grits and eggs. Well, we gonna see how your dick take to hot grits, nigga."

So, Yah finished tying Mamie. Now, she's tying Brickman up to the stripping pole he has in his bedroom. Ms. Smiley came in with the hot pot of grits.

She yelled, "Nigga, where are my guns, my money and I know you didn't smoke a fucking kilo, bitch. I refuse to believe that." She held the pot under his dick and lifted it up to his dick.

That shit started boillin'. He screamed, "I'm sorry, I'm sorry." Then Vah pulled out her silencer and shot the female, Mamie in her right temple. Then they all started looking for extension cords and found some. They wet them and beat his ass until his skin started peeling something terrible. The Jaia stabbed him in the neck with his stem.

They all trashed his house like it was a drug deal gone bad.

* * *

Detective Reese watched Boone leave the scene of the crime he just committed. He thought, *'that motheifucker doesn't even realize his ass* is *dead meat, just as sure as he killed that 'Iil gangbanger. I can't wait to get his funky ass. I just have to come at Boone right. He's not the one to take shit lightly. He wants to be a fuckin' legend of the hood, so he* is *not going down easy at all.'*

Boone had run down Orange Street, turned on Sheridan Avenue, and sat on an abandoned stoop. He was wondering if anyone saw him shoot T.J. He thought if they did, he'd have a posse after his ass. Therefore, he felt he didn't have shit to be sweating about. He wanted to keep slinging his shit, plus he knew he had to take over the L&O area. He wanted to impress Jaia and Vah so they would make him in charge. That's all he kept drilling in his head; also, to make Uncle Muff proud of him. He figured he'd let all the commotion die down and then he would head back up to L&O to finish getting rid of his shit.

Two hours passed and Boone walked back up the block. He stood in front of the garage on Orange Street. He'd seen the 'Iil gangbangers over by the Arab store on the corner. Everyone was crying and talking about T.J. getting killed, especially this 'Iil hoodrat that said her and T.J. were talking about being a couple and how she wanted to be initiated in order for her to be his girls.

She said, "I was only doing it to be with him. I'm a miss my boo, T.J., God rest his soul."

Everyone went and put something personal of theirs in the spot where they found TJ.'s body. They even brought a can of spray paint and started putting his name in the spot, with R.I.P. on the sidewalk.

They all had 40 ounces of Old English beer and a case of Heineken bottles. They were drinking up a fucking storm, getting pissy drnnk. One of them came with at least a case of Henessey. They all were saying, "T.J. my nigga, this is for you, homie," in unison. Customers were coming in to cop crack. They were fucking with them, especially the fiends. One female came to cop and one of the gangbangers told her, being that she was short of money, to show her titty. She then told him she would do something better than that, she'd suck his dick.

He said to her, "Right here in front of everyone, bitch. Wha cha gonna do? Put some kind of sucking my dick show on for a click, huh?"

She said, "Sure, if you're all for it, boo."

She said, "And if you make me cum good, then I'll give you a little more than you came for, bitch. A-ight. Now, get on your knees and get to sucking."

The woman zipped him down and when she bent down to actually give him some head and as she was trying to pull out his dick, he bashed her in the head with a Heineken bottle.

He yelled, "Bitch, I wouldn't let you suck my mangy ass dog's dick. Ya nasty ass hoe. Git the fuck outta here before I have my Rottwei1er fuck you in the ass."

Everyone laughed at that shit. Some were about to piss on the woman. She ran and sat across the street bleeding, but she still needed a hit bad. Boone got up and walked over to the woman and asked her what she wanted.

She said, "All I want is a dime, I'm two dollars short. I told him I'd suck his dick and he gon' hit me upside my head wit that dam bottle. Look at me. I still need a hit. Yo, you got surnmin man?" Boone said, "Yeah rna, give me the eight dollars. I got ya boo, a-ight. Listen, after I give you this get from around here before those Iil niggas kill your ass. If they get drunk enough, they might try to rape you or shove some shit in ya. So, get the fuck outta here rna, bleeding and shit.

Go on, bitch."

Nubian and Lil Kill came from around the comer and asked Boone, "What's poppin, my nig." He told them about the incident that just happened with the woman.

Nubian said, "Them Iil niggas don't know the fucking crackheads and fiends are the ones who bring the money, cause they always find a means to git money and bring customers. They are the assholes who think they're really hustling and fucking the game up being real fuckin stupid. Ya know what I mean. Therefore, that's where we come in and treat'em only right. Ya feel me Boone, cause it's all about the cheddar getting better." They both laughed.

Two days passed since Danny's body had been found. The homicide detectives that were working his case believe it was a gang related killing because of the markings on his body. The area is known for gangbangers and drug dealings.

"Maybe he came to cop and got robbed, then killed and these Iil pussy ass gangbangers wanted to send a message out to someone. It depends on who this dude was affiliated with.

There is a method to these street punks madness," stated the homicide detective, whose name was Kemp.

Detective Kemp had been on the force fifteen years and figured he'd seen it all, until Danny's death. He thought, *'Dam, just when you thought you'd seen it all. Jesus fucking Christ, who'd think to do some shit like this to another human being.'*

Danny's dick was chewed the fuck off by rats and maggots. A stray dog was nibbling on his leg. His body was eaten by a little bit of everything.

"He definitely got eaten alive," Detective Kemp said, "there's more to this killing than meets the eye. I'ma lay on it for a minute. This dude didn't deserve to die like that, handcuffed to a radiator. Whoever killed him definitely wanted him dead. They knew what their intentions were, the handcuffs tell it all.

In the meantime, Vah, Jaia, and Ms. Smiley were back at the same bar toasting to a crime of the time in being partners.

Ms. Smiley thought, *'Therefore, nobody can ever rat each other out.'*

Jaia and Vah had seen and done so much crime in their lives to even ever utter a word of another committing a crime. To them it was their duty, by any means necessary, to kill a motherfucker and keep their hustle proper. Even Ms. Smiley wouldn't have a clue. To them TLC bitches, it's a trauma waiting to happen.

Jaia, said, "Yo, let's go over to that bar called Yana's on Lexington and Sheridan. It's a hoodrat bar, Vah. Maybe we can get a IiI summin, surnrnin ya know. Even though it's supposedly a straight bar wit so-called thugs, maybe there's a good pussy eatin' thuggets there. Ya feel me. Ya never know, my nig. This bar here is lame. Let's be outti. Yo! Ms. Smiley, you traveling or what."

"You know Jaia, you say some of the darnnest shit out of ya mouth. I know ya wit that licky clitty shit. Dam, boo. I don't want to hear that fuckin' stupid ass talk. Y'all bitches go ahead fucking around in Y ana's. One of them niggas in there is gonna try ya dyke asses. Be careful. Them niggas in there don't like not bitches corning where they have their bitches hangin' out, try'na fuck'em, suck'em or pluck' ern. Fuck around and y'all two bitches will be ducking them bullets. Go ahead ya hard headed dyke bitches." They all started cracking up laughing.

Jaia said to Ms. Smiley, "Bitch, you crazy. I feel you fo sho on that shit."

CHAPTER EIGHT

THEY PULLED UP IN JAIA'S spanking new, pretty navy blue Navigator. All heads turned to get at a look at these two gorgeous bitches betting out and the loud music they were thumpin' to. Shit was getting hot. Fifty-cents' "Magic Stick." All the hard core thugs standing around trying to get their rap on saying, "Yo ma, what's good," as Vah stepped out.

She's like, "Nothing a drink can't handle once I hit Yana's. Ya feel me, son?"

He looked at her up and down, "Yo, where y'all from?"

She said, "We from all around and you just happened to be around this time we showed up, boo. Isn't that special."

He said, "I'm all around. I ain't never seen you. So, what's your name?"

"Vah"

He stepped back and said, "Yo, I heard yo name before. That is about it."

Jaia stepped out of the Navigator and niggas started flocking and flossing, smiling all in her presence. She was already buzzin' a little.

She yelled, "Yo Yah, come on. Let's go inside, boo. It's too many clocks out here ticking, ya feel me."

The dude talking to Vah felt disrespected cause she just bounced on him when Jaia spoke.

She said to him, ''I'm olit man. My dawg calling me."

As they both entered Yana's, Uncle Muff was sitting at the bar. They all gave each other sum dap. Jaia' s face showed a big kool-aid smile. Vah caught it. She smiled and thought, *'here we go.'* Uncle Muff was sitting with some female. The jukebox was playing Patty LaBelle's "If Only You Knew," so Jaia went over and put three dollars in and said that if anyone wants to, they can play some music. Then she told Vah to order her a drink while she was staring at the female with Uncle Muff, she felt some type of way. She thought, *'I'ma catching feelings for this bitch, should I tell her, cause it's bothering me to see her with another woman. I'lljust snatch at that bitch and wave her away from my boo.'* She then snapped out of it. Yah's calling her, 'Yo, Jaia, come the fuck over here. Meet Uncle Muffs friend. Her name is Amy."

Next, *Unc* let her hands roam over Jaia's body causing her to make a sizzling·sound of 'Please fuck *me tonight, I am hungry to cum.'*

All the niggas in the bar started making their remarks, "Yo, checkout the muthafuckin' freaks up here in yana." The more they talked, J aia moaned in ecstasy as If Unc was fucking her right there on the dance floor.

Them niggas flipped. "Yo, y' all bitches need to git up outta here with that shit. This ain't" the place for y'all. Motherfuckin git your freak on and shit. Now, if one of y'all wanna hump. my dick and grind, that is another story."

Jaia strayed away from Unc and stepped to the nigga with the foul mouth. She said, "Yo, homeboy. You and yo momma ain't got enough swerve on this curve to make a bitch like me scream for cream. Oh yea, check this, yo momma does and that's straight up, cum up, from the clit up and you nigga wit a foul mouth who disrespect women period. Sho yo momma ain't shit, so I guess that's where you come in, not to be nothing but pure shit nigga. Now hold that, bitch!"

That nigga was vexed. Everybody in the bar said she shut his ass up.

He stated, "Bitch, you got that. Not for long though, ya fucking dyke ass hoe. I'ma see ya. True that," Jaia responded, "Nigga go on, scat. You fuckin bum ass nigga."

Vah stood on the side and smiled. She liked the way Jaia handled his. ass. *Unc* just chilled, still in the cut. Amy was shocked. She never heard a bitch talk to J. Quan like that. She thought *'oh shit, that nigga gone slap the fire outta her ass, soon as she exits the bar.'* So she thought. Little did she know, that'll be the last time he'd raise his hand to hit a woman. J. Quan kept staring at Jaia. She figured she'd butter him up, cause she felt like killing the dude. She stepped to him apologizing.

He said, "Bitch, if you don't" want none of J. Quan Jr., move on, ma," talking about his dick holding it with strength.

She said, "Oh, you wanna stick me wit that. Well, let's see how I'm feeling." She stuck her finger in her pussy to get some of the juices,· then she said to him, "Smell this, boo, then tell me if J. Quan Jr. can handle my sweet smelling' cum, daddy."

His dick did a summer salt trying to get out of his Sean John black sweat pants. It stuck straight the fuck up. Jaia knew she had his ass. She smiled.

Vah's all pooped out. She tells Jaia it's time to, call it a night for herself, which is Jaia's cue to let her know if she's down to leave Yana's too,

As they were leaving out heading toward their car, Boone just happened to come along, He grabbed, them with lotsa hugs, as if he knew them for eons,

Jaia right away pulled him to the side and said to him, "Let me holla at ya, I need you to, do this solid, Also, to prove your loyalty, my nig. Ya feel me. Check it, you see that dude standing in the door?" referring to J. Quan, "I need you to follow my ride cause I'ma make a pit stop down by Washington Park, over in the area called Lover's Lane, with this nigga. See, he is a very disrespectful motherfucker. I gotta show him a lil'summin, ya feel me. I'll fill ya in later.

Yo, Boone, you know that nigga, right?"

"Sho ya right, ma," Boone responded,

They all tallied up in Jaia's ride. She explained to Vah and Unc what was up with J. Quan, She was riding with him in his whip. A Lexus SL300. They rode and J. Quan started. saying, "Yo ma, tell me you ain't no fucking dyke, seriously. If so, I'ma tear that pussy out the frame. My dick is humming for you, rna. I been checking your style out since you walked in the door, boo. You're a fucking dime piece. I knew I had to get some of ya ass, fo sho, So, you gonna make it happen for a nigga, rna. I am dam skippy on this bonding sexual shit." The Lover's Lane in Washington Park was quiet and the only thing you heard was the crickets.

J. Quan said to Jaia, "Listen ma, you wanna play with big boy," referring to his dick, "I need a jump off to stick in your nice juicy cunt, bitch. *So,* are you gonna suck this tip with those gorgeous lips, boo, cause they'd look pretty on my motherfuckin dick. Ya feel me ma, Yeah, come on bitch, get to sucking this big J. Quan's thick dick. It's waiting for ya. It needs you, ya fine ass hoe."

All of a sudden Boone tapped on the window. As Jaia jumped up, J. Quan went for his gat. She already had hers directly in his face. With his dick hard as a rock, she opened the doors for Boone. Boone snatched that nigga out of the car so quick, with his dick hanging limply, J Quan was saying, "Yo, nigga what up with this shit, boy. Who the fuck are you motherfucker?" he yelled.

Jaia said, "Bitch ass nigga, do you know who the fuck lam, boo, I am that bitch, son, and you been violating me all fuckin night." Boone had his gat to J. Quan's head telling him, "One move nigga, ya ghost."

They directed J. Quan up the hill to the handball courts, his dick still hanging out. He was talking about his dick being cold.

Boone and Jaia laughed, saying, "Mutha-fucka, your whole body gonna shiver in a minute, son." Jaia was yelling at J. Quan, "So, you like disrespecting females, huh?" She told him to take off his pants and sit on the bench. Then she told him, ''N ah, nigga, rub your dick on the wall of the handball court. Pussy ass bitch."

J. Quan, fuming said "Bitch, have you lost ya mind, ya freack ass, bitch ass dyke.".Jaia said, "Yo, Boone, take your dick out." Boone looked at her for what she said.

Jaia said, 'between you and me, he gonna suck ya dick and he gonna do it good. I wanna see ya cum, Boone, ya feel, me. This is on me, son, also a chump ass nigga such as this piece of shit."

Boone thought about her saying to him, *'loyalty,* 'but never like this shit.

He's like, "A'ight, ma."

He grabbed J. Quan. "Git on your knees motherfucker. Putting my dick in your mouth is gonna keep you livin' so I gotta cum like rum. If I like it man, I'll see ya around and we can be on the down low, ya heard."

Jaia smiled at Boone, J. Quan got a hold of Boone's dick and started licking the tip, like he had done it plenty of times before.

Jaia kept egging him on. "go ahead, J. Quan, daddy lick it soft and make it real hard."

Boone grabbed J. Quan by his head and began to pump his mouth, telling him, "Man, ya better deep throat this good fucking dick. I'ma 'bout to fuck you all in ya mouth, man. Yo, make my dick stand at attention motherfucker, like it's the fucking general bitch, ya heard. Start slurpin on my dick, nigga. You the fuckin' man." Boone started shoving his dick in J. Quan's mouth, not letting go of his head. He was cummin in J. Quan's mouth saying, "Oh, man, I gotta bust another nut. Come on homey, do a nigga real right. This time let my dick in the back of ya throat. I want you to suck my balls also, a'ight."

J. Quan's mouth is sore and raw. He's like, "Ma, I'm sorry, boo."

Jaia's like, "Shut the fuck up and git to suckin, bitch. Next time ya see me, boo, you'll turn the other way with respect, nigga. See, J. Quan, I got this Smallbany on lock, nigga. You haven't heard, this will be our little secret too, boo. If you ever try to git at my nigga, you'd better come correct. See, I'ina let ya live, cause ya gonua be my ears to the streets. See motherfuker, I'm not herb, I'm that bitch on top." Vah and Unc pulled up by the handball courts to get Jaia. Boone was on his second nut buster. He then wiped his dick on J. Quan's face. He said, "Darn, nigga, you give head better than a bitch." He stepped off.

Jaia hollered at Boone, ya, my nig. I owe you one. I got ya, ya heard."

They all started laughing their asses off. J. Quan stood there embarrassed, as he thought to himself that the shit was kind of good and exciting. Whoa, he noticed he got a thrill from that shit. So surprised at himself, he went on his merry way, acting macho, as if it never occurred...

Unc just stared at Jaia with lust. She was really starting to feel a sexual desire for her.

She can't seem to shake it. Knowing how ruthless Jaia is, she also feels that involving herself with her sexually would be a big mistake for business.

She thought, *'what the hell. I want her fine ass to fuck my face royally. With my loyalty behind it all, I'ma have her. She* is *going to be my boo.* 'Unc smiled.

They were all conversating about the whole situation. Vah's mouth opened wide when Jaia mentioned J. Quan sucking Boone's dick.

Unc went in a shocking movement, "You've got to be fucking kidding me, Jaia." –He continued, "that nigga tryin' to prove his loyalty to ya, Jaia, cause he do not play that man to man shit. So, I think he's desperate to be a part of y'all troopers."

* * *

The next morning Jaia woke up to her phone ringing like crazy. She picked it up and it was Auyna calling collect. They both started yelling and shouting 'bout how much they missed each other. Then Aunya told Jaia to get Vah. on the phone. Jaia three-wayed her ass quick. Now they were all very cautious, especially since they dam sure knew that shit was not allowed. Aunya had explained to them on their first visit how to do it. They talked for a while. Aunya said that she did not want them to visit anymore. It was almost time for her to be released. Six more months they could send her parole clothes; also, her usual stuff for packages. They all hung up at the same time.

Detective Reese was scouring the area of L&O,. seeing if he'd see Boone, cause he definitely got a murder charge on this son of a bitch. Now all he had to do was put it out on the streets, letting these fucking gangbangers know who killed their trooper, T.J. Detective Reese got out of his car and headed toward Boone's car. He tapped on the window and asked him to step out of the car, while showing him his badge. He then asked Boone about the killing of the white dude and asked him if he' knew him. Boone looked at Detective Reese and remembered him from the night on Morton. Boone thought, *oh this cracker thinks somebody* is *stupid. He's trying to play me. Fuckin' cocksucker."* Boone answered all of his questions.

Detective Reese then asked Boone about T.J.'s killing. He said he knew nothing about it and made a smart remark to the detective, "Should I know shit, anyway?" Detective Reese stepped off and headed toward the. stoop where T.J.'s crew as acting as if he'd be questioning them. As soon as he showed them his badge, he said, "You see that motherfucker I just got through talking to? I'ma make it short and simple."

They said in unison, "Yeah, what pig, what the fuck good are you to make any nigga life simple?"

Detective Reese said, "Listen you lil piss head bitch. See, I'm here to let you motherfuckers know that black motherfucker over there killed your sorry ass homeboy T.J., you fuckin' assholes."

They were all stunned "Yo, po-po, you ain't telling us this shit to have niggas at each other, cause we down for ours."

Detective Reese walked away and left it at that, with a smile on his face.. He thought, *'it's on now, it's my turn to get rid of all these motherfuckers. T.L.C. welcome to L&O, get the money girls. Time to* git *paid - ay.'*

The gangbangers stared at Boone. One of em said, 'Yo, that nigga's got our man fo sho He killed J.T. and expects to get paid, slinging on L&O. I don't think so. Let's let po-po go We got that nigga Boone."

Jaia, Vah and Unc were making their pick-up at the spots. Jaia's spots were all good since that incident with Black. Nigga's on the block loved her gangster. She's ruthless, so they all knew she's not to be fucked with at all. That is what the streets are saying. Then they went to Vah's spots where they first met Unc.

All the nigga's were flexin' when they pulled up, respecting their hustle, cause it was tight and a nigga knows if they come at 'em right, they are always strapped.

Unc got out the hoopty and niggas were like, "Oh shit, Uncle Muff, they put you on. It's all good, stay in the game Boo, Ya fell me. They treat a sister right by law." Afterwards, they all decided to go to Julian's on Pearl Street for lunch to discuss something that needed to be dealt with first hand. When they all walked into Julian's, all heads turned, Jaia with her sleek, sexy walk turned heads in a flash, anyway. The waiter led them to a table. Once they sat down Unc said she'd prefer a female waitress. Jaia looked like she wanted to chop her fucking head off. The waiter said, "no problem" Unc gave him a twenty dollar bill and he sent this nice caramel complexion Aisan waitress over to their table. Jaia was heated.

Vah was just watching the both of them, feeling Unc's move to catch Jaia's reaction and it worked.

Vah stated, "Unc you playing with fire motherfucker. Don't' get her amp up. She is not the herb man. I am fore warning ya, fam. If it's real don't test it or play wit it. Go for it, cause she is all yours. I know my dawg. She's feeling ya seriously. She's a straight up keeper, so don't play with her head. Remember she's my dawg and I'll die or kill for her, ya feel me." Unc said, "I got you Vah. Thanks for the info, fo sho."

Jaia said aloud, "Excuse me, I am right here. Yon're talking' about me. Hello!" They both started laughing in her face. Unc looked at Jaia and said, "Isn't it me and you, boo, are gon be as one on the real, ma, cause I'm ready and ruthless as well. Dam sure, for me and mine."

They kissed and sealed a true to game relationship.

The TLC crew started tallying up their monies, as they enjoyed their lunch at Julians.

Now they needed to start moving shit on the real, with Aunya coming home. They wanted her to see their accomplishments in the game.

They decided to let Nubian have Morton, Lil Kill, First and Hudson, Boone, Lark and Orange, who is getting ready to get knocked outta the whole game for life.

Jaia said to Vah and unc, "We need to take a trip Vah, to the old hood Washington· Heights and check out my Uncle Tito, to start getting connected seriously. That motherfucker ain't gonna like that I'm in the hustle game. Oh well, he's a prick. The bastard use to try his ole perverted shit with me. I left that son of a bitch with a painful memory. I burned the side of his face with an iron while he slept. My aunt said I was the devil's daughter. That is when she put me out.. At the same time she explained, no rather she scolded me about how I killed a man in the Dominican Republic."

"I was six years old. This man was beating my father. I guess they came to rob him in his villa. I had went in my father's room in his nightstand, got the gun, a 9mm, and just started shooting. saying, 'leave my poppa alone.' Two of the man'~ bodyguards got killed, too." "It was then my father sent me to New York City to live with my Aunt Lucinda and Uncle Tito, but I barely remember anything. It's all a blur, ya know."

Vah and Unc were like, "Bitch, you're a natural bom killa from the villa." They all started laughing their asses off. Jaia said, "And ya know I haven't seen my father in eighteen years. Even though he'd send some monies to my aunt, making sure I was very well taken care of. In the meantime, I watched my uncle deal drugs and shit. People came and picked up. They'd celebrate getting rid of some of the competition Motherfuckers were coming from Cuba and Columbia, all in expensive gear and jewelry. They'd talk in codes. Yeah, I was in the mix of it all, niggas. I still wonder, cause they was this one guy who use to stare at me all the time. I do not remember his name. He looked so familiar. He wore a pinky ring, oval shape with onyx and a diamond in the middle. It was a yellow diamond-shaped, like a cone. It sparkled so pretty. I always wanted one like that. Matter of fact, I'ma get me one as we speak." She called her jeweler at the Styvesant Mall. She asked Unc if she would like one and she said yes. She automatically got Vah and Aunya one. It was their oath to each other.. She asked Unc if she'd like to get her necks tattooed with their symbol, TLC. Unc said yes. Unc said to Jaia, "Ya know for sho when it's us, it's on for life, boo. True that shit. My word is bond and it's what I live by. I'd never lie to either of y'all, ya feel me, fam."

So Jaia asked if they were ready to make some real monies.. Once she stepped to her Uncle Tito, it's gonna be off the motherfucking meat rack. She made sure her crew was ready to step up and take shit over, including Ms. Smiley. She never cared for that ole hustling, so-called slow ass bitch. *'It's time to move on and move some bricks, like fifteen hundred or so,'* she thought. Now, Ms. Smiley will buy from them pronto, or else shit was gonna get hectic, fo sho Jaia said, "We gon do this bitches, ya heard. Boo-ya-ya." In the meantime, the gangbangers were setting up Lark and Orange for a Fourth of July night, to light Boone's ass up for killing T.J. Boone was chillin in his Audi across from the garage on Lark and Orange. Next thing you know, all these Iil nigga came rushing from around Lark Street and through the vacant lot just shooting. Bullets were flying everywhere.

Boone had his gat, but ducked as far down in the car as he could. It was too late. He caught seven bullets, four in the head, two in the face and one in the shoulder. He was done holding his gat.. Detective Reese sat a little way down in his car. He'd seen it all, so he put his siren on and rushed to the scene. Everyone scattered, but he had every last one of them, so they were all going down for. murder.

He reached Boone's car before civilians began surrounding the scene. He reached under the front seat and pulled a Price' Chopper plastic bag out, it was full of heroin and crack. He thought to himself, *'Oh, there's the rest of my shit,'* then he reached under the passenger's side and found a Macy's shopping bag full of stacked money. He threw the bags in the car. Everyone in the neighborhood knew that Detective Reese was a dirty motherfucker popo.

Detective Reese called back-up on his walkie talkie, also EMS, with a big smile, because his next task was just about to begin. He loved it.

CHAPTER NINE

DA-STEVE JUST HAPPENED TO CALL Detective Reese in the nick of time, finding out that Boone was just murdered. He' d seen the whole incident, therefore, he knew who to arrest.

He said to Da-Stev, "Yo, so I guess we're all going to be in the money, huh, cause I just made it happen for your peeps. Man, I'm laughing like a child with a brand new toy."

Det. Reese also mentioned to Da-Stev about being paid for his efforts.

Da-Stev related to him. "I'ma holla back at yain a half hour dude, a'ight."

Da' -Stev called Jaia and explained that their plan for Lark and Orange is a go. Jaia smiled and told Vah and Unc. They all toasted to that and a new come up for sure in the·makin.

Everyone will be getting paid for their work. She told Da-Stev she was at Julian's and to meet her over on Swan Street, where they first met. She had some monies for him and Detective Reese. Then she hung up.

Vah, Jaia and Unc were enjoying their afternoon with yet another celebration – taking over Lark & Orange.

Jaia said to her crew, "oh, we gonna go pay DaStev some funds and Detective Reese for his services, bitches." Ya feel me."

They all toasted, "Hell yeah, it's on!!!" They all yelled.

Jaia met Da-Stev within a half hour at Swan Street and gave him two duffle bags. One with a Fifty thousand for himself. He was grateful, althoug he felt he really didn't do much. DaStev called Detective Reese and told him he had his goods and plenty waiting for him. He told him he was around the corner on Swan Street. By the time Detective Reese got to Swan Street,.

Jaia and them were gone. He kinda wanted to meet them personally. He felt they thought they were too good to be in his presence. Little did he know they were watching his ass, snapping pictures of him taking the duffle bag with the mqney from Da-Stev. The whole police station lmew Da-Stev was into dealing drugs, so Det. Reese is fucked.

Vah and Unc. said, "Gotcha, Coppa." They all laughed and headed to their cribs to get ready for their trip to New York City. Vah had informed Jaia and Unc about who would be in charge of things while they were gone. Right away they all decided Nubian and Lil Kill would.

"They'll make sure shit is proper, fo sho Them niggas ain't no joke, ya feel me. They been wit us, wit all the shit that's going on in the hood proving their loyalty."

"Sho ya right," Jaia shouted, "them my niggas. I'm gonna holla at 'em, let 'ern know shit is on the rise, ya heard, fam. It's us bitches."

Vah mentioned to Jaia and Unc, as they were pulling off from Swan and First Streets, "Jaia, it's been three years we've been doing our thing. Even with Aunya going upstate boo, we have corne a long pretty well, at a slow pace, which is a very good patient thing to do. So now we are recognized as TLC plus one and that's ya boo, Unc. Now we put our act in motion, showing niggas how we came up to be as one. It's gotta be show time now. We got twenty workers to cover Smallbany. We branch out in the upstate area, and I mean the whole fucking capital region area where these motherfuckers think their shit don't stink in their backyard. They the motherfuckers who putting it in ours. So, it's time for some git rich, git paid and kill' em in the process. Ya feel me. Also, we need to have our peeps keep their ears to the streets for keeps."

Then Vah said, "Oh, yeah. I'm getting a house, too."

Jaia responded, "Oh yeah, bitch. When did this happen?"

Vah said, "While I was going to our crib on Main Street, but instead I kept driving up Western Avenue toward, SUNY, University of Albany and saw a nice house. The Main Street crib will be our laid back apartment, as we've always intended. In all reality, Coco knows that spot, which she is the only one. We know she has po-po all in the mix of our shit, so what I did was move further down Western Street," she laughed, "I felt it was necessary, ya feel me."

"Good fucking move. Ooh, you bitch. Now that shit is slick, but when were you going to tell me, hoe?"

"I just did. Booya motherfuckers." They gave some dap.

In the meantime, Detective Reese burn rushed the seven gangbangers for Boone's murder. He busted in the comer house at 5:30 a.m. bright and early. They never knew he even thought they did it because he was so nonchalant, telling them as if he didn't care one fucking bit. Oops, they were wrong.

Detective Reese knew they hadn't seen him parked down the block. He was yelling, "Get the fuck up you pieces of shit. Ya think ya gonna kill him in my area and think you punk ass motherfuckers are going to get away with some shit like this?' All y'all son of a bitches are under arrest. This place looks like a fucking rat trip and you call yourselves drug dealers, huh.

Y'all should a kept ya dumb asses in school instead of this gang shit. Ya'll don't know shit and half of ya involved in this murder can't even read. Y'all a bunch of illiterate, dyslexic, dumb motherfuckers, but you'll learn now, cause all seven of you will be doing some time boys. I'ma make sure ofthat. I seen the whole thing sitting in my car down the block. Gotcha scumbags.

It's good-bye Irene."

He arrested every last one of'them. It was even captured on Eyewitness News, Channel 6.

Nubian and Lil Kill were in charge of all the spots for pick -up and re-ups, until TLC got back from New York City. They were the only two that knew this, just in case niggas wanted to flip on 'em, knowing TLC were in flight, along with Da-Stev.

Ms. Smiley was wondering what's really going on with the Lark and Orange situation, as far as Boone is concerned. TLC hadn't been keeping her informed and who was this Detetive.

Reese that is always on the scene. She thought something wasn't right. She could feel it and thought she's gotta put some ears to the street for info.

Then she thougth, *'shit, as long as they're giving me my ends, what the fuck do I care.*

Then, too, them bitches is getting to where they're getting too bigfor their britches. I'ma have to slow 'em down a little and let 'em know I'm still the bitch in charge, serving and dealing in the areas I let them enter.'

She made some phone calls and found out a little summin' not to her liking as far as them making a trip to New York City. So, from there she took it as them seeking a new connect, but little did she know the connect was bigger than her. She felt she had to get on her game. It was about to get greedy, fo sho Ms. Smiley had recruited a coupla of niggas. She knew them from her come up days.

Being that Brickman has slipped the fuck up on her supply, he had to die.

Aunya had some pretty big plans and a nice surprise for her crew. She had gotten her. GED in prison. She was so happy about that. and wondered if she should pursue going to college. She knew she needed to get her schooling. She thought, being that she is twenty-three years old now, other than her crew doing good in the drug game, she wanted to do something·legit to keep some kind of safety net within them. She decided real estate would be it, so she can keep the monies rolling in action, as it's being made at the same time. *'I'll be released in a coupla months,'* she thought, *'dam, I never wanna step on state grounds again, especially seeing all these crazy bitches doing any and every thing for anything. Officer's getting bitches pregnant.*

Bitches are committing suicide and sucking dick for gum. This shit is like a haven of Sodom *and Gomorrah The only way I come back is if a motherfucker fucks with me and my crew, but I do not know about that Unc character. I'ma see her when I hit the streets for shoo She better be good to Jaia.'*

Ms. Smiley figured, she'd call Jaia and find out what was really going on. She felt very suspicious of them.

Jaia's cellie was vibrating. She picked up, "Yo, holla." She knew it was Ms. Smiley.

Ms. Smiley got straight to the point. "Yo, I heard, you guys are trippin to New York City, huh." Jaia said, "Yeah, I'm going to check out my fam over in Washington Heights and do a little shopping with my crew. Aunya is coming home soon and I'd like to get her a coupla rags plus her parole clothes, ya feel me.· Also, hit some hot ass gay clubs in the village. It's on and poppin. I'ma stay a coupla days or maybe just make a day of it. I'll know once I hit home and find out what's going on with the family, ya know."

Ms. Smiley comes right out, "I thought maybe you were checking another connect cause my shit ain't good enough for you no more. Y'all really getting ya grind on, fa sho I'd have to respect that. You bitches just remember who put you on the come up. If you're deciding to branch out of here. It's only right, ya feel me. It can cause havoc, ya heard. 1'ma holla back later a'ight. One love, Jaia," and Ms. Smiley hung up.

Jaia told Vah and Unc the bullshit Ms. Smiley was saying to her. They were expecting her conniving ass to question her about their trip.

They all had something for her ass. Vah remembered her setting them with that trumped up ass lawyer for Aunya. Also, they found out about the raw deal she had been supplying them on their package. They were paying her off, to off their shit in her area and the bitch got greedy.

So now they had reason to off that trifling bitch. She thought she was getting away with shit. Little did she know it all added up to eliminating her whole shabang. Its get back time, fo sho, for Aunya too.

Ms. Smiley was really fucking furious. She decided that it was time to cut them bitches down.

She thought, "I made them hoes and I can break 'em quick, fast and in a hurry.' She had called Natalie to have her get some gats ready. She explained to Natalie what she was about to do as far as Jaia, Vah and *Unc* were concerned. Fuck up their spots and shut'em down because she knew they were getting a new connect. She felt they were getting beside themselves. She told Natalie her whole fucking plan. She'd be the first one to put a bullet in all of 'em, one by one, even if it killed her, because she felt dissed.

Natalie was like, "0 shit, Ms. Smiley, that is some fucked up shit, ma I feel you though, ya know. Do what you gotta do. Scared money don't make no money. I'll have what ya need by the time you arrive here, alright Ms. Lady." Natalie said.

Natalie's thoughts were, *'if this bitch actually thinks I'ma let her gun down Jaia and her peeps, she got to be out of her motherfucking mind. Not with me knowing who Jaia* 's *father* is.

He'd hang. me by my dam clitoris.' She frowned at the thought of it.

She had to figure out, about getting to this bitch, Ms. Smiley, before she put her plan into effect. Neither Jaia or Ms. Smiley knew Jaia's father. She smiled. Ms. Smiley was on her way to Natalie's. She told her about the two nigga's she had recruited. She wanted them to start hittin' up Jaia's and 'em's spot.

Ms. Smiley's boyz ran up in Vah's spot in the courtyard, stomping her workers with their Timbs and butting them with their 9mm's and 38 Special's. Shit was getting bloody, taking their monies, shooting at fiends. At Jaia' s spot, they just busted in killing the dealers and taking everything. They even had time to rape one of the fiends. They made her suck the Rottweiler's dick. Next thing you know, the dog started licking her pussy, moaning and shit. Every time the female tried to get away from the dog, he barked and growled at her ass, as if to let her know,*'don't move bitch or I'ma tear your ass up.'* So, the female huddled in a fetal position while the dog kept sniffing her, trying to get her punanny again.

She was already scared and busted up as it was. Then she just broke out and jumped out the dam window. The dog jumped right behind her. She hit the ground so hard and busted her head wide the fuck open. She was sprawled out. The dog just broke his leg and went over to-the dead fiend lickin her blood, sniffing her pussy, growling. Then the dog started biting and chewing on her.

Everybody on the block of First and Judson were in shock at all the shit that just happened. They noticed niggas stepped off in a forest green Range Rover. They had on black hoodies, black jeans and black bandanas, covering half their faces.

One drug dealer named Ron, who knew Jaia, said, "Oh shit, do those niggas know who they just hit. I hope so, if not, they just signed their death warrants. Dumb asses."

Ron pulled out his cellie.He had to let Jaia know what the hell just happened and that po-po is on the scene. Also, that her workers are dead, along with a fiend they were fucking with.

* * *

Kevin and De-La were the henchmen for Ms. Smiley fucking up Jaia's and 'em's spots; They were the same two who went to Ms. Smiley about Black's plans for Jaia. They all knew their spots and they were sure in their glory.

Natalie wanted to handle the situation with Ms. Smiley before Jaia got a hold of her and her peeps. First, she had an attitude about the bullshit Ms. Smiley was pulling. It made Natalie think very deviously and viciously. Natalie was going to kin Ms. Smiley before she went back to Albany.

Natalie thought, *'once she comes out here to Selkirk to retrieve these guns' she was definitely sure that.'* She heard a knock at the door.

"Yo, who dat?" she yelled.

"Smiley," Ms. Smiley yells back through the door.

"Alright, give me a second," Natalie says. She opens the door, "Yo, what's up? I see, you ready to get busy and put those bitches out for the count, huh!"

"Sho ya right," answered Ms. Smiley."

She wanted to blow her fucking brains out right then and there. She could taste her gun powder.. She couldn't believe Ms. Smiley came by herself. That's the worst thing she could have done right about now.

Natalie thought, *'Dumb bitch! It's a shame she trusted me, but that doesn't exist in hustling. She's getting ready to find out. I don 'f care how fucking long I'veknown this bitch.*

There is a bigfish in' the ocean. She's not the one at all compared to the bigfish, fucking with his daughter, Jaia. Manuel Acosta will recognize the honor I have for him when he does find out what's going on in the near future, with his daughter Jaia.'

Natalie was trying to figure out how she was going to kill this bitch and needed to think fast. She was not letting this bitch get back to Albany alive. She remembered that she kept the acid that she used to get the serial numbers off some of the guns she had. Natalie wandered into the kitchen while Ms. Smiley sat in her dining room waiting to get her gats.

Natalie yelled to Ms. Smiley from the kitchen, "So, you're really going to off Jaia and 'em fo sho Wow, they fucked up like that. I would never have thought you'd want them bitches done. Yo, they're getting paid, fo sho if ya do the hustle to the bustle, shit'll come right on the grind. Ya know that Smiley. They earned that shit within three years of their come up, especially in corny ass Smallbany."

Ms. Smiley, said, "Yeah, them bitches are moving shit heavy all up in the upstate area, I heard. You know the streets. are always talking to me to listen. They're even covering Schenectady, on up to Utica. might even be further. This is the shit I'm talking about. They did not confide in me. That shit is a diss, so I gotta get some respect in order, ya feel me. I'm not letting them let it go down like that." She smiled.

Natalie was in the kitchen thinking if she should tell this bitch now who Jaia's father is, so she'll think before she goes fuckin' with the TLB, or should she just honor Jaia's father by taking care of the shit hersefby eliminating this dumb ass bitch.

She thought of the· game of hustling itself, especially if you put yourself out there like that. You get got and Ms. Smiley is getting what she deserves, cause the bitch is sho enuff fucking with the wrong bitches. She is getting ready to find out right now, Nnbian and Lil Kill were wondering what the fuck was going on. All the spots were being hit at the same time. They were thinking why the workers are letting those motherfuckers up in the spots. At first they couldn't understand it. Then Lil Kill said, "Nubian, there's only one way this shit could be happeneing. It's gotta be peeps we know. We all know. But who, nigga?

Nubian said, "Look we gotta straighten shit dut before Jaia and 'em return. If we don't get summin in the making, we ain't gonna live to explain what the fuck happened, period. So, let's start trying. to get some info on some niggas IDing these motherfuckers causing havoc and why, Lil Kill, fo sho-ya feel me."

Detective Reese was enjoying all the violence. At the same time, he was thinking it was because of the shit that happened with the gangbangers. Then, too, he wondered how the fuck TLC got involved. He needed to start hitting the streets and get some serious feedback. He sure had their backs with the monies them bitches paid him for evacuating Lark and Orange the way he did. He needed to get in contact with Da-Stev for real. Shit was not proper, sununin wasn't right. All TLC's spots are being hit. That shit was off the chain. Motherfuckers flocking to death.

Detective Reese's cellie was vibrating. He picked up, "Talk to me."·

Da-Stev's first words were, "Man, what is going on with TLC's spots getting hit up, dude?"

Detective Reese replied, "I was just thinking the same thing and about to can ya ass, DaStev.

Who has put some grimy motherfuckers out there on TLC, man?"

Da-Stev said, "I don't know, but I heard a lil summin like TLC's getting too much grind on here in Albany. They need to be slowed down. I've been listening to the streets talking man.

A couple of hustlers' saw Ms. Smiley's two henchmen coming out of Jaia's spot, where the fiend jumped out the window with the dog behind her. Them niggas had her freaking with the fucking dog. Isn't that some shit, Detective Reese." They both shook their heads at the same time, but didn't know it because they were on the phone afar.

Nubian couldn't believe the monies and drugs were they getting taken for. He had to think quick in order to make things right by TLB, so he needed to listen to the streets fast.

He wanted Jaia to be proud of him. Maybe she would see him as that nigga in. charge who can handle shit when she's away handling the shit to keep all our grinds on and definitely get paid with a bunch of honors, fo shoo He respected TLB to the fullest, although he had a thing for Ja:ia. She'll never know though, cause his pride won't let him tell her. He knows she is wicked and she is into bitches, so what would be the point except to give her gangster ass her props and that butch ass bitch, Unc.

Nubian's cellie was ringing to Usher's song, "Confession," "Yo, what's up! It's Da-Stev' mgga. What the fuck is going on boyee. Talk to me. Have you talked to Yah and Jaia about this shit yet, that's poppin' off, dude? Ya know shit is going to be on fire, once they hear about it.

Nubian, ya better get on ya P's and Q's with this shit, pronto. Let me hit you with the niggas who's trying to shut you down. It's De-La and Kevin, Ms. Smiley's henchmen. I don't know if it's her call or not, nigga. That's how they're getting close to your workers. They know' em, ya feel me."

"So, Nubian, ya ass needs to find out the delio, nigga. Ya spots are getting tore up boyee and it's not over once TLB finds out. Until then, Nubian, watch ya back boy. This shit poppin'like this. Other niggas gonna try ya fo sho, so be ready. It's getting to be grimy time, plus ya need to start trying to get some more workers, fo sho, nigga. Ride or die motherfuckers.

Nubian, do not allow anyone but yourself to enter ya spots, even though I got a gut feeling Ms. Smiley's behind all this. While the TLB's handling business in New York City, that's why she's flippin', ya feel me. Nubian."

"She played herself fucking with them crazy ass dyke bitches. Sheplairi ole got greedy too fast, instead of asking questions. She fucked up. She can charge'her life to game. It's over Jehovah, fo shoo Them bitches gonna put Ms. Smiley's ass in front of her maker in the dirt. True that."

Nubian blurted out loud, "She better be hiding out before I get a hold of her. If I find out she's behind this shit, whoa! Jaia and 'em do not have to rush back at alL I'ma make sure of that cause Ms. Smiley will be done. Word on everything I love. TLB ain't gonna have to worry 'bout shit, as long as I'm running game."

Da-Stev told Nubian he had to take care of business and he'll keep his ears to the street for him, as far as what's going on. He dam sure is gonna give him twenty-four hours to get his· paper before he relays all this bullshit to TLB. They fam.

Niggas all through the hood were talking about it. How one of the mutha-fuckers took one of the workers and made him strip butt -ass naked after beating the dog shit out of him. His name was pee-wee and he cried like a bitch Niggas were laughing. He was only seventeen; still wet behind the ears, always acting like his ass was the H.N.LC. with a pistoL That is really what boost his crying ass ego. The motherfucking pistol, flossing and shit. Everybody was teasing his ass.

The Albany Police Department kept all the drug areas on lock for awhile, so the hustle was kinda strict during that time. Po-po were busting motherfuckers for the hell of it. The areas were making them look like they were not doing their dam job and it's the capital of New York.

Nubian went around to all the spots getting the run down on the situation. It was Kevin and De-La, so *now* he had to catch them uiggas and squeeze them like vice grips for information, fo sho.

He didn't have the slightest idea where tolook for Ms. Smiley, so he had to cellie DaStev.

In the mean time, he'll be hunting them two uiggas down. *'With all the money and drugs they got from us, them motherfuckers should be in Florida by now,* he thought to himself.

Kevin and De-La had met Ms. Smiley's informant at a bar called Dorton's. They had the money and drugs in the Jeep. She asked them if all the spots were tapped out or what.

They responded "We took everything them assholes had in their spots."

Kevin said, "The good thing is we didn't even have a problem getting in the door. You would've thought they'd be very cautious about that, huh? Yeah, that's what them niggas git, trusting a motherfucker in the game It's critical they found out though."

De-La laughed his ass off at that and Ms. Smiley's worker, too. They all started making fun of the shit they did to the so called hustlers, they call themselves.

Nubian just happened to be driving past Dorton's and spotted the forest green Jeep' that his peeps described in the spots being hit. He then called some of his worker's quick and he just sat in his nice little navy blue Jeep Cherokee waiting for Kevin and De-La to exit Dorton's. If that's where they were.

BINGO! Kevin and De-La steeped out with Ms. Smiley's informant. Nubian couldn't make out who the bitch was, but he knew summin was up with her. His troops pulled up just in time as Kevin and De-La and the informant were about to depart.

Nubian and his crew pulled out their gats, had them niggas covered, all three. No, ifs, ands or buts about it!

"Put them bastards in the jeep fast," Nubian shouted, "all y'all motherfuckers. We're going for a ride. Bitch ass nigga Kevin riding with me. And whoever this bitch is," he suggested to his homie, T. Dove, 'snatch her ass and bring her with you, man."

De-La got knocked in the mouth with the but of a .38 Special, trying to slip away.

Nubian stacked all their asses in the three cats, including their Jeep.

Nubian took them niggas where they first met Jaia when she fucked up Black, so De-La knew his entire life was over, fo sho.

As they went down to the basement, there was a pissy, nasty aroma. Once they got down there, Nubian cellied LilKill.

"Yo, what it is. Talk to me fam," said Lil Kill.

"I got these grimy ass henchmen, boyee. So its hammer time nigga, I'm over in the got dam chamber of crucial brutality, dude. Come on over for the show, fo sho, my nig. *Night.* Lil.

Kill, it's on. We gotta get them to spill the beans, huh! Yo, dude you get all our shit back, too?"

Nubian said, "Sho ya right, boyee. Ya heard. One love. Git ya ass over here. Holla back."

CHAPTER TEN

TLC ARRIVED AT THEIR OLD stomping grounds in Jaia's navy blue Navigator with pink.' interior. She started checking the Washington Heights area where she learned her hustling game from family and friends. Vah was smiling and bobbing her head to Jay Z's H.O.V.A., bad ass beat. Unc was amazed to see a block so full of people in transaction.

She kept saying, "Oh, shit this shit is trauma, fo sho This is y'all hood huh! This shit here is the cracker lackin, like Snoop says. Ya feel me. Dam, this is 24/7, huh. Booya-ya."

Jaia's like, "Unc, hustler's don't sleep on this block. There is money to be made, but it's so clustered no space to wander. Can't ya tell bitch." she laughed/'that's why me, Aunya and Vah got the fuck outta here. It's a danger zone to be trying to get your grind on, ya know."

They looked for a parking spot and as she parallel parked, a fiend came up to the Navigator. A Dominican dude came up behind the fiend and did a home run on his back with a bat.

Jaia yelled, "Ouch, that shit hurt," noticing the guy with the bat is her Uncle Tito's son, Juan.

"Que pasa mi prima, Jaia," he turned and told his boys, "Esta es me prima. Oh my god," he says "come get out so you can see mi mami and mi papa."

Jaia's face looked stunned at how Juan just did what he did to the fiend. Now, she sees where she gets her crazy ass shit from, it run's in the family. She smiled. It's her cousin Juan who really justified all her violence before her. It's a family thing.

"Yo, Prima, fo what you been. It's been a long time no see you," Juan tells Jaia. She tells him she has been keeping herself very busy, doing her thang. She continues on to explain to Juan her reason for visiting and that she is indeed in need of a connect that can distribute on time, for as long as she needs it. No repercussionsbehindit.

Juan was like, "Oh man, Papi, is going to be so fucking surprised. He never thought he'd ever see you again."

Jaia thought, *'Yeah, he just wanted this sweet, young pussy. The fucking pervert. His time soon will come. I got shit in store for his ass, too.'*

"Wow, man, Papi is going to be shocked like a motherfucker. I can't wait until he sees you, Jaia."

Jaia says to Juan, "Why you hit him with that bat like that, man?"

"No fucking fiends on by block goes up to any fuckin body's car in my motherfucking face. I own this fucking street, this fucking block. Tu tambien, prima. It's no joke. Anybody who is somebody will tell you or anybody that I am somebody on this block. This block alone.

So you know shit is proper."

"Oh shit. Excuse me Juan, I'd like you to meet my crew, Vah and Unc. She's mi amora.

Everyone meet my crazy cousin, Juan."

Juan says to Unc. "Where the fuck did you get a fucking name like that. Oh shit; you don't lookie like an Unc., but a patita, si (a butch, yes). No Unc. I'm just funnin' with you, okay my man.". They all started laughing. Juan cracked himself up and just caught what Jaia said.

"She is your girl. My hearing must be slippin," all of a sudden he's like, "what the fuck has happened to you, why are you this way, Jaia? Now you know Papi is gonna flip, for real."

"I don't think so, Juan. Trust me, Juan, you will see."

Then Juan looks to Vah, "I remember you hanging out all the time in the block, too." So he got straight to the point, "Are you patita, too? Were you and my cousin rubbing pussies? Is that why you both ran away, to be together? Oh Wow!"

Vah politely told Juan, "You must be out of ya fuckin' rabid ass mind. You got a one track sick ass mind, Juan. And yes, I am a mothefucking patita. How bout that! We all about being family. Something you'd never in your Dominican ass life know nothing about or have a clue without drugs being the sole purpose to keep us family. Moving right along."

Juan all arrogant said, "You still have that snotty ass attitude. Whatchmacallit is ya name, but you are family now, okay."

Vah smiled and commented, "You still an asshole. It's ajoke Juan."

* * *

Back in Albany, Nubian, Lil Kill and their troops were looking at the three assholes who tried to get away with taking their. shit. They thought they'd really get away with no repercussions. Oops! They lied to themselves.

First, they stared with De-La, "Yo nigga, I'ma ask you one time and one time only, bitch ass. Who the fuck is behind hitting up our spots? It's that bitch ass, Smiley. All I want is a yes or no, motherfucker."

De-La responded, "Fuck yo, lil rugga. Suck my black dick, boy. You fucked up. You never let anybody in your spots, period. Only your peeps in power, bitch. It's the game in hustling nigga, you know nothing about, ya little black ass." he laughed.

Nubian pulled out an ice pick. He said to De-La, "Motherfucker, I'ma keep stickingya ass until I get an answer. It's your choice, my rug."

He stuck the ice pick in De-La's right cheek. De-La hollered like a wolf. Still he did not answer Nubina's questions. So, Nubian decided to have a sticking good time in De-La's body.

That motherfucker just kept screaming and calling Nubian a fuck-up. Nubian kept getting more furious at De-La. Then he told Lil Kill to go get him some salt. He started throwing the salt on his wounds, and then he was rubbing the shit in like lotion, leaving De-La hollering.

Kevin's ass was being slapped around by the troops at the same time. All of them were in the same room watching each other being tortured as hell. The female, Ms. Smiley's informant, pissed on herself, realizing her ass is really in for the death penalty. She figured she'd spill the beans on Ms. Smiley, thinking it would get her off death row.

T. Dove yelled to Nubian, "Yo nig, can I get a piece of this good asshole this bitch squeezing back here. I can't help it if I'm a dawg and raw. I don't mean me. No never mind. A tight ass is always on the menu.

T.Dove grabbed the female and tied her hands to the pipe. She was naked as a jay bird with her position in doggy style. He started telling her, "Girl, your ass in mine, boo. All mine.

I'ma fuck your ass up literally and bust a coupla nuts. This is my specialty."

Everybody's looking at T. Dove, amazed that this nigga is serious as all hell. He actually went straight for her ass. T. Dove ended up liking ass because of a ten year state bid. He· had only· been home eight months and hooked up with Nubian quick. He's a straight up homo thug nigga. He is big built, burly and looks diesel. He started slapping the female so she could resist and start trying to jiggle her ass. He started getting excited.

He grabbed that bitch's ass and just plunged his nine inch in her ass gradually, making moaning sounds and telling his troops, "Yo, yo don't know what kind nut ya missing when it come to ass, niggas. This shit is like a rubber around ya dick, hoping ya bust rapid nuts." He started laughing and just kept easing his dick in her ass.

She was screaming and. yelling, "Ya nasty, dirty, grimy motherfucker. You're ripping my ass." She was begging him to stop.

Then he said, "Bitch, is Ms. Smiley behind this shit or what, bitch. Your ripping my ass." She was begging him to stop.

Then he said again, 'Bitch, is Ms. Smiley behind this shit or what, bitch. As a matter of fact hoe, wha ya name?"

She replied, "Oww, oww, ooh, it's killing me. Please stop. It hurts, oh god, it hurts.".

Then another one of Nubian's troopers had some vice grips and came over to where T. Dove was fucking her in the ass.

He said, "Oh shit. I do know ya, scalliwag ass bitch. Your name is Lilly, hoe."

He told T. Dove, "Fuck this bitch hard, nigga. She got one of my homies killed over on Third Street, over her grimy ass. His name was Echo. Nigga was real straight up true dude. Ya feel me. Let me at that bitch: I got sununin' for her."

He put the vice grips on her left nipple, tightened them and started twisting them, saying, "Bitch, ya ass bound to start squealing now, boo. Bitch, you remember me now? took at me.

It's me Keyes." He laughed as T. Dove was busting nuts and this bitch was hollering in agony for her life.

In the meantime, Lil Kill had tied Kevin's dick with his balls, with a telephone wire, pulling the shit tight as hell. Kevin was yelling, "Y' all motherfuckers gonna git yours. True that, fo sho I ain't telling ya shit. Kill me bitches."

So then Nubian came over to Kevin and spit on that motherfucker and started beating him in his face at the same time. He knocked his front teeth out, all of 'em. Kevin's an asshole and ain't trying to say shit, so everyone decided to leave' their asses alone for a coupla hours, with some salt on their wounds to keep them aware of more pain to encounter.

Lilly's ass was raw and sore to the point where it took her voice, also because of screaming at the top of her lungs. Her lungs were out of wind, too.

She felt like dying, but thought crazy *'bout maybe they'd let her live and she could relay a message to Ms. Smiley warning that they're afterher ass or that nig T Dove might put in a word.* She's definitely thinking stupid. She almost forgot about the dude's boy, Echo. Now she realizes they're going to kill her no matter what.

Kevin and De-La were too weak tonY any kid of escape or retaliation of some sort.

They both were bleeding like a waterfall. Kevin could barely see out of his eyes, crying. He was aching, holding his chest. It was how they tied his ass up after beating him in his chest with the bat, let alone his dick throbbing with the telephone wire tied around it in knots. This nigga had blue balls, blue face, just plain ole blue fucked up.

They were all in so much pain that the hours had passed them by. Just moaning, no one called to each other or said nothing to one another. It was moans rather than silence.

One of Nubian troopers stayed behind to keep a close eye on them. They called him Born. He had been with Nubian's troops as a favor to Lil Kill and for the come up in a crew so real. He was shoot' em up bang bang nigga. No shorts or ya life. He was from B-Stuy, do or die.

Born looked over at Lilly. He thought, *Dam, she is kinda cute.* So he yelled to her, "Yo bitch, check this. I gotta treat for you, boo. If you can suck my dick right, I'll talk to my peeps 'bout letting ya ass go, ya heard. Away from these two birds you got ya ass caught up with. Yo, ya hear me?"

He went towards her, zipping down his pants, took hold of his dick and went straight for her mouth. Lilly looked up at him, all tied up on the pipe, opened her mouth and stuck her tongue out. He played with the tip of her tongue with the tip of his dick. That nigga was hard as hell already. Lilly thought, *dam, this'll be quick.'* So she began sucking his dick, soft and slow.

Next thing you know his ass was bustin' a nut.

All he said was, "Ahh, that a girl, You know what ya doin, rna. Yeah, suck soft."

In the process of telling her to "suck soft," his ass was cummin: two-minute man. Then all of a sudden he began shoving his dick hard in her mouth. He had her by the hair and made her look as if she was pumping gas.

"Yeah, on Born's dick." That nigga started wiling, growling and shit, forcing his dick down her throat, grunting like he was about to blow up or something. Lilly was like trying to talk in between him shoving his dick in her mouth, "I can't, I can't, I can't."

Born said, "You can't what bitch? Suck this dick. Oh yes you are bitch. I'ma make sure.

of this shit, ma. Oh you done got my dick in an uproar to nut all in your mouth. Lillies of the field, that's what my dick feels like in your mouth. So now bitch, you best get to sucking hard, cause my dick is feeling kind of ruff. So, you going to ride it with your mouth. Come on bitch, get to suckin'. Suck, suck, suck it, suck it." He started bucking and shaking. His eyes going up in his head. Then he sighed like a bitch..

Although in pain; De-La and Kevin were getting hard off the episode they just saw Born do with Lilly. They wished it would have been them. They knew he had a beautiful nut.

* * *

Nubian and his troops returned to the basement of torture. Born explained to him, his little fiasco with Lilly. T. Dove asked Lilly if she was ready for round two or ready to answer whether or not Ms. Smiley is behind this bullshit. If so, Nubian had to get shit right, bum rushing her and her peeps.

He was in need of some more gats. Jaia knew the connect to that, as far as quantity and quality. He'd have to call on that tip fo sho and not let her know, at the same time., the *real* shit is going down for the cause. He remembered what Da-Stev had said to him, that he's got twenty-four hours to straighten all this shit out before he calls Jaia to let her know what's poppin off with their shit. Nubian felt that the shit was halfway over and he's just gotta get to Ms. Smiley and it would be a slam dunk. He felt that it was all going as planned.

Nubian cellied Jaia, "Yo, fam, what it is, yo. Ya'll enjoying your IiI va-cay?"

Jaia said, "What up, my nig Nubian? Everything all good at the home front. Ain't no fucked up shit to report or 1'd be there in a flash. You got it all under your control, I hope.

Monies making money. Ya feel me."

Nubian declared, "Jaia, I need some more gats, boo. We clocking so much cash, I wauna be safe doing the pick ups. I got a coupla more troopers, ya heard. They all real to the game, boo. So, can you let me in on ya peeps with the gats and get back at me, fo sho, I need' em. We ballin in dough, Jaia, it's flowing with a quickness. Yo, Jaia, holla back. I didn't mean to intrude on your va'cay. True that, boo, a'ight.?

Jaia responded, ''Nubian never that when it's business, my nig. I was wondering if ya ass, if anything, would call and keep me up to date. Listen anyway, I'ma holla at my peeps. Her name is Natalie. She's in Selkirk. You know how to get there, right. She'll know all about you when ya get there. She's cool as hell Dangerous too. A white chick. So get the shit and get the fuck out. Understand Nubian? As a matter of fact, I'ma three-way'her right now: This was she'll know ya voice, Feel me."

Natalie answered her cell phone, "Yo, Natalie, it's Jaia. A friend to the end is stopping by, ya heard."

''Nubian, say 'be real.'

"Be real," Nubian said.

"Hang up, Nubian."

Jaia then continued her little code words with Natalie, so everything was set.

As Nubian hung up from speaking with Jaia, he headed toward Selkirk to Natalie's. He knew that everything would be on point as far as getting what he needed.

Natalie already knew what Nubian was up to as far as needing the gats. She had Ms. Smiley ather house, but Nubian did not know, so he'll be surprised. She also gathered that Nubian hadn't explained to Jaia the crazy shit going on. Natalie figured she'd save them a whole lotsa time hunting Ms. Smiley's ass down, once Nubian entered her place.

In New York City, Jaia wondered what Nubian really wanted the guns for. In the back of her mind she felt summin. Then again, she also knew Nubian would hold shit down. Otherwise, she would not have left him in charge.

Jaia got off her cellie, explaining to her dawgs about Nubian's call.

They were like, "That nigga ain't no joke, so don't sleep on him. Trust me, he's sho nuff loyal nigga, to the heart."

Vah said, Jaia mentioned, that if a motherfucking penny or crumb is outta order returning back to Smallbany, I will kill everything moving in the hood, especially that grimy bitch Ms. Smiley. She'll be done on the fucking spot. I don't give a fuck. Ya feel me, dawgs."

Unc was like, "So check it, where are we staying for the night ladies?"

Vah said, "Hell, let's make a celebration of our stay until we can set ship up with ya Uncle Tito, Jaia. Why don't we call a hotel for reservations? How about the Marriott, fo sho?

Ya know you two are bunking together, cause I'm not in for hearing pussy slurping at all tonight, a'ight?"

They ended up at the Marriott Marquis in Midtown and paid for two rooms right next door to each other. Jaia had a big kool-aid smile on her face, checking Unc out as they entered their room. The room was really nice. It oversee 7th avenue, Avenue of the Americas, and Broadway. They were acting like. there were sightseeing and shit.

Unc touched Jaia's face, telling her, "Baby, this is the moment I've been longing for, boo.

Just me and you love. Alone at last, honey. Now I can show you how much of me wants you, for always Jaia. You need to know my feelings are real, girl Not because of this hustling shit either. You're all I want, love and more of you. Only if you let me, cause you'll have all of me, Jaia. I hope the feeling is mutual and you're just not being a tease or some type of turn on, turn off, boo."

Unc kissed Jaia softly on her lips and Jaia, in return, gave into Unc's sweet tongue. Jaia felt as if she was in her glory cause she had loved her some Unc, and realized this with a kiss.

She was whispering to Unc that she could have her if she wants her because she is feeling her desperately, as if she needs her to make love so sweetly and passionately. Unc is desiring every inch of Jaia. She is in a zone oflove, making Jaia enjoy and feel the love she has for her.

Jaia and Unc are all intertwined with each other. As Unc is nibbling at Jaia's neck, kissing her so tenderly while undressing her, as well she is rubbing her breast in a circular motion. Then she takes her titties and begins licking the nipples, wetting them enough where her tongue slides around her breast, sticking her nipples between her teeth, as if she's biting them.

Jaia is moaning in a sexual, seductive manner, enjoying Unc pleasing and tantalizing her body.

She is kissing Unc every chance she gets and can seeing Unc's eyes she is loving her for who she is. That's very mesmerizing for Jaia.

Unc is feeling all over Jaia's body as if it's a precious jewel. She's letting her tongue roam all through and between Jaia's legs, kissing her pussy and putting hickies all over her belly.

Then she asks Jaia, "Baby, are you ready for me to taste you, boo? Iam sure thirsty for you, Jaia. I have been baby, since we ate at Julian's, love. Now, I'm getting the menu I really wanted that day. It was you Jaia."

Unc's making Jaia so wet. Unc tells her, "Your juices from your pussy are slippery enough for me to suck your clitoris at a pace you desire, honey. Direct me boo, on how you want me enjoying you, enjoying my pussy. Ya feel me."

Unc's playing in Jaia's pussy with two fingers, while licking and sucking her clit. She's in a daze. Unc is staring at her enjoying her so beautifully. She is slurping all of Jaia's juices.

Unc's saying to her, while fingering her to fuck her, "whose pussy is this babe? Is it mine? Is it mine? Let me hear you say, "Unc, this pussy is yours, love. Tell me Jaia. you want me to have it, then give it graciously."

Unc sticks another finger in Jaia's pussy. She is flooded with pre-cum. Unc is ready to go all out but decided she'd take it slow this first time, giving Jaia all this pleasure in making love to her, not fucking her just yet. That is next after Jaia thinks she's all cummed out.

Unc though to herself, *'I've got to hear my baby feel the fuck of it all.'*

Unc was still putting her tongue on Jaia's body. Sucking her toes, licking her ass to her asshole, nibbling to her thighs and back, pulling at her hair, sticking her tongue in her ears. She's just giving the woman she's falling in love with a tongue bath.

Jaia feels as if she's on some type of aphrodisiac, in pure ecstasy, loving every touch of Unc's caressing, especially giving her body her full attention in sexiug her. Unc' s making love to every tense spot. She's feeling the relief of Unc's love onto her.

Jaia's mind I s focused on what's being done in an unexplainable sense of love. The positions she assumed is for Unc to take as much of her as a token of her love to her, as she feels her sexual desire for Unc. Jaia's voice is trying to let Unc know she is getting ready to cum.

She's saying to Unc, "Baby, I'm about to cum. If you keep sucking my clitoris as good as you're doing baby. Ooh, ooh, ooh Unc. This is definitely your pussy baby. Ooh yeah, honey, suck it. Oh yeah, like that ma, yeah like that ma. Ooh, ooh, aah. Unc baby, this pussy is all yours Unc. My pussy is so promised to you, only you. Oh, oh, oh, oh, Unc, Unc, Unc, oh oh god, I'm cumming, cum, cum, cum, ooh, ooh oh right there, oh yes, right there, oh Unc, suck it.

Oh baby, it's yours."

Unc is sweetly tearing Jaia's ass the fuck up. She hears Jaia say, "Baby, come lay on top of me. I wanna cum some more for you, with me. Her and Unc started body rocking. Their pussies kept meeting at the same destination. They were both moaning, saying how good it felt, looking into each other's eyes, feeling the love they want each other to share so sincerely. Both of them were all smiles in the other's gaze, cuming at the same time as one.

CHAPTER ELEVEN

BACK AT NATALIE'S, MS. SMILEY was just jabbering away about her plans to demolish TLC and making· sure everything is as it is, no ifs, ands or buts. *'Them bitches gotta get taught a lesson, fo sho'* Little does Ms. Smiley know, Natalie is getting ready to set her ass afire, as soon as Nubian gets there to purchase some guns. As it is, it's not going down the way Ms. Smiley planned for TLC.

Nubian's cellie is ringing to the tune by Ja-Rule and Ashante, "Always There When You Call." He pickes up and it's Da-Stev. "Yo, what up Nub, yo nig, is everything in order, Nubian?"

"I got themotherfuckers who are hitting the spots along with some Puerto Rican chick named Lilly. Neither one if 'em are saying whether or not Ms. Smiley's behind this bullshit, ya hear. If she is, I'm on my way to Selkirk to get some gats for insurance, ya feel me. I hollered at Jaia to get the info, but did not mention what's going on. I have a hunch she ain't feeling that two bit story I ran down to her about our cash needing more security. That's my reason for getting in contact with her connect for the gats. I feel that Ms. Smiley is behind all this and I'm going after her ass. It's time for her hustling to end anyway. I'll be doing TLC a favor, ya feel me, Da-Stev?"

"That's what I'm talking about Nubian. Be about it all the way live, boyee; cause the game only lasts if you play it to succeed nigga. You 'bout to blow up on the strong arm tip handling your army and yours, my brother. Let Jaia and 'em know you are the man, Nubian.

Get your props right, ya feel me. I feel ya on that information about Msc Smiley. So do you, so make it right so we can all get paid. TLC is getting ready to rise, my nigga. Remember, you're helping to put them in the game to riches, Nubian. So listen, once you go do your thing with picking up your shit in Selkirk, go back to the basement and get rid of those birds, OK. You don't need 'em for nothing. Ya mind is made up to eliminate her and her peeps. Clear all of 'em the fuck out from the face of the earth."

"Yo, listen. I'll keep ya up to date on the inside of the police department and their scoops for the streets. Yeah, I'm in like that, so I can keep my peeps on point, ya feel me Nubian. Shit is bout to blow up, fo shot I'ma make dam sure we all git our shine on. Let motherfuckers know TLC are Nubian's Queens on the game board and are passing go on the Monopoly, ya heard. It's a given as long as I'm breathing. I like seeing females In control, hustling. They're treacherous, up front with everything, cause they know they gotta be harder than the hext nigga getting paid... Believe you me TLC is in a class by themselves. Them bitches is bad. They're no fucking joke to be played with, at all ya get caught slippin', that's an ass whipping, depending on whatever one you try a stunt on, Nubian. Stay with 'em my nigga.

Guard them with your life, ya feel me. You'll end up controlling an empire of hustling in the game of murder, money and mayhem and the next nigga to be on top of the game once all is good and they're gone. Ya feel me, lil nigga?"

Nubian felt some type of way about Da-Stev's last remark. He just let it roll. He knew he had to keep a leash on this motherfucker with shome shit comin flip like that outta his mouth. So, now he had his binoculars open wide on Da-Stev's ass, fo sho Da-Ste was letting Nubian know in a sense, he could be his own king of hustling, if he really wanted to. He figured he'd try and put some shit in Nubian's head. He had seen the expression on his face that the shit that slipped out of his mouth was foul as hell.

"Well," Nubian says. to Da-Stev, "nig, I gotta blow away dude and go handle the chicken heads real quick. Bust on out to Selkirk, ya feel me, Da-Stev? I appreciate ya schooling my nig.

It's all good. I'ma be about it, fo sho Long as my peeps are the TLC, it's fam and who we be.

Later."

Nubian drove Lexington Ave. and. went in the basement when he arrived. All three bodies had been shot the fuck up as if they were a target range practice. Nubian's face and had a kool-aid smile. He said, "Yo, I came back to dead these motherfuckers."

T. Dove replied, "I beat ya to the puuch. Ha ha ha ha Yo Nubie, now let's go nail this bitch Ms. Smiley to the pavement. It's on and popping. My guns are huugry for some more bodies to put a nigga's ass, ya feel me. I'm done here. Come on Nubie, direct me."

Nubian, T. Dove and Lil Kill jumped in the Jeep and headed for Selkirk to see Natalie.

T. Dove asked Nubian, "Yo, Nubian, nigga, you ever get your dick sucked? I see it's get money all day with you, nigga. So you ever take abreak for some hoe to suckie suckie or fuckie fuckie?"

Nubian cracked up, "Yo, T. Dove, you ain't right to be on my dick like that, boy. Just cause you ass is sexually freaky ass dude, who like poking and shoving your dick in ass doesn't mean I'm not getting my dickie suckie. Ha Ha...""

"I feel you Nubie. I'm just funning, man. I needed a laugh."

Lil Kill was like, "T. Dove, you should be the last nigga asking if and when anybody gets" their dick sucked. The way you fucked Lilly in her ass, you should never want anybody to put, their mouth on ya dick. Yo, your dick is for ass, period! I believe that is the only way your crazy fuckin' ass can nut up anyway, ass man." They all laughed goofing on each other.

Da-Stev actually thought about his last remark to Nubian and felt he is the type nigga that" is up on game, is a very loyal soldier and slippin like that around Nubian could cost Da-Stev his life. He knew definitely to always be on point around Nubian. He realized fuckin'up any way toward TLC is a fucked up way to die. Trust and believe TLC is loyal, not to mention Nubian is in love with Jaia. It's like a fuckin' stick of dynamite. He could not believe he endangered his life like that with a dumb ass remark to "Nubian, of all peeps.

He figured he'd wait out the outcome. If Nubian became suspicious of him, then he'd have to put some sort of back up plan into effect, for real. He thought hard about not dying in these streets, especially the way TLB and 'em like to torture a motherfucker. Ain't no fucking way that shit is jumping off on me. Nah, fuck that! *'gotta stay alert, fo sho,'* he thought to himself.

Da-Stev happened to see Detective Reese as he drove into the ghetto Price Chopper parking lot on Delaware Avenue. He needed his vitamin drink shit. He figured if Fifty-Cent owns it and looks the way he does, whycan't he - he's selling mayhem too!

He smiled and beeped for Detective Reese, "Hey, my man, what it is dude?"

Detective Reese walked toward his car, "You tell me son. What is going on with TLB and their spots? Does this mean no more free money, Da-Stev, cause I haven't the slightest idea what the fuck is going on man. Can you fill me in or should I just get ready for dead bodies to be laid to rest throughout Albany?" He laughed.

"Then I guess it's time to get paid again, huh, only this time it's about not arresting TLB'speeps. Oh yea, Da-Stev listen, this is between me and you. I have a buddy of mine who's transferring, a detective from New York City. Check this, the motherfucker is just as crooked as a limp dick," he laughed so hard, he choked. "He asked if he can be put on too. Not that I mentioned your information. Never that, Da-Stev."

Da-Stev says, "Well, let's do this once he's settled. Oh, I get it, he'll be your part'na, right? Hell yeah, tell 'em he's good to go, Reese." He continues, "First you gonna give me some shit on him. I can connect with him to make sure his ass is in order to be dirty and know if the peeps he's been fuckin with are a'ight, Reese. This way no one gets played, ya feel me, and everybody gets paid. It's all in the game of hustling. Yo, you know that Reese. It's all good especially in the hood, dawg."

Back at Natalie's. Natalie wanted so bad to get rid of Ms. Smiley, but instead she decided to keep that bitch hostage until Jaia and 'em return from New York City, where they're enjoying themselves on the rise.

Natalie decided not to inform Nubian of her capture of Ms. Smiley, cause then she'd have to explain herself. She is not about to explain shit. She knew she had to get ready to go into her living room and throw some acid in her eyes, just a little and gag and then hog tie this bitch.

Natalie yelled, "Yo, Smiley, come in the kitchen for a minute. Help me with these gats, a'ight?"

Ms. Smiley is like, "Bitch, you the gun runner, hoe. You should be making trips back and forth. I'm paying to see your ass sweat," she laughed and headed towards the kitchen.

Natalie was bending down in the cabinet where the sink'sat, as If it's difficult, "Whew.". Ms. Smiley was coming toward her saying, "Natalie, are the guns stuck in the fucking plumbing pipes or what?"

As soon as she got "what" out of her mouth, Natalie threw the acid directly in her eyes and said, "No bitch, you just got stuck fucking with the wrong bitches. How 'bout that bitch!"

She laughed out loud.

Ms. Smiley was yelling and screaming "I'ma kill you, ya white fucking cracker ass. Ya ass is dead bitch," she kept hollering.

Natalie cold-cocked that bitch with the butt of her .38 Special Automatic. She knocked her ass out. Then she hurried up and stuffed all kinds of dirty rags she cleaned her floors with, in her mouth. She duct taped her hands and feet, then duct taped them all together like she was a pig ready to be barbecued. She then rolled her ass into her walk-in pantry with the quickness.

She knew Nubian would be there any minute. So she had to clean up shit. She didn't want Nubian to be suspicious at all.

'Whoa' she thought, *'dam good thing I did this fuckin shit in the kitchen. 'Yeah, a bitch like me* is *definitely on point.'*

Nubian started thinking whether or not he should take this nigga, T. Dove, to Natalie's spot. He knew better though. T. Dove had always been desperate motherfucker, by any means necessary. He was definitely not to be trusted. He felt Jaia would blow him a new asshole if he did or if anything happened to Natalie.

'Nah,' he thought, *'he's not gonna fuck up like that.' Before they hit the highway, he asked T. love and Lil Kill where they wanted to be dropped off.*

Lil Kill looked at him, "Yo Nubian, what up with that nigga?"

"Jaia's orders, a'ight."

Nubian said "I bullshit you hot, dude. Yo, you know how she gets down nigga, ya feel me. Where y'all motherfuckers wanna go? I'll pick y'all asses up on my way back."

T.Dove said "Yo, what kind of shit you trippin' on Nubian? We go too far back for thinking dumb shit, dude. Yo, motherfucker, it's a secret or some shit? What?' Fill me in dawg."

Nubian responded "Like I said to both y'all niggas. Jaia's orders, ya feel me? That's all that needs to be said, no more, no less, with no disrespect. Tell my niggas. Lil Kill yo, you should know how the fuck Jaia's ass is. She's a stone cold bitch. Word up. First of all, if you fuck With TLC that is your life. Second, if you fuck with her money, that bitch will go King Kong or Scarface on your ass, all at once. Keep in mind, niggas, she is fucking ruthless. But ya know what, that's my queen, motherfuckers. She's bout it, ya heard. The sadistic bitch, fo sho Ya feel me.

CHAPTER TWELVE

AUNYA'S EXCITED THAT SHE HAS four months before she's released. She can't wait to be with her dawgs again. The good thing is that she got her GED. She can not believe it herself and won't until she starts making it work in terms of taking some college courses in real estate. Then shit is on and poppin, fo sho.

Aunya really thought hard about Jaia's and Unc's relationship, as far as hustling.

Although her dawgs are still on the grind plus one added to TLC, shit is all good. She still feels some type of way about Coco's. bullshit. She has held on to that the whole time being incarcerated. She wonders why TLC hasn't done not a dam thing to Coco to defend her honor, she can't understand that crap. No matter what, we represent. Hopefully they have a good reason for not killing the bitch. Her anger does not want that bitch Coco to think she'd gotten away with a fucking thing; She'll definitely have to shed some light on shit once she hits the streets. She fought with herself long and hard, whether to stick to the game or become legit.

It felt weird to because she never accomplished shit in her life except to become a part of TLC, and that's in rare form. She takes pride in TLC's accomplishments, wondering in the long run if she can run the empire herself, if anything were to happen to Jaia or Vah.

'Fuck around and depending on what's good in the hood, if I have to, every-fucking-body would git got. It's all about me now. lam the focus,' she thought.. Next, Aunya thought about this female she'd been seeing for a while in her dorm unit named Kenyetta, aka Labu. She's a very lovely shy woman. She's Korean and AfricanAmerican, with a dark complexion, light brown eyes, with a mole in between her lips and nose. A shape like Lauren London.

Aunya's thinking, *'Tm feeling Labu, maybe I'll take her home with me.'*

She's a sincere woman who understand Aunya's ways. They've grown to be exceptional of each other. Labu will be going home two months before Aunya to Miami, Florida.

Where she's from. She has been in jail seven years, a flat bid. Her time has come to go back to Miami.

Her people's are in Washington Heights, which is why her and Aunya became so connected.

They do care for each other very deeply. Labu is twenty-six and has no kids. She's been down since she was nineteen years of age. Her parents disowned her when they found out she was in a New York State Penitentiary. Labu managed through all those years of incarceration, and she knew Aunya would be her savior to her having a life to die for.

As time got close for both of them to part, their relationship became unbearable because they were in love with each other. It would be so hurtful to actually be without one another.

They were *for* each other, ride or die. Aunya had some serious thinking to do concerning Labu, as far as not being in each other's presence. Once she is gone her heart will hurt and her emotions will be devastated. She cares very much for Labu and feels she needs to be there for the one man she loves, she thought. It'll be something to be considered for the sake of her love and relationship. She'll hook up Labu to Jaia andVah, so she'll be taken care of until she is release. Moreover, so they can continue being as one not having to be without each other.

Labu loved herself some Aunya since they first got together in the yard nine months ago.

She was watching the paddleball court and spotted Aunya kicking ass, talking shit to her opponents.

"Boy, she's tearing their asses up," she said to the girls sitting on the bench with her.

From then on she felts she had to get with Aunya. Labu introduced herself and it was a wrap.

Aunya was all hers with her fine mannish features and looking sexy as ever.

"Yes, she's mine. I love her dearly." Labu keeps that to her heart. If any bitch has words regarding any type of issue affecting her partners, it affects Labu deeply. She'll jump in an argument in a minute, ready to beat a bitch down about Aunya's ass.

Nevertheless, Aunya's making love methods are wonderful. They've spent quality time to have such good sex on their units. The rush of fucking is so enjoyable and pleasurable with the way Aunya has total control over fucking me lovely. *That's what makes us so compatible,'* she reminisced and thought to herself *'for one thing she knows how to suck and luck me right.*

M-m-m, not only is she very good to me and respectful, she know s how to treat a woman.'

Their good-byes to one another were an emotional task. Aunya has explained to Labu the situation when she hits Albany. She'll be taken care of until she comes home and she'll be fine where she'll be living and that she will be keeping in contact with her at her apartment on South Main Street. She decided not to go to Miami, and instead chose to go to Albany to have a life with Aunya.

Aunya told Kenyetta, "Do not do a motherfucking thing until I come home baby, cause you'll be a'ight. You're maxed out of the system, love. That's a good thing, boo.

Back in New York City, Jaia, Vah and Unc were having a good time. The services at the Marriott Marquis were nice and relaxed, however, they all decided to go down to the Village, Washington Square Park, where they met. Aunya was all they talked about once they settled at their destination.

Jaia's music was blasting going down Fifth Avenue. She is on shit. Niggas whistling and shit. Every time a nigga even thought to look her way driving, she'd reach over and give Unc some tongue. Unc gladly responded. They both were lusting for each other, listening to old school Chaka Kahn's 'Sweet Thing.'

Vah was the back seat driver thinking to herself, *'I'm happy for both of 'em, but I wish I woulda took a fucking cab instead, so I can get away from these two fucking lovebirds. I gotta go find some bitch to play and lay, like Frito 'so'*

Jaia yelled to Vah, "Yo my nig, you a'ight? Do not think I's forgot about ya playa, ya feel me. So what up, is there anything you'd like to do in particular, besides getting your pussy sucked, bitch? You can't tell me with all this kissing and sucking me and my boo doing here ain't getting ya all juiced up in your panties, dawg."

Vah said, "Yo Jaia, you come out ya mouth with some of the foulest shit, bitch. Ya disrespectful bi-atch. You just keep ya fucking thoughts in your clitoris, bitch. Let me worry 'bout my shit getting sucked. You a sick ass motherfuckers, but I love every bit of your crazy ass, for life, cause only fam can come at me like that. Now go stick ya tongue back down Unc's throat. Make that bitch choke, ya feel me dawg. I luv ya both, true story. Yo, let's park somewhere."

They were on West 4th Street and Avenue of the Americas. They found a spot and jetted toward the park. Heads were turning, they were turning theirs too. As they got to the entrance of the park there was a homeless woman with a cart filled with what might have been her entire belongings, for everyday survivaL Unc walked toward the woman and gave her a twenty-dollar bill Jaia and Vah looked at her, she said to them, "It's always good to give back when you can spare it. My moms always said that to me as I grew up. I kept it to my heart, especially when I see homeless people or anyone who needs to eat, ya feel me."

Here goes Jaia, "Well then Boo, you need to open up a shelter with the money you're handling, for real love. That is if you really feel for it that way."

Vah's response was, "Fuck both y'all bitches with this sorry ass sentimental, lovey dovey bullshit. I'll see y'all hoes feeling soft from fucking and sucking each other's sense loose.

That's all the fuck it is, ya fuck buckets! Ha, ha, ha."

They were all laughing so hard, Unc said she was about to piss on herself as they went and sat on the benches in the circle part of the park with their colds beers. Some dude approached them saying he's got good crank.

Vah jumped up, 'Motherfucker, do we look like we smoke that shit nigga? Yo, you best get the fuck up from over here son. Fo real, nigga." The dude looked like he just hit the streets from Sing Sing or Dannemora.

"Ah fuck, that nigga's dieseL"

He looked at Vah and politely said, "Yo Boo, you did not have a scream on a nigga like that, rna. I'm getting my hustle on, tryn'a servive after I did a five year stretch. All I'm doing is getting my food to eat, ma, that's all So, all that shit and drama, Boo, kill it cause neither one of us is gonna bust a grape in this gay ass park.

"Yo, why you so hostile, ma? Chill It's not that deep nigga."

He started laughing at her he called Vah a nigga, like she's a dude. She kinda laughed to herself He introduced himself, "Yo, what it is? My name is Damian."

Everybody introduced themselves. Jaia, Unc, and Vah all looked at each other. Unc was puzzled. Vah knew a good hustler and sensed it, with him out here in Washington Square Park doing this shit. I can imagine his skills, she thought.

Yah's like, "Yo son, you got skills, I'ma test ya waters dude, a'ight?"

She gave him her cellie number and told him to give her a call in two weeks, if he's still in the streets or alive.

Damian's feeling curious, so he's like, "Is it anything better than being in this park?"

"In two weeks you call and you'll answer that question yourself when I pick up on your cal! ya feel me."

He walked away with a smile. He kept looking back at them.

Unc said, "Vah, I was hoping that nigga did not want to whip your ass like you stole some shit from him. He's fuckin huge, bitch. Didn't you look at that nigga as he approached?

What the fuck is wrong with ya eyes in broad daylight, bitch? Everybody was cracking up.

Jaia told Vah, "Ya fuckin fool. Yeah bitch, you ain't got it all in ya head, Ned."

They all headed toward the pier. Vah was hoping she'd meet some cutie to profile with her, at her side. She was feeling kinda lonely. A restaurant in view caught their eyes, called the Riviera Cafe, a block before the pier. As they entered the atmosphere was beautiful. The waitress escorted them to a table with a view of the streets. There were people hustling and bustling to wherever they were going. It was all good.

Jaia said, "It's all good."

Duc said, "Baby, you like this place? If not Boo, Vah can stay and we'll just find one that you'll enjoy, love." Unc was just kidding, messing with Yah.

Jaia said, "You better leave my dawg alone, Dnc."

Unc frowned at what she said. It kinda stung her and made her think that these two bitches would seriously kill her funky ass. She thought out loud, "Fuckin with either one of them, I'm dead. Just saying her name made me realize, bitch watch ya tongue. These bitches were not to be underestimated. Fo sho."

Ms. Smiley has regained consciousness and is wondering what the fuck is going on. It' s dark as a motherfucker in here. She thought. She realized she can't move or say shit freely.

She's wondering, again, what the fuck is going on. She can't remember just yet cause her mind is fogged. Her fuckin head is pounding like she got hit with a fucking brick. 'Ooops,' now she is remembering, *'that bitch Natalie threw some acid in her eyes.'* That's why it's so dark. Once she came to think clearly about her situation, she remembered every freaking detail. *"Oh, that bitch,'* she tried to speak but smelled the rag she had in her mouth was one of Natalie's nasty ass cleaning rags for her guns.

Ms. Smiley tried her damnest to move any part of her body, but she was hog tied. She couldn't move shit so now she kuew she was fucked royally. However, she couldn't for the sake of God figure out what the hell Natalie had her hemmed up the way she did. Then again, she's thinking, *'what the fuck is going on,"* wishing she could hit the door with herself to get attention.

She heard voices outside of the closet as she's wondering what the fuck is going on and why the fuck she's in the dark tied up like a hog. She'd thinking, *'this is some real scary shit.*

My eyes are in pain, I'ma bout to shit on myself cause I sense my death near. What the fuck is wrong with this bitch Natalie. She's lost her ever lovin' motherfuckin' mind. What? Is this bitch on crack or something? She's kidnapping my ass for money or my supply. What the fuck is going on here. I don't understand, but what I do know fa sho, this ain't no joke.

This shit is for real and this bitch is going to kill me. What the fuck is going on?' Suddenly, her cell phone is vibrating in her pocket, she wishes she could answer it so she can tell who ever it is what the fuck is going on. *'At this minute that is a great thought for wishing, yet, I'd hope for some truth to it 'cause I dam sure need it, fa sho, right now with the quickness.'*

The conversation she could hear was about gats, the price, the kind the dude wants, plus some ammunition. *"Dam,'* she thought, *'this nigga sounds like he's about to go to war or some shit. He sound like whoever gets in his way, papa and all, are some dead asses on the real tip.'*

The dude then just said to Natalie, "Yeah, I gotta do some work in keeping my spots on lock. Sometimes shit gets kinda hectic, ya feel me."

Ms. Smiley wondered if the dude she heard was new on the block. She thought to herself. *'Wherever he's hustling, shit I couldn't get to him anyway for some business. If only I could get out of the closet.'*

She kept trying to pull herself loose, instead she felt the rope cutting into her skin. She felt blood dripping with the sizzling from the acid coming out of her eyes. She could not believe it one fucking bit. All of a sudden she heard something scattering behind her. Then she heard a scratching, then she smelled it.

"It's a dam cat, oh my god, un-fuckin real."

Next the cat's, "meow, meow." I don't believe this bitch put her un-neutered nasty ass fucking cat in this hell hole of darkness with me.

She listened to Natalie tell the dude, Yo Nubian, just tell Jaia and 'em all is well, alright," with a smile on her face.

Natalie knew Ms. Smiley had definitely heard every word she said to Nubian, fo sho After she closed the door behind *him,* she went straight to the kitchen pantry, let the cat out and shut the door without even saying a word to Ms. Smiley.

She picked her cat up, "What's the matter with lil Pussy Willow, huh Pussy Willow? Pussy want some milk or some Fancy Feast, beef flavor, your favorite. Pussy Willow. Mommy can do that love. Yeah, you were caught there with that greedy, grimy bitch baby, I know.

That's why my Pussy Willow was scratching to get out of there and away from that played out bitch, huh?"

Then Natalie rubs her nose on the cat and says aloud, "Yeah, she wanted to kill TLC, Pussy Willow. I couldn't let her do that now I know Jaia's father is Manuel Acosta. She doesn't know anything about he drug lords. She's Smallbany, but I'ma hold her ass here until Jaia and 'em come back from New York City. Nobody knows this bitch is here and in my food pantry at that. See, the dude, Nubian, that just left? He bought the guns and shit to hunt ya rotten ass down bitch, like the scum you are lady."

You got no respect for the game, which you'll learn in death. I'ma kill ya ass slowly, fo sho, Smiley. Ya hear me there? Yoo-hoo, yoo-hoo. I hope you hear me in there, honey. Ya fucked up. I knew I'd seen Jaia somewhere before when you first brought her here. She is the picture with her father in Florida -- Miami, as a matter of fact. I met him at the NRAS convention. The man is made of money, girl. Something you know nothing about. You're petty Smiley and you're too comfortable as far as hustling. Ya dumb ass came here without anyone bitch. Ya dead as a door knob."

She could hear Ms. Smiley scuffling and grunting, switching she could kill her were she stands.

She thought to herself. *'Nah, cause she's tied up in the closet like a fucking animal. I got a big ole grand finale death for this bitch.'*

Meanwhile, Nubian's back in Albany distributing his gats. T. Dove and 'em are getting all trigger happy and shit. They're going around Swan Street bad mouthing Ms. Smiley's name, daring any nigga to step to him. He got summin' for their asses, fo sho He saying some awful shit about her. Niggas in the street are looking at his black ass as if he just came out of a psycho ward, namely the Capital District Psychiatric Center.

T. Dove offered anybody with any info on her whereabouts a reward, so some knucklehead could step up and snitch for some dough.

One dude, named Adidas, took a chance. He said he heard some niggas that work for her said she's out of town visiting her peeps or some shit. Adidas is a stone cold liar. He's been trying to get with TLC's crew for the longest, since they stepped on Swan Street. That first day he'd seen Aunya and 'em knock that bitch out in broad daylight, before they put Nubian or T. Dove on three years ago. So, by any means necessary, he wanted to be put on. He said, "I heard also, she was trying to get some gats. Where, I don't know or whether it's for sho, my nig. Ya feel me? If you're looking in a sense of burning her ass, then maybe it's true about the guns, ma'an, ya heard, dude?

CHAPTER THIRTEEN

Detective Reese's new partner, Milford Gadson, was ready to be down with the bullshit. He looked like Mark Wahlberg, who used to be a rapper back in da daze. He seemed too anxious and Detective Reese couldn't get with that shit.

He'd say to Milford, 'Listen ya city slicker motherfucker, you need to relax here in Albany. This is the capital, man. It's not as fast and wild as New York City. You can sleep on shit every now and then and watch these motherfucking drug infested hood rats kill each other.

It'll make your job much easier as far as arresting them, cause ya dam sure can't lock up the dead." He laughed, so did Detective Gadson.

Detective Reese had filled Detective Gadson in on all the fucked up, crooked shit happening in areas he controls. He even mentioned the catastrophe TLC asked to be created over on L&O.

As he continued to tell Detective Gadson about all the episodes and havoc, his cell phone rang to the song of John Cougar's "Hurts So Good." Detective Gadson was shocked as hell.

He cracked up and said, "you're old as fuck, listening to that shit. It's time your ass retires Reese."

While Detective Reese was on the phone, he was making all kinds of frowns answering the other person on the line.

"Yes, no, why? Just tell me what the fuck is going on Captain Faulkner. Ah-huh. Well right now I'm over on First and Judson, sir."

Captain Faulkner couldn't stand Reese. He knew he was a dirty, rotten, fucking cop. He also heard a lot about his new assigned partner, Detective Gadson. With the two of them together all hell is going to break loose.

He was digging in Detective Reese's ass asking, "How the fuck are all these murders taking place, in which a got dam thing hasn't been done in solving not one fucking case? Oh, except that gangbanging shit. Now, that's a collar, Reese. I still do not understand if your eyes and ears are open to the streets, why haven't you brought me anything on my desk! As a matter of fact, what the fuck happened with that Ms. Smiley character? Didn't you have her under surveillance? Tell me something Reese! Or the incidents over on Judson with the fiend and the dog jumping out of the window. Got dammit Reese, ya ass is grass if I don't have something soon Detective. And I mean get your riff-raffing ass on it and detail everything in your report.

Understand?

"Yes, Capital Faulkner, I'm on it. Sir."

When Detective Reese got off the phone, Gadson laughed at his ass.

He said, "Man, he got you by the balls, son. What have been doing? You know you gotta give him something so he'll stay off your ass. He sounds like he doesn't care for you much, man. Something is up with the Captain as far as you. I'd advise you to lay low in whatever you're doing, but give him a case you're solving in the process to keep him at bay. Do that until we start getting this money you claim is so easy to come by doing our job. Who's this TLC crew, Reese?"

Da-Stev pulled up in his Denali, a brand new one. The shit was beautiful; a silver one with burgundy interior.

He called to Detective Reese, "Yo what it is, man. Long time, no see."

"You see me now, my nig."

Detective Gadson was shocked that Detective Reese was talking to Da-Stev like a black brother or shall I say, hood talk.

"Da-Stev, this here is my man, I told ya about, Detective Milford Gadson. A-ight, Detective Gadson, this is the motherfucking man, right here. He's the nigga ya really wanna roll with, ya feel me."

Da-Stev responded, "Yo Gadson, this is the only white nigga I know in the hood and a fuckin po-po at that. Ha, ha, ha. And, what you might be partnering up with his dirty ass, as well as yours. Huh, hmm, let me guess, a white African nigga. Ha, ha, ha, ha. Well dude, what's on the menu besides when Jaia and 'em come back? I'll tell ya what, let's start rounding up Ms. Smiley's peeps, okay Detective Reese?"

Detective Gadson says, "Yeah, his honkey ass needs to give Captain Faulkner some results. A whole bunch of shit has been going on. He's vexed at his acting nigga in the hood ass." They all laughed.

Da-Stev said to the detectives, "Until TLC lets me know what is good, then' I'll let ya'll know what is good fellas, cause they're on the rise in the mix." The time for Labu has come. She has maxed out, fo sho She has dreaded the day, as far as parting form Aunya, period. Although, Aunya has hooked her up upon release, to stay at the South Main Street apartment until she comes home in two months.

Labu is crying up a storm saying, "Baby, promise me you'll come directly home to me.

We'll be sharing a life together, Aunya, isn't that our promise to each other, love? I love you, Aunya and you're going to be very proud of me when you get home, baby. I'ma ride-a-die bitch for you, boo. Bet that. I'm all yours, ma, and, honey, call please. Aunya, will I get to meet Jaia and Vah? Are they going to be there waiting for me Babe?"

"No, they are not. They are taking care of business, Labu. Listen, I'm only gonna say this once. Do not fuck with Jaia and ah until I come home, a-ight. Just lay around, wait for me to call, ya know. Stay busy, somewhat, and Labu, don't fuck around with no one on the drug tip, period. You have enough money to shop for clothes and food, plus there is a surprise for you when you get to the crib, a-ight. Labu, I'ma miss you a lot love, but it won't be long baby, cause I'm out of here soon to be with you and we make it happen. It's all about us love, you'll see. I got a lotta love for ya."

Aunya continued, "I warma make you so very happy. You'll never want for nothing except what we have for each other, baby. That is as real as it gets."

The officer yelled, "Kenyetta McMichael. Pack it up, inmate, you're out of here. I'll see ya when you come back in a coupla months. Your vacation is over, girl. Now it's time for you to go home and spin on some dick. Leave the gay shit for the staying in jail duration."

Labu answered the female officer by telling her, "Check this CO, my girl is seeing to it that I go home to everything you have worked hard to get while watching over me during my seven years. So therefore, I walk right outta the gate into money, an apartment, oh and it didn't cost me shit, except conversation. How 'bout that, ya bum ass officer." She had to laugh at that, cause in all reality, it's true.

Everyone was saying their good-bye's and shit.

"Later, bitch."

"Don't come back, hoe."

"Labu, be safe."

"If ya decide to come back, I'll be here."

"I'll be here for another ten years, so drop back in, a-ight." is what Officer Hill said, "which is when I retire, girl. Have a nice life. Now go on over there with ya friend. Get the good-bye's and hugs over with in the bathroom."

"See ya, Labu."

Aunya was telling Labu the do's and don'ts, for real. So there is no question to be asked as to why this or that and everything remain kosher on her way out of the facility. Aunya explained how Vah and Jaia hooked Labu before they left for New York City. Everything she asked for was in her property, keys and all.

Labu looked at Aunya with lust and love, telling her, "it's that time, baby. Call me tonight, please. I'll be waiting by the phone to hear ya voice, instructing me to orgasm, baby.

Yeah, girl, some phone sex. Oh baby, I can't wait. Well honey, this is it. I love you Aunya. I'll talk to you tonight, love. *You* have all of me. I'ma prove my love to you by tomorrow when you call. You're going to love me even more baby, cause I'm doing it for Aunya. That's my loyalty to you, for real, rna."

The bus ride for Labu was tiring. She caught a cab from Albany bus terminal to the apartment. She entered and was in her glory. She couldn't believe the hook up Aunya hooked her up with. She looked all through the apartment; everything she needed, even food was stacked. Now Labu had to get on her job and Find Coco's ass for locking her baby up.

'Hell,' she thought, *if it weren't for Coco, she'd never met Aunya. She'd really like to thank her, fa sho Instead, she needed to prove her love for Aunya and let her know she is that bitch by killing Coco's ass before she gets out of prison. She had all the information she needed.*

The bitch still had the same job since she had Aunya's ass locked up years ago.

"Well," she said out loud to herself, "she will not be returning there by a long shot if I have anything to do with it. She's got to go."

Labu was trying on all the beautiful clothing Jaia and 'em left for her.

She thought, *'Wow, they have beautiful taste.'*

She was checking out her Prada, Blahnick stilettos and her Phat Farm outfits, also Docle Gabbana shades. They really went all out for Labu and she doesn't even know 'em at all. She has heard so much about them though, she feels as if she does know them, especially when Aunya talked about Vah. It kinda made her curious about her. She knew she had to be just as ruthless, from some of the shit Aunya had told her about Jaia. She went into the kitchen and on the refrigerator was a note addressed to her telling her, "'Welcome Home' and sorry they couldn't be there to meet her. There was an envelope on the table for her. She walked over to the table and low and behold, there was a set of car keys.

Labu's like, "Un-fucking-believable. That's my baby, Aunya. Thank you Lord for putting her in my path."

She stepped out of the house, onto the front steps and pressed the button on the key ring to see which car was hers; it was a nice silver 2009 Lexus. She was overwhelmed. Labu could not believe this was happening to her. After she went and played around in her new car, she went back inside and took a nice hot bath in some Beyond Paradise bubble bath by Estee Lauder.

She was so refreshed, she sat and watched some videos on BET's 106 & Park. She made herself some popcorn and relaxed.

Back in New York City, Jaia and 'em finished their nice meal at the restaurant. They decided they wanted to hit the club scene. They went over to a club called Crazy Nannies ~ wall to wall lesbians having casual conversations. All Vah wanted to do was fuck. She needed her pussy sucked, licked and plucked with some tongue.

Unc's proud having Jaia on her arm. She felt dam good. She was checking out the atmosphere, heads were turning as they headed towards the bar. The music was a mixture of rock, R&B and house music. It was cute and cozy, fo sho Vah was definitely getting an eye full of all the chicks. She could eat up every last one she's seen so far, she thought. Then too, she was horny as hell. As she went to order drinks, a nice looking female accidentally bumped into her. It was crowded and Vah's eyes did a double take at this fine piece of specirnen. Vah's mannerism's started working overtime.

"Oh, excuse me love. I am totally sorry miss. May I buy you a drink for disturbing your thoughts by bumping into you, love?"

The female looked at Vah and smiled, "No, it's my fault and let me buy you a drink.

Sorry miss, may I ask you your name?"

"Vah. And yours?"

"Seasonn, Yah. Your name is very rare, Vah. I like it, it's different."

"Thank you, Seasonn."

Seasonn was smiling acting shy, as Vah stared at her in to a zone. They both caught their look for each other. Vah asked Seasonn to dance. She accepted.

Jaia and Unc were watching Vah, thinking, *'oh shit, she got some pussy, fa sho'* As they looked at one another, Jaia said to Unc, "Yeah, she did her thang finding some pussy, huh, boo. She is not bad looking woman, looking like Jada Pinkett Smith."

* * *

Detective Gadson thought to himself as he listened to Da-Stev and Detective Reese conversate, *'this guy, Da-Stev, got some shit going with the drug game and I am aiming to find out. The way him and Detective Reese come at each other* is *too corny for me. Plus, I don't like no black motherfucker thinking I'm eating out of the palm of his hand for shit. I am the law and he will recognize. I don't give a fuck how crooked I am. I am in control of shit in my space. Detective Reese* is *like a kiss ass sucker on the take for pennies.'* Da-Stev though about Nubian and the last time he had talked to him as far as controlling TLB's shit and the remark he made about trying to school 'em. He felt it was time for Nubian to get got and he knew he had to get it done. That racist new partner, Detective Reese has for a true partner in crime. As soon as he gets up with him, he'll let him know without Detective Reese knowing at all It'll be between just them.

He called Detective Gadson to inform him of a duty he needed done as soon as possible.

Definitely before Jaia and 'em return. This way they'd think it was Ms. Smiley's doing any fuckin way. Yes, he has a plan.

Detective Gadson answered, "Talk to me, and this better be good."

Da-Stev explained that he'd like it done pronto. He put Gadson on three-way to listen in on Nubian's whereabouts' to have his soft ass killed Nubian answered, "Yo holla. What up Da-Stev, my nigga?"

"Nubian where are ya? I need to get at ya with something, a-ight. True that, ya feel me, Nub." "I'm over on Robin and Sheridan, Da-Stev, doing a little summin with this shawty, understand. I'ma be out in about a half hour. So where you be? I'll catch up to ya Da-Stev. As a matter of fact, I'll call ya. One, I'm out.

Detective Gadson heard every last worked that transpired. He just had an easy target. He said to Da-Stev, 'I know we'll be seeing each other later for the results of this episode and paid in full, huh Da-Stev? Yeah, you the man."

"This is between just you and me Milford." He called the detective by his first name to assure he it's kept information among us, as he stared straight in his eyes.

Detective Gadson is the grimiest fuckin po-po you'd ever meet. He had the motherfuckers shook in New York City, for real. So, he needed to relocate, not just for himself but for his daughter. She's attending college at St. Rose, which is where he moved close to on Western Avenue. He bought a nice house. His daughter was so happy. Her name is Maria.

She is everything to him since his wife died at the hands of a crack head mugger. She stabbed her five times cause she did not want to give up her wedding ring and chain her daughter had gotten her for Mother's Day. It was a tragedy on a subway train station in the Ridgewood section of Queens.

This is why Detective Milford Gadson in all actuality despised drug dealers or users. The murderer who killed his wife is white and that is what really eats at him. He really wants to blame African-Americans for the infestation of the drugs because he has arrested so many black drug dealers.

He's being patient waiting until Da-Stev gives him the right-away to take Nubian out. He couldn't wait.

Da-Stev thought about how Jaia will get down to the bottom of Nubian's death. He thought, *"Oh well, another one bites the dust."* Ha, ha, ha. *"He's too soft a nigga. This is a man's game, not no love on hold shit. Nubian is not cut out for this. He's only trying to prove summin to Jaia. Nah, that nigga gotta go, fa sho'*

CHAPTER FOURTEEN

LABU GOT UP EARLY. SHE sighed, "Oh yes, it's my second day of freedom. Thank you Lord, but I gotta represent my baby, avenging her status. As for Coco, that bitch is ghost with the quickness." Labu got geared down in some Apple Bottom Jeans and a baby blue wife beater, some brown Timbs. She was on her mission toward Wolf Road, where she remembered Aunya telling her about Coco's job at Rite Aid, and the IHOP where the incident happened. She waited in the parking lot of Rite Aid.

Aunya described Coco to a tee, and who'd not know if it weren't for the scar.

Labu spotted her. She was vexed. Her mind snapped summin' serious.

She waited until Coco went to get into her little Honda Civic Accord. Then she came at her on the driver's side and called her name. Once Coco rolled down the window, that was the last time she saw anything.

Labu said to Coco, as she shot her in the head, "This is for Aunya, bitch!"

Coco's eyes were wide as ever with the shock of her last breath. Then Labu took a picture of Coco, slumped over in the car.

Labu walked away and got into her own car, with the biggest Kool-Aid smile.

"Yeah, that's for my baby," she said. "Something Jaia and Vah should've taken care of before I even had to kill you, bitch. For my Aunya," Labu thought to herself.

She ended up going to McDonald's on Central Avenue, next to Westgate Mall.

She was enjoying her freedom, thinking about her love of life, and knowing it was about to be count time in the penitentiary.

After a while, Labu decided to take a ride around Albany. She was cruising down Central Avenue and noticed the change in environment, compared with where she lived.

She was driving toward downtown, passed Ontario, and turned onto Lexington Avenue. She saw she was definitely the hood. She thuoght about all the conversations she'd had with Aunya and what areas Aunya had told her about, as far as when she did her thang, until the incident with Coco.

Labu made a left on Orange Street, headed up to Robin, and sat for a bit, wondering how it was when Aunya was out her on the street with her dawgs. "They were vicious, I bet," she thought. Labu was missing her terribly. Her heart was hurting, fo sho Nubian called Da-Stev to let him know he was about to be out from the shawty's house he slipped into. Her Dad and Mom were at work. As he exited, he gave her some bills and stepped. As he walked toward his Jeep, he saw Labu sitting in her silver Lexus in a zone.

Nubian was like, "Wha' up, Miss? You a'ight?"

Labu said, "Oh, yeah. I's just thinking about my boo. She's upstate. She'll be out in two months."

Nubian continued, "Dam, as pretty as you are, baby, you're into chicks? Dam, niggar ain't got no kinda shot at ya, no kind of way, huh? Boo, your shit is on lock down by a bitch!"

Labu replied, "Niggar, I think you need to watch ya motherfuckin' mouth, fo sho, talking 'bout mines."

Labu was ready to blow his fuckin' head off. If only he knew that was just what she got through doing to a bitch for hers, as in Aunya. Labu knew instinctively that Nubian dealt drugs, just by his demeanor, the arrogance. She had been around dealers long enough to know them, before doing her bid of seven years. It was as if once you enter the game of hustling, everything else seems to hang in the cut all the time.

All of a sudden, as quick as Nubian was standing there talking to Labu, all she heard was POP-POP. Nubian went down.

She was like, "what the fuck, yo!!"

Labu got the fuck up outta there as fast as hell. She could see the car in her rear view mirror and knew the person driving it was Caucasian. She never looked back, wondering what the fuck the nigga's name was.

She thought to herself, "Like maybe he's important to the hood, in order to be killed in the morning. Dam, these days killing a motherfucker is some anytime of the day shit."

The white person in the brown Seville looked as if he could have been a narc or something. Labu just hoped whoever it was doesn't come fucking with her, 'cause she is dam sure ready for their ass.

Nubian's body lay in between the curb and a car. No one really noticed shit except Labu, and she got the hell out of Dodge. So, his body was just another statistic for the morgue.

Nubian thought he had breathed his last breath. He couldn't imagine Jaia and 'em without him, also who'd want him dead?

"It's Ms. Smiley", he thought. "Oh God, please somebody, please help me." He tried to get up, stretching his arms and grabbing the handle of the car that he had fallen up against. He had been shot twice. Once in his chest and once in his abdomen. He felt the shit burning, praying to God he'd make it to the hospital quick. He was losing a lot of blood.

* * *

Labu hurried and drove fast back to where she was talking to the guy who just got shot. She pulled up to where he was reaching for the car door. She skidded.

"Yo nigga, come on. I'ma help ya up and drop ya ass off at the hospital. Don't say shit. I don't wanna know ya name or nothing. I'm just doing a good deed, man, a'ight? So chill, okay? I'ma get ya there quick."

Nubian said, "Albany Med."

Labu dropped his ass off and kept it moving as fast as possible. She remembered Aunya told her not to go anywhere near any area where T.L.C. made their spots. She also wondered if the guy even noticed how she looked.

She thought, "Oh well. If so, I got summin' for his fuckin' ass. The feeling is mutual. Let that dude come in my space if he wants to. He'll get his ass shot the fuck up!"

* * *

Detective Gadson sped off after he shot Nubian, hoping the nigga was dead as a door nail. As he slowed down on Clinton and Swan, he spotted this white chick looking like she was selling sex. He felt he could use her mouth for some dick suckin' after that incident with Nubian.

He called her over. She was kinda skeptical, 'cause he looked like a po-po to her.

Little did she know she was 100% right. He told her she didn't have to worry about him hauling her ass in, if she'd only ride with him and give him a nice decent blow job.

Detective Gadson asked her name.

"Marsha," she replied, "... and even if you're not busting me, I still wanna get paid, ya know, 'cause I do not smoke no motherfuckin' crack. I like the profession of being a street hoe, ya know. It's the excitement of watching men who like getting their dicks in all kinds of nuts to be burst, and the extreme they'll go to for the nut that is getting busted. To me, it's funny 'cause some of ya'll toes will curl and ya asses get to twitchin' and shit. Anyway, I'ma suck ya dick with the utmost pleasure, 'cause ya gonna nut up for sho I promise you." She smiled.

* * *

Da-Stev was waiting for a call from Detective Gadson. He wanted to know if Nubian was history. He found out the little whisp been fuckin' with hustling, but his ass is outta the game now. He knew Detective Gadson had something on his ass, because he still didn't know Nubian is a part of T.L.C Now that's what was going to put Da-Stev's ass in line with T.L.C., their main man Nubian, if they ever fonnd out his ass was behind Nubian getting shot. Period.

Da-Stev felt he should call Jaia and Vah, so he could make himself look good in their eyes. He though about that long and hard, knowing he's behind the shit. Also, that he used the Ms. Smiley situation as his tactic for informing T.L.C. of everything that has been going on the whole week they've been gone. He really did not want to interfere with them getting a new connect.

It meant more for him too, in the process of T.L.C. becoming top dawgs in the Capital Region area. He needed to find Ms. Smiley now, being that Nubian got shot, in order to make his shit look legit. He had to find her and kill her dead, in return making T.L.C. think he'd avenged Nubian.

"That'll work," he thought.

* * *

In the meantime, Nubian was at the hospital dam near dying. He was wondering if and when someone will notice he's not around. The female he had been talking to when he got shot and actually came back for him to take him to the hospital, has his cellular in her car. He had tried to put a text message on his phone, saying Da-Stev is the only one who knew he was on the street. He had to quit, though, when he started feeling the pain of the gunshot wounds.

The other reason he'd connect Da-Stev is because of the quick glance he got at the driver. He remembered that Detective Reese sometimes drove the brown Seville. He figured Da-Stev was behind this shit, because he caught on to that nigga's thinking. He's the grimiest of 'em all.

Nubian prayed, "Oh God, if I get through this, all I have definitely is one score to settle with Da-Stev. I want his head on a platter, fo sho I'ma show motherfuckers the deadliest shit in the game, especially anybody who fucks wit me or T.L.C."

The doctors said Nubian is lucky to be alive. He just lost a lot of blood and needed the bullets to be removed.

* * *

Detective Gadson drove down by the truck stop and parked in between two trailers. He told Marsha to get to suckin'.

She answered, "Listen up. Like I said, I'ma make ya toes curl, po-po."

His dick was laying limp on his lap while she was yapping off at the mouth, looking at it. She noticed he had a strawberry birthmark on his dick. Marsha was gagging, laughing her ass off. At the same time, she was like, "To top it all off, you got a nice size penis, dick, popsic1e. It looks pleasurable."

He smiled at her admiring his dick. He started getting a hard-on, saying to Marsha, "Come on. It's waiting sweetie, for you to suck it and lick it like the popsicle you'd like it to taste like. Ooh yeah, Marsha, that's right girl. Suck it. Suck this big piece of strawberry dick."

Then he went on to say, "You sure can suck a mean dick, Marsha. Ya suckin' has made my shootin' a nigga all the more pleasurable this morning. Shooting my guns twice in one morning is the shit." He oozed with pleasure.

Marsha was thinking what the fuck his ass was talking about. Soon enough she'd know, 'cause word travels fast on the street, especially here in Albany. She'd find out what his ass has done. Information is money.

She thought to herself, "When the time is right, and I hear whispers in the street, it'll be time to get paid off his ass."

* * *

Labu was back at her crib, wondering what the fuck just happened with that dude.

She couldn't believe it. She was minding her business at that dam time. She began thinking if she should mention it to Aunya when she calls. She figured she better not.

Prison phones are monitored.

She thought, "My baby will be home soon. I'll just tell her then. Her, Jaia or Vah might even know the dude."

She kept up front what Aunya had told her specifically, so she better not mention shit. She felt she should relax for a minute and get her bearings together. Maybe make herself something to eat, like some salad.

Then she started thinking about Aunya sexually, in the position she had herself in laying on her sectional sofa. Touching herself, she began to get wet and juicy. Pussy hotta than a firecracker. She was in a fantasy of Aunya just sexing her. She knew she was in love.

* * *

After Detective Gadson busted his nuts all up in the hoe Marsha's mouth, he thought of the female he had seen talking to Nubian after he shot him. He was hoping she had not got a good look at him, 'cause if so, he'd have to kill that black bitch too.

Marsh was like, "This is some kind of morning. Shit ain't right," she told herself.

* * *

Nubian was at the hospital with Lil Kill and T.Dove looking over him. They both were wondering what the fuck had happened. Who'd want to kill their hornie?

"Shit is about to get critical, fo sho up in Albany," said T.Dove. "We ain't letting it go just like that. It ain't fucking happening. If that bitch Smiley is behind this shit, that bitch is totally fucking dead, ya feel me dudes? I'm blowing my guns all up in a nigga's ass, anywhere I see her peeps. I am fucking vexed. It's definitely an all out war!"

T.Dove's temper was getting out of control. Lil Kill said, "Yo, T.Dove. Check yourself before ya wreck yourself. Chill. We on it man, no doubt. Fo sho, nigga. We just kinda relax a bit, ya feel me?"

* * *

Da-Stev was sitting back in his Denali, wondering if Nubian is sure enuff dead and thinking Detective Gadson should be beeping him any minute on his cellie. He knew his shit better be correct when T.L.C. confronts his ass about any foul shit that has been happening, since they've been gone. Da-Stev knew he should've called them with any jump off shit. Them bitches sense when a motherfucker ain't right. Fuck up their shit, and all hell breaks wild.

Detective Gadson finally beeped his ass, so Da-Stev drove to a pay phone and called him on his cellie.

Detective Gadson says, "Yeah, speak."

"Meet me at McDonald's on South Pearl and Madison."

"Later."

They both hung up, driving toward McDonald's. Da-Stev was coming from First and Judson, Detective Gadson from Cagney's on Central. Both on the move. T.Dove and Lil Kill just happened to be coming from the hospital after seeing Nubian. They spotted Da-Stev's Denali going down Central Avenue, while they were at the stop sign on Lark.

Lil Kill said to T.Dove, "Yo, isn't that, that niggar Da-Stev, Nubian always talkin' to? He's fam with Jaia and 'em, and he kinda oversees shit. Well, let's check this motherfucker out, fo sho Maybe he can up some info on this situation with Nubian. I hope the fuck so. Ya feel me, T.Dove?"

T.Dove responded, "My dick is getting hard just knowing somebody gonna get got."

CHAPTER FIFTEEN

NATALIE'S MIND WAS RACING A mile a minute. She was so anxious to actually kill Ms. Smiley. It had been a day and a half since she put her in the closet. She was thinking that the bitch was definitely starving by now and probably looking like a sea creature and shit.

She opened the closet and started calling Ms. Smiley names, "Yo, bitch, I guess your ass is so hungry, huh? Oh well, check this. I'm gonna let you eat a half of my ham sandwich. I gotta let you live until Jaia and Vah come back from making their connect. If you try some ole' you gonna see if you can escape shit, bitch, I'll have to shoot a mud hole in your black ass. Anyway, you're not going no fucking where."

Natalie slapped Ms. Smiley in the face and said, "Fuck it." Then she took the glass ashtray and busted Ms. Smiley upside her head, saying "You know what? I can't stand your got dam ass, bitch. So-called hustler. You ain't shit. I guess you won't be running shit no more, babe. Not even your mouth. Nubian and them is taking care ofya peeps as we speak, tearing shit up in the hood. By the time I'm finished with your sorry ass, they'll be scraping your ass up outta the fucking streets, bitch!"

Ms. Smiley could not speak, with the dirty ass rag Natalie had her gagging on.

She stared at Natalie, looking as if she was pleading for her to let her speak, just for a second or so. Natalie looked back at her, letting her know she's going to kill her, and at the same time giving her back a stare that says, "Uh uh, girl. Forget it." She felt no pity at all for this bitch. She knew that in the long run, she'd be rewarded lovely.

"Understand, trust, and believe they are going to get down to the bottom of shit.

Shit is getting ready to hit the fucking fan, Natalie," Charles said, "... and there is a whole bunch of shit going on in them got dam streets in the hood. So anyway, babe, are ya gonna let me knock them boots tonite? 'Cause you got that good pussy, boo. You make mother:fuckers dicks scream all nite, Nat, and I'm 'bout due summin' summin'. Ya feel me?"

Natalie responded, "I sure could use a good fuck tonite, plus you got that good Mandingo dick. Makes a bitch holla confessions, 'cause that shit fills up this pussy like Mr. Softee ice cream fills a cone. First, I have to get rid ofthis bitch here, some company I despise. It's all business. Give me an hour, and you can just come on over with that scrumptious dick of your that my pussy will gladly be honoring." She hung up.

Natalie's thoughts were running wild, wondering who in the fuck killed Nubian.

As far as she was concerned, he was untouchable, being that he was with Jaia and 'em.

She thought to herself, "Something is very fucking fishy and definitely doesn't smell Kosher at all." She looked as Ms. Smiley. "Bitch is behind this shit."

She said to Ms. Smiley, "Answer me by shaking your head if you do not know who tried to kill Nubian."

Ms. Smiley shook her head no. Natalie took the tape and gag off her mouth. First thing she says is, "You fucking dead, bitch!"

Natalie punched her in the mouth and said, "Shut the fuck up, bitch. Whatever it is you trying to say, motherfucker, it doesn't matter, 'cause ya shit ain't platinum. No way, bitch."

* * *

Nubian way laying up in Albany Medical Center Hospital, trying to figure out what the fuck is a narc doing out in the morning getting' at him. He remembered the car and if anything, the female who drove him to the emergency room would have seen who it was that shot him. He had to get in contact with her, to thank her for saving his life, and he was also wondering who the fuck the narc was. The thing is, he doesn't even know who she is or where to begin looking for her. He's never seen her before in the hood.

He thought, "Oh, shit. There is some shit going on. Sum serious fucking shit.

Whoever it is actually wants me dead, fo sho Well, that shooting wasn't a successful one. It's not like they aren't going to come for me again. Dam, maybe I should give Jaia and 'em a call, to let them know that shit is getting hectic, somewhat."

"Nah, I got this," he thought. He reached over to the night stand and grabbed the pitcher, to pour some water out in his cup. As he did, the nurse came to let him know there is a Detective Reese to speak with him about the shooting.

Nubian said, "Let him in. I have nothing to witness at all, 'cause I did not see anything or anyone."

Detective Reese heard every word Nubian said. "Well, Mr. Nubian Fields," he responded"...I guess there will not be too many questions to bother you with. I do have to ask you one thing, though. Do you know a Ms. Sheila Grimes, a.k.a. Ms. Smiley?

Word on the streets is that you're at some at some sort of tug of war, Mr. Fields. The streets are being filled up with her peoples all over the hood, coming up dead. She is nowhere to be found. You're in here with two gunshot wounds. So, Mr. Fields, explain to me what the streets are talking about, ifit's not you and this bitch going at it."

Nubian just looked at him, so Detective Reese continued, "I'll tell you what. Do not fuck with me, alright? Whether you want to believe it or not, Mr. Fields, I am your lucky charm or I can be your worst nightmare. We are counected through some resource investors. Soon enough, you'll get it."

Nubian said, "Check this out, Mr. Po-po. Whatever the streets are telling your ass, you need to find the head nigga that's in charge of talking. Maybe then you can succeed in preventing me from getting shot the fuck up! Yo, it was a narc's car that was being driven, when I was being shot at. Now, what the fuck you po-po think of that? I think that's all the fuck you need to know. How 'bout that, or was it you coming up in here pretending to do your so-called investigating? Now, you tell me summin', summin', Mr. Po-po man."

Nubian was really getting worked up now. "What the fuck am I supposed to tell you to help you? 1'd really like to know my dam self. Is it possible for you to get the fuck out my room and go investigate what the fuck I just told your ass, in plain English, so I can get my shit right and my health together, a'ight?"

As Nubian kept talking about the incident, Detective Reese's eyes wanted to actually pop out of his head. When Nubian said he'd seen a narc's car, that shit puzzled the hell out of him. He wanted to ask Nubian some more questions, but thought he'd better not, even though he began to get real fucked up senses about Nubian's shooting.

He had to do some serious researching into this situation. Now he felt somebody was trying to put some shit in his oven, let alone if T.L.C. finds him accountable for trying to shut them down.

He thought, "Where the fuck is that bitch Ms. Smiley? Oh, fuck this shit. I gotta get on my P's & Q's. Shit is getting hectic, I dam sure need to find out what the fuck is happening, especially If there is one of mines is involved."

Detective Reese thought hard. Real hard. He started thinking all kinds of shit and did not want to believe that his new partner, Detective Gadson, was involved in some kind of way. It seemed possible, although how and through who, he didn't know.

All he said to Nubian was, "Right now you need to nurture your wounds and consider yourself lucky to be alive. I'll be getting back to you soon enough, Mr. Fields. Good day."

Outside of Nubian's room, he called Da-Stev. He thought maybe Da-Stev knew something, 'cause Nubian just messed up his head. He needed to get to the bottom of all this drug dealing bullshit.

* * *

Lil Kill and T.Dove followed Da-Stev, then they both were wondering where he was headed in such a hurry. As they drove, they saw him stop at McDonald's. Over on the drive-thru side, they saw a white dude who looked like a narc, pull up by Da-Stev's Denali.

Lil Kill said, "Yo, my nig, this politickin' shit looks kinda fucked up. Nubian told me that Da-Stev had inside info all the time for T.L.C. when it came to hustling. Maybe Da-Stev is trying to find out the delio about our nigga Nubian. Ya feel me, dude?"

T.Dove said, "I ain't try'na feel no goodie two shoes shit when it comes to no popo.

Any and everybody who got a plan and scheme, we don't know what the fuck they're in cahootz 'bout. Let's just feel this motherfucker Da-Stev out. Once dude takes a hike, we shine on his parade, ya heard? I sense a bunch of fishy shit going on that ain't kosha by a long shot. I'ma 'bout ready to make some noise with my guns, fo sho, if this nigga Da-Stev does not come out his mouth with the shit I'm expecting to hear after he got his info from po-po."

Lil Kill shouted to Da-Stev, "Yo, yo my nig! What's good, homie? Is everything, everything man. Is it possible you've got some info on Nubian being shot, dude?"

Da-Stev's voice was overpowering, yelling, saying, "Yo, who the fuck shot my boy? Yo, I ain't feeling that shit! Not at all. When did this shit happen, yo? Fill me in, fam!"

T.Dove looked at Da-Stev, amazed. Da-Stev looked shocked, as if he really didn't know what was going on with Nubian. T.Dove was feeling Da-Stev's vibes, so he let him carry on venting, but he thought to himself, "When he's through venting, I will mention his nice lil' convo with po-po. There's sho 'nuff some explaining to do about the meeting that just took place at the McDonald's drive-thru parking lot."

CHAPTER SIXTEEN

JAIA AND VAH ARE ON some real loving shit with their boo's. At the same time Seasonn is one serious bitch with Vah. She is no joke and Jaia is crazy 'bout her style in every way.

She admires her gangster attitude. Little does Jaia know, Seasonn is a hardcore ride-a-die, classy-ass motherfucking bitch. They all had a beautiful nite at Crazy Nannies. It's where a wonderful friendship began, as well as a soon to be relationship between Vah and Seasonn. Their shit was on fire for each other, seriously. Both of them took a cab back to Vah's hotel room at the Marriott Marquise to continue their escalating feelings for one another. They were talking all nite; kissing and fondling one another, letting their minds go wild in a fantasy for each others touches. Then they fell asleep passionately in each others arms. When they woke up they stared at each other with pure lust. Vah held Seasonns' face with her lips, smothering hers all at once.

In desperation she said to her, "I want you, babe and only you, if you'll let me have you this morning for some good lovin breakfast, boo."

They both removed their clothing, their bra's and panties. Vah was in a trance at how lovely Seasonns' body was. It was shaped so well and pretty.

She said to Seasonn lovingly, "I'ma love you like I'm eating my favorite meal, cause that's exactly how you look to me right about now, baby. A good lovin taste of you this morning will fill me up."

Seasonn was ready for her luscious, gorgeous chocolate lips. They were shaped to tear her ass up something terrible. She could not wait; she actually began purring like a cat for Vah to taste her, fuck her, play with her. She was ready with full force of loving Vah back. Seasonns' pussy was getting soaked with her juices flowing all through her insides as Vah played with her clitoris.

She moaned in a soft, sexy voice, "Oh baby, you're making me feel so good, baby. My pussy is throbbing all for you, Vah. I love your name baby; it turns me on. It makes me feel so attracted to you; it draws me to you, boo. I want this pussy to be yours only, Vah. I need for you to show me and make me feel what you can do to my juicy wet, slippery pussy that your fingers seem to be enjoying; getting me so turned on to you, baby. So Vah, take this pussy, love."

Vah stuck two more fingers in her twat, slowly. It made her buck like a horse. She felt her pussy was definitely being made love to once Vah started licking and kissing her clitoris, fingering her at the same time.

"Dam," she whispered, "ooh ooh ooh Vah, oh yeah oh yeah, right there Vah, oh oh oh oh baby, you know you know, it's good love, it's good girl, yeah that's right fuck this pussy, come on baby, make your pussy cum; this is yours, isn't it, Vah?"

Vah was working her ass. She was begging Vah to stop; telling her she had enough, she was cumming too much. Vah was wearing her ass out and claiming her pussy so she never goes elsewhere.

She has four fingers in her pussy; gliding them in softly and slowly. It was making her ass go fucking crazy. Plus, she was sucking her clitoris slowly. The girl was going nuts, busting nuts; playing with her nipples.

She then climbed on top of Seasonn while she was cumming. They both began to body rock in motion; moaning, sharing so good lovin' conversation. They started rocking to the same rhythm that felt so good. They were telling each other how good it was for both of them to be cumming at the same time. They were feeling the voices of their sexual encounter together.

"Ooh baby, let's cum for one another,' Vah stated, breathing heavily.

They were riding each other; cumming together, calling each others names, ooh-ing and ahh-ing. "Oh baby, this is so good, can you make me cum all day, baby," They both smiled.

Vah replied, "Quite frankly I can, smiled.

Seasonn said, "Baby, do your thang. Your freak for the taking."

Just as they were going for round two, banging, calling their names at the door. Vah Was like, "Let me handle this, babe.

Jaia and 'em at all, when it comes to me makin' love to mines. Hold up a'ight, I'll be right back. You keep that slippery, silky, nice juicy wet pussy I have to attend to, more heated, boo. Please, I'm not done by any means, O.K."

Vah went to open the hotel room door and Jaia entered saying, "Oh no bitch, I know you ain't in no sucky fucky mood early in the morning, my dawg. I'sa comin' to invite you and my sister-in-law out to breakfast or we can have the Continental breakfast, whichever you prefer, Vah and Seasonn."

Jaia said Seasonns' name so loud, as if she'd be coming out of the bedroom, as she was looking toward the bedroom.

Vah told Jaia, "Listen I really need some me-time with my boo, dawg, ya feel me. So can you please leave us the fuck alone, so I can fuck, suck and lick the cum off my boo, ya heard. Now, get the fuck outta here and take ya rugrat, Unc with ya.

"Ya know I love you Jaia forever, dawg, but this one time I need not to be disturbed. Unc, take this bitch wit ya, go fuck her, eat her pussy, do something. Lay her ass down, stick ya fingers in her ass, make her sit my nig, cause you are in charge, aight.'

They all started laughing. Jaia and Unc were on their way out the door, giving Vah some dap.

Seasonn came out of the bedroom, butt ass naked, laid on the couch, legs spread wide as an eagle.

Vah said, "Your pussy looks beautiful. I'ma taste it so slow, baby." She started tonguing her pussy, licking in and around her asshole.

She had never let anyone go back there. Vah's lovemaking was exceptional in her book. She freaked every minute of her tongue lashing.

Then she said, "Hold on a second, I'll be right back. I gotta surprise for you. I hope you're ready. I'ma 'bout to fuck you hard boo, into oblivion with my motherfucking strap-on. You ready for that, girl. I'ma make you feel so damn good, sugar."

Seasonn told Vah, "I'll tell ya one thing, you better know how to work it girl, as if you're the only man in my life. And me, I'ma ride or die on your ass, Vah. You dam sure better fuck me to the kingdom and I cum.

So come on honey, lay it all on mamma. Take this pussy. Show me what ya working with Vah, put some love on my handle, it's opening for you, babe."

* * *

Jaia and Unc went to breakfast in the hotel dining room.

Unc's like, "Wow boo. Vah has met her soulmate, ya think not, huh? She's a keeper, I bet to the fullest. She is a'ight, whaddya think, babe?"

"I think the bitch is stacking paper legitimately, plus she is all class With so much etiquette. She is a down chick and if Vah goes ga-ga for her so will we, ya feel me. A family of down sadistic bitches. Boo-ya-ya."

Jaia was real happy for Vah, as well as herself, for having partners With them on the rise.

"Shit, we'll be glowing like a pretty rainbow."

Jaia stopped wondering about Seasonn and Vah and began thinking about Nubian and Lil Kill and what was really going on with their spots and monies. She decided to give Nubian a call to say hi and not make him think she's checking on him. She had just spoke with him a day or so ago. She really gave it some thought. Not that she's at all worried because she knew and felt with Nubian, shit stands correct back in Albany.

If anything, he'd definitely call her or Da-Stev if shit starts poppin' off with her troops. At least she hoped the motherfuckers would. If neither one of them didn't inform her of havoc happening with her monies, they might as well wish themselves dead, straight like that, no dam questions asked at all, bottom line.

* * *

After Labu had her little sexual fantasy of Aunya and her, she felt like the lady she should be for her baby. She misses her so, but it won't be long and Aunya will be cuddling her so closely. Labu was hearing this sound like a vibrating in her Louis Vuitton coach bag. She grabbed her bag and took out the cellie, noticing the shit was not hers, at all. It stopped vibrating and she opened it up and looked at the screen.

It read, "Holla back."

'Who was the caller, she thought.

She did recall when she returned from that episode where the dude got shot. She had been out of it when she was cleaning out her car where Nubians' blood was on her back seat. She had thrown his cell phone in her coach bag and totally forgotten about it. She was getting curious about who would calling him, like it's her business. She wanted to return it to Nubian, but did not want to draw any type of attention to herself by visiting him at the hospital. It would look like she was one of his ole hoodrat girls.

'Never that, Aunya would kill her ass, fo sho,' she thought.

She couldn't figure out a way of getting his phone to him. She did even know his full name, except his first name, Nubian. She had gotten that off his voice mail, being curious and very nosy. She still couldn't figure out who had called him, cause the number displayed 'unavailable' on the screen.

"Dam,' she said to herself.

Labu decided to chill until she could think of an idea as far as getting Nubian's cellular phone to him.

* * *

T.Dove told Lil Kill they needed to get on their grind and make things shine with Nubian out of commission, by killing all nigga's existing that assisted Ms. Smiley. He felt he needed to start represenitin' shit, fo sho. He asked Lil Kill what he thought of the scene with Da-Stev and Detective Gadson back at McDonald's.

Lil Kill's like, "Yo dude, summin' up. We gotta keep all ears to the street and if there's anything to do with our crew, that motherfuckiri' DT is going down, fo real nigga, true story. When it comes to the hustling game, a bullet ain't got no name, understand? Yo, T.Dove I gotta head back to the hospital, so I can run this by Nubian, ya feel me. He on a need to know basis, even if my nigga is on the lay-away. He'll fill me in on that motherfuckin' Da-Stev. Plus, I wanna know if he's talked to Jaia and 'em about any of this shit.

"If Nubian's on point he'd want to inform them cause somebody is out to kill his ass, fo sho, so he needs to let his peoples know. I gotta go T.Dove. Shit is funny, ya feel me, dawg. One love, I'm out dude."

Lil Kill dropped T.Dove off over on Judson and First and headed toward the hospital.

T.Dove went up into the spot where three of his workers were counting money. They had just re-upped and were real busy.

One of 'em named Sincere said to T.Dove, "Yo man, wha up with Nubian, he alight? When ya see dude, tell 'em we all are on findin' the nigga who did that to him. We got the hood on lock and our loyalty lies with him, ya heard."

"I feel ya, Sincere. That's peace, I'll let him know," said T.Dove, "now how's business goin' and what's money lookin' like dudes."

Another dude who was up in the spot comes all out loud, "What ya think homie, we ain't up in here re-upping for nothing man. We're ya busy neighborhood drug dealers, dude."

T.Dove jumped up, went over to the guy and said, "Yo, you young ass loud motherfucker, ya think this is a fuckin' joke, bitch. Ain't no fuckin' comedian in this camp nigga and ain't no time for no show boating, bitch ass nigga, like yourself. Anyway nigga, you best keep ya ass over at that table, bitch. Keep on packin' up our shit to put out there to get paid. Better yet, go get us summin' to eat. I'ma chill for a little bit wit ya'll, a'ight?"

* * *

Da-Stev was wondering what the fuck were Lil Kill and T.Dove doing following him. He really needed to be more careful, he thought cause he has one strike against his ass concerning Nubian. Quiet as it's kept he knew his ass was definitely dead meat, if the T.L.C. crew finds out he took out their trooper. Da-Stev knew sure as shit Nubian was dead, because neither T.Dove or Lil Kill mentioned that it wasn't his cellie's ringtone, "Killin' Me Softly" by Lauren Hill.

"Yell-o, talk to me," Da-Stev said.

Detective Reese started telling Da-Stev about Nubian being at Albany Med with two gunshot wounds.

"He ain't talking, don't know who the shooter is and shit, but: he did mention it's a narc. Where he's coming from with that I haven't the slightest fucking idea man. I know everything is about to be hectic in these streets with his two ole homies gunning in the hood for some information.

"You know Da-Stev, I can't have that right about now with this sorry ass Captain Faulkner chewing my ass out, so I'ma give you a chance to talk to T.L.C.'s crew and Nubian over at the hospital. It does not have to be an all out stupid, bloody neighborhood war, O.K. I'd also hope if there is a narc, detective or rookie involved other than you. Know what I mean? I need to get a hold of this situation and find out who is putting this shit out there. So, have you seen Ms. Smiley lately, Da-Stev?"

"Nah."

Detective Reese looked at Da-Stev and said, "Yo dude, is there something you need to tell me or is there anything I need to know. You look as if you have something to say that is heavy on your mind. I'm here to listen, man. Talk to me."

Da-Stev's like, "You know I haven't called Jaia and 'em to let them know about Nubian yet, cause I just found out a little while ago. Can you believe this shit happened this morning. It's crazy, man. So, how's Nubian holding up, does he need anything? Thank God he's not in critical condition. He'll just be a little sore once they let him sign out."

"I never said he's in any kind of condition, Da-Stev. You're giving a diagnosis like I mentioned it and I didn't."

"Lil Kill and his homie T.Dove explained to me what happened, but any-fucking-way man, you sound as though you're investigating my ass, po-po. What the fuck is it Detective Reese, am I a motherfucking suspect? If so, ya ass better be kidding nigga, fo sho."

* * *

Nevertheless, Jaia and 'em were ready to go and make shit happen with this connection they're about to lay on her Uncle Tito. She felt, if anything his fuckin' perverted ass owes her anything she'd hope for. Especially, because his nasty ass was trying to get at her in a sexual manner during the time she stayed with him and her Aunt Rosa. She'd never understand why her aunt turned on her like that when her uncle was the one who was the culprit and trying to actually bust her cherry.

She thought to herself, 'He's the motherfucker that should've went down with the quickness, but I guess the bitch been married to the scumbag for so many years, she's used to his dumb ass shenanigans. I am her niece and I do not understand this situation, but as soon as I get my shit right on my shine, both these so-called familia's are gonna get theirs. Right now I need 'em, until then I'll play my cards right.

"I can't remember too much growing up, being here in Washington Heights being so pleasant, but I've learned quite a bit to where me and my crew will dominate the drug game to the max. I'ma see to it as long as we are family, not like this corny shit my aunt is living in. She is so, so beautiful. I wonder how she spent her younger years before she met my sorry ass Uncle Tito. She looks like she's been through a hell of a lot in the midst of living with him, or shall I say married to the piece of shit. I can imagine the slimy shit my uncle has done to Aunt Rosa. He has her head all fucked up, on top of controlling everything she's about. I wonder how she stays so non-chalant being addicted to him like she's on some ole dope fiend shit.

Jaia came up outta her zone and said to Unc, "Remind me to holla at my Aunt Rosa, babe after we make this move on this connection with my Uncle Tito, a'ight love" Unc said, "Yeah boo, you got that right on the tip of my tongue, Jaia. Girl, you know I luv ya babe, ya my shining star boo." They both laughed, then kissed.

* * *

Vah's cellie was ringing like crazy. Her ass knew it was Jaia and that she was having a lovely time with Seasonn. They both enjoyed every moment of each other. Vah learned that her baby owns a stripper's club and a coupla brownstones in Brooklyn over in the Crown Heights area. Vah was impressed, but she wanted Seasonn to come back with her to Albany. Seasonn declined. She has a life in the city. She told Vah she'd love to see her again and that she would be in the Albany Capitol area in a coupla weeks on business and she wants to see her then. And, if Vah is good to her maybe she'll consider relocating. Her shit is on lock for Vah. Seasonn actually hated to see Vah go. She is definitely going to miss her and her good lovin'. She couldn't believe how an aggressive attitude, thuggish lesbian could be so attentive and so romantic. She is a beautiful woman on the inside. They both shared quite a lot among each other, but 'money comes fast' is both their mottos, that's why they hit it off so well.

Seasonn doesn't agree with Vah being into the hustling shit. Although, she knows that is who she was when she met her and she is not trying to change that at all, knowing the ugly consequences, even though she is going to be there for her baby, no matter what. Vah belongs to her and she is gonna find out when Seasonn takes the trip to Albany. She is not letting Vah get away from her by a long shot. She thought to herself, 'this pussy here is all hers as long as she wants it.'

It surprised her; the fact that both of them had a very serious conversation in terms of the bad and good in both of their lives and keeping it real. Also, it turned the both of them on more toward each other. Vah told Seasonn, she's by her heart where she tattooed her name, as Seasonn did hers. Which is where they were when Jaia called.

Jaia explained to Vah she'd be meeting with her Uncle Tito in a couple of hours, if she's ready to make this power move and to bring Seasonn along.

Vah's like, "Hah, she's a'ight where she at, dawg. We'll just be playing it by ear for now, but you best believe we're connected bitch, fo sho. She's mine, ya heard. That is my boo, sho enuff, Jaia. I care for her a lot."

"Bitch, you're just fucked out Vah. All that sucking, fucking got you all domesticated, bitch. Snap out of it hoe. Earth to Vah, earth to Vah," Jaia kept saying.

Unc was cracking the fuck up saying, "You two are some funny asses, Vah. Your ass needs to snap back to reality, cause this doesn't sound like you. Remember you were making fun of me and Jaia? All of a sudden ya clit done found a lick, isn't that something how the table turns so quickly, nigga. Git yours, bitch. She's a keeper too, so I'd advise ya black ass to snatch Ms. Thing up, ya feel me. With her fine Jada Pirikett looking self, but never anything as fine, sexy and beautiful as my Jaia. Never that, Vah. I'll give you ya props homes, that's about it, dawg."

"Why gee thanks, coming from a bitch with a name like Uncle Muff, until I cut it short to Unc."

Unc's smirk to Vah's statement was like, 'dam, here she goes wanting recognition.'

"Yo Vah, so what do ya think about this connection? Jaia is ready to go all in nigga, so you gotta represent, as well. We're all 100% at all times my dawg, straight to the grave, Vah. I love both you and Jaia, but I love fucking my baby." She laughed.

Vah's like, "Oh, you got jokes nigga, a'ight. You better like fucking her, cause Unc it'll be like your cradle to the grave. If she ever think you'd fuck somebody else or got another bitch on ya mind. Ha, how 'bout that, bi-atch!" Vah laughed.

"Now unc, let me spend these last hours with my baby, and I'll call you and Jaia when I'm on my way back to the hotel. Then, we can take care of business, OK."

Seasonn kept saying her tattoo was burning and that they can they go and get some ice to put on it. It is right above her right breast, as is Vah's. As they are walking down the Avenue of the America's toward Bleeker to get the ice,

Vah noticed the dude Damian, so she yelled out his name.

He responded) "Yo wha ma? Whoa boo, is this female all you," looking at Seasonn.

"Yes she is, nigga. Now check yourself dude. Listen up, we, I mean me and my peeps, who you seen me with when we first ran into you in Washington Park, we making shit happen tonite. So, bust this, would you want to work with us up in Albany, Damian? We already got shit on lock, but we could use a good worker, ya feel me. As long as you respect me and mines and definitely my motherfuckin' dawgs, you'll be a'ight, ya feel me. So what ya think, dude? Let me know within the next three hours, cause we outti like Gotti, headed back upstate. We ridin' our hoopty and no, you can't ride shotgun nigga, cause I can't. That's if ya trippin' with us on the highway."

Damian tells Vah, "Yeah ma, I'm trippin' with ya'll and I respect you and yours. Trust and believe, you got my loyalty royally, boo. I am that motherfucking nigga, Vah, a-ight. That is on everything I love, ma. I have two seeds, boo. It's hard as hell out here for a motherfucka, understand, so if ya willin' to help me get on my grind, yo, I'm all in on the strength of you. I'ma feel pride rise, feel me Vah, so let's do this. Thanks for looking out for a nigga, bossy."

"Yo Damian, I'm spendin' these last few hours with my boo, so I'ma git up wit ya later dude, fo sho."

As she was leaving Vah told Damian she'd catch up with him later.

These two guys, one Puerto Rican and one Black, had made a provocative remark to Seasonn, thinking that Damian and Vah weren't paying attention. Before Vah could say anything Damian hauled off and punched the Black dude right in his fuckin' eye. Then he snatched the Puerto Rican up so quick and body slammed his ass. Damian, Vah and Seasonn started kicking the shit outta those two fuckers. They were screaming and hollering for them to stop, while apologizing for saying anything to Seasonn.

Vah wanted to actually shoot their asses, but knew better being on a New York City street like that. She knew she would not ever see the streets again, with so many witnesses down in the fucking village. The guys got up and crawled away all fucked up.

Seasonn could not believe her own reaction to the incident herself. Yes, she loved herself some Vah. That was it, she would kill someone over her boo.

Damian was like, "See, I told ya Ma, my loyalty lies with ya'll now. It's my duty, ya heard. Well, I'ma scoot up on outta here, give you ladies your quality. Until next time.

One. Peace out."

Vah's mind was on how Damian did his thing on the two dudes.

She was fuckin' amazed. He handled that shit with no regrets of a flinch of an ounce of pity at all.

She said to Seasonn, as they pursued walking down Bleeker toward the Pier, "Are you okay, Baby? You're not shook up or anything or disappointed at the way my boy handled shit, are ya, Ma?"

She said, "Hell nah, I kinda thought it was noble of you Boo. It just made me want you even more Vah, so let's get to steppin' so you can go handle ya business. Oh, and keep homeboy by your side, but never let him know what ya right hand is doing. Everybody got game, a'ight. Now, is there any where you'd like to go eat?"

"I'm already caught up in my menu before me, Boo. You know it's you Baby."

Detective Gadson was vexed at the fact he did not kill.

Nubian on the spot. It fucked him up because there would be a lot of repercussions behind the misfortune of a demise so calculated. He realized he should have gotten out of his car to make sure Nubian's ass was dead, even if he'd had to kill the bitch that was talking to him. He knew it was sloppy of him, so he had to make it right or else he'd have to clean the shit up somehow.

He thought to himself, 'I'm going to start by finding out who the bitch was that sat in the Silver Lexus. And, what in the hell was she doing at that time in the morning, knowing Nubian just came from his shawty's, busting a nut. Did he think he was a Cassanova or sometirig. Shit, I'm not that good in fucking back to back like that. I gotta catch up with that bitch. I'll check with the Department of Motor Vehicles and see what's up.'

Next, he figured he'd go on up to Albany Med and check shit out or kill his ass up in the hospital on the spot. He's gotta make this shit right, like he was suppose to have from jump street. He knew Nubian had a coupla dudes looking out for his safety, which would be from now on. He knew that, fo sho.

When Da-Stev called him with the news of Nubian being alive, Detective Gadson believed that if Da-Stev could've blown his fuckin' head off over the phone, he would have cause he was one mad Black motherfucker.

He then thought, 'I'd better watch my back. I can't believe I fucked up like that and fuckin' Nubian is still alive. I wonder if Detective Reese got wind of this episode and what his take is on it. Being that his monies is from T.L.C.'s crew. If need be I'll have to take his ass out and got dammit, I will. I wonder if that bitch saw me. Only she can I.D. me. I have to do some real back tracking if my ass don't wanna be found out. Not that it's my career, but my life, as well, fucking around with these got dam drug-dealing dealers. They're more notorious than a fuckin' precinct.

Then his cellie rang, it was Da-Stev.

He yelled at Detective Gadson, "Yo honky, you need to get on ya job, motherfucker and get rid of that bitch ass Nubian. I mean right now dude, not another motherfuckiri' minute, home slice. Shit is critical in the hood and money is stagnant."

CHAPTER SEVENTEEN

EVERY DRUG DEALER IN THE hood was talking about what happened to Nubian and not understanding where is this bitch Ms. Smiley. One small time hustler Sam was running off at the mouth about where the fuck are Jaia and 'em. If they were around shit wouldn't have went down like this, at all. He was getting pissed off, cause he admires T.L.C. a lot and knew motherfuckers, if anything, would not try no crazy shit that is happening now.

He figured they must be out of town, so he felt he would be their ears to the streets. If and when they do return, he'll have enough dam information for 'em. It'll be a book.

He needed to get on his mission, if he wants to be a part of the T.L.C. crew. He doesn't give a fuck that the name of the abbreviation - T.L.C. - is what it is. It's the money he's all about, so it's time to cruise the hood.

All of a sudden he heard a bunch of nigga's going at it.

'Ah man," he whispered, when he saw who it was. It was that boy T.Dove. He had this dude up against the side of the diner on Lex and Orange, across from Ms. Betty's store, fucking his ass up.

He kept knocking that dude in his jaw asking, "Yo money, I'ma ask ya ass again where the fuck is your peeps Ms. Smiley, nigga? I ain't playing, it's your life son, do or die."

He grabbed a pipe off the sidewalk and started beating the shit outta his legs.

He said, "Boy, you ain't going no where until I'm done whipping ya fuckin' ass for some information, and that, you're going to give me motherfucker. What's ya name again, nigga.

Although all I see is Ms. Smiley's feature's all over you, bitch ass. So, listen up pussy, you either tell me something good like Chaka Kahn or momma say knock you out like L.L. Cool J. I like L.L. better, so what's it gonna be J.B. You rather take this ass whipping boy, huh! Talk to me."

J.B. poured out all info for T.Dove, telling him that Ms. Smiley might've put a hit on Nubian and T.L.C. He couldn't say it was so, cause he has not seen the bitch. He told T.Dove how she is missing in action and one of her workers, Dolce has been feeding them work and that she'd went to cop some gats over in Selkirk.

J.B. was yelling, "I do not know the motherfuckers' name except she is a white bitch. That's all I know T.Dove, I swear man. Word up, nigga."

T. Dove started beating J.B.'s ass like a runaway slave. He told him next time he better have something better to tell him and where Dolce's nest drop-off and pick-up were.

J.B. gave him the location. T.Dove cold knocked his boney black ass out like a light. He thought about fuckiri' him in his ass, for a minute, but then again, he really wanted his dick sucked.

'Nah,' he thought.

He'd rather wait until he runs into Dolce. He likes the way his name sounds, so the nigga might have some sweet lips, but he prefers ass. It's his nutta butta. T.Dove smiled at the thought of manhandling a man's ass. Crazy sexual shit excites T.Dove whenever ass is involved, male or female.

* * *

T.Dove stopped by Yana's, sat at the bar talking to the barmaid Brenda, looking at her ass.

"It's looking kirida thick back there B."

She's like, "Yeah, it's a doozer, man. This ass is a Miracle on 34th, ya feel me? Jingle bells on up in T.Dove, cause I know you're and ass man, boo. I gotta stay on my toes around you and your dick, a'ight. So, have another drink on the house."

He said, "Dam B, why you so cold to a nigga? All I wanna do is romance and finance our quality time, girl. You want that Mandingo hulk of mine to take you on a fantastic voyage."

They both had to laugh at that shit.

B said, "If I didn't know you any better, you actually sat here in just ten minutes, fantasized about my ass. Yea, ya did motherfucker. Check this, ain't nothiri' happening. How 'bout that. Now, laugh to that, fuckin' creep. Now, put some money in the jukebox, boy and cut out the bullshit with ya crazy ass."

He said, "Alight B, if I didn't like ya ass, your ass wouldn't even bother with an evil ass, mean broad like you, but there's some sweetness in you B, but baby not enough for someone else."

He left going to the location J.B. had told him, to find Dolce. J.B. gave him a pretty good ass description of him. he caught him jumping out of his cream color Bonneville '09. That shit was the sweetest of cars.

He thought, 'After I take care of Dolce, I'ma take his ride. The nigga looked like Omario. I knew with a sweet sounding name like Dolce, this nigga had to be sweet looking, fo sho. I'ma have to man down this motherfucker. He's definitely gonna try some ole get away shit. It's a good thing I got these handcuffs in my possession from the other night when I fucked that freaky bitch. I rode her ass all night, plus the bitch was handcuffed.'

T.Dove started getting a hard on, so as Dolce began to enter the building, he called his name. As Dolce turned, T.Dove went straight for his 45 Auto.

"Motherfucker, if you even breathe hard, ya ass is sho- nuff dead, bitch. I just wanna ask you a coupla questions money, a'ight and you're going to answer them, ya feel me. Let's just hurry up in the building, dude. Is anyone else up in this joint? Don't lie to me, cause I'll kill them right where they stand, D, fo sho, so think safe, nigga."

Standing in the vestibule T.Dove is staring at Dolce's ass, like he cannot wait. Dolce, on the other hand is waiting for T.Dove to fuck up with one false ass move, so he can fuck his ass up. He is not the one to let a nigga think he is getting away with shit. He keeps his body in shape with calisthenics.

His built showed somewhat, but he felt kinda short compared to this motherfucker.

'He's fucking diesel,' he thought, 'I'ma have to try to kill his ass, cause he dam sure is going to kill mine, no questions asked after he gets his info. It's written all over his face.

T.Dove said, "Yo Dude, is there anybody else up in this crib? This is the last time I'ma ask you again, my patience is getting short, nigga." He slapped him with the pistol.

"Nah man, ain't nobody up in here. It's my stash house.

Now, if ya gonna rob me motherfucker, then do so, so I can go about my day nigga, cause ya really don't know who you've just fucked with, my man. How much money ya want, who sent ya, come on man, it's gotta be something boy, especially when you running up on me with a gat at me dome, nigga. Come on let's rectify this shit, ask me something. I'ma make it worth your while if ya don't kill me. I'll pay you double or triple, more than the grimey motherfuckers who sent ya ass and are paying you is that peace or what, my brother."

"Listen up man, first of all I am not your brother bitch, nor from another mother or descendent when it comes to getting mines. So, take your fucking ass up these steps and let us see what we'll be working with Dolce, a'ight. I'm seeking some monies, information and fun, bitch. You'll find out. Now, get the fuck going up these stairs, motherfucker. I'm not going to say it again. I'ma just put a cap in your ass, fo sho."

Dolce did as T.Dove told him. Once they entered the apartment they were in the living room.

T.Dove said to Dolce, "Yo man, so where's shit at, and I'm only gonna ask you once dude, ya feel me. Yo, this crib is hot, it's nice and homey. I like this."

He noticed a heating pipe in one corner and a radiator, figuring he'd handcuff this motherfucker, so he can get some ass.

Dolce was watching T.Dove's every move, even his eyes. Once he noticed his eyes roaming the room, he punched him right in his jaw, realizing it did not phase him at all. T.Dove looked at Dolce, snatched him by his Sean John shirt, along with his Gucci white platinum chain with a medallion of the Celtics, off his neck, in the process. He then threw his ass across the room where he smashed into his fifty-two inch screen Plasma.

T.Dove said to him, "There's your debut, bitch," and went over to pick him up, kicking his face to a pulp, "I guess you do not look like Pretty Boy Floyd anymore, nigga. Now, see you gonna show me where every fucking thing is, or else I am going to start torturing you. That's my specialty, bitch ass nigga.

T.Dove then yelled at Dolce to get his hands out, so he could handcuff him to the pipe. He threw Dolce's ass toward the floor.

"Motherfucker, move when I say move, bitch. Yeah, just like that, ya feel me, son. We getting ready to have some kinda fun, Dolce. First, tell me where shit's at dude, or it's over rover."

He yelled at the top of his lungs, "Yo man, it's under the rug, under the floor board. Yo man, please uncuff me dude, ya got everything. I got money, I got drugs, I got jewelry. Yo man, you definitely been paid, bro. Don't hurt me man, please."

Next thing you know T.Dove cold knocked Dolce the fuck out like a light. That nigga looked like he was in a fucking coma, fo sho. T.Dove smiled cause he still had skills in puttiri' a nigga to sleep with a Banaca Blast Punch. He uncuffed him, then he dragged his ass across the living room, across the dining room and into the bedroom. His eyes got wide at how big the bed was and how the setting of the room was. It had a wide Plasma T.V. and surround sound with speakers in every corner of the room and a hope chest at the end of the bed. He sure was in his glory because his time with Dolce's ass is going to be a fuck to remember.

"Now, that's wassup!"

* * *

Seasonn was really feeling Vah and needs her to have something to remember her by, while she's away from her. So, she decided to let her have her black Mercedes 250 LS 2009, with burgundy interior. She knew her baby would look good in it. She'd let Vah know once she'd be on her way, after they shared a coupla hours together. This way her boo would be ridin' in class on the rise with her crew.

She thought to herself, "Jaia is a down chick, fo real dough.

I admire everything she is. I'd put my life in her hands, so I know my baby will be alright. They are very, very close.

I can feel as much, as I care and I feel I love Vah already.

Both them bitches would kill me without a doubt. They play for keeps. Their hearts are each others. I would not ever offend my boo, by trying to use my love to come in between them.

I'm dead if I try. I know dedication when I see it and they are that to each other. I cannot wait to meet the other half or quarter of their whole name, Aunya. Gee, they are some down bitches, by their law and theirs is dangerously devastating, if you fuck with any of 'em, fo sho.'

She decided to go to Motown Cafe on 57th and 5th Avenue, for what seems to the last of her seeing Vah, but little does Vah know Seasonn is not going anywhere. Seasonn explained to her boo that the restaurant is upscale.

"It's the best only, for my baby," she said to Vah, "I'ma spoil you boo and keep you happy. Dam it's only been almost two days and Vah you do make me feel beautiful honey. I mean that from my heart, love."

Vah said, "Baby, how 'bout we go to this place called One Fish Two Fish Restaurant. It's on 91st and Madison Ave." "O.K.," Seasonn replied.

She agreed with anything for Vah right about now. She was horny as hell, so as she drove toward Madison she asked Vah to play with her punnanny. Vah obliged addictively.

Seasonn said in a seductive voice, "That's my baby. You are that bitch, ma."

Vah was playing all in Seasonns' pussy. She kept opening her legs wider every time she took her foot off the gas pedal. Then she put the shit on cruise control and let Vah control her sexual need for her. She was so wet and juicy, wishing they were back at the hotel. She knew one thing for sure and that is, she'll definitely have Vah by her heart where her name is tattooed forever. She smiled a big ass grin.

As they arrived at the restaurant, they were escorted to a table. They got some stares because both women were gorgeous and they knew it, so did the other customers. Some snickered and Vah caught it, so she blew a kiss to Seasonn. In return, she took her boo's hands and looked into her eyes.

At a tone where people could hear, Seasonn said to Vah,

"I love and care for you Vah, very much, even though I only just met you. Baby, I'm all yours."

People looked and kinda cheered in a soothing way seeing she let her love be known publicly.

Two guys that could've been partners said, "It's a beautiful thang, Ms. Thang. God bless you, both."

Vah was so overwhelmed she grabbed Seasonns' face gently and kissed her and told her she loved her, too.

"Now baby, can we order and eat. I'm starving and we only have and hour a half left with each other, love."

Seasonn smiled.

CHAPTER EIGHTEEN

NEVERTHELESS, NATALIE'S DECISION TO LET Ms. Smiley live had come to an end.

She said, "Fuck it, it's time and this bitch is of no use here in my closet, taking up space."

She then yelled to her, "Listen up bitch, I'ma give you one chance and one chance only, to let ya black ass out of this shit. Tell me where your stash is and the monies bitch. After I do get what I want, I'ma let ya ass go, bitch. Now check it, I am going to take the gag out ya mouth, so the only thing I need you to explain to me is the whereabouts of the stash and cash. All that other shit ya got to say babe; keep it under wraps, cause ain't nothing happenin' 'bout that, bitch."

She took the rags outta Ms. Smiley's mouth, so she could get her to talk about givin' up her shit for her life.

Ms. Smiley starts to actually plead for her life. She figured that all that egotistical attitude shit, fronting about being fearful, a bitch in charge mood needs a change for her to beg Natalie not to kill her ass.

The first thing that came out of her mouth was, "Please do not kill me Nat. I'ma give you all the money you want or will ever need. Please believe me, I'm good for it love, I do not want to die. I wanna see us all make monies, Nat. Check it, the stash house is over on Park and Dove. The keys are in my pocket in my wallet, two keys, downstairs door and up the stairs. The money and drugs are under the throw rug in the living room, under the floor boards, under the love seat, a'ight. All ya want Nat. There, you satisfied now.

Then she went on to say, "I am in a lotta pain bitch, seriously. Tell me the truth, all that shit you said about Jaia is true, fo sho. I have nothing to do with none of it, except what I came here for. To get the gats. Now how the fuck did you know 'bout Jaia's biz? What you some type of motherfuckin' undercover DEA, FBI, shit bitch."

She started yelling, cause now she was getting mad.

Natalie's feeling pissed off at this bitch raising her voice, so she slaps the shit outta her.

"Shut the fuck up. I'ma give you something for ya pain seriously. You'll be alright."

Ms. Smiley's phone's vibrating.

Natalie goes over to her, pulls it out of her pocket and looks at the screen. It was someone named Silver Fox. As soon as Natalie read the name out loud; Ms. Smiley's eyes grew wide, because that's her big connect, Reyes, a bitch not to be fucked with, at all. Which is why she's in this situation, hog-tied getting all fucked up.

Then Natalie goes to the kitchen and comes back with a syringe.

Ms. Smiley's like, "Oh nah, come on Nat, not that."

"Yeah bitch, this will help everything go away for a while, especially until I go to your stash and cash house and get mine. You'll be nice and high in that closet, all cozy. So, you'd believe once this heroin hits your system boo, maybe you can fantasize being on an island or some shit, while I'm getting paid with your shit Smiley. That's the game of hustling, having no shame at all, it's getting it."

Natalie's singing, "I'm not a gold digger, no no, but you about to be a broke nigga. Ha ha ha," she's laughing her ass off.

Meanwhile, Ms. Smiley is starting to nod, "Dam, this shit is smooth as hell," she stated.

Natalie's like, "Oh dam, this bitch is about to throw up."

She ran to the bathroom, got a bedpan and placed it in front of Ms. Smiley's face, so she could throw up, and that she did.

Now Natalie said, "You can enjoy that high, fo sho. Why don't you go to dick land or pussy land, either or is wonderful, girl. I am getting ready for some company, so I'ma have to throw ya ass back in the closet for a couple of hours, boo. I'm getting ready to get my freak on, girl, so you can imagine being in there hearing how I am about to get my pussy tore up inside, the fuck out. The nigga got some Kunte Kente dick."

She stuffed her mouth with the rags again, took her nodding ass back in the pantry.

"Lay down bitch, enjoy that high, you'll be feeling it for a while."

Next, Natalie's doorbell rang. She knew it could only be her one and only nigga, Charles.

As he entered he called out to Natalie.

"Come here with your white Gabrielle Union looking-self.

My motherfucking' bitch, come let daddy take care of that sweet marmalade pussy."

"Come on Charles, let's go in the shower to start this fucking off fresh."

"I hear that," Charles responded, holding his dick, knowing he's about to fuck the wholly shit outta Natalie, cause she is a bonafide freakazoid. Natalie knew she had to hurry up and get this fuck on, so she could go to get this money at Ms. Smiley's stash. She should focus on this nigga, Charles fucking her right now, but the money and stash keep actually breaking her concentration in trying to be fucked hard. That is what she wanted, to relieve some tension.

She was thinking, 'this is just the right medicine, some big black dick.'

The crazy part about her thinking was she knew Ms. Smiley would be listening and Charles doesn't even know she's there.

'Isn't that something,' she thought.

It excited her to realize that. It kinda made her want to sound like a good sexual show was being performed.

"Ooh, ooh WEEE," she laughed and snickered.

* * *

When Dolce awakened, he found his whole body in a position that puzzled his ass, something freaky. He was on his stomach, arms spread, a pillow under him, like the shit has his ass propped up in the air, butt ass naked. It fucked him up.

"Yo nigga, what the fuck is up. What the fuck are you doing, man. Yo, come on man, untie me. It do not have to be like this man, ah ah ah. What the fuck, man. Yo dude, come on man. Yo, I told you where shit is nigga; yo motherfucker, i hope you not goin' do what I think man and fuck me in my ass.

Nah man, come on," T.Dove yelled.

"Yes I am, Mr. Sweet Ass Dolce, pretty bitch-ass motherfucker. Yea, ya begging like the pretty bitch you are nigga. I like it that way; when you so-called sorry motherfuckers' hustlers got game. So now nigga, ya gonna back that ass up on my dick, Mr. Macho Man. Who the man now nigga, cause it sure ain't you dude.

"Get in position sweetie, I'ma give you some big ass penitentiary time dick, Dolce. It's thick and strong enuff to bust a whole new asshole in ya fuckin' shit. Yo, you do feel kinda slimy back there. That's because I put half of a jar of Vaseline up in your ass boy, so my dick can slide somewhat and I'll push the rest of the way, ya feel me. Don't worry - you will soon."

T.Dove exposed his dick. Dolce was screaming and yelling.

"Motherfucker you gotta be crazy."

"Check this my nig, me and you are gonna be like Dolce & Gabbana tonite, boyee., I'ma git mine. That is what it is. If I don't get none, it won't be no fun. Yo, so I know you weren't lying to me about where the money and drugs are at. I hope not, but let me check anyway, to make sure."

T.Dove left the bedroom and went straight to the living room.

He yelled to Dolce, "Yo nigga, under what couch boy."

"The love seat motherfucker; the one over where the entertainment shit is at. It's under the floor board, so you gotta move the couch to the side, you fucking dummy."

T.Dove said, "Bitch-ass, what you call me."

He ran in the bedroom, slapped his ass, rubbing it.

He was saying, "Soon enuff me gonna take care of ya, a'ight."

Then he rubbed his finger past his asshole.

Dolce's like, "You are a sick freaky motherfucker nigga. When I had the chance, if I'da had my pistol with me, you would have never been able to get at me the way you did, boyee."

"Oh well, you blew it Dolce, and now you are going to be my bitch. Til' death do us part. That is the only way, ya heard."

T.Dove was laughing up a storm.

"Please man, whatever ya name is, homie, please don't fuck me in my ass, man. Come on man, I don't wanna go out like I am some type of punk ass faggot, bro. Don't do me so shameful, dawg."

"Yo, go ahead beg. I'ma check out what's under the floor board. It better be worth me letting ya ass live, Dolce. I am serious."

He lifted out the big black garbage bags of money. The fucking hole in the floor was as long and wide as a safe, as if they had it built in the floor.

He thought to himself, 'hell, he owns the fucking house, so it's a possibility.'

He couldn't believe his eyes. He got four bags of money, and six kilos.

T. Dove yelled, "Jackpot homie. I could do my own shit. Yo, hey hey it's your birthday."

He went over where he saw some Cognac in the china cabinet, got to drinking, singing about how he's getting some ass, fo sho, of Dolce's. He was rubbing his dick. M-M-M good. He started getting his swerve on sipping Cognac, feeling himself with Dolce in the next room, scared to death.

He knew he was going to meet his maker after this crazy motherfucker fucks him in his sacred place. God knows he'd never imagine some heinous crap like this happening to him, ever. Since being in the drug hustle, it would've never occurred to him that he'd end up in a predicament such as this. So, he now believes anything is possible. He began thinking of all the hideous shit he had inflicted on people on his way to where he is now, as Smiley's worker.

Then he thought to himself, 'where the fuck is this bitch at. I haven't heard from her ass in almost two days. There is some fucked up shit going on, it got to be with me in this situation. She needs to be calling to check in with Silver Fox hooking us up with some raw cocaine. She has never been late either. Who the fuck is this character that has me hostage?'

Then Dolce came to his senses, he recalled Nubian being shot; that's the word he heard on the streets. He started wondering if that's what this was about, other than him being a part of Ms. Smiley's crew.

He called T.Dove, telling him all loud, "Yo my man, if this is about yo boy Nubian being shot homes; I did not have anything to do with dat man, seriously. I do not want to die man, and if you really gonna fuck me in my ass, shoot me quick. Yo, you better be glad you got me tied up, bitch ass nigga. It was a lucky punch in order to get me knocked out like that, sucker ass nigga. Why are you doing this to me man; tell me something, man. I do not wanna die this way."

"Oh well Dolce, that's the way it is. You know what it is."

He was standing in the doorway all prepared to jump his ass. He walked over to the bed and patted Dolce on his ass. then he started rubbing his ass in a circular motion, getting his hard-on as he is, thinking of the feel of Dolce's ass clamped around his dick, as he pumps in and out.

T.Dove climbed on top of the bed looking at homeboy's ass something serious, licking his lips, he grabbed his ass and spread Dolce's ass cheeks, staring at his asshole.

Dolce was shouting, yelling for this nigga not to do that crazy shit. He was begging hard.

"Nah nah nah man, nah man, don't do that, don't do that. Nah, come on man."

Next thing ya know T.Dove is shoving his dick in Dolce's ass furiously, viciously. His ass was on fire from him pumping hard. He could hear the sound of T.Dove gritting his teeth as his dick was tearing Dolce's ass apart.

T.Dove was panting, saying, "Who's ya daddy bitch, cause I'm riding this ass nigga. It's good boy; you got some good ass. I'ma ease my whole dick in further man, cause I wanna hear you scream like a bitch, bro, a'ight. Now let me fuck your ass and get my nut on boy."

Dolce's screams were sounding like his flesh was a part of the Passion of Christ movie. His whole world ended on this shit. He'd rather be dead after this. He'd kill himself, if he thought this dude would let him go. He kept pulling and trying to get loose.

'No can do,' he thought.

He was cutting into the skin on his ankles and wrists, hollering from pain. Real excruciating, tormenting pain.

"Oh god, stop nigga. Ya killing me man. Stop! Oh stop please, oh god it hurts, it hurts," he sobbed in anger, hurt and pain.

T.Dove was enjoying this fucked up shit he was doing. It's only because when he was incarcerated at the very young age of seventeen, He had been continuously raped in jail. This went on until he became a man at the age of twenty-seven. In return, he built up his strength and power and body, so he would not be a victim anymore. He became the rapist in the penitentiary, as horribly quiet as it was kept. He also killed quite a few other inmates. Torture became and addiction, especially when he's in action. He thrives on it. It's a fuckin' rush for his ego, fo sho, especially when it's a man who thinks he's in power or can't be got. T.Dove gets off on it, cause he knows and feels the wrath of such cruelty with no one to spare his shamefullness. There were nigga's calling him out his name, but he held his head high on lock down. It made him become a wild, human predator in any way, shape or form of body, he is in a class by himself, fo sho.

CHAPTER NINETEEN

JAIA CALLED VAH TO LET her know she was going shopping and wanted all of 'em to make a day of it. She told Vah to bring Seasonn, so she could show her some love, being that she is Vah's girl. They had at least an hour and a half before meeting their connect, so she told Vah to meet her and Unc at Sak's 5th Avenue. Vah felt beautiful about that, cause in all reality it was a ladies day thang. She really did want Jaia and unc to get to know Seasonn as she was feeling her, as well. She did riot want Jaia to think her boo was going to be a part of their crew, cause Seasonn has a life of her own and she accepted that. She'd explain it all to Jaia and Unc once they've had some time together.

They all met at Sak's on the dime. Jaia gave Seasonn a hug and Unc gave Vah some dap. Once they entered Sak's, Seasonn already was going toward the Men's cologne. She got Vah some Banana Republic and Burberry, 25 oz. each.

"Yo, she ain't no joke shopping," Unc said.

Jaia looked at Unc and Vah caught Jaia's look.

She said to her, "It's all in fun, boo. Don't act like that."

Then Unc went over to the shoe department and saw some Jimmy Choo four inch heels for Jaia.

Jaia flipped, "Whoa baby, these are the shit. Ima rock these, ma. You want me to wear them for you, honey, I will, love, even while we're going out the store, if you'd like."

They were going buck fucking wild, shopping and having fun. They tried on some dresses and everybody was laughing their ass off. Vah had tried to put on some stilletto's and dam near broke her fucking neck. The ladies did their thang trying to look like thuggets. In spite of it all, Jaia and Seasonn realized they have a lot of class, which is what makes them beautiful women. They both could not look like bitches even if they did their best to. It wouldn't work, at all.

Unc and Vah were admiring their the women in their lives, smiling and feeling so good inside about 'em; knowing every man that passed them with their wives wished to have a piece of their boo's, which is not happening ever, if they have anything to do with it.

The customer's in the store were staring at them smiling, as if Jaia, Unc, Vah and Seasonn were some type of celebrity, or singing group. The floor sales people were carrying their items of clothing. They had all gotten new suits, such as Armani, Donna Karan, Versace, Jones New York for Jaia and Seasonn; along with some Dolce & Gabbana and Chanel shoes, and Coach bags. Vah got Seasonn and her unisex Kenneth Cole suits. Them shits were hot. Seasonn s' heart melted, fo sho.

Unc and Vah got them some Sean John and Perry Ellis.

"My new found look is a done deal, as far as change," Unc stated "Oh, I gotta get me a nice linen suit, too. It's a must, it's my suave look."

Vah said, "Oh yeah, long as you are swaying your ass Jaia's way, you can swerve and sway all day, nigga."

They both laughed.

Unc's like, "Oh nigga, you got jokes, huh, a'ight. We both are on point boyee, ya feel me. It ain't no fucking around with our honey's, Vah. They're like diamonds and pearls and mine is all my karats and more, most def."

As they were having fun, Jaia noticed this female boosting shit, but she kept it on the low. Once the booster caught her eye.

Jaia's like, "Excuse me miss, I was wondering if your name is Dunk."

The female said, "Am I suppose to know you or something, miss. What is your name?"

Jaia responded, "Oh yeah, now I remember you. You're related to that crazy ass Juan."

"Yeah, I sometimes cop my shit from him, the fuckin' nut. That shit he be wearing is all what Iam boosting doing now."

Jaia said, "Oh, so you still on ya grind. Well, check this meet me outside. You'll see a Navy Blue Navigator with pink interior, boo. I'm coming at ya, eight. We gotta do some business Dunk. It's all good, ya heard."

Dunk looked at Jaia and 'em, "Check this out, I'm 'bout money Jaia, gettin' mine, gettin' paid. I see from the looks of you, there won't be no delays. That's real, it's all good. Ima do ya right Jaia, bet that. I like ya style and flow."

Dunk already had some shit outside she had boosted earlier from Bloomingdale's over on 59th Street and Lexington Ave., so her shit was set as far as getting monies.

Now Dunk remembered when Jaia use to chill out on the block where she had copped her shit from Juan, Jaia's cousin. She knew the family was fuckin' nuts for violence when it came to hustling on the block.

'They had it on lockdown,' Dunk thought, 'back in the day.'

Then all of a sudden there was this big ass crowd of people, all excited.

They were saying, "Oh my god, it is her, oh wow unbelievable."

"It's wonderful."

Some of the customers were all choked up, tears coming down their faces.

Jaia and 'em were like, "What the fuck is goin' on, yo. What is all the commotion about."

Unc inquired and Seasonn looked with amazement.

"Oh shit," she blurted out, "is that, what's her name, Halle Berry?"

"Yo word," Unc yelled, "hell yeah."

Vah said, "She's with an entourage fo sho, ya feel me."

Jaia's saying, "Hi Halle."

Seasonn calling out, "You look beautiful, Halle."

Unc caught her wink.

She thought, 'Yeah, I remember that statement she made on Oprah. Bitch, I am here, I'd leave Jaia's ass in a minute and Jaia would hunt me down like a bounty hunter, fo sho.'

Vah's like, "She's no comparison to my baby Seasonn. I do not see it."

Unc said to Vah, "Nigga, you in love talking that crap. No disrespect to you Seasonn. I'm just teasing this nigga Vah."

"Did you mean what you just said baby, huh," said Seasonn to Vah.

"Yes I did, love. I meant every word I said, honey. There is a whole lotta love I wanna give ya, Seasonn."

"Oh shit, Unc," Jaia said, "Baby, we should be getting ourselves together ladies. It's about that time yo, for the show to begin."

"Hold up, hold up," Seasonn said, "I need to say something to Vah. Honey listen, I want you to have my ride. The Benz, baby because my love is hard for you. Please do not say no. Take the got dam car, Vah."

Jaia and Unc said in unison, "Bitch, take the dam car. It's outta love, not the sex. Maybe that is what the sex is worth."

"Shit if it's that good," Jaia said, "then we should try and bottle that shit up and become rich and forget about the drugs, ya feel me."

Everybody laughed at Jaia's words of joy. Her eyes were focused on Dunk. She was cleaning house since the sales people were watching Halle Berry. Jaia was smiling at her and nodding her head, letting her know she is good to go. Unc, Vah and Seasonn kept their sales person busy with their shit. Everybody in the game of hustling knows the next hustler. It's recognized in different forms of making money.

The time has come to depart for Vah and Seasonn. Outside of Sak's, Seasonn had to catch a cab. They were expressing their good-byes with enough hugs and kisses to last until the next time. Vah had hailed a cab, Seasonn got in, they both were blowing each other kisses, as the cab faded away.

* * *

Vah was ready to do this she stated to both Unc and Jaia. "Let's get our bags and shit and put 'em in the trunk and get the fuck outta Dodge tonight, after handling our business dawg, a'ight? It's time for us to shine bitches."

As they headed toward their cars, Vah thought about Seasonn for a second. She appreciated her giving her, her hoopty. It's a prize, it's a sweet ride.

'And it's all my boo. Now it's time to get on the grind, get this money, make riigga's work,' she thought to herself with a big smile on her face.

Vah followed Jaia in her car to go up to Washington Heights. They played like they were racing on the highway, passing cars recklessly. When they arrived on the block, Juan was waiting.

"Yo mi prima, I thought you'd probably say fuck it. Guess not, but Poppi is waiting Prima. He doesn't sound to happy about this shit. You wanting to deal in pettico, tu es tambien. So, you better make him a fuckin' believer, yo or he's gonna rain on ya fuckin' parade, yo. Mommy wants to see you too, Jaia. She's doing okay, so Prima they're waiting for you upstairs. I so Suggest you leave your little patita's in the car, yo. It's better if you deal alone, mia."

"No it's not, just in case I can't make it, yo. These are my dawgs, so where I go, they go, understand. Trust me, Uncle Tito's not going to have no problema tu tambien. I got this Juan, it's all good. Thanks for the info, yo."

She signaled for her dawgs to follow her upstairs to her uncle's. As she entered the apartment Aunt Rosa was standing there.

She said, "Como esta, bien nina. Your uncle's in the den mia, okay."

She pointed in the direction of the den.

The apartment looked like a mausoleum of statues. All kinds with some candles and shit, a fuckin' machete in front of the porcelain statues. The atmosphere was kinda fuckin' creepy, just to get connected. There were many candles with all kinds of saints and shit. Vah and Unc had never seen no shit like this before, in their lives. It seemed kinda weird to them.

Jaia was used to this. The whole time she lived with them; the room with the saints and the candles was the same as when she left, when her Aunt kicked her out. She doesn't regret it at all.

'Not one bit,' she thought.

As she and her dawgs entered the den, her Uncle Tito stared at her as if he wanted to fuck her right then and there. Unc saw it and knew she'd have to kill the yete motherfucker, fo sho. For now she let Jaia handle business. Sooner or later there will be a whole lotta consequences behind the shit.

'I can see it already,' Unc thought to herself.

Vah asked Jaia, "Yo, you sure everything is everything dawg. The vibes feel hectic, yo. I do not trust this dude, uncle or not, ya feel me."

Unc said, "Yo Vah, be cool. It's about being paid and rising as high as we can. Listen to this cornball for what we need. As long as the product is right for the price, we good"

Jaia's Uncle Tito called her by his pet name for her. He'd always call her Ju-Ju.

"Yes uncle, let me ask you a couple of questions in terms of your request of me and me honoring it."

"Ju-Ju, es ta-biers. This is a very serious situation that I have to consider, as a part of you being involved and protected, entiende. Although, under the circumstances of your departure, Yes I do owe you this honor, mia. So here is the deal. You only deal with me for any re-ups. That goes for all you patita's, entiende.

"Here is the deal today as we speak. I'll give you twenty five kilos, fifteen on consignment, Ju-Ju, if you can handle it, mia. I do not want you fucking around over my shit, riot having my money, entieride. Ju-Ju are you ready for sure. Come closer, I need to say something to you nina, privately. You know I'm sorry Ju-Ju. If we're going to be doing business; we need to let by-gones be by-gones, verdad."

"Only on the strength of business," Jaia replied, "I'm all about getting paid, making my life comfortable for me and mines, uncle. I just feel this hustling is in my blood, as well as yours. You know I guess it runs in the family."

Tito's wondering if Ju-Ju remembers when she lived in the Dominican Republic with her father, his brother, Manuel.

'Why doesn't she ask about her father. Is there something she actually doesn't want to find out. I am not going to push the issue, as far as Manuel. I am going to watch over her in her time of need.'

"Ju-Ju," he called, "listen give me some information about where you'd like everything to be delivered. It shall be done."

She goes to hand him the money.

He then tells her, "Keep it, we're familia, Next time, if you get rid of that as quick as you say you can, we'll be able to manage what you want. It's a done deal. Ju-Ju just be careful. I am here for you and you'd be surprised who else is connected. That's all there is to know. Go with ya crew, make the streets yours. Once you deal in this career of hustling everywhere you deliver is your area and everything becomes done on your terms."

CHAPTER TWENTY

As Labu sat in her living room chillin' watching the 'Resident Evil' movie, she heard Nubian's cellie ringing to the tone of Nelly. She hurried toward the coffee table, picked it up, opened it and answered.

"Hello, is anyone there?"

"Yo bitch, what the fuck are you doing picking up my boy's phone. Yo, is there something going on as to why you handling Nubian's cellie bitch, cause I know he did not give you shit. If ya ass stole it hoe, he's the wrong motherfucker to be stealing from, so you better be sucking his dick lovely for you to have his cellie. He had to give you permission, if ya head is good. Who the fuck are you anyway?

Labu continued, "Yo, where the fuck is Nubian? Put that nigga on the phone with the quickness, yo. I mean right now, bitch."

Labu was talking so fast she'd blurted out her name.

"Tell him it's Jaia hoe, a'ight. How 'bout that. Now go get him now."

As Labu pretended to get Nubian, she is in total fucking shock. Now she knows why Aunya told her ass to stay put. She is nervous like a bitch, wondering if she should tell Jaia about Nubian getting shot or if she already knows.

She was thinking to herself, 'I doubt it, the way she sounds over the phone, like a bitch in control and seductive.'

She could hear Jaia talking to others saying that something ain't right. That a bitch is answering Nubian's cellie **and** that shit is not kosher at all. Also, that she's gonna have to let his fuckiri' ass know it's a crucial situation, when you let pussy come between ya business.

"He's gots to get his shit right. We are not going to ever have our motherfuckin' crew infiltrated over no fuckin' bitch or a nigga. That's a motherfuckin' fact, ya feel me."

Vah responded, "You got dam right, because then we gotta go through the bullshit of hunting this bitch down. Sex is a motherfucker, yo. We all know."

Everybody laughed.

Unc replied, "What's taking him so long to come to the phone, yo. That nigga best no be whipped, not when handling my shit. Yo Vah, you think shit is kosha or is this ass fuckin' up shop. I'ma have to call Da-Stev, see what it is. Yo, call Da-Stev on your cellie Vah, while I got Nubian's bitch on this line, fo sho. Let us play connect the dots, yo. I think it's time we find out what the fuck is sho-muff going on with our troops.

He continued, "I'ma tell ya'll right now, motherfuckers dam sure is gonna get got if our shit ain't right. That bitch Ms. Smiley is the number one candidate on the chain. She kinda started smellin' her ass once we got our hustle on. Yo, what is takin' this motherfucker so long to come to the phone, yo. If anything this nigga Nubian better tell me some good shit, fo sho."

Vah dialed Da-Stev's, no answer - voice mail, Then Ms. Smiley's, no answer.

'Whoa,' she thought, 'that's really strange; no one answering their calls.'

She repeated aloud to Jaia, "Yo Jaia, this shit is weird, no one is answering Da-Stev's or Ms. Smiley's."

Jaia replied, "But we gotta bitch answering Nubian's, isn't this a motherfucker. Let's see if she can fill us in on some information."

"It's time for us to get out of Dodge," stated Unc.

Vah replied, "Yeah, after Tito let's us know when he can make it happen. He needs to tell us personally, ya feel me.

"That way all is taken care of," Jaia responded.

"We are truly on our grind, yo," Unc said to both Jaia and Vah.

Jaia heard a voice saying, "Hello, hello, you there."

She put the phone to her ear, "Yo, I'm listening."

Labu disguising her voice said, "Listen up, I'm gonna say what it is you need to know Jaia, then I'ma hang up, a'ight. So your ass needs to listen closely. I just happened to be parked on the block, Nubian's talking to me. Then, all of a sudden, this Caucasian guy in a Seville started shooting at him. I rushed him to the hospital. That is how I ended up with his cell phone yesterday, ya feel me. So, now Ms. Thang you take it from there. Check out ya boy. I hope he is a'ight."

Click, the phone went dead.

Jaia got really hysterical, cause she kinda cared for him a little.

Vah said, "Bitch, calm down. We'll get down to the truth. Right now, we need to take care of this money we 'bout to make. Nubian's come a dime a dozen, girl. Shut that noise up. Oh, I almost forgot to fill you in on this; Damian will be ridin' with us back up to

Albany, a'ight. He'll be my soldier. He's ridiri' with me in my boo's sweet present to me, her car. Booya-ya.

Vah continued, "We have to be crucial sometime in our thinking, even if it's with our own worker, yo. It's a give and take in this money we'll be gettin', so it's always good to recruit nigga's in our journey. Also, to stay on top of the game, because it'll turn a motherfucker against us quick and we're all females, so a nigga looks for our weakness, tryin' to play us or using that macho egotistical bullshit, especially tryin' to fuckin intimidate a bitch. So, from now on bitches, it's grimey time."

Unc asked Vah, "So what we need to do now is kill some time until Tito puento here let's us know what it is we're going to do, fo sho. we yell, let's stroll through the hood, see what's good."

They all headed out of her uncle's crib. Jaia stopped in the kitchen to speak with Aunt Rosa, to let her know that her uncle had apologized. She understood her aunt's position, living with Uncle Tito and that now harm's done. All she wanted is for them to communicate because they are the only biological family Jaia knows. Aunt Rosa always loved Jaia. She hugged her with a loving squeeze as if she missed her dearly wondering how her life has been.

"Oh well, what's done is done," she said to Jaia, "life goes on and you keep it moving on, as long as God allows you to breathe in the process of your endeavors. There's always consequences, unless you choose to settle your life, sooner or later, if not, until then - yes, our lives will get the better of us, Jaia. I give you wisdom in what you're about to endure, but you already have a secure and protected life, no matter where you are. In due time everything will come to light. You shall no longer be left in the dark, as your journey awakens you. Please do keep in contact. I'll be waiting to hear from you to share bits and pieces of your empire."

"Yo Jaia, are you comiri' boo. We are going to the corner store to get some forties yo, so do please hurry up. I do not wanna be without my boo," Uc was singing.

As Jaia listened, she felt what Aunt Rosa was saying seemed weird in a sense, like she talked in riddles or some shit. Nevertheless, when Unc called, she started smiling ear to ear.

"I'm comin' baby. Aunt Rosa, I'm doing my thing, but I promise you're the only family here I have. I need to keep in contact. I promise I will."

She was gone with everything her Aunt said on her mind, and held it to her heart. Curiously, Jaia thought there was something her aunt needed her to know. In time, like she said, she will inform her.

Jaia's cousin Juan was calling her, Vah and Unc. He wanted to show them how the money is made in his neighborhood. As they followed he'd told them what they're about to see is real fuckini' sick shit going on with this drug they're selling.

"This vision is real and raw," Juan warned.

Unc was like, "Oh shit, whoa boo; is he kidding about the shit he is getting ready to show us. Well, I guess we'd better get our stomach prepared for some ole griminess shit that's getting ready to be presented, yo."

Vah told Unc, "Yo, you ain't never been inside of a full blown crack building, not house bitch, building. These are known throughout the four boroughs. Maybe after you check this scenery out, you'd want to open up a couple buildings in Albany. Not apartments Unc, buildings, but Albany is smallbany. New York City is huge, my nigga. It ain't the Big Apple for nothing. Albany is the bite they took out!"

They all laughed.

"We are going to keep that bite of Albany going strong, ya feel me. So Unc, you 'bout to actually get a degree in the field of how people go to the deep end for drugs, boo. Learn from this town girl, it's an experience you'll never forget, fo sho - ya heard."

As they walked down 181st Street, they entered this apartment building. Juan tapped on the door. The worker looked through the glass, noticed him and opened the door. A well built Hispanic dude.

Juan called his name, "Ramon, this is my cousin and her friends. I am coaching them on how to make more money by keeping customers at bay, amigo."

They laughed.

While they were walking, they looked in each apartment, because the doors were left open and each worker had guns protecting their customers, while they enjoy getting high. The potent crack they were selling on the premises kept customers from leaving the building for days. They made it their homes, as if were their lives, being in the building, addicted to this shit.

"It's something else," Jaia thought.

"Dam, you mean it's money to be made like this, yo. Ya gottas be fuckiri' kiddie' me. Vah, look at this shit."

One female Puerto Rican was getting fucked all up in her ass, fucked in her mouth; looking like she is on a roller coaster from dick to dick. Then there was this Black girl, licking this homo-thug nigga's asshole. He was enjoying every touch of her tongue. He then fed her some crumbs of crack; she takes a hit and starts licking his ass again.

"This shit is off the chain up in here," Unc said, "I never would have imagined a building like this existing, in my life, at all.

Here goes Vah again, "Bitch, cause ya ass ain't nothing but a suburban bitch."

She cracked up, "Ha ha ha."

As they kept walking through the hallways, this beautiful looking Brazilian woman came running out of one of the apartments with a gash on her arm.

She was screaming, "Help me, he's trying to kill me."

Ramon stood there with his 9mm, waiting patiently for the guy to actually come running out after the beautiful woman. Right then a man did. He was a medium height older man who looked to be in his mid-sixties.

He called to the Brazilian woman, "Come here to me, my wife."

He had a knife in his hand. Ramon cold-cocked that motherfucker in the jaw. It was if the man was in a zone, even though he snapped outta that shit, quick.

Juan said, "Kick his ass. Then put his ass out. If he gives you a hard time, kill him."

Jaia said, "You see the crazy shit up in here, prima. It's no fuckin' joke, entiende."

Then they all went on the second floor and saw some guys in a menagie trois at the first apartment door they came to. Then there were about four other guys giving head and sucking dick as they went from one dude to the next. Some were sitting on the side, getting high; waiting their turn.

Jaia had seen some crazy shit once in a while in the hood when she lived there, but riot up close. Now, knowing her Uncle Tito's running all these activities going on; she understood his dumb ass perversion toward her.

Vah noticed a boy over in a corner in the hallway. He couldn't have been no more than ninteen years old. His eyes were bulging out of his head, sin all scaly and his mouth was oh so nasty, looking like Pooky in New Jack City. She couldn't believe her eyes as she got closer. He looked as if he'd been in the building forever, deteriorating in that corner. His hair was so matted; it has a solid gray brick look. The clothes he wore were torn and shredded.

Vah went to say something to him; Unc pulled her ass back.

"Bitch, you do not know what that little bastard got."

Vah said, "Bitch, you ever snatch me like that again, I'll break you fucking jaw; scaring the shit outta me like that, bitch."

"Yeah a'ight, I shoulda just let his ass jump on you, bite ya ass to death, motherfucker. See how long you would've stared and been amazed at that, ya fucking emotional dummy."

"Yo Unc, check yourself," Vah yelled.

"You got that, yo," Unc replied.

As they went on throughout the building, time passed long enough for Juan to get a call from his father, for Jaia and 1 em to know what his plans were for delivering their goods. So, they headed back out of the building.

"Yo Juan, you got shit sewed up here, man. Making money is all it is, son," Vah said to him, "I'ma try a little something like this up in Albany. Maybe it'll help to become a patita baller, entiende that," she laughed.

Unc, Jaia and Ramon didn't understand a dam thing she said. They laughed for the hell of it outta respect for Juan's cousin and feeling glad that this tour through the fucking building was over. Juan is around this shit twenty-four seven and he even gets his dick sucked every now and then.

As Jaia entered her uncle's apartment, he directed them toward the den. He took Jaia to the side, whispering in her ear that he did not want Uric to ever come to a pick-up. He felt some type of way about her; he got bad vibes. So, out of respect for her, he had to let her know, with them doing business together. He remembered Vah, so she wasn't a problem. He always knew that her and Jaia were going to be best friends forever. To him she's family, so he's protecting her, as well. Unc is a different story, though.

Tito also regretted trying to molest his niece when she lived with him and Rosa, because he sees revenge in her. Now he knows, with her into the hustling, it's going to make her become as powerful and strong as her father. He knows that her wrath is going to be unpredictable. He has to prepare himself, He explained the deliveries and drop-offs to Jaia, Unc and Vah.

He told them, "May you prosper in millions, ladies. Be safe."

"Let's roll, it's time to hit the highway, fo sho."

Jaia's jammin' listening to Whitney Houston's, 'It's My Pride".

"But it's okay, I'm gonna make it anyway; pack your bags up and leave', her and Unc were singing their asses off.

Vah called Damian ahead of time, so he'd be where she could pick him up. He was there. As he climbed into the car, the first thing he was boasting about is her ride.

She smiled, "Well nigga, it's a go, dude. I spoke with Jaia and 'em. You'll be my soldier, ya feel me. You only take orders from me first, then Jaia and Unc, understand. We do not step on toes in our crew, ya feel me. We're like family, as one, let alone dawgs for life. Nothing comes in between us, nothing. That's fo sho."

Damian tells Vah, "Listen boo, all I'm about is feeding my family, by any means necessary, ya feel me. My loyalty lies with you and ya crew. You'll *see.* I am straight Vah, so don't come at me about no trustworthy shit. My word is real forever. Now, let's go on the road to riches. I'm ready, yo."

They laughed as they drove.

CHAPTER TWENTY-ONE

After Natalie got her fuck on, with Ms. Smiley in the pantry hearing every sound of her being fucked beautiful; she had to tell Charles she had enough. He likes when he does that to her and his reason is there's another female waiting on him. So, he fucked Natalie hard and long, until she could not take no more. It had only been an hour and forty-five minutes.

'Dam, he's good,' she thought, 'he tore my pussy up.'

She had a little limp, 'cause he got all crunked up in her shit. She finally got herself together, looking nice and spunky ready to go check out the stash house over in Albany. Had Ms. Smiley not been rolling, bumping into the door, Naltalie would've just jetted out of there. Instead, she stopped to talk a little; letting her know that she'll be taking her ass with her. She told her she'd be in the back of her Jeep, a nice Pathfinder, with tinted windows. She had the bitch hog tied, so she won't be going nowhere no time soon, at all. She is all fucked up. Natalie kinda felt bad for her, but she knew if she started letting the mushy feelings in, she'd end up dead fucking with the bitch.

So, she dragged her ass to the garage, pushed her ass in 'Once I get the stash,' she thought, 'it's over for her. No more will she dock in Albany, period. Oh no bay; today is her last living day.'

Ms. Smiley knew, fo sho that it's over, for real.

She thought, 'If only I wasn't tied up, let alone being fucked up. I know she is saving me to kill for Jaia and 'em when they come back from their connect. Dam, I should've had someone with me. Got dam, I can be so careless. I got too comfortable, so it is what it is.'

Natalie reached back to remove the gag from her mouth to let her get her last words out, begging for her life. Natalie turned on the air conditioner and put her windows up. Now, she is ready to go on her way and take Ms. Smiley's shit. She don't give a fuck either; all she cares about is gettin' paid, right about now.

Turning on her CD, she's listening to Lil Kim's 'Mafia'. "This song is the shit," she said to herself.

Then to Ms. Smiley, "Yo bitch, you a'ight, bundled up back there like a hog tied pretzel, boo. It's only right, it'll be over soon."

Natalie arrived at the stash spot, asking Ms. Smiley what the number was. She obliged. The block was quite clean and looks very well organized. She took out the keys and she opened the door. As she got closer, she heard loud music. It was louder than a mother. She was surprised the neighbors were not complaining.

'Oh well, it's still early,' she thought to herself.

As she put the key in the door, where the loud music was coming from; she cracked the door slowly like she was a cat burglar. She heard what sounded like voices, as if someone was having some freaky ass sex.

'That accounts for the loud music,' she thought.

The smell of sex was all in the air. She heard a man's voice.

'Probably he's having some S&M shit going on, with a little deviance.'

All of a sudden there was this scream. It sounded muffled, but it was a man.

'Oh my god, it's two men, macho fags getting it on. Oh, I'm gonna peek and see this shit and how they're doing it to one another.'

She went into the living room, saw the bags of money and the drugs and her eyes got wide as hell. T.Dove was talking to Dolce's ass and fucking him hard.

"Yo nigga, didn't I tell you to say I'm ya daddy, bitch. See, I'm a grown man in your ass, try'na get nutted, dude," T.Dove said as he pumped Dolce's ass.

Then he started going fuckin' buck wild on Dolce's ass. Next he pulled out a box cutter, slicing his back as he's pumping his ass.

"Nigga after this good fuck, you ain't never gonna want no pussy again."

Dolce's mind was in total shock. He felt numb, weak; he just wanted to die.

T.Dove kept pumping saying, "Yeah, so I guess ya stank ass boss bitch ain't gonna like having ya ass around no more. Now, where the fuck is Ms. Smiley, boyee."

Natalie could not believe her ears.

She thought, 'What did he just say.'

Then, she heard him say it again to Dolce.

She figured since homeboy wanted Ms. Smiley so bad that she'd deliver the scank ass bitch to him. She hurried out, grabbing three bags of money, took four kilos, as T.Dove kept torturing Dolce. She flew down the stairs to her Jeep, having an awesome plan. She opened the doors throwing the bags and shit in, as Ms. Smiley tried to say something. she gagged her mouth, cause she did not want this bitch hollering while she dragged her ass into the vestibule of her stash house. Boy, did she have a surprise for her. As Natalie left, she stepped back, took the gags out of Ms. Smiley's mouth and her ass started screaming up a fucking storm.

"Yo, you white ass bitch, after all I've done for you in servicing your customer's, hoe. You actually going to leave me hog tied in this fucking hallway like this. Bitch, if I ever get out of this, your ass is dead."

As Natalie walked away she said, "I do not think you'll ever get outta that there bitch, because there's this black dude upstairs torturing your homeboy bitch, looking for you. Oh and check this out, he's fucking him in his ass. Your boy is strapped down for the taking, bitch. As soon as he's finished with him; hearing your loud ass mouth, he'll probably fuck you in the ass too, ya know. He really seems like an ass kind of guy. Chow, babe."

She was gone, fo sho, money and all; happier than a faggot in Boy's Town. She was wondering who the dude is that was torturing Ms. Smiley's worker.

She was thinking, 'If I would've stayed a little longer to listen, maybe I'da found out. Oh hell, sooner or later I will.'

* * *

Ms. Smiley was thinking, 'Dam, I can't hear shit over this loud ass music.'

At that moment it stopped.

She heard this fuckin' guy yellin', "Yo, what the fuck happened to the thee bags of money and four keys. Is there a fucking ghost up in this piece."

He saw the door was cracked open a little. He pulled out his gat, a .45 caliber Baretta, walked toward the door; opened it, looked out, down the stairs and saw Ms. Smiley hog tied.

He said, "Yo, what the fuck is going on bitch. It's nice to see ya dead looking ass."

He ran toward her as she tried telling him about Natalie.

He said, "I have no idea who the hell you talking 'bout, but I'ma find her ass. Get my fucking money, yo."

Ms. Smiley's like, "Check this out, I got more where that came from. Please just don't kill me."

"Bitch, I just found your stash and everything. You telling me there's more where that came from. I don't believe ya ass. You might be setting my ass up, bitch."

'POW' - he shot her right between the eyes, went back inside, grabbed the shit and saw Dolce for the last time. His ass was bleeding like a water faucet. T.Dove stood there feeling as though he shouldn't leave him suffering like that. Tied up, he patted him on his ass.

"Yo dude, you had some dam good ass son, but I can't leave you like this so I'ma do you a favor, a'ight."

Dolce whispered, "Please kill me, please kill me."

Dolce shot him in the head, got the fuck outta there and headed straight to the hospital to see Nubian to let him know he killed that bitch Ms. Smiley, fo sho.

Now, he needed to find the bitch that took his fucking shit. He's in a very dangerous mood to the point of no return. Although, he knew that he had to relax in order to think clearly, so now the shit was hitting the fan all over Albany. On his way to see Nubian, he was hoping and praying his boy is better.

He thought to himself, 'It's time to tear shit out the frame.'

As far as getting his grind on, he definitely is telling Nubian about the drugs and money. They're like brothers. Nubian always helped him as far as putting him on to get paid. They go way back when. T.Dove's life has been a fucking massacre. If it weren't for Nubian keeping him head strong, he'd probably be in a mental institution. Yet, he's almost there being in the streets; believe it or not. All the crazy shit he does is his process to sanity.

Once T.Dove got to the hospital he saw Lil Kill.

"Wha up, my nig, greater potato boyee. Yo son, I just came from letting off my guns on that bitch we been hunting, man. The fabulous Ms. Smiley. Yo son, it's strange though the way she landed in my lap, man. Un-fuckin-believable. I' was doing her home slice Dolce something terrible, dawg. Ya know how I am, but not for nothing, let's take this conversation up to Nubian. He'd love to hear this, a'ight."

Lil Kill and T.Dove knocked; then entered Nubian's room.

"Yo boy, when are you outta here, man. You should be ready for anything coming at ya now, ya feel me. That's fo sho," declared Lil Kill.

T.Dove got right to the point of telling Nubian about killing Ms. Smiley and her boy, Dolce. He went into detail, in which neither one of them wanted to hear that graphic shit, especially being done to a nigga.

So, T.Dove's like, "Yo, now we gonna knock off the rest of her crew or see if they wanna be down with us or what. Am I right, yo. We are goin' to make that happen, ya feel So, being that the bitch is truly dead; I shall say so myself, we need to find out about what motherfucker is trying to take Nubian down. Quickly."

Nubian sat up in his bed, remembering the female who helped him. He recalled she was a Caucasian. He definitely did not think it was Detective Reese who tried to hit him, but he needed to find out with the quickness before Jaia and 'em get back. It should not be long. As he thought of them, his phone rang. It startled him. He picked the phone up.

"Yo, who dis."

Nubian couldn't believe his ears. It was Jaia. He was wondering how the fuck she found out about him.

"Oh shit, it is a small world."

Jaia asked Nubian is he was alright and why he didn't call her to let her know what was going on with him. She wanted to know how he could keep something so important like this, from her and the crew. She was asking him what the fuck was he thinking and telling him that this ain't no pride shit going on in her stable.

Lil Kill was motioning to Nubian.

"Yo, that's the boss lady, man?"

He shakes his head yes. Then, Lil Kill tells Nubian he's going to the vending machines.

In the meantime, Jaia is lighting his ass up. She made Nubian feel like a piece of shit and he was the one laying in the hospital.

He thought, 'At least this bitch could've had a little ass sympathy.'

She told him about the hoodrat answering his cellie; explaining that she was the one who drove him to Albany Medical Center hospital. Then she told him that the bitch had the nerve to hang up on her. Nubian kinda smiled, cause Jaia hadn't shut the fuck up since he answered the phone, so it was a relief to his mood.

T.dove kept reaching his hand out for Nubian to give him the phone, so he could talk to Jaia. He wanted to tell her he was the one who killed Ms. Smiley and has been with Nubian twenty-four seven. He felt the it's a must that he meet up with his payee's. He needed to inform them of the shit he confiscated at the stash house. He also wanted to prove his loyalty to them, even if it meant stepping on Nubian's toes. He always gets his. That's his motto.

Lil Kill came back with a whole bunch of munchies for them Nubian was still getting his ass chewed out. One thing he did mention to Jaia was that he was the only one she left her number with to contact and did not expect to get gunned down.

Jaia said, "Yeah, I suppose ya right Nub, but check it we got another bonafide worker named Damian. You can school his ass on the area, a'ight. You, what's good with the monies. Everything is good and Lil Kill; he's doing his thang or his part looking out for you Nubian, taking care of business while you hold up nigga. I hope so dude. Listen, I am almost in Albany. I'll be dropping by to see ya as soon as I hit town, ya feel me. Then we can discuss whatever. Yo, we gotta set shit up different, so we all keep connected. Have ya heard from D-Stev, Nub."

Nubian's thoughts of D-Stev trying to kill his ass cluttered his head, but he wanted to handle the shit he knew about Da-Steve himself. He felt that nigga is gonna feel the fucking wrath he has in store for him, for a lifetime.

He answered Jaia telling her that he'd only been in the hospital a day or two and soon he'd be released. He hadn't answered her question about Da-Stev; instead he asked her about Vah and Unc. He wanted to know if they were a'ight.

"Yeah them bitches are fine. Yo, you won't believe the shit my cousin Juan has set up on his block. When the fiends cop their shit Nubian, in a fucking building, yo. The whole scene is fuckin' wack when you enter. It's like you never, ever leave that shit, you. I'll explain more when I see you, a'ight."

Vah thought about the young boy she had seen in the hallway. It kinda fucked her up. She'd though he'd looked familiar, with all the dirt and grime on his ass, she couldn't tell who the fuck he looked like period, but she felt he had been someone she knew, fo sho."

* * *

Labu could not believe she had stayed inside the house for at least three days, since the shit with Nubian. Then she had spoken with Jaia. She knew that should've told her ass to stay put, because now they're on their way back to Albany and shit is about to get hectic. She knew grimey nigga's were getting it now with no questions asked. She knew she needed to stay put. Just then, the phone started ringing.

The operator said, "Collect call from a correctional facility."

Labu accepts.

Aunya's voice sounds like she's a puppy in love, but firm, also. She is all into Labu.

"Baby, what's up, love. I miss you, ma. It won't be long boo. So, do you like the crib. Tell me what you been doing since I last spoke with you, when you were all in a rush to see your new car. I hope you love it, baby. I hope you love it, baby, My dawgs got some taste in fashion, bet that. So have you met them yet. Oh nah, I forgot they down in New York. Well, can't say too much, ya know, on prison phone, boo.

"So let's give them something to listen to boo, by us having phone sex. Labu, I want you to stick ya middle finger in your pussy, ma. Just right up there now."

Labu tells Aunya, "Baby, you don't want me to wet my finger with my saliva"

"Nah, I just want it done boo, after you've taken your finger out; I want you to suck it like peanut butter is at the top of your mouth. Then, I want you to lick ya finger babe, please. I'd like to hear it Labu, O.K."

Aunya had Labu's ass going. She was getting all juicy and wet, feeling her boo through the phone; laying in her bed with her legs wide open. She was facing the mirror where her vanity set is; admiring herself and getting off on Aunya's phone sex. She started moaning. Then she told her to hold on a minute because she needed to put on the speaker phone, so she could bust a nut and cum.

Aunya said, "Damn ma, you thirsty, huh, for me. I miss teasing and sucking your clitoris, so softly and tenderly Labu; touching every inch of your being, as mine to make love to, baby. It'll be like a mouth move, boo. Then, it's me and you, Labu, ya feel me. Babe, more than anything in this whole wideworld, I do not want to stop loving you. Just do not; I repeat, do not hurt me ever, babe. You promise."

Labu answered, "Yes, the same goes for you, too. No lies, no secrets; all honesty and trust, Aunya. O.K., ma."

Labu seductively continued telling Aunya, "Number one love. This pussy is all yours forever. You can have it whenever you want, even our phone sex. It's yours baby; morning, noon and night, love. Oh baby, what is it you'd like to wear home to me. Let momma know honey and it'll be there overnight. Would you like for me to come pick you up, baby."

"Nah, I'ma enjoy the scenic sites, a'ight. I want to be ready once I get out of the cab, boo, coming into the house, Labu. Then, you'll be mine all night. I want to suck, fuck, make love and cuddle up to you, giving ya all the love you missed since you were released boo, ya feel me.

"Continue playing in my pussy. I wanna hear your wetness over the phone, Labu. Spank your ass, and tell me that you're being a good girl. Ooh, ooh, Labu, that sounds very slurpy, ma. Oh yeah, I hear it. Keep playing in that nice, pretty, silky pussy. I cannot wait to rub my tongue all around; inside and out, especially licking my baby's asshole. You know it, fo sho, Labu. You're mines, girl. Aunya, I'ma send you a nice letter with my cum all on the letter, baby. How 'bout that boo," Aunya chuckled.

"Just kidding, love. Oh baby, you are making me so dam hot in my pussy. It's ya voice, honey. I miss everything about you. Rub your clitoris, Labu. It's going to get better, ma. You are so juicy wet, girl. I can imagine your fingers getting all your wetness on 'em."

"Ooh, ooh, ooh Aunya; I feel like I'm getting ready to cum, baby. It's oozing, honey. Ah, ah, ah, ah, ah; I love you s0000 much. Hurry home, love. Oh baby, that was terrific, girl. Promise you'll do that again to me, O.K."

"I promise, Labu."

Aunya then asked Labu, "So, have Jaia and 'em called you at all, to meet ya pretty ass, baby."

"Nah, boo."

"Well, maybe they are really busy taking care of a whole bunch of business. I haven't been able to reach them either. Them bitches are straight up handling shit. Boyee, I cannot wait until I hit the streets, love. I do miss my dawgs, 24/7. We are all as one boo, fo sho, ya feel me. Labu, if you need something to do baby, start looking for a house, cause we are going to need it when I get home, a'ight. I know you're not familiar with the area, so now you can get some idea of where we should rest our heads, ma. I love you and I want the best for us. That we shall have. It'll be even better once you are in my arms again. That is what really matters."

Labu wanted so badly to let Aunya know that she'd taken a ride down to the hood and got caught up in a shooting. Instead she left well enough alone.

She thought to herself, 'I'll wait until she comes home. It'll be better said than over the phone. I wouldn't want her putting me out, thinking I wasn't keeping it real with her. She might go on some crazy ass, wild fucked up spree, insinuating I'm actually fucking that nigga, Nubian. Then all the shit with Coco would kick in mentally and all hell would break loose. I can't have my baby thinking no type of crap like that; with her being released soon and being in jail. Oh hell nah.'

"Labu, Labu baby are you still on the phone."

"Yeah honey, I'm here."

"Well what the hell you got on your mind so heavy that got you in a zone ma. I've been yapping for a minute and I know you did not hear shit. You didn't answer me, yo. What's good, Labu? Tell me is there something I should know, ma. Keep real, keep it simple, if it's anything."

"Nah baby, I just happened to start fantasizing, listening to your voice. It took me away baby, seriously. My love is deep, so you mesmerize me everytime, my sexy ass bitch, Aunya. Ooh that does something to me. You are so sexy. Ya know that's right baby, with your muscular self. It's a turn-on with your very, very sexy walk. You're so versitile. I admire that about you, baby and respect the goodness you bring me. Ima 'bout to get wet all over again; hearing your voice talk so softly, Aunya."

The automatic operator intervened letting them know that they had sixty seconds left on the phone call.

Labu was thinking to herself that she wanted to tell Aunya the situation and she should tell her to call right back. Then she thought, 'Nah, let her call again tomorrow.'

She kept saying to Aunya, "Baby, I love you more than life itself; can't wait until you come home, ma. My pussy is missing your caressing tongue."

Click, the phone shut off.

Labu sat feeling sad. The love she had for Aunya is really from her heart. It's the most beautiful, loving, awesome internal feeling to be in love. This is her first time.

* * *

In the meantime, Jaia and 'em are getting off the exit in Albany.

"Hallelujah," Vah said, "it's time to get paid. Sho ya right. We have a lot of dirty laundry to clean up. Damian, here is where you earn your stripes, nigga. You'll be chillin' with me at my crib up on Western Avenue, dude; only for a second. Nah, I'ma just get you ya own shit until you can get up on ya shit, ya feel me. As a matter of fact, it's a favor, a'ight. I really do not like a nigga up in my domain where I rest my head any ole fucking way. No offense to ya, my nig."

* * *

At the hospital, Nubian, T.Dove and Lil Kill were all'up in his room laughing and talking about the shit that happened with Ms. Smiley.

"It's all hilarious if you ask me, Nubian," T.Dove said, "I cannot understand how the bitch ended up at that dam stash spot."

Lil Kill replied, "As you can see T.Dove, she was dead on it."

They all cracked up laughing, "Yo, it's all about getting money."

As T.Dove began to talk again Jaia and 'em entered the room.

Nubian looked toward the door and said, "My bitch, my true dat nigga, ride or die and her dawgs. The powerful T.L.C., ya'll came right on time to help my ass outta here, fo sho. I am being released as we speak. Yo, Lil Kill, did you get the gear that I asked for. Give me my boxer's; I don't want none of ya'll seeing my hamlet with a handle, ya feel me."

Everyone laughed.

The nurse entered the room, "Okay everyone, please will you exit the room so Mr. Fields can prepare himself to be released. Thank you."

She was a pretty caramel sistah, with a plump ass, light brown eyes and dooby hairdo.

'Fine piece of meat,' Nubian thought.

He was fantasizing about how he could bang his hamlet all up in her. He asked her for her number. She declined, so he told her, "Maybe another time in life, boo."

She answered, "I am not your boo, Mr. Fields, so let's leave it at that and get you up outta here so you can go be with your extended family that you have waiting for you, okay."

The nurse came pushing Nubian in a wheelchair to the desk nurse, so he could sign out. As he did, everyone was figuring out where to go as far as getting shit back on point in the hood.

T.Dove sat and listened to all the rigor mortis shit that was being said. He looked at Damian and remembered that he looks familiar, as if he had been up in the joint when them nigga's did that shit to him. He would get up with him later, but he knew fo sho that Damian ain't no fucking joke. He was thinking that if he was with T.L.C., then he's down by law.

'Me and that motherfucker there go way back. I'ma refresh his memory, although when your ass is locked down, ya ass do not forget shit, cause shit is the same basically, twenty-four seven. Other than a face, that is the only fuckin change in jail.'

Nubian said, "Yo fam, let's roll over to my crib, cause I need to talk 'bout some serious shit, ya feel me. It's only for a minute, cause I got a lotta shit on my mind."

In the parking lot of the hospital, Vah introduced Damian and, Nubian introduced his peeps, then told everybody else who are the head bitches in charge."

Bang, bang, bang, bang!

"Oh shit," everyone ducked and ran behind cars and vans, "what the fuck, yo."

Jaia started firing her 9mm Glock, saying, "Yea, yea come on, ya fucking pussies."

Damian was shooting his gun, protecting Vah. T.Dove was blowing his shit wide, all in the parking lot. They were all jumping in their rides. Unc had been in the Jeep all along, asleep; jumped up ready like a motherfucker.

"What the fuck and who the fuck, in broad daylight would do some crazy shit like that. Yo, let's bounce, sirens on the prowl. Nobody got shot, right; it's a good thing.

Vah yelled, "It's time to dead some bitches and niggas. This is the type of shit I've been waiting for. Nigga's challenging our strength. Well, it's time to show the piper, cause I'm not paying 'em shit but, no mind.

Now everyone settled in, grabbing forty ounces outta the fridge, cause that's all up in the shit. T.Dove was rolling a blunt, especially after that drive-by stunt.

Unc's like, "So, who is it ya'll think plugged some chumped up ass nigga's to try and take us out. Not one; all of us. We are never going to be in the open like that again, all at once, ya feel me."

Vah intervened and said, "As of today, we're all going to rise in an empire of money, mayhem and murder. We all are nigga's in control to take over the whole Capital District Regional area, yo. So we have to prepare ourselves, by taking what we want. Ms. Smiley is just the beginning, my nigga's. I've been hearing shit's hectic, because of the situation with Ms. Smiley, in which T.Dove; I honor you for taking care of that bitch, true dat.

"No more slow motion on the streets; everything is all 'bout to shine something fierce. Stepping on some heads to get messages across of what we're cracka-lacki lika that, yo. Nubian, is ya ass well enough, up to fending off the enemy for battle, son? Whoever is all in the way; dies, that day.

Vah continued, "Listen up everybody, it's like this; T.L.C. supplies, you all apply, ya feel me."

T.Dove stated, "Ain't nothing and no one 'bout to shut shit down on our ladies and bread & butter, ya heard. So, let's act like, instead of the men of the house, be the man hustling in the street to eat. That's the delio yo, for real, on the strength of Jaia and 'em. We go hard as if it's our own, understand."

Damian agreed declaring, "Sure, ya know that's right. Our loyalty lies with each other."

Jaia's frowning and says, "However long ya loyalty lasts, you all will be taken care of financially. If you decide you've had enough, just don't come in my backyard. If it's gonna be a hustling thang, then I gotta go to war with ya ass, ya feel me. It's not going to be pretty if I get ya ass first."

Unc looked at the expression on each and everyone of their faces. She could tell them nigga's were ready to die for the cause, as long as they're getting paid, tearing everything outta the frame in the process."

Vah mentioned Aunya being released in a few weeks and how she is a straight up dawg, like them. They are the ones who started this shit, fo sho.

Unc felt kirida left out, as usual, when Jaia talks about herself, Vah and Aunya. She's suppose to be her boo, although she's starting to see another side of her, that's ugly.

CHAPTER TWENTY-TWO

DETECTIVE REESE IS ALL IN questioning nigga's about that bitch Smiley. He could not believe she had been hogtied like a fucking animal. The scene actually fucked his eyes up, seeing her like that. Then, to go upstairs, seeing Dolce's body sprawled out, with his asshole looking like he'd been fucked with a plumbing pipe.

'Unfucking-believable!'

He's thinking to himself, 'What in the hell is this world coming to. I guess revelation has its' course on some.'

He knew he had to let Da-Stev know the shit was so crazy. Ms. Smiley's cellie is vibrating; he picks it up,

"Hell-o, Detective Reese here."

The person on the other end hangs up. He figured it might have been someone wanting to cop, so he gave the phone to a rookie and told him to take it to the phone company to trace all calls, and have them go through it with a fine tooth comb.

"Get every call listed on it, pronto. There is much more going on here than meets the eye. Isn't that a blip."

As he giving orders to the rookie, his walkie-talkie is relaying an incident report about the Albany Med shooting.

"What the fuck is going on around here. Dam, it's an all out fuckin war zone."

Just then he remembered the name on the screen of Ms. Smiley's cellular phone. Silver Fox. He had never heard the name before, so now he will work on finding out who the fuck is that. He decided to call Da-Stev.

"Yo man, this shit is off the fucking chain. Yo, you won't believe who was hogtied, dead in front of me over on Park Avenue. I guess this is one of those stash houses. There is a safe built in the fuckin' floor, maybe this shit was a robbery, or did they just plain keep both these dead motherfucker's hostage or something, for a while."

Da-Stev yells, "Yo motherfucker, stop babbling bitch, who the fuck it is, man."

"Ms. Smiley and some black dude tied up, face down on the bed. His asshole had been fucked out something serious, DaStev. I would riot wish this shit on any man, ya heard. It's a horrible sight, boy. Whoever did this left a serious message. I am about to find out.

Yo Da-Stev, have you ever heard of the name Silver Fox, floating around anywhere we should know? Look into it for me, a'ight. The name showed up on the screen of Ms. Hogtied's cellular, so it must mean something. We just gotta figure out who, what, where they are, you know. Another thing, I am looking into who tried to kill that kid, Nubian Fields."

Detective Reese continued saying, "Wow, it's hot as a firecracker out here. It seems as though there are some pissed off people in the Capital of Albany. I gotta try and shed some light on this shit. Yeah, that kid told me that the dude that shot him looked Caucasian, like a narc. Also, there's this young lady that can I.D. him, so I need to find her before whoever tried to kill Nubian, will soon be after her ass; especially if he is one of my guys in the po-po department. I really got my fuckin' work cut out for me, up to my ass, fo sho. Captain Faulkner is really up in my ass wanting these fucking crimes solved, or somebody brought in, arrested and booked 'Dano'," they both laughed.

"So Da-Stev, do you have any idea what is going on in the streets. As a matter of fact, aren't T.L.B. ya so-called family, nigga? Why haven't ya ass been over to see Nubian? Aren't you overseeing his ass while they're out of town, man? I would have thought you'd be the first on the scene when I went of the hospital to question his ass."

Da-Stev answered boldly, "Nah, I have my own shit to worry about. That is more important than some hoodrat nigga getting shot. It's all in the game itself, when you play the part of being in charge. There's a whole bunch of consequences and mayhem. It's do or die; each man wants to be on top of their shit. I've been running here and there to Massachusetts, Jersey; trying to find a nice laid back crib, ya know. I planned on being settled man, getting up putta this dumb ass hustling, for the next motherfucker, ya feel me. Detective Reese, I just want enough to bounce; make me and mines comfortable financially. I got some stash, ohter than wasting my dough on trying to flash and shit. That is what constantly set a motherfucker back, if they're not too cautious with their monies. I am a bonafide miser yo, it's a must."

"So you been house hunting; is that right? You do not strike me as that kind of guy, Da-Stev. You seem like an all around 'I'ma get mine no matter how I get it', kinda nigga. If anybody I can remember ya ass is a sho-nuff killa from Manila man.

So, don't go trying no 'changed settled bullshit-ass coca mammie' story on me, of all people. Remember this is me you're talking To Detective Reese, ya phony motherfucker.

I got your bullshit in my pocket, as well as you having mine. We're dirty together, bitch ass nigga. I know you're up to something. It'll come to the streets as well as to light."

"You know Detective Reese, fuck you cracker; also the horse that galivanted your ass up in these streets. Fuckin' grimey ass pig. I'm glad we've finally let each other know the real deal about the way it is, on the strength. So whatever it is you trying to git at, save it bi'atch honky. We go deep in dirt motherfucker, on my undercover shit and in the process, busting your crooked ass. Now the game is being fucked up all around you, sonofabitch, and I do not need you blowing smoke up my ass, as well. So, we know where we stand, as far as our positions, right? You stay the fuck outta my way. I'm warning you only this once. I will definitely let ya fucking ass keep being crooked, and my flunkie bitch, a'ight. How 'bout that Detective Reese. You have a very incriminating day."

Da-Stev had called Detective Gadson wondering when the motherfucker was going to tell him that a bitch identified his ass from when he shot Nubian.

'Unfucking-believeable!'

Da-Stev started thinking how Detective Gadson left some important information like that. He fucked up, fo sho. He decided he needed to confront his racist ass about a job fucked up, all the way around the whole nine yards. His stupid ass had been seen, so what could he be thinking. He thinks just because he's a detective that he can't get got in Albany.

He thought to himself, 'That dumb ass isn't thinking with a full deck; he's acting off the chain. I'ma have to try and clean up his mess somehow, someway. I have to find the female who can I.D. his ass. I need to see Nubian. He can shed some light on shit, if he doesn't feel like I tried to kill his ass. The only thing I can do is try to weigh this shit out. If push comes to shove, I can just blame it on Detective Gadson. Then too, by not admitting or owning up to it, I'll take Gadson's ass out, if it has to end up being that. Whoa, that is a whole lot of killing just to make it right, but what the bureau don't know won't hurt 'em. I've been undercover for years, way before Jaffa and 'em to try and get at the Silver Fox syndicate. I had to start small time and so far so good.

He continued with his thoughts, 'Hell, I get a family to feed, what the fuck. Also, I enjoy doing this shit, it's kinda glorifying, Ole stupid ass Detective Reese has no idea which syndicate is behind Albany's little drug dealers. This is out of his league. He'll crumble in their hands. Arid, he did mention the Silver Fox, so something is about to jump off, as if someone fucked up their peeps. Dam, could Ms. Smiley have been connected. Oh shit, all this time. Wow, she kept that shit under wraps. I wonder how the detective came to know the name, other than the cellular phone. If they even have a hint Detective Reese is throwing that name around, that's his ass.

Then he thought, 'I need to get with Nubian. I'm going to try and holla at a nigga and see what type of response I'll get.'

Da-Stev dialed his cellie number, a voice answered and it was not Nubian's, but a female voice, "Hell-o, hell-o."

Da-Stev listened to her voice. He thought quick, 'this must be the bitch that I.D.'d Detective Gadson.'

First, he asked her, "Where is Nubian?"

She said, "He's in the hospital, and who are you?"

"I'm Da-Stev, his homeboy. Yo, how you got his cellie?" "Why you asking so many questions, like you po-po, nigga; instead of finding out whether ya boy is dead or not. So, this is riot customer service bitch."

Click!

Da-Stev's pissed the fuck off at that bitch.

He thought, 'It had to be the one he'd been talking to that morning, and she ran his ass over to Albany Medical Center Hospital, fo sho. She sounded like she needed to hear some reassurance for Nubian, so I can't blame her. I gotta get with Detective Gadson. Let me try his number again. He seems as though the motherfucker is ghost. Yeah, he knows he fucked up, which is why that bastard is not in my sight. If I knew any better, I believe a cop is hiding from me. Ah, ah, ain't that right! It's okay, cause Jaia and 'em gonna do his ass in once Nubian starts talking.'

He decided to call Jaia.

"Yo fam, wha up babe? You back in town or what, Ms Lady, or should I say, ladies. You were missed, that is fo sho, ya heard."

Listen up Da-Stev, don't jive time me, motherfucker. Why in the fuck did you riot call me when all this bullshit went down, man. That ain't right, nigga. You know and I know it dam sure wasn't no fun, cause me an my dawgs couldn't get none of the action. I specifically left my number to you in case any crazy shit happened, until I made the connect, motherfucker. And, you did not even bother to even holla at a bitch. Unfuckin-real. Even though my nigga's lit their asses up, huh. So, what's up with ya po-po? Did he get any of my workers or what? Nah, everything is everything, Jaia, all is good."

"Yo Da-Stev, the shooting with Nubain; do your boys have any info on that yet?"

"Jaia, I didn't call ya ass, because Nubian wanted you to trust him to handle shit, and he did like a trooper; shot and all. That nigga's real for ya'll. He ain't no joke boo, when it comes to representing. Oh, and his right hands T.Dove and Lil Kill; them two nigga's are veteran's of the streets. It's do or die, no lie. They're like fuckin bazooka ready, full force, for anything combat-able. I spoke with them before I left to handle some business in Massachusetts. I'm trying to get into real estate, you know, so I can legitimize my money by spreading it, ya feel me girl, it's only right."

"Yeah, yeah right Da-Stev, which reminds me that I need to contact my accountant, Ms. Pitcher, so she can get on the fuckin' ball making my monies legit, quick. Yeah, MC Hammer my shit, our dough gonna be rollin all up in our pockets, trust and believe dude, it's on. Oh yeah, I heard Ms. Smiley's outta commission, too. Yo, do you know who knocked her off, man. None of my peoples know. Find out from your Detective Reese for me, a'ight, Da-Stev."

"Yeah Detective Reese said the bitch was hogtied. Can you believe that, and acid had been thrown in her eyes. That's some shit. She suffered. He said she was held hostage for some time. It fucked me up how he described her death. Not that I give a fuck. It's as if someone's trying to let nigga's know if she got, got; so can everybody in her stable. It's a lot behind this whole situation, other than you guys. Oh yeah, ya'll need to watch ya back, too, okay. The game just got uglier, until you all set shit straight the way you like it, ya feel me, Jaia. I am here with anything you need, ma. Yo, you ever heard the name Silver Fox? It's a very powerful name, dealing in drugs in the capitol area, so be alert. Once you enhance your empire, it's no turning back. It's about the 'I don't give a fuck, get paid, kill 'em, get 'em outta the.

Jaia felt there was something Da-Stev is not telling her. He seems edgy and kinda withdrawn, so she felt since that is his persona now, it's time to keep an eye on his ass with all the shit that popped off. You can't trust anybody when it's time to make moves on millions. That is me and my dawgs' goal. It's funny Da-Stev did riot know who killed Ms. Smiley. He's usually up on everything in the hood. It's odd to her, his riot knowing, being he is the one who turned them on to the grimey bitch. Sooner or later, it'll come to light and that's when I protect my nigga T.Dove."

She asked Da-Stev if by any chance they can hook up, and if he will find out the arrangements for Ms. Smiley's funeral, in the hood. Arid, to holla at a bitch, so she can pay her respects to Ms. Smiley for putting them on to making money and for dying before she killed her, her motherfucking self, fo sho."

"Yo Da-Stev, I gotta go, boyee. Oh yeah, Vah and 'em said hi. We got our work cut out for us, ya feel me. One love, nigga. Holla back, when ya find out that info I asked about, alright."

Da-Stev hurried up and called Detective Gadson to let him know he had spoke with the female who'd seen him, which Detective Reese told him those were Nubian's exact words.

Gadson's phone was ringing, "Yo, Gadson here," he answers.

Da-Stev yells, "Man, where the fuck have you been, white boy. I been trying to track your ass for a day and a half. Yo, so you decide to be outta sight, huh? Don't tell me ya ass is on some ole running scared shit. Nah, I don't wanna hear no dumb ass motherfucking shit like that."

Da-Stev went on to explain the situation about what Detective Reese relayed to him and the phone call to Nubian's cellie with the female answering, who can I.D. his ass.

Detective Gadson got all excited. He knew he had to kill that bitch, fo sho, now that he's thinking clearly. He remembered that the car Nubian was leaning on was a Silver Lexus. It won't be hard to find in the hood, which is where he'd start looking. Maybe ask some questions pertaining to the shooting in the area.

He then said to Da-Stev, "So, how do you want to handle this, man. Let me know something, dude. I'm all in for whatever I got to do to clean this shit up before any and every thing gets outta control and out of reach. I mean now, A.S.A.P.!"

"yo, you fuckin ain't right. Ya ass is going to clean this fuckin mess up especially with me having summin' to do with the fine fuckin mess you made. Dam boyee, first job ya fucked up. Some crooked ass detective you turned out to be. Can't even kill a motherfucker right. Yo, it's been how long you been on this job? How many motherfuckers have ya ass killed legally? Maybe that's why you fucked up illegally. I guess the law agrees with your so-called crookedness, huh? Or it's waiting for you to hang your dam self. Hell, you're halfway there any ole fucking way, at the way you pulled this wack job, Detective Gadson."

CHAPTER TWENTY-THREE

JAIA, VAH AND UNC COULD riot believe most of the shit.

Nubian and T.Dove were telling them that happened since they were gone.

Vah's like, "Un-fucking-believeable."

Unc said, "This shit is like a fucking movie. T.Dove you have done some treacherous torturing my man, but I like it very much."

Jaia kept giving him his props, fo sho. She felt she had to organize shit to the fullest keeping them protected. Now she truly is out to kill, no if's and's or but's. She informed T.Dove he'd have to take over L&O and Judson, First & lex drop-off, pick-up.

"Not the same time every day. I'll beep the spot that needs to re-up. One will come out to get the re-up and the other will go get the money. When the one that gets the re-up is on the way back, the other will wait at the corner for the one that did the pick-up to come outta the building. Got it? It's a go for spots, ya feel me. Everything is in order as planned. Listen up, everybody is on point. There's seven of us. We need to stay connected and in contact as much as possible."

If we feel anything is strange or bad vibes or somthing ain't right, like being followed then we'll know shit is getting ready to hit the fan fo sho, ya'll. It's on and we have to be on point like and all points bulletin, ya heard. Another tharig do not, repeat, do riot trust anybody outside this circle we've just built, understand fam? Yeah that's us fam. Now Nubian, who is the bitch that answered your cellular nigga, told me you were in the hospital."

Nubian being honest said, "I do riot know her at all except that she saved my life, because I would have bled to death. If she had riot rushed me to the hospital. After she took off the first time she heard the shots and returned to drop me off at the hospital emergency entrance. That is all I remember of her, rio name, no shit. Yeah though, she sho nuff is in love with her woman. She made that loud and clear before I got shot. She dam sho gorgeous. Why is it that all the good looking women like rubbing pussies, man. That is some shit."

Vah said to Nubian, "Yo nigga, respect my lifestyle. If it bothers you get the fuck outta here 111 nigga. Go find that hood rat bitch you were laying up with when a lesbian sistah saved ya black ass, boy. Oh by the way, you should be thanking her trying to eat her pussy, but you don't know nothing 'bout that. Your a stick and move guy, huh?"

Everybody started laughing.

Nubian shot back, "A'ight you got that, I'm good. Ya right 'bout my life being saved. I need to try and get at her, fo sho. Yo Lil Kill, let me hold ya cellie man."

Nubian dialed his own cellie number. Voice mail. He smiled.

"Dam, my voice mail sounds nice."

He left a message.

"This is Nubian. Can you please call me at this number, A.S.A.P. I would like to thank you for saving my life. Please, it'll mean a whole lot to me, ya feel me. It's important to me."

The voice mail clicked off.

Vah said to Damian, "Yo my nig, you'll cover my spots up at the courtyard on Morton Ave. The whole area is ours, ya feel me." Lil Kill and Nubian, you two and some of your troops know these areas like the crack of ya asses, so you all will oversee the drop off, pick up at your own discretion. Only you and your troops will know among one another, who'is who a'ight. NO everybody in rio stash house at the same time. Always have someone outside looking, lurking fo sho, Definitely know whats going on at all times. Even some fiends - hit them off. They're our ears to the streets."

Unc said, "There is one thing. I'd hope no one subjects themselves to beating up on fiends. That's a no-no in our areas. They keep money flowing. Another thing, no tricks to suck ya dicks on our time, understand. Yo, let ya workers know, no slip ups - personally I'ma kill that ass for real. All we got for now is money on the mind, and the mind on the money."

T.Dove spoke up about the drive-by, "That shit seemed kinda weird, as if they were directed at my riigga Nubian. What's up with that? Who wants ya ass that fuckiri bad, out for the count, especially on hospital grounds! They wanted to send you to the morgue, boy? Did you fuck a virgin and her daddy is a drug lord or something? Shit, ya ass is hot, nigga."

Nubian answered, "Dam it's been so much killing going on since Ms. Smiley. Who started that dumb ass shit by getting greedy. So, her man and 'em are still retaliating until them motherfuckers think they're gonna kill us all. It ain't going down like that, not by me, understand? I'ma start blasting nigga's as I see 'em on the streets. Get 'em before they get me. Sooner or later those chump ass nigga's will get enough after seeing their peeps dying faster than a bullet. Hell, they might just wanna sling some shit for us."

Jaia interjected, "Nah nigga, that where ya wrong now fool. If ya believe for one second any of them motherfuckers ain't thinking bout blowing one of our heads off if they can get close to us. Nigga please, now I know ya ass on some ole Mister Rogers shit. That shit sound fuckin crazy Nubian. And, you don't think they'll want revenge, nigga. They been with that bitch Smiley for years. Whoever they believe killed her is going to feel their wrath. Number one, her boys feel ya taking food from their mouths, the whole sha-bang. This is a job on the real, whether society wants to accept it or not.. If they legalize it maybe it would and just be grounded in a different format."

Vah shot back saying, "Yo, hold the fuck up with your 'so I'm for the economy' bullshit speech."

Everybody laughed and Jaia was on some attitude shit now after what Vah said to her.

She just said, "A'ight you got that, Vah."

So Vah pulls Nubian to the side and asks him if Damian could bunk with him for a minute.

Nubian agrees.

"He's gonna look out for ya ass until shit calms the fuck down in the streets, ya feel me."

Everybody dispersed for Nubian's crib and went on to handle business. Jaia and Vah went on to cool down their thinking and get to drinking. As they entered the bar, J.Quan was sitting at the bar. He just stared at them going to the back to sit at a table.

He got up from the bar, went over to their table and politely said, "Yo Jaia, there is word in the streets that the bitch Ms. Smiley is affiliated with some organization with a bitch in charge named Silver Fox. By killing Ms. Smiley you and your peoples signed a death warrant, ya heard. So a lotta nigga's wanna get at ya'11. At the same time, although that is out there, they actually know you guys were in the city making a new connect when she disappeared."

He left it at that and walked away from the table.

Vah looked up toward the bar and saw T.Dove sitting pretty talking to the bartender named Brenda. He is a funny motherfucker telling her 'yo momma' jokes. She definitely was enjoying his company, but still does not trust the motherfucker as far as she can see him, but at the same time there is a true loyalty about his blackass, fo sho.

They sat at the table thinking 'oh shit.'

"This here situation is all the way live ya'11, now we been put on," states Jaia, "it's time we start asking motherfuckers as we kill 'em in Ms. Smiley's crew, 'who the fuck is a got dam Silver Fox, a dude or a woman, yo?' We need to get on this wagon, if not I feel a fucking war and we're going to be sitting bulls, yo. It's crunk up time."

Unc told Jaia, "Boo, we've distributed our business at hand. All we can do is wait out our opponents. They'll come around sooner than we think ma, a'ight. It's all in the hustling we happen to come across a bitch deeper in it than we realized, ya feel me, Love. It's gonna be fine, usually this type of chaos dies down, fo sho."

Jaia responded, "I wonder where that crooked ass fucking Detective Reese is during all this time. Is he on our payroll anymore of what, or did Da-Stev give us a one shot deal, dealing with him. Let's find out our got dam selves a'ight, cause that money we funded him should've went a long way, even if he is a gambler. Listen up, we have to start making some serious moves as far as knowing our surroundings, especially if we are going to take the capitol of New York by storm."

"Yo Vah, who was that chick we met that work over in the legislative department. We've met quite a few people here in Albany along our journey." She's just someone we had drinks with when we were down in the city at the club. She said she worked up here. Anyway Unc, what is it you think she can help us out with? She could patch us into some things going on here in Albany that maybe could be of use. And Vah, she had kind of a crush on you, dawg."

"Oh hell nah, not when I just got me a wonderful bitch in my life. Have you lost ya fuckin' mind Unc."

"Well Unc ain't doing no shit like that, not with me being in Albany at the same time. I don't think so. Check this all is fair, let's just kidnap this bitch, see if she knows or has heard anything about a Silver Fox, plain and simple bitches, a'ight." Vah you set the shit up. I'll take it from there just torturing her per-say."

"Yo Vah, we have to check in with our accountant, Ms. Louise Pitcher. I was meaning to do that two days ago. You should also be interested in checking on your shit, Unc and Vah. Maybe we should send Ms. Pitcher and appreciation gift or a thank you, one, whichever; she'll still be getting paid in full. I kinda like her myself. She handles money in a delicate manner and keeps us up to date and on time with our scheduling and our drops to the bank. Maybe we should take her out for drinks one night or buy her some tickets to a game or show.'!

'Unc, don't you know that white nigga that works the Palace Theatre ticket office? As a matter of fact, let's get us all some tickets to see a concert there. How 'bout Usher?

Yea, oh shit let's do this. Vah call Ms. Pitcher boo, so she can hang with T.L.B. Show her a beautiful time. Come on we got things to do like head to the mall, Crossgates and get some gear ya'11. One more drink, them we outtie. True dat. Vah did you tell your accountant to meet us at the mall? We're treating her to the whole nite out. Boo—ya—ya!"

Jaia ya ass is fuckin' crazy bitch. You feeling yourself. Yo we gonna drop my baby car over on Main Street. Oh shit, Labu ya'n, we gotta get her too, fools. Ohh ohh wee, we gonna have a ladies night out even if ya ass is a butch, aggressive; we're all women hoes, ya feel me."

They arrived at the Main Street apartment to pick up Labu on their way to the mall. They were riding high in Jaia's navy blue Navigator, all pretty, sexy looking women.

Jaia went up to ring the bell. Labu let her in, then everyone else followed. They all introduced themselves to Labu, letting her know they are all family and that Aunya's peoples is their peoples. They wanted Labu to feel comfortable in the presence of them. Vah went to the living room and turned on the stereo she had picked out when they all used to share the apartment way back when. It was nice to know that someone else was enjoying the luxury she started with her dawgs.

"Yo Jaia, come here."

Vah called to her in the living room.

"Remember this jam, boo. We all used to fuck shit up in here dancin' all crazy. Yo Unc, watch this. I'ma put it on Jaia."

Vah started dancing all funny, everybody was laughing. There was a phone on the stereo shelf just a ringing. Jaia looked at it and thought,

"Wow, that's strange, it looks like Nubian's cellie." She turned to look on the end tables and saw a pink cellular phone.

"Whoa, why two phones. This bitch better not be cheating on my dawg or I'll bat the holy shit ouuta her ass."

As Labu's talking and funning with Vah and Unc, Jaia's carefully listening to her voice. The cellie is still ringing next to the stereo.

She informed Labu,

"Yo La, yo La, ya cellie is dam sure ringing off the chain here next to the stereo."

Labu said, "Jaia answer it, we family boo. It's all good.

As Labu realized the phone Jaia was getting ready to answer was Nubian's she wanted to change her mind quick, but it was too late.

Jaia answers, "Yell—o".

No on answered.

CHAPTER TWENTY-FOUR

NATALIE HAD LEFT MS. SMILEY to her death. She knew that the guy torturing that dude in his ass would definitely kill her no doubt. Now she needed to figure out what to do with the drugs she took from the stash house. She knew if Ms. Smiley talked the dude would be looking for her soon. He'll be wanting his shit back. She rode around Albany all through the hood. She was hoping to see somebody she knew so she could get rid of the cocaine. That's what she really needed to do, fo sho.

As she rode down Lark Street faces started to look familiar. She couldn't remember of they were customers or nigga's that had to be taken out or killed. Most likely that is what it was, her doing what she does best; killin' a motherfucker for a living, since she'd been introduced to guns.

Natalie thought, 'It would be real nice to see Jaia and 'em right about now. Maybe they'd take this fuckin' cocaine off my hands. I feel kinda nervous ridin' around with this stuff in my Jeep. So, it's time to take my ass back to Selkirk. Tomorrow's another day.

A few days passed with all the bullshit that happened. Natalie ended up going to Ms. Smiley's funeral, held at Garland's Funeral Home on Clinton Ave. Everybody in the hood that was somebody attended. The place was packed. All kinds of cars lined the Avenue. Crackheads and fiends stood outside waiting for some drug dealers to disperse, so they could cop a hit. Adrianne, the hoe from Swan Street was boasting about how long she knew Ms. Smiley. She was saying good things to the others that used to cop from Ms. Smiley when she was a street hustler.

Jaia's crew passed through the services to pay their respects. They got dirty stares from the other drug dealers representing. If all could pull out their guns and blow Jaia and em's heads off they would, right in the funeral home. Every nigga in the place had mad hate. They knew how ruthless T.L.C. had been in their days, so it's a fo sho showdown if anyone dared jump off on one shot on them bitches, which they knew better with ole crazy ass T.Dove dressed to impress to shoot off his guns on command. As Damian stood by just in case. No one knew who he was, but they knew his ass is a NYC nigga, always at attention for T.L.C. All eyes watched as T.L.C. viewed the body and kept it moving. Jaia dressed in her nice Dior black dress with her black Jimmy Choo's, and Vah and Unc had on nice Armani suits with Stacy Adams gator shoes, ready for anything. It was like a fashion show as far as they were concerned.

Jaia stated, "These half ass country bumpkin motherfuckers. They're corny as swine. Yo, let's bounce."

It was one hell of a feeling walking in there and coming out alive," Unc commented, "did you see them motherfuckers all up in there wanted us dead as a door knob. Ain't that some shit not really knowing who the fuck killed her grimey ass. Hell, whoever it was beat me to the punch."

"I do not give a flying fuck, money is money; the bitch got greedy as hell, plus whoever held her hostage, isn't that something," stated Jaia.

Jaia caught Natalie's stare and hollered her name, "Yo Nat, what it is girl?"

"Ain't nothing, business as usual."

"Yeah, she was a good client in my book, that's why I'm here, ya know."

"So what's been up with you, Jaia. Ya need anything girl? Let me know. Listen I need to talk with you when you get some time. You and your crew. A'ight, it's all good." Jaia looked at Natalie, "Whoa, now that bitch is money twenty-four—seven. She is definitely a soldier for a white bitch. I like her alot. I could use someone like her in our stable of mayhem, cause that's all it's going to end up being anyway."

* * *

Detective Reese was scoping out the people entering and leaving the funeral home, paying their respects to Ms. Smiley, like she's some fucking martyr. The bitch is a drug dealer for godsake.

'Isn't this shit ass backwards,' he thought to himself.

He thought that all the little street hustler's he busted in his days, more that he cared to remember. He spotted a beautiful woman. She had to be Dominican, he thought. She was talking to this Caucasian female who also was gorgeous. He wondered who they were. It came to him that it could be Jaia and 'em, but then again Da-Stev never described them to him, so he'd have to guess on this one.

"Go figure."

There were so many females that were in trios, it fucked him up. Little did he know he was partially right. It was Jaia talking with Natalie. He knew he needed to get with Jaia. If only he knew how she and her crew looked.

He remembered he had his camera in the trunk, so he went to get it. He dam sure was gonna take pictures and then ask Da-Stev who is who. Right then he saw Da-Stev exiting the funeral parlor. He quickly cellied him.

Da-Stev was busy trying to get the fuck outta there. There was too much tension going on and if something jumped off he didn't feel like being in the mix of it all. He just wanted to pay his respects. He glanced over to see a couple of new faces in the crowd and wondered who they were. It would only be a matter of time and he'd find out and hoped the connection would lead him back to the Silverfox.

Da-Stev answered his cellie, "Yo, what up, it's me Reese. Listen I need a description of Jaia and 'em, man. I do not even know how them bitches look."

He told Detective Reese, "You see the Dominican and Caucasian females huddled conversing. The Dominican is Jaia. When she steps off you'll see her entourage follow. Listen I do not want to describe at any time, fucking prisoners over the cellie, ya feel me. Check me later, a'ight. It's too crowded."

As soon as Da-Stev hung up, Vah stepped over to Da-Stev.

"Yo son, what's cracka-lackin. It's sure a publicized funeral, huh? I guess the capitol truly liked this Smiley character. She had shit on lock, fo sho. Nigga's in the hood respected her wack ass hustle. Can you really believe that shit, son? What I do not understand is how she ended up hostage. I don't get it at all, and who, for what and why, other than our little mishap; which we did not have anything to do with at all, ya feel me. So these dudes all up in this funeral can think what the fuck they choose to cause me and my dawgs are ready for whatever these nigga's wanna come our way with. We'll just have to start busting caps all in motherfuckers domes."

"Dam Vah ya'll are some treacherous bitches. You at Smiley's fuckin funeral, yo. You know me and her go way back. She's a trooper, no matter, whatever took place; it's all in the hustling. It looks as if you and your Lesbian Hustler's crew are taking over from where she left off, huh? I'll tell you summin though, ya'll have a lot of bridges to cross coming up in Albany thinking you're gonna take ove just like that. You know there's others to see, confront and answer to than just Ms. Smiley. Ya'll getting ready to find out. It's not as easy as you think. But don't sweat it. Whatever my boy Detective Reese gets run by him down at the station, he'll let me know. Then I'll let you know, a'ight Vah. Oh yeah, I forgot to mention that there was some money and drugs that were taken from the stash houses too. There was a safe built in the floor. It definitely had all the drugs and money in it. The forensics results told a lot because of all the residue of chemicals inside the safe."

"Excuse me a minute Da-Stev. Yo Jaia, Unc can you please come over here for a minute"

As they approached and gathered around Da-Stev, Vah asked him what the situation is with Detective Reese.

Is he still on the our side or what? I sure do not recall you informing us of anything during the whole duration of mayhem. You have been slacking up nigga. So what is wrong with this picture, Da-Stev?"

Jaia yells, "I know you ain't still waiting on fucking me at the hotel, as in three years ago dude. I thought we were better than that. We accumulated a family status."

Da-Stev's like, "Whoa, whoa, whoa, wait the fuck up ladies, it's not that complicated or deep. Dam, chill the fuck out, stop jumping the gun, yo; let a nigga breathe some answers to ya fuckin' questions, a'ight. As for Detective Reese, he's been chillin'. His captain has been digging in his ass deep about all this shit that's been going down in his area. He wants some answers to solving these murders that have reeked the streets. Hell, bodies been turning up all over, ya feel me. But, we good as far as he's concerned; ain't nothing poppin' that he won't be stoppin', yo. Oh and bout that fuck Jaia, i want you to end up begging me for some of this good dick in the long run. Until then, it's all good, ya heard family."

"Yeah, a'ight," Jaia responded and smiled.

Unc asks Da-Stev, "Yo, wha up with this Silver Fox person? Are we supposed to be aware or summin'? Yo, keep us on that. I think there is more to the moral of this story of Ms. Smiley."

"Yeah, so we're finding our, huh?"

"So we better be expecting unwanted company in our area take us out of commission, man. What are we trying to get to or what's all this bullshit inconspicuous fucking lollygagging for; the fucking birds, yo. Let's do what we gotta do$_{t}$ all to get our grind on. Fuck everything else."

Nubian ended up driving by the funeral home. As he got closer to where everyone was standing around conversing; he knew it was bullshit if it was pertaining to Ms. Smiley. As he passed by he saw Jaia & 'em talking to Da-Stev. If looks could kill that nigga Da-Stev would've blew up literally, like a bomb.

He snapped out of his trance when he heard Jaia calling him over. He stopped.

"Yo Jaia, wha up?"

Yo, Da-Stev got some good info for us as far as the streets listening or people talkin'. It's all good I suppose, huh! I'll get back to ya later, Nubian. We all are going to eat at this nice restaurant called Thatcher's. It's a cozy, quiet joint, ya know."

Jaia's mentioning of food drew Unc's full attention.

"A'ight let's roll yall., it's getting our eat on right about now. Right, boo?"

They all jumped in their rides and headed up Lark Street straight toward the restaurant, passing L&O, music banging playing Mary J. Bilge's '411', nigga's checkin' them out flossing. Jaia was hollering out the lyrics while Unc was playing with her nipples and fondling her pussy. Jaia was loving every touch of Unc and smiling.

She said to Unc, "I love you Unc, baby. We are going to rise up together fo sho, in style and class even if it means a massacre to get there, ya feel me babe."

"Yes love, I am feeling all of you as much, Jaia. You are my ride or die love of my life, boo. It's a heart of stone for you, Jaia."

Vah was riding behind them with Damian riding shotgun. T.Dove was riding in the back and asking Vah if she knew whose peeps were in the front pew at the church.

Vah said, "I really do not know. I never knew whether of not Ms. Smiley had family or what. If so she kept it private. It's a good thing in this hustling game. I have to say Ms. Smiley was a fine ass broad, fo sho. She had some nice fucking lips."

Damian responded, "You gotta be kidding me, Vah. The bitch has passed on and you're talking 'bout her fucking body parts. Well, did she ever make you think she'd give a broad a chance?"

"Nah," Vah said, "but she was alright on the real tip."

T.Dove interjected, "Hell, I could've got me some head if I'da known she had some sweet lips as ya said, Vah. I missed out, huh?"

"Yeah motherfucker, when it comes to you nigga; yes she'll wish she were dead for real T.Dove fuckin' with a mean ass dick the bruiser like ya self."

"So she is lucky. Yeah, how 'bout that Damian?"

They all laughed their asses off.

Vah popped a CD in the player. It sounded awesome. It was the new joint by Patti Labelle. They all got into it. Vah was thinking about Seasonn and what she was doing, if she was missing her of what and should she call her and tell her she wants to go up to see her for a little while. Then she thought about Seasonn having a business to take care of and decide to call her later on that night.

"Yo Vah to earth, Vah to earth," Damian kept saying so she would drive because the light had changed.

"Yo Vah, wha up with you in a zone and shit nigga, ya ass missing ya boo, huh? It be's like that Vah and especially in distance. It's a killa yo, trust me. I know from my time in Sing—Sing; my shorty out here with my seed. It's a terrible felling yo, right?"

T.Dove replied, "Yeah nigga, I lost a lot of family and peoples yo, fuckin' in jail doing all that time. Nubian's the only nigga that kept it real all of our lives. I am in debt to him seriously. I'll die for my nigga Nubian in a heartbeat, ya feel me. He stuck by me for years doing my bid like a trooper. I owe him big time."

"Alright the reminiscing shit is over rover. It's time to fill up our guts, then hit them streets for info on this Silver Fox son of a bitch. Plus we are going to need to re-up soon, so we'll be talking to Jaia's Uncle Tito, or shall I say Jaia. Look at them two nasty bitches all up on each other, thinking nobody can see them through the tinted windows. Them fucking freakazoids. They never get enough of each other."

Vah kept going on about her dawgs.

"Now watch how they look at us after fucking and sticking fingers all up in a bitch. They funny."

"Ha ha ha," Damian and Vah laughed and T.Dove holding his dick laughing.

CHAPTER TWENTY-FIVE

DETECTIVE GADSON WAS TRYING TO figure out a plan to try to kill Nubian, again. His mind is all fucked up over this shit. He needs to chill seriously or fuck up royally are his intentions. He never thought for one second he actually missed shooting Nubians' ass and killing him. So now his ego is getting the best of him.

He said, "Fuck it!"

He jumped in his pick up truck, a blue Ford 4WD, nice and big. He drove on over to where Nubian lives on First & Swan. He's waiting until he sees someone come out, then he'll just start blasting his ass away. Detective Gadson felt some type of way over his fucking up, until he recalled that they all keep a close guard on Nubian. He decided he's wait anyway listening to his soft rock radio station shaking his head to Nickelback's latest song. He went into a deep zone remembering his wife when she was alive. Her name was Lauandrea. She was the love of his life. He hasn't been right since her death. He thanks God they have a Beautiful daughter who looks exactly like her mother. She has his arrogant, conceited ways and it eats his ass up. Lauandrea was Asian and had long jet black hair, beautiful hazel eyes and a body to die for. Her familiar looks are of The Black Widow, champion female pool player. Detective Gadson could still not sometimes believe she is dead and gone. As a father he has done an excellent job with his daughter Andrea. She's in St. Rose College getting good grades so he is as proud as can be.

All of a sudden a loud bang, bang, bang sounded and all these guys in cars came flying up the street shooting at Nubian's house. He was parked across the way and sunk down in his truck so he's not seen. He couldn't believe this shit was happening. It took only a second to actually get his bearings together. The fucking street was hotter than a firecracker and he wasn't about to jump out of his truck talking about 'hold your fire I'm a detective from Albany Police Depatment, Homicide.'

He thought to himself out loud, "Fuck that, they'll never blow my fucking head off."

He got a good look at, at least three dudes is a black Audi.

They all were saying, "Let's blow this fucking house to shreds, ya'11. That's an order. We have to take these nigga's out for the count, fo sho. Whoever comes out of that house right now. Kill 'em."

One of the Puerto Rican dudes said, "Any and everybody, a'ight. Yo, this motherfucker is a piece of dead meat."

They started pouring gasoline all around the house, but nobody ever came out so they decided to smoke 'em out. Detective Gadson just sat watching the whole scene play itself out.

'Whoa,' he thought, 'what the fuck just happened."

He started his truck up and got the fuck up outta there. He did not even bother to report it. He wished he could've been down with the Puerto Rican dudes, but he knew he would've stuck out like a sore thumb. He drove toward Clinton Avenue and Swan and decided to head up to Central Avenue to the Chinese place, next to the check cashing joint. He liked their General Sal's chicken. In the meantime he called Da—Stev.

"Yo, wha up; talk to me."

"Gadson here. I got some information that'll make you smile. Check this out, meet me at H.J.B. Washington Park entrance off of Henry Johnson Blvd., O.K. Right now. I'm in the Chinese restaurant. Fifteen minutes tops, Da—Stev. Out."

Da—Stev 's mind was racing at what Gadson needs to tell him so he left quick fast in his Denali and headed toward Central Avenue. He crossed over to Western Avenue and parked his Denali, then walked the rest of the way. Detective Gadson was sitting there eating his food. He offers some to Da—Stev and he declines.

He tells Gadson, "Yo c'mon with the story, man. I rushed over to hear about what you got to tell me. Do not keep me waiting until ya ass finish eating ya fucking food. You gotta be fucking kidding me. I'll walk the hell up outta here so_get to talkin' white boy."

Da-Stev paused for a moment waiting.

"Dam, come on Gadson," he shouted impatiently.

Detective Gadson explained why he went over by Nubian's in the first place.

Da-Stev yelled, "Listen white boy, leave that Nubian situation alone motherfucker because if Jaia and 'em catch ya ass they'll torture the truth outta ya ass before any shit like that jumps off. I swear I'll kill ya fuckin' ass first, bitch. Now you done fucked up my status messing with ya so-called wanna be po-po ass. I'ma say this once man, leave that issue alone. It's a done topic, yo. Somebody else is gunning for Nubian's ass. Our plot has thickened. We don't need to dirty our hands anymore man, so leave it alone. Wow, so you mean to tell me they actually burned the house up, seriously. Whoever it was wanted Nubian's ass bad. Was there anybody inside that you know of. Did anybody get killed or what Gadson?"

"Nah, I do not know to be honest. I was in a zone thinking about Lauandrea, my wife. She's deceased. Then these Puerto Rican guys in a black Audi came and you know the rest, Da-Stev. It happened so fast, man."

As they sat in the park they saw the fire trucks and police headed toward Nubian's.

"Well, if anyone is dead; we will hear about it soon," stated Da-Stev.

Da-Stev's cellie vibrated, he picked it up.

"Holla at ya boy."

It was Detective Reese informing him of the incident over at the house where Nubian lives.

"They have found a body. So they are going to need somebody to go ID it at the morgue."

Da-Stev was shocked and feeling relieved hoping it's Nubian.

He went to the morgue and when he saw the body he could not identify the body because it was so crisp. He relayed this to Detective Reese and told him whoever it is has a bullet wound in his chest, so it's hard to tell. He told him he'd get back to him as soon as they clear shit up, and for Da-Stev to let Jaia know what is going down. Then he told him what he thought about the situation.

"Dam, somebody wants this Nubian fella dead bad. Do you have any idea what is up with this cat man, cause now his house is burnt. I mean burnt, dammit!"

"Yo detective Reese thanks for the information, I'll let Jaia and 'em know pronto, ya feel me. They're going to cease a whole bunch of shit in the hood. It's going to be on and poppin' now. I guess nigga's is coming outta the woodwork. Ya think it's a hit on this kid or what. Maybe it's some of Smiley's people retaliating about what went down with her death. You know she definitely was a connected sistah, so maybe it's her peeps. Well, we'll find out along with everyone else tryin' to get at him."

"Da-Stev, so you know something I don't and need to spit it out? Is it this Silver Fox person? I'ma find the fuck out, you'll see; then I'll have something for the captain to get off my dick about, huh? So I gotta go until next time. Be safe Da-Stev, these streets are looking for bodies to cover 'em. Oh and Da-Stev, let Jaia know that someone is gunning fore her boy, a'ight and tell her I informed you, man. This way they'll know I am true to the game, ya feel me yo. I'm out."

After speaking with Detective Reese, which actually confirmed Detective Gadsons' story; Da-Stev's mind was racing a mile a minute. He was wondering what the fuck was really going on. He needed to find out, even about who the Puerto Rican dude is that's hunting Nubian. The shit sounds fucking wack.

Detective Gadson was relieved at the fact someone else was finishing what he tried to accomplish as far as killing Nubian. He recalled what the guy said while shooting into the house.

"Yeah motherfucker, it's a pay back for the nigga's who tryin, to get paid by death. Well, here's to yours, bitch ass." Detective Reese just happened to drive through the park headed over toward Madison. With just a glance, he saw both Da-Stev and Detective Gadson sitting on the bench by the statues at the entrance on Henry Johnson Blvd. He could not believe his eyes, but he dam sure knew on thing; that them two motherfuckers were up to something; which he was about to find out.

Then he thought, Oh yeah, Nubian said that it might've been a narc that shot him."

As he stared at them conversing their facial expressions projected the conversation was intense. He should've gotten binoculars so he could read their every expression. Next time he will because he knew there will be a next time. He decided he is going to stay on these cats like white on rice because they are devious. They will be under surveillance because one of them has gotta go.

"I'll go to Jaia and 'em my dam self and put them on to those two or have them play against each other once I stumble on their plan. By the looks of their body cues these boys are serious."

As he drove on through, not once was he noticed or recognized.

"It's a beautiful day in the neigborhood," he thought.

He knew when he called Da-Stev to tell him the incident that Detective Gadson must've been right at Nubians' house.

"For some reason I'm feeling there's a connection with all of them. It's not a pretty one. I need to get with Jaia and 'em. Something is not right when it comes to those two congregating. It's hazardous to the health of whoever is in their plan. It could only be one thing and that is death. Just knowing them two, it's all it's about; even though they've been acquainted for a while. They are dirtier than money itself. I'ma take my ass to the station and do a little paper work to figure out what the fuck is going on with Da-Stev and Detective Gadson."

As Detective Reese turned toward Madison and Lark he saw Marsha the prostitute. He beeped his horn and yelled, "Yo you, hey lady, yeah you, yo come over here."

As he double parked, she walked toward the car.

She's like, "Yeah well, what the fuck can I do for another po-po. What is it with you guys, your wives ain't sexing ya'll asses right or the Mrs. ain't into sucking ya'lls dicks? Oh no, the Mrs. won't let hir dick her ass up, ha ha ha. That's a good one, huh?"

Reese retorted, "Shut up bitch and listen, alright? I'ma ask ya a coupla questions being that I usually see you all around selling your ass. Now I know your ears stay listening to the streets talking so what is the word on the street, Lady. And, why did you say for another po-po?"

Marsha began to tell Detective Reese about the trick that she picked up on Clinton Avenue a couple of weeks ago. She told him how he was talking in riddles and shit about shooting his guns off twice in one morning. She described the cop even down to the strawberry on his dick.

Detective Reese looked at Marsha and started laughing his ass off.

He told her, "Yo Lady, you are a funny bitch. Ya know I bet you make a motherfucker holla for a dollar, fo sho. You are alright by me. So now listen up, me and you never has this conversation. Right, Lady?"

Marsha said to Detective Reese, "Nah, unless you paying me for my time you just took up for your own personal use; you know one hand washes the other, Mr. Policeman. So what do you do for me.?"

Detective Reese was looking at Marsha like, 'bitch if you do not get ya hoeing ass up outta this car, I'ma wash your ass up in the street by dragging you a mile a minute.

He said, "Lady I'll owe ya one. O.K. You have my word on that. I'm good for it fo sho."

Detective Reese thought long and hard about what Marsha said to him. She had described Detective Gadson to the tee. Now he needed to find out why and what the fuck he has gotten into with Da-Stev concerning Nubian. Why would they want him dead. He knew some serious bullshit was going on and fucking Gadson thinks he's gonna come into this town and start killing up the peeps that are feeding his gambling debts. He was thinking are these dumb motherfuckers stupid or what. It is his fucking area so Da-stev must want to start a war. He began thinking about letting Detective Gadson know that the nigga Da-Stev is undercover because then he would definitely kill DaStev without a doubt. He thought long and hard about putting them two at each other's throats knowing they're scheming behind his back. He decided to start a file on both of them. He knew he had to because when the tough get going he'll have something to work with.

He would have some insurance to work with as the plot thickens. He liked the idea of inquiring and finding out what they are in to. He had his own ideas already and figured that Da-Stev is behind all the shit with Nubian. Da-Stev is the one who put the hit on Nubian through Detective Gadson which fell through. So he knew now they had to be planning on something else, unless the information he had just fed Da-Stev concerning the incident over on First Street, they think the problem has been solved and think Nubian is dead. If it is him he knows he's got both of them cocksuckers right where he wants them.

He knew he needs to get at Jaia and 'em with his thoughts. He first had to get some proof. He had to get to the woman who took Nubian to the emergency room. He would track her ass down because she is his proof. He had to get to her first before those two kill her ass. He had to get on his feet solving this shit. He hoped he could make it to her on time. First he had to get to Nubian's stubborn ass to see if he'd listen to what he has to say with his bitch *ass.* He knew he would once he laid the information he has on his dumb ass. He would have no choice with his sorry ass life and he'll be thanking him along with Jaia and 'em. He decided to try and ease up on them. Also, he had to find out if it was his ass burned in his house.

CHAPTER TWENTY-SIX

Vah and Jaia and Unc decided to ride by their spots to check on the workers with their 9mm Tech 9 on their sides. They went over to the courtyard first being that it's on the first hood stop coming from the crib Unc rented in Mt. Hope, over on Chestnut Road.

"Them bitches are serious as a motherfucker; no shorts on cash or nothing. All the shit with Ms. Smiley, they have to come at nigga's hard."

As they entered the coutyard a couple of Unc's boys approached them.

"Yo Unc, what's good? I heard 'bout all that dumb shit but we still on our shine over here for ya. True dat, ya feel me.

"Yo who that," one of the dude's yelled to the dude talking to Unc.

Unc said to Rahmel, "He with you? If he is, that nigga better respect yo, or his young ass is got with the swiftness."

He said to his boy, "Yo son lay back, these are our peeps running this empire, yo."

He said, "Unc this is my nigga The D. He holds shit down right, no doubt. Nigga takes heads off."

Vah walked over, "Ain't enough of profiling. Let's pick up and roll, plus pay ya'll boys and step the fuck off."

The D looked at Vah and said, "You are a bad bitch fo sho. I respect ya game 24/7. If ever ya need me, let Rah know; he'll let me know and I'm there."

Vah's like, "I feel that. Enjoy the day nigga."

Jaia told The D, "What is it you about nigga? What is it ya asking to offer?"

The D told Jaia, "I can show you better than I can tell you 'bout my skills."

He turned around and called Rahmel.

"Sorry son."

"For what," Rahmel replied.

The D shot that nigga right in his fuckin' head, straight like that.

Jaia stunned said, "Yo son how long you knew that nigga."

"Ah about two years. We met when we were at this little juke joint called Bottoms Up. So he wasn't all that, ya heard. So I'm down all the way live like the Wild Wild West, ya feel me. Excuse my for the mess."

He called a couple of other dudes.

"Yo clean this shit up. take this nigga body, throw it in the sewer in pieces, ya feel me. Got my drift; now move it son."

Vah called out, "Yo The D that shit's a'ight, so you got heart huh? It's all good. You just take care of all this area for us. We'll treat ya nice and we are treacherous as bad as a fiend. So let's not get it fucked up cause you decide to kill one of your homies and what do you think we know of you now?"

The D lied, "We know fo sho we gotta take ya ass out for real" Vah said, If ya head get too big and greedy in our stable there is enough for everyone to eat. Ya never get full in this game of hustling. It's too much to eat; a whole lot to swallow, ya feel me The D. But you are the motherfucking man, I'll give you that. Yes we need you in our crew, money."

Jaia's cellie is ringing. She picks up and it's Labu.

"Yo what up fam? I'm just bored as hell sitting in this crib. I also called to thank you all for that shopping spree, girl. I had a very lovely time. Oh yeah, Aunya called. She'd like to find out if the plane tickets are at the Buffalo airport for the day she is released. It's only three more weeks. I asked her if she wanted me to handle the transportation. She told me nah that her dawgs got everything. So what am I chop suey?"

"Oh Labu, she's very caring and compassionate for hers and we have been there for each other on the real. We all each other got with no disrespect to you. That's just how we all get down for one another. You'll see once she is home in your arms. Things and your feelings will be totally different. We all respect each other to the fullest. Please let my dawg know that everything is done, a'ight. The tickets are a done deal. There will be a limo to pick her up at the facility in Albion, okay. She is going to be fine. Also, we all should be waiting at the Albany airport when she arrives. Is that cool with you Labu or do you prefer just yourself waiting for her? We can respect that yo."

"Jaia you all would do that for me? Ah, ah that shit is nice, but nah cause you guys are all she talks about. It wouldn't be fair."

"But Labu, she knows we're always busy making money."

"Dam Jaia, you sound like you leaving time for us to get our fuck on fo sho."

"Sure ya right. Once Aunya's home we will hang out more often. Right now though we're makin' shit happen so our dawg can get paid, lay back and drink some lemonade in the shade, Ha ha, ya feel me girl? I want the best for you both and more, a'ight. Yo Labu we'll get a limo at Albany airport too so you guys can really ching ding. Is there anything else I can do to accommodate you Labu? Please let me know, love. Me, Vah and Unc are here for you, ya feel me. Labu, it's all real and all good. Real people do real things fo sho."

Labu suddenly blurted out of nowhere, "Jaia I know who tried to kill Nubian. I was there that morning talking to him, but I did not know he was a part of your crew. It happened so sudden. All I was doing was driving around checking out the Albany area, then all that shit jumped off. The only reason I'm saying something is because we're family and Aunya had told me to stay put as far as being around the house. My first time roaming and look what I get into. A fucking shoot out bullshit. So my thing is this, if Aunya finds out she'll be pissed."

"Yes she will Labu. Also though it's not your fault, so be easy on yourself. She should understand especially being where she is right now, although I'm not going to say no more about my dawg. She's not here to defend herself. Anyway, soon enough you can tell her the whole situation. My thing is this, who is the motherfucker that tried to take my boy Nubian out? Did you get a good look at him, Labu?"

"Yeah it was a white dude. He seemed like he could've been a narc. If I was to see that fucker again; yeah I think I can ID his honky ass."

Jaia told Labu, "Let's lay on this for a day, a'ight. I'll get back with you."

* * *

In the meantime, Detective Reese wants Da-Stev to get him in touch with Jaia and 'em. He needs to relay this information to them without Da-Stev picking up on his vibes about his dirty ass. He's totally pissed off about Detective Gadson, but instead he went around the hood looking for Nubian or anybody that is affiliated with them, so he rode back through the park. Them two asshole were still yapping off. He decided to call Da-Stev.

Da-Steve answered his cellie, "Yell-o talk to me."

Detective Reese responded. "Listen I need to lay some information on Jaia and 'em, so is it possible they can be contacted as soon as possible, Da-Stev? It's concerning the Silver Fox man, so I'd like to deliver it personally, understand?"

Da-Stev's looking all around the park. At the same time he's trying to tell Detective Gadson that it's Reese on the phone and to see i he sees him in the area.

"Oh yea, well I can give them a call; how about three-way 'em?

This way ya'll can set a place, a'ight. There ain't no checking shit once shit hits the fan with his trac fone, so he's not worried."

He told Detective Reese to hold on a minute while he called. Then he told Detective Gadson he would get with him later. He did not trust Detective Reese. He knew him too long and felt he had been up to something and for Detective Gadson to sit tight because shit is getting hectic in the hood and he needs to find out.

Detective Reese spotted Detective Gadson leaving the park while he was still talking to Da-Stev. He then heard a female voice.

"Holla at a bitch."

He looked at his cellie.

"Oh shit, this broad's a hood rat for real. Yo, I'm here.

It's Vah," she said to him. "Yo dude, we 'bout to be out by King's Chicken a'ight, in twenty minutes."

"I am around the corner as we speak Ms., I'm out."

"Yo Da-Stev, it's all good. I'll talk to ya later man.

Later, replied Da-Stev."

Da-Stev was wondering what the fuck Detective Reese was up to mentioning some Silver Fox shit.

"If only he knew that is the reason for my undercover sheistyness. I could care *less* about all the other bullshit that I put in the game to get Jaia personally. She's gonna find out sooner or later once I'm done with what I need to do. As for Detective Reese, if his shit for Internal Affairs is free; but I do need him for some menial things when I wrap shit up. If any of TLB get wind of that stupid ass Gadson pulling the trigger on Nubian all hell is gonna break loose. Now I gotta keep an eye on what's about to jump off with Reese and Jaia and 'em at that chicken joint."

As Vah, Unc and Jaia headed over to meet Detective Reese, Unc's wondering why it is he wants to see them face to face.

"Summin' ain't right. Yo Vah, all this meeting shit does not sound kosher to me, ya heard. My man sounds desperate. Ya'll know it's all about the Benjamin's with this kat fo sho so we 'bout to pay for info."

Jaia cut in, "We been working with this dude for a while. It keeps our shit running smooth in the hood like it should. We really cannot complain, except for them getting at Nubian. Vah, what's up with that situation, what gives?"

"Well Damian and T.Dove are babysitting his ass. We have to get nigga's squealing and snitching for ours, ya feel me."

"I am going to start laying the lead to the head," Unc stated.

"Yeah if ya do boo, take that nigga The D with ya. He's hell to pay a motherfucker death for answers, cause babe I really couldn't stand it if anything happened to you. I do love ya Unc."

"I love ya ruthless ass too, Jaia."

"A'ight that's enough bitches of that mushy shit hoes. We're out taking care of business. Save that 'I wanna fuck you' shit for later. Now is seriously not the time."

Vah had to say that because she knew Jaia and Unc were more into each other than making money on the rise. She knew she'd have to keep checking them two motherfuckers because were about to get reality kicked all up in their asses because they weren't about to fuck up the Benjamin's and Grant's for her.

"Yo check this Jaia, why don't you meet this Reese dude and Unc and I will catch up with you later nigga, a'ight?' Nah better yet we'll wait in the parking lot next door, okay? It would not look good in public. You got that dawg, being I am not really equipped to handle scum like po-po on the take without a doubt. Sho ya right."

"Yo Unc, you must've realized you are a fucking cocky bitch, right nigga,? Vah smiled.

Unc's laughing, "Yeah man, I most definitely know, fo sho."

Jaia went into King's Chicken and ordered a chicken breast and biscuit. She figured she might as well nibble on something sitting there with her louie vitton pocketbook and Baby Phat gear on and some Timberlands, smelling like Pleasures. She saw this white guy enter and as he did her cellie started ringing.,

It was Vah.

"It's him. That's the car Labu described that was involved in the shooting."

"A'ight later," Jaia clicked off and slipped her cellie back in her pocketbook.

Detective Reese walked up to the counter and ordered some shrimp popcorn, a piece of chicken and a ginger ale soda. He sat down at the table where Jaia was sitting near the window. Vah and Unc were cruising the sidewalk.

Detective Reese introduced himself. He remembered her from the funeral talking with Natalie.

"Well, well, if it isn't my little secretive so-called boss Jaia. Am I right, sistah. It's all good. It's finally nice to meet with you. Of course you're already familiar with my name and status. I'd like to get straight to the point. It's to my knowledge from my investigation and as far as I can see that it is one of your very own deceiving your crew trying to get rid of Nubian."

"Who the fuck are you claiming this crock of shit, nigga. I know the whole dam scheme ain't for some dough bitch, cause you got a bad ass gambling habit; so what the fuck is the real deal, yo."

"Listen up ya fucking dumb ass broad. You think I want cash. Nah bitch. It's not that type of casino, just to let you in on it. I wanna be in like flint on your take, but not by trying to take or get money in scheming off you. Hell nah. This information is for free. Also, ya have to let me handle this my way for you, a'ight. Is it a deal? Do I have your word Jaia. We need to work out this situation very discreetly only among us. Do you feel that is possible Jaia? We will keep our normalcy in order of operation. As for the information I originally came to let you know, is none other than Da-Stev, Jaia."

Jaia's face looked like it exploded with pure hatred. If the top of her head could open for some air, it would've been all over the King Chicken restaurant. Jaia called him all kinds of liars and shit. He told her it's hard to swallow and for her to drink that shit and chalk it up to another lesson learned in the game of hustling.

"It's what you do with the info now that it's yours. That's the delio, ya heard. So it's ours fo sho. We are definitely going to make an example out of him and his partner. Between me and you, you have no idea what a grimey motherfucker he is.

He is an old partner of mine from New York City. Yes, he's homicide Detective Gadson. We need to keep him on the low, Jaia. His ass is mine, so don't worry ya pretty little heart about him at all. I'll handle shit with your presence once we wrap it up, ya feel me. Things are kinda hectic out there in the hood with your peeps. Oh yeah, Nubians' house has burned down. A body has been discovered in the debris, but they haven't ID'd the body as of yet. Oh well, let me call the coroner's right now."

"Hello Albany Medical Center, How may I help you?"

"I'd like to be connected to the forensics lab."

"Let me connect you to their operator."

"Oh okay, thank you ma'am."

When he got through to them they told him the body they identified was that of Joseph Murphy. His street name is Lil Kill.

Jaia said, "Oh shit my nigga. Yo Reese, this is a done deal on dat nigga Da-Stev and Detective Gadson, a'ight. Do what ya gotta do."

"There is another situation that needs attending to Jaia. A chick by the name of Silver Fox. See I saw her on the screen of Ms. Smiley's cellular phone. I am surprised Da-Stev hasn't kept you up to date about the streets hearing this name. It's suppose to be some type of drug syndicate here in the capital region. I've been tailing their tracks on my own little time. It's bigger than us. I assume that bitch Ms. Smiley was affiliated with this Silver Fox. I guess they feel you or shall I say TLC has knocked her out of the box. So be aware, a'ight."

"Yo Detective Reese, my people had nothing to do with her being killed. Nobody knows who, what, when or where the fuck she showed up from. That is the weirdest shit I've ever encountered."

Vah is just watching getting a good glimpse of Detective Reese talking to Jaia. Suddenly she sees Da-Stev's Denali in her peripheral vision. He seems as if he's trying to ease in by looking inside King's Chicken peeping Reese's conversation with Jaia. Detective Reese's back is against the window. After he got a good look he continued to drive on, not noticing Vah staring at his ass.

Vah stunned said, "What the fuck just happened."

All puzzled she went over to where Unc was in the parking lot and told her what just happened. She decided to call Jaia to let her in on Da-Stev's showing up.

"Yell-o Jaia, holla back."

"Yo that nigga Da-Stev was easing up looking in the restaurant at you and Detective Reese. Do you know what's up with that Jaia, cause he sure looked like he needed to kill a nigga quick, fo sho."

"Well Vah, I just got information on Da-Stev's sorry *ass* with a whole bunch of other shit. I'ma hit ya with it all. As soon as I finish up here with our inside informant, a'ight. Back at ya dawg."

Detective Reese said to Jaia, "Yo, do yourself a favor and watch ya boy Da-Stev. Do not play him close. Although you guys been associates for years now; just stay alert at all times. You'll soon enough get what I'm saying to you. I wouldn't put it past him if he followed me here fo sho, a'ight. Listen up, I'm outta here. Here's my card, private number on back. Don't file it, dial it. A nigga needs some funds, ya feel me jaia?"

"You know you are a cool ass white po-po, plus ya ebonics are hype nigga."

Detective Reese smiled at what Jaia was saying about his crooked ass for a detective, then he left.

When Jaia got outside she told both Vah and Unc everything that was said between him and her in King's Chicken. Unc wanted to hunt Da-Stev's ass down to torture him.

Instead Jaia suggested, "Give it some time. When we do get his ass boo; you can have him personally. I knew he had been acting kinda distant since we've been back from New York City last time. As a matter of fact, it's time for one of us to make a trip soon."

"Oh yeah yo, we gotta give Aunya a coming home party. We need to get with Labu within the next two weeks ya'11. How bout we give it at my crib." Jaia said, "Let's first see how Labu feels, a'ight? Vah why is it she's not hanging with us? You ever wonder why Aunya told her to stay put?"

"Jaia, that ain't none of your fucking business. She just wants her there when she comes home. She is very obedient. She must love herself some Aunya, huh Unc? Wha ya think man?"

"I am not even going to comment, cause whatever my boo asks, oblige, as long as it's not hurting either one of us."

Jaia continued, "So anyway, Detective Reese *says* we do not know who the other dirty po-po hired to kill Nubian. Labu does, ha ha ha ya'll. Once Aunya comes home we'll explain it all to her. Until then we need to stash Labu someplace. If she is seen, it's over. We're not about to let that happen dawgs. Unc call Nubian, Damian and T.Dove and tell them to meet us over in the courtyard. We about to shift some head in Albany. Oh, we have to find out what really happened with Lil Kill. Summin' up."

CHAPTER TWENTY-SEVEN

Meanwhile T.Dove was at L&O picking up cash where he runs into the nigga Sam. He tells him about what happened with Lil Kill and the Puerto Ricans chasing him into Nubians' house and how the dudes burned it down.

T.Dove grabbed that nigga.

He said, "What," all loud.

Sam said furiously, "Yo man, get your fucking hands off me. I'm on ya side nigga. I know how crazy ya ass is. Them ya boys. That's why I came straight to ya nigga; putting you on T.Dove. Yo listen up, there they go right over there parked in that black Audi. The Spanish dude with the blunt puffin' is the one who shot Lil Kill. Them other two burned the house."

"Yo lil nigga, you sure," T.Dove said to Sam.

Yeah nigga, I'm sure. I was right there when the shit jumped off. Lil Kill was tearing their asses up in the dice game, celo won all they shit. It's a sad thang, cause them nigga's are some losers. Ask everybody on the block, right there on the corner of First & Swan. He dam sure tore their pockets up T.Dove. I tell you no lie, man. Them nigga's was heated.

I guess they did not know who they were fucking with, huh?"

"Nah, they dam sure didn't. Yo Damian, Nubian we 'bout about it yo; revenge is a motherfucker yo, especially when ya ass don't know what the hell is getting ready to jump off at ya last sight of life. Yo, let's do this like a motherfucking brutus. Holla!"

Damian, T.Dove and Nubian all approached the Audi with their guns pointed directly at all them migga's in the car. It was as if how the west was won. T.Dove noticed the Puerto Rican dude noticing them coming directly at them.

He yelled to his two homies, "Oh shit ya'11, nigga's comin' at us."

Those were his last words ever.

All three of them were shooting all at once, shooting anyone they saw moving in the car. After they finished the fucking car looked like connect the dots with bullet holes. Everybody in the hood just shook their heads as if to say, 'don't fuck with them nigga's?

Other were saying out loud, "Glad that's them motherfuckers and ain't me."

The crowd dispersed. Everybody definitely ghost. Sirens heard within blocks approaching.

T.Dove's cellie was ringing as they got into the Jeep. It was Unc explaining that Jaia needed to kick it to them and for them to stop by the courtyard pronto.

"A'ight," he answered, "on our way up, yo."

As Vah and 'em entered the courtyard her cellie rang. It was Seasonn.

"Hello my number one love. It's been acoupla weeks, babe, I figured you were very busy after I tried a few times to call ya, boo. I miss you terribly love. And, the air is wonderful. When I'm drivin' I feel I'm all love. We've repeated our episodes over and over again, Seasonn. Oh shit, I'm just rambling on baby. I'm thirsty for yo honey."

Seasonn surprises Vah by telling her she is at the Crown Plaza downtown.

"Oh baby, I can't wait to see my one and only love of life. I could show you better than I can tell you. Are you real busy right now, boo? If so, I am not going anywhere until you get your pretty chocolate ass in this room with a whole lot of energy with a strap on or ya tongue, Vah. Now call when you are on your way."

She gave Vah the room number and hung up, called the front desk and told them she'll be expecting a guest. They informed her they would ring her room when her guest arrived.

She had bought some nice sexy lingerie she wanted Vah to take off her with her teeth. She had a very special sexual treat for her boo. Seasonn has never felt the way she does for Vah for any other woman she's been with. She's stuck like chuck on Vah and lovin' it.

She smile and said, "Yeah, that's my bitch, yo.:

Vah was so overwhelmed to hear form her baby that nothing is going to get in the way of her going to see her boo.

"Yo, listen up peoples," announced The D as everyone entered the courtyard.

All got silent at once. Vah was looking around, staring at how many workers they have in the courtyard.

"Dam," she said, "whoa, we making ours for real."

Seeing them all there brought her attention to where they were three years ago. It was a beautiful sight to see. TLC was sure enough getting paid. Not in full as of yet, but soon to come for sure.

"I'ma lay it down like this to my main soldiers," Vah said to them all, "you know who you are. We 'bout to blow up in the whole tri-state area. We have clientele all over, ya feel me. Now's the time whether or not ya *ass* is on for real. From now on it's do or die. There are a lot of motherfuckers gettin' ready to come at us hard, ya feel me. Since Smiley's misfortune we're all making all the dough coming in and leaving, so everybody gets paid. Ain't no reason to get greedy tryin' to knock TLC outta the box. ears are always on the speakers of the streets. Ain't nothing I don't know, because I do not speak what I know. It's better left unsaid. Any of ya'll motherfuckers in here part of my crew, trust and believe ain't nothing I do not know. Ya know ya'll shit ain't none of my business, cause what we deal in is all 'bout business. The fuckin' drug business is all we have in common, true dat.

"Our boy Lil Kill has met his maker over a fuckin' dice game, so ya'll nigga's know it ain't a game, it's all 'bout the Benjamin's. We need to stay on our P's & Q's at all times. Everyone is gonna git at our crew at any given time.

After ya asses leave outta here, every second is not promised to you. Our lives in dealing is on borrowed time, fo sho."

Jaia cut in saying, "There is these motherfuckers out here tryin' to get at Nubian. We are not sure who yet, but we have an idea. So, ya'll need to look out for ya boy and keep ya ears to everyone who talks about the streets' information. Nigga's do not agree with us putting shit on lock down in Albany or the Capital Region area. Who gives a fuck when it's all about money. I know I don't cause I'ma git mine regardless or somebody's head gotta sho nuff be put on full blast, ya heard.

This nigga Oops yelled, "Five 0 is on the move, yo. We need to wrap it up Jaia and Vah. The precinct is already looking for a reason to try to put a demolition order on the building, blowing it off the block. And, no disrespect to you all."

Oops knew the schedule for the Morton Avenue area. It's his hood since birth. Every nook and cranny Oops had mastered. Jaia told every last one of them to be aware of this Silver Fox. Whatever the fuck the name meant in general, but she felt repercussions on the rise of her empire. All had to be in order.

Vah had explained to her H.N.I.C. of some spots to spread the word that they heard to their troops. The one thing they stress is to treat customers right.

"Ain't no dogging 'em and shit, but be careful whose mouth ya put on ya dick yo and just make sure in the process you do not fuck my shit over, a'ight," Vah explained.

Unc sat in the cut as usual listening to her boo give the thirsty motherfuckers pep talk, seeing in them nigga's eyes if they had the chance to fuck her any kind of way, they would. Not on her life though. As she scanned the crowd she saw this female she remembered from back in the day named Mia. At the time she had a train ran on her ass. Fourteen nigga's were all up in her pussy, one after the other, busting nuts. Her pussy was dripping like Niagara Falls cum. That shit was hilarious. She handled it though, like a trooper. She wanted to seek revenge because she went to rehab after that and got cleaned up. Found out she had the House In Virginia (H.I.V.). Now she looks more beautiful than ever. She's getting her grind on with one of my troopers. Oops, as a matter of fact.

Unc went over to her and stated she remembered her.

Mia in return said, "I remember too."

She went on to tell her that whatever is needed to be done for T.L.C. to let her be down loyally.

Unc was the only one who tried to go to her aid that awful night, but to no avail. Them nigga's did not quit. The only reason they did not fuck with Unc at the time was because of Amadeus. Mia will always be thankful to Unc.

Oops was trying to listen to their conversation. Unc asked him if there was something wrong with his hearing. She then suggested he get up outta hers, talking to Mia and quick. She told him if he had any sense that he's one less nigga to worry about.

Oops strayed away feeling embarrassed in front of Mia. He also knew not to fuck with Unc or even let her hear his voice mumbling back at her flip outta her fucking mouth. Not with her main man's there. He'd definitely get got on the spot. No joke. Oops looked at Unc with a vengeance in his eyes, with his head held down though.

Across the way Damian caught his look. He knew he had to watch this kat. He could tell he has some larceny in his heart. He knew he was going to have to shut the nigga down. He's got his number fucking around with any type of brutal thoughts toward Unc. He decided to get to Unc first about the chump ass nigga Oops. Damian was serious as hell. He'd take care of that in due time.

Unc was telling Mia that she'd need her guarantee so to be ready when she hollered.

Mia replied, "A'ight, one love Unc."

While they prepared to go their separate ways out of the courtyard, a nice handsome man came out of the blue in an expensive Brooks Brothers suit. The nigga looked like he just bought the whole block of buildings, including the courtyard. Right then this female came out screaming.

"Yo stop that nigga there looking like GQ. He just raped my kid. She's only twelve years old."

Oops turned to see that it was his aunt yelling. She's a smoker for sure. Everyone looked up at Oops. He ran and grabbed that motherfucker and started beating the shit out the nigga. All of a sudden the dude started getting the best of Oops, fuckin' his ass up. Jaia found a pipe.

"This niggas' ass gonna get done."

She put the beats on the motherfucker. She couldn't believe when she she heard what Oops aunt said he did to her daughter and she got madder than a bitch. All who were standing around asked Jaia if she was alright.

Vah answered, "Yea, her ass is all right. He just helped her to let off some steam."

Damian asked Vah if she wanted him to get rid of the piece of shit, referring to the dude. She nodded her head yes. Damian yelled out to everyone in the courtyard to stomp the nigga to death. All who wanted to be a part of the crew demolished the dude. He was done. There was about fifteen nigga's with timbs killing his ass, let alone Jaia whipping his ass with the pipe. He looked homeless, fucked up and then dead. That's some shit.

Vah yelled, "This is the kind of filth we do not want up in here. Understand. Kill it and get rid of it. I enjoyed the show. Later, fam."

T.Dove was laughing saying, "Dam, all you could see is this fly ass nigga ready to exit the building looking like he had taken care of some serious business, ya feel me. The next thing you know the piece of shit is a rapist. Oh well, you did not even hear him try to defend himself because too many motherfuckers were dead on that ass. I swear I never heard a peep outta him. Maybe just a moan."

He continued laughing his ass off.

Oops hollered, Let me get a shovel and scrape this chump *ass* GQ looking nigga up off our sidewalk up in here, in the courtyard. His dead ass is taking up space."

Mia spit on the body as she passed. Remember her shit and how the niece of Oops feels.

CHAPTER TWENTY-EIGHT

AFTER DETECTIVE REESE LEFT FROM seeing Jaia, he thought long and hard about Da-Stev and Detective Gadson trying to get rid of the kid Nubian. He knew he was not going to let that shit happen again, not in his realm. It doesn't even mix like it's all right. He knew he needed to get with Detective Gadson quick if he wanted to stay on his good side. He would not want to leave Nubian alone.

'Truth be told he is fuckin' up our crooked money, so he needs to recognize. Da-Stev is setting his ass up for a fall,' he thought aloud.

Da-Stev was setting himself up for a fall knowing Detective Reese knew how he feels some type of way about Jaia. She is a very beautiful woman, dangerous and cunning. He likes that in a bitch. She dam sure is hell on wheels always ready to burn rubber.

Reese had gotten a hard on thinking about Jaia and was sitting in his car rubbing his penis and smiling; looking devious as ever imagining himself fucking the shit out of Jaia. He would cum and then she'd put a leash around his neck while walking on his knees like a dog and his tongue would be hanging out and he'd be panting. He saw in his mind Jaia dressed like a dominatrix, all leather, spiked hair, stilettos and a whip whipping his ass; as he's barking and howling. He sat there imaging all kinds of freaky shit he'd like to encounter with Jaia. He knew it would never happen unless he had a machine gun on her ass or a grenade.

* * *

Finally he came out of the zone thinking about who the hell is Silver Fox. He called Detective Gadson and told him he needed to see him immediately, no fucking excuses and hung up the phone. He knew he'd be sweating wondering what it is he's so anxious to talk to him about. It will be eating at his brain until he decides to call Reese back.

Nubian, Damian and T.Dove decided to check out DiCarlo's strip joint on Central Avenue.

"Yo nigga, is there a lot of po-po up in that piece, Nubie? If so dude, I do not want no part of it. I can get a bitch off the street and tear her ass open for what I pay to see a bunch of hoes do on a pole. That shit ain't happenin' nigga. You and Damian go on, I'll check yall later, ya heard," Damian declared.

T.Dove jumped in his GMC Yukon. It was a gift to himself from the money he had gotten when he fucked up Ms. Smiley's homeboy Dolce. He came off lovely as far as cash, so he split it with Nubian. they both kept it between themselves. He can honestly say loved Nubian like a brother and respects that he kept it between them and not mentioning it to Jaia and them. When he told them the story he said whoever put Ms. Smiley in the vestibule stole everything while he was in the bedroom fucking Dolce in his ass. Everyone left it at that and had laughed at the whole scenario. T.Dove told them Dolce's ass was some good old shit and he was satisfied. He recalled Ms. Smiley trying to tell him about a female who had held her hostage. That's all he could recollect for now. He hopes it will all come back to him in the near future. when it does he has some devastating plans for the bitch.

He blasted the music riding toward Delaware Ave. and headed over across town listening to Chingy sing "I like it when ya doin' it right there, right there," as he's singing along.

"Wow," he thought aloud, "it's been a year and a half since I've been released form the hell hole of a prison, I'd rather be put in a body bag before ever returning."

* * *

Jaia and Unc decided to go make some lovin', while Vah went to spend some time with Seasonn at the Crown Plaza being that all is good in the hood for them to chill. Damian was on his own going to DiCarlo's. Nubian decided to go hang at Bogie's, a club where the college brat packs hang. It's close to St. Rose College. Bogie's plays a little bit of everything, but especially rap music. They sometimes have guest appearances. It's a club that parties hard.

Nubian stopped there and entered. They were playing Lil Wayne. He's bobbing his toward the bar. All he wanted was a Heineken. He got it and went over to the pool table and saw a couple of white chicks being silly. Once they saw him approaching he smiled at them.

He was thinking to himself, "Yeah, check it bitches, I got a big black juicy dick ready to run like and express train through all ya'lls' pink pussies."

As he got close to them they were both snickering.

He went up to them and stated, "Do I look funny or summin'?"

"Oh no," said one of the females shyly, "it's just that I like ya jeans, they're Rocawear right?"

"Yes they are, would you like a pair or summin'? Yo what's ya name boo?"

"Maria."

"Nice to meet ya, mine's Nubian. Yo let me holla at ya girl, I mean if ya can, a'ight."

"Dam," Nubian thought, "Im'a have to take this bitch over to T.Dove's if I'ma get some of that pussy. I know I'm sure gonna try. She isn't bad looking at all, looking like a New York City dime piece. She got it in her and I'ma get me some, fo sho. Now let me have a couple more drinks cause this is what it is for now."

They were feeling the drinks after a few drinks, good conversation; so good like it should never end. He was feeling horny and could feel from the conversation and the look in her eyes that she was too.

He straight out said to Maria, "Yo I'm ready to bounce boo. Yo ya bouncin' wit me or what? I wanna fuck you down."

She was so giggley it kinda annoyed him, so he was thinking for everything she's so silly about he'll fuck her harder, then she will feel what could possibly be funny. He knows he's definitely getting her pussy tonight, no doubt.

"Yo come on," Nubian demanded.

Maria said good—bye to her friends.

They all yelled, "You go girl. He looks like he can do some damage, girl; so we better see you walking like a cowgirl next time, bitch."

Everyone parted, laughing, saying goodnight.

Nubian ended up going to the Holiday Inn on Wolf Road.

It was almost 2:30am so it doesn't matter if it's just for a few hours.

Nubian said, "Yo Maria, what we looking at here, a couple of hours or a day boo? I ain't spending my dough on this hotel if we ain't doing shit, ya feel me. I could drop ya ass off home girl, so is it on or what? Yo you steady giggling, smiling being silly intoxicated and shit, so what is so fuckin' funny boo?"

"It's just you're so rough around the edges, like real thuggish Nubian."

"You do not have to be that way with me, okay." Oh yes.

"Oh yes I'd love you to fuck me if that's all you're waiting to hear. Rough ride this pussy, Mr. Thugaliscious," She smiled shyly.

He was shocked like a motherfucker and couldn't believe what this white girl was saying to him.

"So it's all good boo, huh?"

She said in return, "Trust that, my nig."

He laughed his *ass* off.

"Come boo let me put some of this mandingo dick on ya ass my bitch."

She told him, "Oh you on some get back shit."

He stared at her like where the hell was her slang coming from."

"Yo where you from boo?"

"Queens, New York, born and raised. I came here to go to college, a nice private one called St. Rose."

Nubian replied, "Oh yeah that's hot boo, keep going do not ever stop, a'ight."

She responded, "A'i ght."

He actually liked Maria, she kept it real with him all night. He decided that whatever happened from this night on she is his. They finally made it to their room overlooking the indoor pool.

"It's really nice Maria."

"Oh man we 'bout about it, fo sho."

Nubian is laughing at her and staring at her at the same time.

He said to her, "Dam ya kinda pretty girl. It's on boo."

He's thinking, 'dam I'ma sure make her mine seriously. She sounds like a down chick, even if she is white. That's what will make it right in my book.'

Maria couldn't believe she was in the hotel room with this nigga, but she sure wanted some of that dick. He seems as though he's packin' all puffy in the front with a good size looking bump. Out of all the black guys she had detested while living in Queens. She couldn't believe it herself. Yes, she had black friends, of course, but never felt a connection. She realized it was her dad's wishes.

Then she thought to herself, 'as of right now, the hell with my dad, I'm getting me some of Nubian's dick. He's fine as hell. He seems so thuggish; I like that, that shit turns me on for real.'

Nubian grabbed Maria's ass, "Get over here girl, fuckin' time."

She said, "And I'm on time boo."

He stared at her, "Yo you sure ain't no blackness in you boo?"

She smiled sweetly, "Nah baby, but what I'm about to put on ya, ya gonna think twice about a black sistah again. How 'bout that Nubian, I ain't playing. Come on, let's get it on."

She started kissing his neck, chest, massaging his balls and playing with his dick. She's dying to kiss him all over so he can get chills from her tongue licking his ears.

Nubian slid his hands around the back of her neck and pulled her to him. He stuck his tongue so deep in her mouth, she made a moaning sound as if she was trying to tell him how good it is. They were tonguing and kissing passionately as if they both never want the kiss to end. Maria wants so bad to really go to sucking Nubian's dick. Little does he know, although his tongue is in her mouth it felt like a thick penis that came alive with some movement. She was in her glory feeling so horny. He's bringing that character out of her and she's enjoying it truthfully.

CHAPTER TWENTY-NINE

DAYS HAVE PASSED SINCE THE courtyard meeting. Jaia went and got Labu and took her over to Vah's. For a couple of days she'd stay there and then move her around from place to place. This way Detective Gadson will not be able to pin point where Labu will be staying until something is done about his ass. Jaia is getting ready to put fire to his dumb *ass* for fucking with Nubian. Da-Stev also.

It's just a matter of time. Jaia is wondering who is keeping Nubians' time and she's noticing he is always talking about his boo and shit. Plus the bitch is white. In Albany there are no boundaries as far as being involved with someone of a different nationality. All are welcome.

"It's cute as long as that nigga is rolling in my dough and ain't fucking with my flow, he a'ight," she thought.

Then she yelled to Unc from her bedroom.

Unc, come here boo, I got summin' I wanna show ya love. Please ma."

Unc yelled back to Jaia, "Yo I'm watching the NBA Playoffs. Oh yeah Jaia, Seasonn says hi, I just got off the phone with She asked if we'd like to go to Oh Bar's bar for a couple hours boo. Later if you'd like. So do ya wanna go Ma, huh?"

"Yeah, only if you come in here so I can show you summin' Unc."

Unc told Vah they'd be there in a couple hours because she's gotta sex up her boo first. She'll be good after sexing her.

"Later Vah."

Unc ran into the bedroom and stopped at the entrance. Jaia had her legs wide open, pussy looking pink and juicy, playing with her clit and sucking on her finger. Unc's eyes filled with lust at the moment and she went directly to Jaia's pussy, kissing it as if it were Jaia's lips kissing her back. She was feeling her to the max that took her mind to a whole new stratosphere. Unc was acting all thirsty tasting and literally trying to suck Jaia dry.

It was turning her on more and more hearing her moan to the effects of what she was doing to her. They were both getting all soaked up in the pussy, ready for each other to bust a nut, as Unc would put it; thinking it as she has Jaia going crazy ready to cum all in her mouth.

She can't wait so she was teasing Jaia's clitoris. First she was sucking it with a rhythm, then she'd slow it down, inserting her fingers in and out of Jaia's pussy; playing with her desire to cum. Jaia was begging her so softly.

"Unc please baby, yeah just like that Ma; I wanna cum baby. I wanna cum Unc, 000h yeah Unc, 000h Unc I wanna cum, baby come on yeah suck it like that, 000h 000h Unc."

Jaia grabs Unc's head and keeps it in a motion to the rhythm she likes her to suck her clit.

"Oooh," she hissed, "yeah baby like that Ma, now it's good so good Unc. I love ya ass boo; you gonna make me cum in a 000h 000h 000h ahhh, oh yeah baby. I'm about to cum baby, you gonna taste my cum, rub it all over your face, oh 000h I'm cummin cummin cum cum, oh baby it's good, it's good oh hell yeah it's good baby, it's good."

Unc is feeling very proud of herself, making her boo cum with some head and of course a couple of fingers to help the process along.

"Maybe she is satisfied," she thought, "now I can go finish watching my game, then we'll go meet Vah and Seasonn."

* * *

Meanwhile, Da-Stev sat home wondering if, Detective Reese had mentioned anything to Jaia and 'em about him being connected to Gadson. If so, he knew they could not touch him at all, but then with them you can never be sure. He needed to get with Jaia and 'em to let them know about the Silver Fox and that is who he is really after. Silver Fox was involved with Ms. Smiley and if they are on to him he has to be sure they don't put him six feet under. He knows he has been kind distant from TLC lately and realizes if he's going to get on their good siCe has to switch the shit on Detective Gadson. That will be the only way to straighten everything out and by killing him.

"Oh fuck," he thought, "boy I gotta get outta this shit fo sho, if it's the last thing I do. Somebody gonna die and it ain't gonna be my ass."

He called Nubian, but the voice mail came on, as usual. He felt Nubian had an idea, but wasn't sure if he was involved in trying to kill him. Now he needed to get on the ball quick. His time was running out with TLC. He recalled that Aunya should be coming home soon, as in about three weeks. He knew they were throwing her a 'welcome home' party, although he couldn't guess where.

Then he thought, "Probably at some ole Gay joint. Hell, I like being surrounded by pussy anyway, so it'll be a pleasure."

He turned on the T.V. and put on the news. It was reporting a shoot out over on Orange Street and Northern Boulevard. A guy by the street name of J.B. had been shot several times in broad daylight. The newscaster said there were two gunmen in black hoodies and bandannas covering their faces. They had walked up to J.B. and asked him some questions about another individual named Dolce. Then they both began shooting at him, jumped in a black Cadillac and took off.

"That is all we have on this story, back to the studio."

Da-Stev turned the T.V. off trying to figure out if those two guys were constituents of the Silver Fox.

"If there's anybody with even a little information, they're dead on the spot fo sho," he thought.

He needed to get- over to the hood quick and start asking some questions. He needs to get in TLC's good graces again by clearing up some shit for them.

* * *

Vah, Seasonn, Jaia and Unc were all at Oh Bars enjoying each others company; playing pool and listening to some juke box music. The gay guys in the bar were acting all flaming and shit. The bartender kept watching Jaia. She caught his eyes on her so she stepped to the bar.

"Excuse me," she said, "but do I know you from somewhere?"

He said slyly, "No, I just like looking at ya. You're so beautiful looking, that's all. If it's a problem I'll stop. I'm sorry, My name is Demetris love, and yours?"

"I'm Jaia, those over there are my peeps. Oh, can you please send another round to our table, please."

She handed him a hunfred dollar bill and told him to take ten dollars for a tip.

He smiled, "Thank you, Jaia."

She walked back to the table where Unc and them were and explained to them what was said between her and the bartender. Unc turned and looked toward Demetris. At the same time this female had approached the table. Vah and Jaia were shocked. It was the female Free-Free. She had appeared with Coco in court when Aunya's case was sent to county court. Vah went to give her some dap and she did not respond.

Instead she said, "Yo, you know Coco's dead right? She was killed about a month ago in the parking lot coming out of her job. Shot dead in the head yo, slumped over in the car. I attended the funeral. It's sad motherfuckers have to go around killing each other like that. Ya'll wouldn't happen to know anything about that, Huh?"

Jaia's mouth froze wide open looking at Vah. They both couldn't believe their ears. Free-Free was staring at them feeling like those bitches are so full of shit. Coco had explained to her about them being into hustling and drugs.

Free-Free was thinking it could've been them who killed Coco, then again they seemed just as shocked. So Vah introduced her to her boo, as well as Jaia. She called over to Demetris to give Free-Free a drink on her, but she declined and said she'd never drink with scumbags such as them, called them murderers, then stepped off.

Jaia was ready to blast the bitch dead on the scene, instead Demetris came over and asked Free-Free to please exit the bar. Otherwise, he'd be forced to have the police escort her off the premises. She obliged without an argument.

Free-Free was pissed. She really cared for Coco. They started dating after the incident, so she was heartbroken and wanted to seek revenge. Inside herself she felt that Vah and Jaia were not responsible for Coco's death and Aunya couldn't be because she's still incarcerated.

"I think I just fucked up with them. Oh well, I'll know soon," she thought aloud.

She was walking down Madison Avenue toward Washington Park and she got close to Knox she had this strange feeling come over her of being followed. As she realized she was she hastened her pace. All of a sudden the person was right up on her and shoved her into the bushes.

"Yo bitch, you say one word, ya ass is done. You hear me. Now walk slowly until I tell you to stop."

He took her over where the dogs play in the grass, where there were a bunch of bushes in the middle of the field. He then tied her to a tree.

"Yo what the fuck are you doing man? Don't so this to me. Yo come on dude, please I'm begging you man, nooooo. The guy stuffed her mouth with his sock.

"Shut the fuck up or I'll kill ya quick bitch. I just want some of that *ass* boo. Also, to let you know you don't fuck with people outside your league. That's a no-no bitch, so I'm forced to teach you a lesson with the pleasure of getting my rocks off at the same time."

He tied her so tight around the tree you would've thought she loved Mother Nature's creation. She could not get a good look at the guy to save her life. Everytime she tried he would turn her head facing away from him. He found a two-by-four about three feet and put it in between her legs with each end settled on her ankles so she couldn't move her legs at all. He then pulled out a razor and began cutting her pants down the back seamy. She had on some Calvin Klein jocks.

He laughed, "Oh shit, you are wishing you had a dick, huh bitch. Well check it, I'm gonna give you some and until I bust a nut I'm not going to stop a'ight, so you might as well loosen up ya asshole babe, cause nobody can hear ya. It's just you and me love in these bushes."

He had some Vaseline that he put all around her *ass* and on his dick, enough where he felt it would slip in easily. As he pulled her *ass* to him he shoved his dick so far up her ass, she screamed a blood curdling scream, as tears poured down her cheeks. The humiliating pain she felt made her feel numb. That is exactly where her mind went was numb, as well as her body. He was just ripping her ass wide open. He was busting nut after nut, telling her she has some good ole tight *ass.* He started slapping Free-Free's ass. She had already passed out, while he had his dick jigging her in her ass. He could not believe how good it felt. He was in his glory. If he could take her to a hotel, he'd fuck her ass all night. He definitely was satisfied, so he removed the two-by-four, untied her, picked up the two-by-four and began beating her in her face while she was still unconscious.

He thought, "She never felt it coming anyway. Now bitch, Jaia and 'em are not to be fucked with."

T.Dove happened to coming from Dunkin' Donuts. His GM Yukon was parked in front of Oh Bar's. That's when he saw Vah and them through the window. Jaia's face had a look of shock on it. She was listening as he recalled what he just did to the bitch Free-Free and how much he enjoyed fucking her in her ass. As he was telling them the guy behind the bar came over who had escorted her out.

"Well, they won't have to worry 'bout that bitch no more."

He went on to tell them how he spit on her, wiped his dick off and kept it moving as if it did not phase him at all. He then left the bar, walked to his Jeep in front of Oh Bar's, looked back at his peeps through the window, smiled at Jaia as she caught a glimpse of him getting into his Jeep. He couldn't help but think that what he just did to Free-Free was some ole misery shit with the two-by-four.

"Boy that's a classic."

He sped off into the traffic, popped the CD in, turned up the music and thought to himself that he didn't even have to pay for ass tonite. He was happy about that for sure.

CHAPTER THIRTY

MEANWHILE, BACK AT OH BAR'S bar Jaia and 'em were talking about what the female Free-Free had said about Coco being dead. Vah couldn't believe it and both of them knew neither one of them killed her.

Jaia said, "Maybe someone got to her for summin' else she did. Vah the bitch is grimey, that's why she's dead, ya heard."

"Dam Jaia, do you have to speak so ill of the dead?"

"Yo bitch, do you remember what that dead hoe did to our dawg, huh nigga? Hello Vah, calling earth to Vah."

Jaia is really irking Vah's nerves at this point.

"A'ight Jaia it's all good, yo I'd really like to know who did her ass in, ya feel me. Not to mention Aunya is getting ready to hit the bricks in a few weeks. Yo yo yo is it on or what fam, we have to give her the big ole welcome home bash, ya heard Jaia. We gotta decide where we're going to style & profile our nigga when she's free yo. Let's make it a party she'll never forget. Oh yeah we have to tell Labu that her time is short for her boo. She'll be very happy about that. I'll hook her up with her soon on that matter, a'ight. It's going to be the fuckin' bomb diggity yo. I'ma make sure of it."

Unc cut in, "I cannot wait to meet Aunya. Ya'll truly have a bond. That is a beautiful thang. I wish I dam sure had peeps like that in my life, who could've been there for me. Some people just have all the luck and are fortunate. She is blessed to have such great people as the two of you. It's wonderful. Anyway, who'd like to play some pool. Our party is just getting started."

"Hey-ee," the bartender called over to Jaia's table, "ladies are you ready."

Everyone in unison yelled, "Hell yeah, bring it on Demetris."

Vah and Seasonn got up to dance to the old school joint 'Show Me Love' by Robin Bass. They were all over each other. You could tell they wanted each other bad. Jaia was telling Unc she saw T.Dove outside. His Yukon was parked right in front of the club and he had winked at her. Jaia was wondering what he was doing in the area. She thought maybe he had gone to Dunkin' Donuts. If she remembers correctly he did have bags in his hands.

She then remarked to Unc, "Oh okay."

She responded to Jaia, "Boo let's not think about anybody else other than you and me. It's just us tonight, a'ight ma. Look at Vah and Seasonn, that's you and me; all day everyday."

Unc started rubbing Jaia's pussy through her pants under the table reminding her of whose pussy it is. Jaia was feeling all tipsy and horny trying to get Unc to leave quickly because she is ready to fuck hard.

She whispered in Unc's ear, "Baby let's go please."

"Hold on Jaia, we came with them so let's wait to let 'em know we 'bout to leave, okay love. Shit they look like they are ready to fuck too. Look at 'em."

"I know dam well Seasonn is just as horny as I am Unc. Fuck that, let's go dammit."

Unc just happened to galnce out the window right then and saw these two guys with hoodies staring inside at them. She wasn't worried because she 's strapped and as soon as she let's Jaia, Vah and all of them know that them two nigga's will be part of the sidewalk fucking around with them when they are trying to get their fuck on.

"Are them nigga's crazy or what," she thought out loud.

Right then she let everyone in on what was going on before they all stepped out of Oh Bar's.

As they exited the club, Vah had her peripheral vision on alert while Seasonn held on to her hand and they walked around the corner on Madison to get to where the car was parked. As Unc and Jaia followed they expected something to jump off. Instead, the two nigga's were across the street shouting at them calling them lesbians and telling them how they need some dick to get over eating pussy. Unc got so pissed off, she ran across the street to where they were standing.

"Yo young nigga's, ya'll want some of this butch shit. Come on ya fuckin' punks."

She pulled out her Glock and as they saw it them nigga's took the fuck off running and yelling to each other.

"Yo man that dyke *ass* bitch got a fuckin' gun. Let's roll dude."

Unc began laughing at how fast they took off. Vah and 'em were cracking up. Jaia was calling to Unc to come back across the street.

"Come on boo. They don't want none of you. Lame *ass* nigga's."

They all parted laughing with Vah reminding Jaia about Aunya's bash and getting in touch with Labu and getting a hold of Da-Stev to find out what is really going on with him. They didn't want to believe what Detective Reese was telling them and if it was true find out what the reason was behind it. They knew Da-Stev because he was the one who helped them get their jump off by introducing them to the bitch Ms. Smiley.

As Jaia and Unc headed home to Colonie, the same two guys with the hoodies from Madison Ave. followed them. Jaia looked in the rear view mirror to see how far back they were. She needed to get at her gat before they came up on them.

She told Unc, "Let them motherfuckers come up to the plate where their asses will be read about in the paper, huh boo?"

Unc was about to answer her boo when suddenly them nigga's hit them from the back.

"Oh shit baby, they wanna play smash cars, crash 'em up, a'ight!"

Jaia smiles and steps on the gas. Her Navigator started flying down Western Avenue. There wasn't much traffic so she automatically stopped her hooptie, jumped out and ran toward the Nissan shooting her 9mm. Unc was right behind her. Them bitches were furious.

Unc's yelling, "Yeah nigga's, I didn't wanna shoot ya asses back on Madison. Now you've done tried my patience fucking with me and my boo."

Them motherfuckers were looking all shocked at the both of them, like thy lost their fucking minds.

"Yo Lee, these bitches are crazy man. We're done."

They could not move. Jaia and Unc had them. He looked over to Lee.

"He's dead. One to the head," Jaia declared, "Get outta the car nigga. Come on boy, it's time to let the cat out of the bag, bitch ass nigga."

They took his *ass* over to the basement over on Lexington. Unc called Vah letting her in on the situation and to meet them in the basement.

Vah got up fast and got dressed. She told Seasonn she did not want her to be a part of what was going down and how cruel they can be in torturing a motherfucker.

"I respect that, baby," Seasonn said.

Vah kissed her so softly and was out. She could not believe that the incident happened not to far from her crib. She couldn't wait to see these clowns who tried to take out her dawgs. She wanted to know who the hell' sent someone after Jaia and Unc. She knew the time had come to pay the piper. She wondered who the hell the motherfucker was and knowing that they all have been getting paid lovely. All she could think of was that somebody wants in and whoever it is, somebody is about to get got. She knew it could be anybody and that they could trust no one. As she drove she was thinking about so much and it was getting her vexed at the whole situation.

Vah arrived at the basement within twenty minutes. As she was going down the stairs, all she heard was a crying sound and humming. Then she heard Jaia.

"Yo nigga, who is it that put you on to us? What is your name money? Come on say summin' boy. You and Lee had a whole lot of say before nigga."

Unc walks over to him with a lit cigarette and sticks it on his neck.

"Now I'ma ask ya *ass* one more boy, why were you put on to us, for who and what's ya fuckin' name nigga."

He is in pain screaming, "Yo ya'll bitches is outta the ordinary. I was paid by this broad. She did not give me no name. I didn't even see her face, but said to make sure one of ya'll was killed; said she'd give me the other half of the 50 G's after the job is done. That's all, I swear."

The dude was scared to death. He knew his life was over either way. He did not deliver, except for himself into their hands. They had his *ass* hanging from a pipe, butt ass naked. Vah had an extension cord; she walked over to the guy and began beating his legs and hitting his penis. At one point she struck him continuously and he hollered like she was his momma.

He pleaded yelling, "Please stop. I'll tell you whatever you want to know. No more, please."

Vah kept on beating his ass.

She told him, "Talk nigga, talk. I'm not stopping unless you mention a name motherfucker. If not, I'ma beat your skin off your *ass*."

She continued whipping the shit out of his natural born ass. He was screaming helplessly.

"A'ight a'ight stop yo stop, listen I know I heard her boy calling her name. It was Sheila. That's it, that is all I know. True dat, word. Ouch, oh shit, dam, ouch, 000h I'm hurting bad. Ya'll please do not hit me no more with that extension cord."

Jaia declared, "Nigga I'm next whipping ya natural ass bitch. You know some shit boy, I can feel it. Ya ass is definitely gettin' ready for another motherfuckin' ass whipping. Ha ha ha ha ahhh, so come on out with it boyee, ya heard."

She began beating his feet. HE was in agony.

"Oh lord," he yelled after she whacked his feet again, light 000h ahhh, shit there is this dude they mentioned. His name is Milo, He's suppose to be taking ya'll off the count." Vah stated, "Say what? You got to be shitting me nigga."

"What gives, Sheila and her crew are on some get back. What the situation is, I honestly do not have the answer, for real yo."

"Well," said Unc, "I do"

She shot that motherfucker up. All he was doing was babbling on trying to prolong his life.

"Uh uh, I'm not in the mood, ya feel me dawg."

Vah wanted to know who Sheila and Milo were and what they want with T.L.C. and why?

"Yo peeps gunning for our *asses* and we don't even know who the fuck they are or what they want with us. Maybe it's that Smiley shit, ya think?"

"Nah."

Jaia remembered that nigga Black.

"Remember that nigga Black and how ya crazy ass killed him. Dawg, that could be retaliation bitch, ya heard."

"You got a great memory when it comes to your shit all the time Jaia. That's my dawg. So let's get T.Dove and Nubian to clean this piece of shit up outta here and let 'em know the delio, a'ight."

CHAPTER THIRTY-ONE

NOW THAT THEY'RE ALL TOGETHER again, they decided to go see Labu. She was staying over at the South Main Street crib where they'd let her stay for a couple of days. Labu was happier than a motherfucker to see them. When they arrived suggested they all go out for a while.

"Fuck it ya'll let's go to DiCarlo's, the strip joint or would ya like to go to Shenenigan's up in Schnectady," Jaia asked them.

"Yeah I do," Vah yelled, "and let's go get my baby so we can flirt while the dancers or strippers shall I say, think about tipping us fly ass bitches for watching them do their thang."

Unc hollered, "I know that's right. Booya-ya!"

Vah called her boo telling her to be ready and outside so she can swoop her gorgeous ass up off her feet, so they can have an adventurous evening.

Seasonn responded, "Baby you're talking right up my alley. Maybe if it's a nice place I can buy it or at least invest if their management is on the fucked up side of the game, ya feelin' me baby?"

"Yes I am. Okay love, see ya in a minute, a'ight."

When they arrive to pick up Labu, she felt kind of guilty since she'd explained the Nubian situation. Even though they did not hassle her about it. It was because she felt bad about not telling them about Coco also, which she just wanted to prove her love to Aunya when she comes home.

Jaia called to Labu, "Girl we 'bout to go have a ball, all of us fly ass hoochies. Yeah Vah and Unc too. the manly hoochies."

Vah was like "Yo Jaia shut the hell up a'ight. Oh yeah Labu this is my number one baby Seasonn. We all family, ya feel me Sis? You gonna be okay. Now let's go see some titties flapping, ass clapping and pussy yapping."

Everybody laughed so hard at Vah's last remark. Then they went on to enjoy their eventful night ahead. First they stopped off at this Italian restaurant to get their grub on. It definitely got the night off to a nice start. Labu was riding in the back listening to Jaia and Unc play around with each other.

Jaia says to Labu, "Yo you a'ight back there? I know you miss my dawg. I do too. You saw her last about a month ago right? You should be good cause she'll be home soon hanging, ya feel me, then you'll got tired of her."

Unc tells Jaia, "Baby please with that weak shit you yapping about. We been seeing each other about a year, but it's funny because you have your house as I do mine and we're still always togther. I am always at your crib, so who gets tired of who boo? Yeah I thought so. Pay that shot she just said no mind Labu. True dat, girl. Jaia's not going anywhere, nor am I. I love her crazy ass too much, ya heard. I bet you feel the same about Aunya, huh? I am looking forward to meeting her, her and my boo and Vah are definitely T.L.C. fo sho."

Jaia intervened and told Labu, "Has Aunya ever explained to you why she's doing time?"

Labu replied, "Yes she did. It's over though cause my wifey comin' home in a coupla weeks, ya heard. Oh yeah, which reminds me where will we be throwing her welcome home party? We all need to get together to discuss it. Maybe we can have a motherfucking chingding, huh?"

Everyone including Labu shouted, "Hell yeah!"

Labu got so excited talking about it. she could not wait and her pussy got wet just thinking about Aunya coming home. She went in a trance with her thoughts.

Unc was calling Labu's name, "Yo babygirl, snap the hell out of it a'ight. Where is ya mind? Back in prison with Aunya, huh? It's almost over babygirl. She'll be here with ya ass soon. Come on now, we're here at Shenenigan's. Let's roll up in this piece and walk through for a minute."

Jaia had on her regular Baby Phat jeans, as did Seasonn. They were not dressed to impress, they just looked like a bunch of feminine dyke's. Pretty ones at that, coming to get their freak on. You could see that is what the men were thinking as they entered the club.

"Whoa it's really packed in here, huh Vah," Seasonn nudged her.

"Yeah baby, it is."

All heads turned in their direction as they headed straight for the bar. Everyone smiled as they sat down. The waitress came over and asked what they were drinking. All of them ordered. As the night went on a couple of the men made comments but none where they felt they'd have to shoot them. They entire evening was enjoyable. Labu kept feeling as if she was being stared at. She happened to catch the eye of this one particular man.

'Damn he looks familiar. I've seen him before. He looks like this C.O. I knew from Albion. Hell all of them look alike. Once you've seen them motherfuckers everyday for seven years. Yo, it's crazy,' she thought.

She continued having fun and not letting that ruin the night. If she did know him, she'll remember him sooner or later.

Detective Gadson was sitting directly across from Labu, Jaia and all of them. He only remembers Labu from when he shot Nubian that morning. He is wondering if she remembers him. He kept staring at her and could see she is looking his way and is not sure who he is. He sees her just shrugging it off by the way she's looking at him. He's contemplating following her when she leaves and is in disbelief that he found her in a strip joint.

He's thinking, 'Isn't this a motherfucker; she must be some sort of dyke.'

Detective Gadson decided to call Da-Stev and let him know he's found the witness. He's sure she won't be able to identify him Because he's sitting here right in her face and she can't tell who he is.

He dialed Da-Stev.

Da-Stev answered, "Yell-o speak."

"It's me Gadson. You will not believe this shit. I found.

"Who?"

"The girl."

"What girl?"

"From the shooting incident with Nubain."

"Oh shit, ya shitting me. Where the fuck at Gadson?"

"Over here in Schnectady at Shenanigan's strip joint."

"Get the fuck outta here. Are you serious?"

"Hell yeah man. She is with these other chicks. They all look like a bunch of fuckin' dyke's. You know something though, they're all pretty. What the fuck, a man can't enjoy strip joints anymore.- Hell, they look prettier than these crack heads and dope fiend bitches on stage, got dam. The ones that aren't doped up look stressed the fuck out or abused physically man. She is here with some pretty decent looking women.

Anyway, it seems she doesn't remember me Da-Stev. I am sitting righh across from her and she doesn't recognize me. I'm thinking about following her, but there is no need man, at least that's what I'm feeling because she really looks like she's never seen me before."

"And what is that look?" Da-Stev asked.

"Well, she looks right past me."

"A'ight Gadson that's all on you, but if she does you, just remember white boy; you don't know me. Is that understood?"

"Yo Da-Stev, I got this buddy. See ya later."

"Yeah thanks for calling and keeping me informed."

Labu know who he was. She just played it off so he would not approach her. She knew if he did Jaia and 'em would start shooting up the place. Now that she actually had a good, decent look at him she realized who he was. She decided to take out her cellie and try to get a picture of him. As soon as she took it out she was able to snap a picture. She played it off by telling everyone the girls looked too good not to remember, so she was snapping a couple shots of them. She said she couldn't help it, at which time the bouncer came over and told her to put the cell phone away. She had already took the picture she really wanted, of Detective Gadson, so she put it right away. She hoped that Gadson had not caught her when she took the picture.

It didn't take Labu long to realize who he was after she first saw him. She got back into the swing of the atmosphere hanging with her boos' family. She felt honored that they thought enough of her to come get her to be in their presence. Unc was throwing dollar bills up on the stage with Jaia telling her that is all she better be throwing to them bitches. Vah and Seasonn were enjoying throwing their dollar bill together and telling each other who to give or throw their dollars to. Labu did not bother, she just participated in the excitement of being a part of Aunya's family and it being something fun. She really thought it was funny how all the perverts up in Shenanigan's were staring at them more than the strippers. It felt weird to Labu, but they all went on with their shenanigans up in Shenanigan's for a couple more hours.

"Is anyone ready to hit the road jack?, Seasonn asked.

Everyone replied, "Yes ma'am.

Jaia told Unc, "I know you ready, right boo?"

Vah said, "And if she isn't, what'll you do make her be ready? Yo Unc, you need to let her know who is in charge in your relationship nigga, and the motherfuckin' boss, ya feel me?"

Vah winks at Seasonn and whispers, "Watch this."

Vah continues aloud, "So Unc, who's the boss in your relationship?"

Jaia interrupts, "Unc don't listen to Vah's black ass. She'll have ya ass choked the fuck up, up here in Shenanigan's. I'd leave ya ass in a heartbeat."

Vah keeps on, "Unc you gonna let her control shit just like that man? You got to be kidding nigga."

"That's just it Vah, I'm not playing with you when it comes to my boo."

Jaia yelled, "That's my baby. Sure ya right."

Everybody got their gear together and left nice tips on the table with empty bottles of Moet, Cristal and Heinekens. As they were walking out Jaia caught the way Detective Gadson was staring at Labu.

She said to him, "Excuse me with your. Jordache look, do you know her from somewhere, cause you damn sure act like she's blinding you or summin' summin'."

"Oh I'm sorry, I just got caught in a zone cause she reminds me of my daughter. I kinda started missing her," Detective Gadson responded.

"Well I suggest you hurry home, after looking at all this good ass and pussy. You hurry home to tuck her in daddy," said Jaia laughing.

He did not find that amusing at all. It pissed him off. He wanted to slap the fire out of Jaia's ass.

"Smart mouth bitch," he turned back toward the show.

Jaia told everyone that they should chill over at the crib with Labu. Everyone agreed.

"There's enough room if it's okay with Labu," stated Jaia.

"I'm all for the company," she blurted out.

"All right, the night is set," declared Jaia.

Everyone was cozy in the living room checking out the alcohol in the china cabinet making sure there was soda and juice.

Here we are, all of us. We're family to each other."

Seasonn was thinking to herself how beautiful it all is and how much she loves them all. She decided to break the news to them about why she's been in Albany so frequently. She then asked for their attention as she made sure they all had a drink in their hands.

"Listen up everybody. My reason for coming to Albany so much..."

She paused and told Vah to come over to her so she could hold her hand. Then she continued her speech.

"...what I wanna say is guess what I've bought?"

Everyone was saying at once, "What Seasonn? Come on with it now girl."

"Yeah baby, spill it yo," Vah stated.

"A'ight, here it go. I've just bought a store front and I'm renovating it into a strip joint."

"Oh shit, oh fuckin' shit yo," they all said to her.

She said, "Yes, so I can be closer to Vah. I lover her, fo sho. Also check it, we can have a big nice welcome home party for Aunya if you guys like. It's all on me. I'll hook it all up for Shock Calla Balla to come so you all know who's in the game. That is competition, ya heard. So we, nah, I mean you guys will be on point about some of these knuckleheads. I'm acquainted with them through my businesses. There's some cut throats out there you guys and I know enough info on who's who okay, so talk to me."

Vah was stunned at how Seasonn was in describing the business she's into. There's really more danger, as well as doing her shit. She knew from what she said about her new found business that Seasonn is a bad bitch and the best part is she's all hers. She realized what a blessing it is to have her and was thinking how they click like a seat belt.

She said softly, "I love that woman. It's all good."

She snapped out of her thoughtrs to everyone taking about Aunya's homecoming.

"is it possible to have Aunya's welcome home party in the club?"

"is it all right with you Labu? She's your boo, so let's get to cracka-lackin' on that," Unc laughed.

Seasonn asked for any ideas for the name of the club. She told everyone to put on their thinking caps, like it takes a rocket scientist to name a strip joint.

"We do have a worry about getting the system in there and the stage. I want some cages and shit/ Nigga's are gonna crawlin' up the wall for the bitches I'ma have up in the club. They have to be finer than us to make any kind of money to match what we will be putting out for a show. I know all the good looking strippers put together will never amount to my good looking self, though."

"Yeah I know that shit is right, yo. We are all too good to be looking like getting on some stage. Only for our loved one maybe." Everyone said in unison.

Jaia let it be known, "huh, not me unless I am scheming to kill a baller, shot caller in the game cause sooner or later one of 'em gonna play themselves. Shit gonna get hot like a motherfucker, ya feel me. Only reason a nigga wanna flex his ego is because we're female, ya heard. We gonna have to let 'em feel the powers behind our empire.

Seasonn if I may ask, can we all be partners in this establishment? Then we can all make money. As a matter of fact, more money among us?" Labu is amazed at how they all just put a plan intact to make it work. She realizes she has become a part of it and knows how fortunate she is. She feels dedicated to Aunya and her dawgs, all of them. She is feeling really good and smiles at the thought of what a nice week it has been so far.

CHAPTER THIRTY-TWO

NATALIE THOUGHT HARD ABOUT THE last time she saw Ms. Smiley. She hooked into some information saying Milo was out for revenge. It was connected to the death of Ms. Smiley because some peeps she knew got at her about it. She recalled the name vaguely and the face and all she had to do is see his ass once. Also, some other connection mentioned the Silver Fox, so now her antennas were up for sure.

She knew Jaia and 'em have a storm to get through with the drug syndicate. What they don't realize is Jaia and 'em had nothing to do with the murder, so she has to put the message out there to let everyone know who wants to get at TLC to fuck off royally. She knew she had to load up on her ammunition baby sitting her girls. She knew shit was getting ready to get hectic and as long as she is living she does not give a fuck when it comes to Jaia. She respected her father Manuel too much, knowing she is his daughter. Natalie was going for her props so she definitely has to get to the streets. She had to see Jaia and 'em anyway about the cocaine she's about to give them. It was from Ms. Smiley's stash house where that nigga was fucking homeboy in his ass. She knew that nigga was packing big time. It kind of turned Natalie on seeing him enjoying some shit like that so much. He really reeled in on that dude's *ass.* Thinking about it she knew she'd hated to bump into him in an alley. She also realized it had been several weeks since she heard from Jaia and 'em, so she decided to give them a call.

"Yell-o talk to me," answered Jaia.

"What up Queen Bee, it's Natalie. I thought I'd give ya a call Missy, being it's been a while. What's good Jaia, yo what up ya bad ass bitch?"

"It's nice of you to call Natalie. I had just spoke to my boo about contacting you soon, so you beat me to the punch. What do I owe this pleasure? Oh before you begin Nat check it. My road dawg is getting outta prison in a couple weeks. We're having a welcome home party in her honor at Vah's girl Seasonns' new club she just purchased. It's a strip joint. You know we all on lickety clit atmosphere, so no disrespect to ya, a'ight. Your *ass* is more than welcome to attend bitch. As a matter of fact I'ma need ya ass there. It that cool wit ya Nat? Bring some of ya peeps a'ight? The more the merrier. And if all the pussy and ass is a bother, I'll get some dick up in the joint for ya, ya heard Nat?"

"I'm with that," Natalie replied, "on the real Nat I need to get at ya 'bout some ole money making shit you'll see fit, a'ight. Yo Jaia, A.S.A.P. on that. It's all good and let me know if you need anything. I just got a new shipment. I have something especially for you girl. It's right up ya alley boo. It'll sho nuff make you shine inside fo sho Jaia. So what it look like huh? Can you make it happen as far as when we can hold it down or what?"

"A'ight bust it. I'ma be out in a half hour. Yo Nat is it okay if I bring my peeps, partner in crime as in significant other? She is down for the cause all the way. Then if I can't then she can, ya feel me? Yo Nat let me ask ya summin. Nah better yet I'll wait until I see you yo. A'ight later. Holla back.

Jaia was wondering what it is Nat could possibly want as far as making money. She thought that white bitch was doing her thing selling her guns. She knew she had something she'd like as in a gun. She probably got a hold of the Mother of Pearl chrome plated forty-five. It's awesome and if she has it Jaia wants it.

"It's on. I'ma hit Nat off lovely. I know that's what she's talking about. My nigga white and nice," she said aloud.

Jaia told Unc she'd like her to ride with her over to Natalie's. Unc agreed although she just came in the door from checking the spots with Vah.

"Anything for you love, you know that, but at least let me get a whiff of my boo's canteen," she replied to Jaia.

Jaia started laughing.

"Unc you always got some ole cute shit to say when it comes to trying to get at me coochie boo, huh?"

"Ya damn right Jaia. It's mine ain't it? As long as I want to kiss it or lick it or choose to stick it and satisfy it completely with no complaints; you should oblige boo boo. Daddy doo needs to be submissive to you sexual healing girl. Now come over here and let me tongue kiss your clit. I wanna show you summin Jaia."

"Boo stop playing. If I let you tongue kiss my clit; you are going to make me cum, huh? I believe so Unc, I feel you honey. Yes I'm all yours."

Jaia took off her sweats and Unc placed her head in between Jaia's legs. She propped her right leg on the ottoman so Unc could get all up in her pussy. Unc was licking and kissing it. Her tongue was warm, wet and slippery. She was sucking Jaia's clit softly. Jaia was motioning her head as it was bobbing on her clit.

"Damn this is good Unc. Yeah come on baby, make me cum. Show me, show me."

Jaia kept saying she really needed to bust this nut in a minute. She was smiling licking her lips at Unc, feeling her clit ready to explode at the drop of a dime. She could not believe it.

She whispered, "Like that ma, yeah like that ma."

She continued to motion Unc's head and it got good as she began to cum so smoothly.

"She sighed, "Ahhh baby! Okay let's go on over to Nat's and see what ole girl is trying to get at whoa. Unc baby you drive; I'll direct you okay honey? Go wipe ya face first with my cum all over it like it's a face mask or summin. Come on, hurry babe."

"Now boo you know your cum juices are a facial for me babe. Why do you think my skin looks so silky with a sheen love, cause it's my boo's extra special cum cum."

Jaia laughed her ass off.

"Bitch you crazy, but you mine. I'm loving it too, but I know one thing fo sho; you dam sure better let the next one know and that's for real Unc. Your fine sly ass is mine 'til death do us part, way apart as in six feet under, ya feel me unc."

"Yeah Jaia, I'm in love with ya gal, can't ya tell. So I advise you to let the next motherfucker know and I mean both of them. Do you feel me? Now that we got those feelings out of the way, come on babe. I'll be starting the Navi up while you get your ass on a timer a'ight, so we can jet over to your home girl Nat's place. Damn, come on now Jaia!"

"Unc didn't you say you were going out to the car? now go the hell on. Shit I'm coming baby, okay?"

Unc's playing the rap music all loud in Jaia's Navigator bobbing to the beat smiling, staring at Jaia as she gets in the Navigator. She pulls out and heads toward the highway and down Wolf Road, off of Sand Creek wondering what it is Nat has for her babe. She's thinking it better be good after what she just put on her boo and had to stop getting Jaia's juices all on her face. Just thinking about it made her shake and get a chill. She smiled looking over at Jaia, then gave her a kiss at the stop sign.

"Ahh thank you honey," Jaia said, "Yo Unc I wonder what is the delio with Nat, huh?"

"We'll soon find out boo. If anything the bitch Nat is gonna come correct. I don't give a fuck what it is, ya heard?" replied Unc.

* * *

Damian's life in Albany became a life of leisure and he had a pure commitment to T.L.C. They were his new found family. His trips to New York City for visiting became business trips as we. He'd go down to see his baby mama in Harlem and could not wait to get the hell away from her to return to Albany to continue his protection with Jaia and 'em. T.Dove had become his right hand partner in crime. He saw that T.Dove was one crazy torturing motherfucker. He witnessed one of T.Dovels outbreaks on L&O. Damian actually felt sorry for the dude and his woman Vanessa. He had slapped the shit out of Vanessa. She was a nice red bone lady and looked good. T.Dove complimented her hair style and she responded with a sly ass remark insinuating T.Dove was some bum ass nigga. He called her out.

"You chicken neck bitch. I oughta kick you square up in your *ass,* ya stinking looking hoe."

He slapped her and her man came storming up to T.Dove. As soon as he got within reach, he knocked that nigga out for the count.

Damian yelled, "Oh shit my nig, oh shit my nig. Yo T.Dove boyee, you good nigga."

Vanessa attended to her man.

"Wake up babe, babe wake up, come on Ned. Ned, Ned, Ned, git the fuck up. I can't believe you didn't see that shit comin'. Ya ass is usually on point. I guess some are quicker than you Ned. He got ya ass good baby, so let's get up and get the hell up outta here."

T.Dove looked at Vanessa.

"Listen bitch I need my dick sucked and you look as if you can handle my shit. It's made for your throat, so I don't give a fuck about ya man Ned here. Now let's roll before I knock ya ass out too, ya disrespectful bitch. Come on, leave his ass right there unless you want a bullet with his name on it. It'll be a gift," T.Dove said to her.

From then on Damian knew T.Dove wasn't playing with a full deck at all.

CHAPTER THIRTY-THREE

AUNYA'S HEART BEAT PROFUSELY EVERY time it gets one day closer to going home. Albion has some bullshit going on up in it twenty-four seven. As long as she is not a part of the sick demented crap that she sees and hears, she does not give a fuck. Aunya's in her cube listening to them bitches in the cube next to her eating pussy. They know they can't let out the good sexual feeling of moaning and groaning with the officer up in the bubble. Even if he doesn't give a fuck of paying it any mind as he believes we think. It's all a bunch of bullshit especially if you let him watch. If the sergeant or lieutenant or even the superintendent make rounds all shit will be shut down. As a result you learn to lick, slurp and suck and eating pussy quickie quickie. It becomes the norm. If you do **A** become a part of you will not be slowly sucking and eating in a satisfying real cumming order. When you do all hell will break loose at any given time.

The bitches obsessed and jealous over any other bitch. Even if you're looking at a woman who passes you everyday for however long you're sentenced; shit gets fucking crazy.

Aunya began thinking aloud, "Damn I got a couple more weeks."

She wondered what ever happened to the bitch that got stomped so badly. They took her to SHU. She couldn't remember her, but she'd never forget her. Then she met this one female who had just gotten out of SHU from doing two years in there. Every little noise bothered her and she ended up going right back for tearing this ladies' ass up with a can top. That bitch had about fifteen cuts all over her body. Blood everywhere. They shut the dorm down and put it on lock down until the next day. Some of the officers got with some of Aunya's associates who in turn use to get her cologne. The good shit, Calvin Klein, Burberry and Black Polo. So Aunya's stay had its' good, bad and ugly days. All it took was some good conversation with the male officers because their country bumpkin asses don't have anything exciting going on except these women from all over New York State. They get to be in control aside from their crunch and munch bitches whom they're tired of. They can't go no where so they let the women in prison take them on sexual excursions, something their own hoes know nothing about. This is some real barn yard shit in Albion. These motherfuckers chew tabacco and have all kinds of crazy ass tattoos. These upstate region rednecks will put some fire up in a females ass.

Aunya knows a lot about the corruption going on so the officers do not mess with her. She has information of them they don't even know she has. She passed it on to the other officers who know each others dirt. The other officers look out for her to make sure nothing happens to her. She even had a lieutenant in her pocket in case anything was to get really fucked up. The lieutenant is connected to Jaia's people on the outside. That is why Jaia is untouchable in Albion among all fifteen hundred women there. No inmates were aware of her business not even Labu.

Recently she heard a couple of females who just came in from the streets talking about the drama in the hood which involved her peeps. She remembered Nubian from Jaia telling her about him taking care of L&O when she got knocked. This one female got caught up in a gang banging shooting about a year ago involving a dude named Boone's. Child Protective Services came and took her son she had by a nigga named T.J. He was killed by Boone's. She realized that it's been a menace in the hood. She heard so much about the streets while she's been incarcerated. Prison is just the street behind bars is all and your ass cannot face shit physically. All is known through the grapevine in any penitentiary. That in itself is a true story in life.

All she was feeling right now was the beauty of freedom and the day she walks out of prison. She promised herself she will not return. Only in death is her motto. There is one officer she has had the hots for since being in Albion. She made all kinds of play for her. She did take to Aunya and reciprocated with a kiss. Aunya tongued her down. where they were.

"Whew! That was a beautiful kiss."

It was all they could say once their tongue's were out of each others mouths.

Aunya told the officer, "Too bad you're married. I'd sho nuff wait for you to come home everyday, but see what you and I do can't go hand in hand, so we can only leave this little situation where it's at babe and that is between you, me and God."

They both were agreeable.

As days went on the officer caught feelings toward Aunya. She had to respect her so she changed her bid so she wouldn't have to see her as much.

If Labu found out anything about that shit she probably would end up back in prison, so Aunya knew not to play herself too close. She feels Labu has a mean streak in her gorgeous ass. It's what attracted her to Labu, her aggressive attitude.

Aunya knows she's in love for real and is a lesbian whose love is dedicated, so Labu is stuck like chuck.

Aunya began thinking beyond Labu about Jaia and 'em. She noticed they hadn't mentioned Da-Stev. She recalled hearing some rumors about Nubian being shot. She thought maybe they felt they didnt' want to involve her too much in their activities because of her being incarcerated and their over protective ways. So far doing time has been a breeze. She has no need to complain. Finding out about Coco being dead was a bummer and she would like to know who could've done the honors. She feels it was Vah and the others, but they aren't saying. She's thankful to God for being in prison because of when the robo cops come to inform her and question her. as if she had literally killed her. She was scared to death thinking the homicide detectives were re-arresting her.

She remembered how her throat got dry and hands got sweaty. If she hadn't known any better she would've wet her panties. She kept kept her cool knowing she was inside at the time of her death.

She told them flat out, "Listen, I had no idea that bitch was dead. Why the fuck are ya'll in here questioning me? You should be out there finding out who wanted her snitching ass dead. Yeah, Ms. Coco got got. Isn't that pitiful? Well fellas, it wasn't me!"

Aunya laid it on them hard. They were gilling here as if they wanted to kick her smart mouth ass. They weren't hearing shit she said. They insisted she had something to do with it. Coco had assured them before that Aunya and her dawgs were drug dealers and cold-hearted. After the bullshit interrogation they came to the conclusion they couldn't connect Aunya or her dawgs to Coco's murder.

"We'll be keeping an eye on your dyke ass once you're released. We know your crew are making a name for themselves in Albany and all around the upstate regional area. So, if you know what's good for yourself then stay as far away form them as possible."

"They're not felons or ex-con's and don't even have a police record. They're the only family I've ever known, we're all as one. Here the two of you crackers are wanting me to confess to a fucking murder. I have no idea about that and on the other hand I am in prison for slicing that dead bitches' face. Obviously I don't give a flying fuck. Now I am dismissing myself unless you have another type of crime to re-arrest me for or pin on me."

Aunya then removed herself from the office where they questioned her. As she headed toward her housing area and was walking through the sally port, Lt. Benson asked her if everything was okay. She explained everything to her so she could let her peeps know. Lt. Benson was the shit. A fine ass bitch and down by law. She is a black ass redneck and will fuck someone up in a heart beat. She talks all that smart ass ebonic talk. So no one better come at her like she don't know shit. She's been doing this type of work for twenty plus years. She's a cock diesel lady, but very feminine and very pretty. She runs around Albion with a fine tooth comb on her shift. The white male officers do not care for her, but know they better show a black sister some respect. She's earned it and eats it up when it comes to the male officers. She knows some of her officers are corrupt, abusive, racist and they know she better not catch them, although she has dirt on quite a few of them. She knows they're having sex with the female inmates and most of them are married. That was the kicker in her analogy. She did not become lieutenant being a goodie two shoes having to deal with the fucking crackers. In the process they made it hard for a sistah. She laid something on her superiors. Her position was waiting for her although she never thought she'd get transfered to a women's facility. In the long run they'd kept their word. Soon she'll be able to retire and will be hooking up with Jaia and 'em. Through the grapevine she got hooked up with them. Aunya hadn't even known she had eyes on her all the time. She just found out on her way out the gate. She had to make sure she didn't mess up with a short and shitty attitude just for Lt. Benson.

The Lt. had to help Aunya on her way out of prison, knowing Jaia and 'em were waiting patiently to throw her a big bash to welcome her home, the whole shabang. Although she could care less, she was doing Da-Stev a favor. They been aquainted since way back in the day. She still kind of has the hots for him. If it weren't for inmate Mirayes she would have never known Da-Stev existed anymore so she was a blessing. This time she's not letting him get away from her. Her nipples get hard just thinking about his fine hood rat looking self. The thug shit turns her on.

Little does Lt. Benson know Da-Stev is now married. She has plans for him, but she doesn't know he has a thing for Jaia. He is getting to know her intimately, being loyal and gaining her trust. Forget the undercover shit, they're making money. Lt. Benson has no idea and her mind is going in all sorts of directions with no idea what's really going on. She is planning what she is going to do when she retires in a couple of months. The thought of it all is wonderful for her. She is excited about being able to keep a closer eye on Da-Stev.

CHAPTER THIRTY-FOUR

Meanwhile Detective Reese had been prowling the neighborhood for informants who'd know anything about what Da-Stev and Gadson are up to. So far he could not come up with anything which made him more determined than ever to get information. He was kind of upset that these two motherfuckers would leave him out of anything that jumps off in his perimeter.

"What the fuck is the police department coming to? We're all pretty much corrupt and now this Silver Fox character is intervening. Something is not right at all and I'm aiming to find out," He thought aloud.

He continued, "I'll be damned if shit is going to happen again and I'm not aware of it. Somebody is getting their *ass* blown away fucking around on my turf with my bread and butter. It ain't no joke so these two kats better get off the piss pot because I'm getting ready to get shit on all of them. Sneaky bastards gonna do some crazy ass shit getting shot."

Detective Reese decided to call Da-Stev.

"Yo little nigga, I need to talk with ya ass and I mean quick fast and in a hurry yo. It's about the Nubian shooting so pronto ya ass on over to the Elbow Room bar. Understand. No if, ands or buts, over there now, ya heard."

"What the fuck ya *ass* all riled up about, ya mangy motherfucker. Detective Reese, what it is yo? Ya dick stuck on Jaia and 'em yo? A'ight I'ma meet ya *ass* over at the Elbow. Chill the fuck out. Whatever it is ya ass spitting out about Nubian. Honky tonk better be worth my time white nigga, ya feel me yo? I'm out."

Da-Stev hurried and called Detective Gadson.

"Yo man the ole geezer Detective Reese just called and wants to relay some information about Nubian being shot. I have no idea what that motherfucker is up to Gadson, but we may have to take his *ass* off the count. If his ass gives any indication he's on to us it's a wrap on his fucking pension, ya heard," Da-Stev explained.

He continued meet at the Elbow Room on Delaware Ave. a'ight. lma hit ya up on the cellie if his information is crucial. I'll just call you once our conversation is done, then maybe he can have some sort of accident on the way out of the bar. You know what I mean? Get rid of the motherfucker point blank Gadson. Maybe you'll be successful this time. If it weren't for the sloppy mess with Nubian we wouldn't be under surveillance asshole. Straighten all this bullshit out. Take his nosey ass out, ya feel me and do it right this time."

Meanwhile Detective Reese was sitting at the bar in the Elbow Room thinking of how he's going to approach the situation with Da-Stev. He knew he had a death sentence once he told Da-Stev he knew about Nubian being shot. He know he better prepare himself for a real live shoot out because Detective Gadson is not far behind. He most definitely needs a plan for making an exit and quick.

Just as Da-Stev entered, he saw the deviousness in his face.

"I gotta take this nigga out quick, but I don't think he's stupid enough to pull any shit in here so I know his buddy is waiting in the cut," he thought to himself.

Da-Stev said to Reese, "A'ight honky tell me what is on your mind concerning this Nubian shit and what your info entails that will haunt me. What gives?"

Detective Reese held on to his gun which was under his jacket, letting Da-Stev see him so if he was thinking about making any sudden moves he'd blow his ass away. He began telling Da-Stev the minute he figured everything out telling him if there is an all out war then it's time to face the music.

Da-Stev sat and actually took all Detective Reese's information in.

He said to him, "Listen ya dumb ass honky, if that is ya reason for thinking Detective Gadson shot Nubian then you got it all fucking wrong asshole. What do you care about a low life drug dealer killing our kids in the neighborhood? You cannot even protect them, but you get paid to do dirt. Kiss my ass Detective-Reese. Ya ass is just as foul as the shit that reeks our streets motherfucker."

He continued, "What the fuck are you really saying ya washed out piece of po-po. Like you came to terms with being some Captain out to save some drug dealing bitches. One of their own motherfucker. Ya need to go get ya mind right and retire honky."

He went on to remind Detective Reese how the job has worn him out. He told him how Nubian has been seeing Detective Gadson's daughter. Detective Gadson is very prejudiced and thinks the world of his daughter. It's her and him since his wife died. He would have a real serious issue with a nigga taking a black man out. To find out his daughter is getting served with some black dick and loving it and enjoying the lifestyle would eat him alive. Da-Stev knew that Detective Reese did not know about Gadson's daughter and Nubian so he gassed the situation up to the fullest.

Sort of shocked Reese says, "Well I'll be damned. Of all the college pussy flying around here in Albany, he ends up with Gadson's daughter, Andrea. Whoa, un-fuckin-belivable. No wonder he's losing his mind."

He warned him what a prejudiced, sadistic guy Gadson is. He believed Da-Stev was up to something with all that was taking place. he knew he had an idea of wanting to change a nigga to his liking. He didn't find the information credible concerning Gadson wanting Nubian killed. He didn't buy that crap by a long shot.

Reese said to him, "You need to tell that asshole to back off. It's not that serious and he needs to back off with his personal family affair shit on these streets. And another thing, if I walk out this door and there's some shit waiting on the other side, then I know my suspicions are true about the both of you. So you need to make a call to ya boyee nigga, ya heard? How 'bout that Da-Stev?"

Detective Gadson was waiting patiently for Detective Reese to exit the Elbow Room so he could kill him. He was sick of Detective Reese's pitiful duty as a crooked cop, good cop gone bad bullshit. He's going to give Reese a bullet to die fo. He doesn't know what Da-Stev just informed him of, which Gadson doesn't have any idea about his daughter or that Da-Stev is undercover.

Da-Stev tapped a code into his cell phone letting Gadson know that it is not what they had planned. If Reese had suspicions about him playing them both, so he could believe in having his way with ole sexy ass, beautiful Jaia. That's all he cared about in his heart. Suddenly he heard a couple shots outside the bar and thought Gadson got his code late, and killed Reese.

"Oh shit!"

He rushed out as fast as he could and saw some young kids playing with chery bombs and fire crackers in the air. He could not believe his ears. The young boys were no more than twelve or thirteen years old.

Detective Gadson caught their *asses* and threw them up against the squad car with pleasure. Gadson wanted the opportunity to bust the young nigga's, especially since Da-Stev sent him the message about their mission with Detective Reese. He had a field day arresting them. the onlookers and citizens were yelling.

"Lock their young black asses up. Them little dumb motherfuckers. Maybe they'll get some education being in prison."

One old white man who recognized the boy told Gadson that he was the one who had slapped him two weeks ago. He was walking down Delaware Street with his wife Ava, who is black. the boy told the man, "Yo whitey go with your own kind. Isn't it bad enough ya'll white motherfuckers had us as slaves bitch."

The boy then stepped off with his gang of boys laughing and telling them how he pimp slapped the man. The man told Gadson, "So I guess I get the last laugh now. Little bastards, why don't they want to better themselves for unity and a positive life for themsleves."

Gadson responded, "Sir, your name is?"

"Kenny," the old man replied.

"Would you like to press charges on this little nigga?"

Kenny said to the him, "Officer, that is not appropriate language. It's racist, and no I do not. He'll learn his lesson from where he's going anyhow. Thank you officer, have a fine day."

Kenny then left the scene.

Detective Gadson called for the paddy wagon. He was thinking what a jerk the old man must be not to want to press charges and get these little gang bangers off the streets of Albany.

He thought to himself, "Damn I wonder why Da-Stev called off killing Detective Reese. He could not wait to be rid of him, so why?"

He let all the other officers on the scene know what happened and bounced. He headed for wherever Da-Stev wanted to hook up. Then he hit him up on his cellie.

Meanwhile, Detective Reese was so angry at the fact his notion was on point and they were trying to set him up to be killed.

"Isn't that a bitch," he thought, "them to scumbag bastards. Well, Da-Stev has an idea I'm hip to Jaia and 'em. Then the bullshit as far as Nubian. He's been a detective too long for all this brand new shit. They call themselves pullin' shit on an old timer like me. Pay back is a motherfucker."

He laughed and knew that they don't see it coming. He was fantasizing about his retirement and going to the Bahamas. He was going to go to Florida, but changed his mind to go where the good young pussy is at. He thought about the broken language he does not understand and some fine ass native would be sucking his dick inside her BA-HA-MA-MA mouth.

* * *

Jaia and Unc arrived at Natalie's.

Unc declared, "Straight up bitch, this better be better than what I was doing to my boo, ya feel me?"

Natalie responded, "Motherfucker I don't even want to go there with that ole freaky gay shit. Ya'll enjoy."

Everyone began laughing.

"So what's good?" Jaia said to Nat.

"Well I got some snow white a buyer traded for some guns. I thought you guys might want to get rid of it. Just give me what ya think is enough money, ya feel me." Nat went on, "Jaia I feel we cool like that. You can look at it as a down payment to fit in with you and your TLC Crew however you see fit. So holla at a bitch when it's right."

Unc cut in, "It's better than what ya nasty ass was doing nigga. Yo Nat you a funny bitch yo! I'ma let my boo answer that shit. It's tasty."

Unc laughed at the expression on Natalie's face.

Jaia yelled, "Stop fucking around Unc. And what do you think about what this queen bee white bitch talking 'bout. Come on Unc. Dam Natalie you got my baby cracking up yo."

Unc stopped laughing.

Unc asked, "Well how much snow white you got?"

Natalie looked over toward the sink.

Unc stated, "Oh shit Jaia, come look."

They both looked at each other and went to question it but thought better of it and sat down in the kitchen.

Unc said, "We'll run it by Vah and see what she says and we good, a'ight Natalie?"

"Take the shit with ya'll asses alright. I do not want that shit in here. Bad enough. I got these damn guns up in this motherfucking house, ya heard? Fo sho that is looking at a bid of about twenty years by itself."

Jaia interrupted, "Oh, so Natalie you've done some jail time before, huh?"

"Skid bids," Natalie replied, "not compared to what I'd be doing if I got caught with all this shit up in here. Now take that crap and get the fuck outta here and ya'll bitches call me when shit sounds right, okay? Always remember I got ya backs bitches, ya feel me, from the heart, not trying to sound all mushy and shit. I respect ya'll game and it's all bitches. That's rare. And ya'll are all fucking, licking and sucking pussy. Ain't that some shit."

Natalie was laughing so hard her stomach hurt. Then she led them out of her house feeling a part of something and it involves all women. She smiled and thought to herself that they, meaning them are going to the top. She had their backs. She's the babysitter, little do they know. She meant it with her life. She knew a lot of nigga's are going to die messing with her crew. She vowed it to be word on her own life. She knew she'd gain respect and be honored by Jaia's father. She realized Jaia does not know she's the daughter of an icon drug dealer whose empire is the Dominican Republic. He's a avocado eating yet-tay. She knew if anyone got a hold of her thoughts she'd be a dead white bitch.

"Yo let me get outta my head and get my grind on," she thought aloud.

Jaia and Unc were on their way back to Albany.

Unc asked Jaia, "Yo boo, what is it Natalie is seeking by giving us this stuff just like that? What's up with that? You think she wants in on our crew boo?"

"Baby she is one of our crew. That white bitch is bad and no joke. Whatever she got going on in her head for us, it's about protection, cause she has the ammunition."

She let Unc know that she is game with Natalie and she is on their level. She also told her to keep a close eye on her and to watch Jaia's pussy closer. She thought maybe Unc's suspicions of Natalie could be worth the thought. She laughed at the possibility. She recalled her teasing Unc and knew Unc would take that pussy in a minute. She loved when Unc would tear her shit up and with pleasure.

CHAPTER THIRTY-FIVE

AUNYA WAS SITTING IN HER cubicle feeling the effects of going home in a couple of days. She knew her dawgs done hooked a bitch up for her welcome home shabang. Labu, her boo is definitely giving her some of that twat once they're in the car. She doesn't even want to go too far without Labu not giving her some sweet loving that she so desires of her. She really misses Labu alot.

When she is finally home with Labu she's going to show her how she loves her with her all in all and in between because she is her true love and she is going to let her know it is real. She never loved a woman the way she does Labu. All her other relationships were abusive. They were all women who were jealous and possessive. Labu is really her first girl from prison.

She started thinking more about Labu being home without her and how much she loves her. Then Aunya's jealousy began kicking in and she knew if she finds out she's been messing with anyone since she's been home she's going to hurt her. She even had Jaia and'em keeping an eye on her and the reports have been good. She's been a good girl.

She knew her dawgs were also racking up the money and getting paid. They kept their word just like they said they would when they began on their grind. They held shit down since Aunya had been knocked. She wondered of her crew had her in the cut with the money they accumulated. She felt bad about doubting her crew in her thoughts especially knowing they took care of Coco. Since being in she's felt overwhelmed about the situation. She knew it was because of her that the Albany Police Department had their attention. Other than the dirty po-po her crew had in their pockets. She started feeling some type of way and had to shake the thought.

She then turned her thoughts and smiled at the fact she'll soon be home with her baby. She was excited about meeting Vah's new woman Seasonn. Her name rang some bells in the prison from the females who worked in her strip clubs. They said she is a bad ass bitch not to be fucked or reckoned with at all. Her game is tight is the word she heard. She never heard a fowl word about Seasonn and kept hearing how she is no joke. She was anxious to meet her sister-in-law. Word has it she's an awesome chick, but my bitch is better once she starts making her cheddar.

As Aunya fantasized and explored her upcoming freedom, she could taste the streets and getting back to L&O. She has a lot of plans and that kid Nubain has got to get to stepping. He's going to feel some wrath over her spots. She knew she had to inform Jaia and 'em about the name being raved about throughout the prison, which is Silver Fox. She heard about what Silver Fox is trying to do in their area where the money is being made. She knew shit was going down once she gets to the streets.

Finally she thought how happy she is knowing she is maxing out. Her shit is official. No reporting and all that goes with it. She has too much illegal shit to do anywany.

* * *

Da-Stev and Detective Gadson ended up meeting at Yana's over on Lexington Ave. Everyone in the hood already knew about Gadson and figured he was hasseling Da-Stev. If only they knew they were going over what happened with Detective Reese.

"Unbelievable," Da-Stev told Gadson, "it's not a good idea right now. Jaia and 'em are so suspicious because of the Nubian incident and Reese informed them. We gotta figure out another angle and quick yo. check it, if Jaia and'em are giving a welcome home bash for their crew member coming out of the joint, I know some names of who will be in that piece that night. One is the female you think saw you shoot ya boy Nubian. We can get rid of quite a few that night. Maybe we'll plant a nice welcome home bomb, ya heard. We'll see yo."

Gadson's dick got hard at the thought of having Nubian and Reese in the same place at the same time. Da-Stev was calling his name and noticed he was in a zone.

"Yo motherfucker what kind of shit ya *ass* thinking. Let me in on it."

The other people in the bar stared at the both of them. They were probably wondering if there was going to be a fight because of the sound of Da-Stev's voice. All of a sudden there was this big loud noise coming from a crowd of people outside the bar. It was this woman beating her daughter. She had run away from home. She was only thirteen years old and left home to be with a little bum ass nigga.

Da-Stev played it off with Detective Gadson and told him out loud in front of everyone in the bar.

"Go do ya fuckin' job po-po."

Gadson went out and jumped in front of the mother, showed his badge and the crowd dispersed calling him all kinds of cracker and other derogatory names.

Gadson could not wait to get out of there and called it in on dispatch. He told the girls' mother if he has to he will lock her up. She then went on her way with her daughter. You could hear her yelling at her as they walked off.

"I'll kill ya *ass* first before I'll let you think you can run these streets. I'll put ya ass away and you better not be pregnant bitch. If you are you're getting rid of it, ya little hot ass no good motherfucker. Hurry ya ass home."

Detective Gadson could not believe his eyes when he saw his daughter Maria in the car down on Lexington. As he left the scene, he got the shock of his life. As he stared, Nubian stared back. Nubian was wondering why this cop's look looks so hard. He figured maybe it's because he has a white chick in his car. Whatever it is, Nubian felt bad vibes about Gadson staring at him. He told Maria he was letting her off on Central Avenue and for her to get on the bus. He demanded her to do so right then. He didn't want anything to happen to her. He cares a lot about her, but not as much as Jaia. She's his one and only heart if ever a woman was. She's the only one, his gangster queen. He never gave up trying to see if he could get rid of Uncle Muff by having T.Dove handle her gay ass. Although, he'd like it even more if he could fuck both of them at the same time. It made his dick stiffen up to a tee. That's when he'd be ready to fuck Maria hard the way she liked it, doggie style, thinking about his fantasy. He'd have her hollering his name, pulling her hair like it's a leash around her neck.

He snapped out of his thoughts, he was feeling some type of way about the cop. He felt he should let Jaia and 'em know something is not right with this dude and ask them to check his credentials.

As Maria got on the bus she felt something wasn't right with her boo and knew it was something he had to straighten out quick. She left that thought and turned on her IPod and listened to the hip hop music heading home.

Gadson had to hurry home hoping all the way that the girl he saw with Nubian was not his daughter. It it was she had a whole lot of explaining to do. He thought maybe he was imagining things or just plain over worked. Also he had not been spending any time with her and thought it might be his guilt. He sure was getting ready to find out as soon as he gets home.

"Damn what if it's true. That would mean I've been trying to kill her motherfuckin nigga *ass* boyfriend. Ah shit. I don't wanna believe that crap. I'm going to have to wait until I speak with Maria."

He started thinking about what Da—Stev said about the homecoming gathering for the friend of TLC, Jaia and 'em's crew. He thought maybe he could kill two birds with one boom at the soiree.

He began laughing heading home to find out about his daughter hoping the information is not true. If it was he knew he'd have to kill her ass too. He'd be so furious if it's true.

Just the thought of his Maria with a drug dealing nigga.

"Oh hell no," he thought, "her bringing home a nigga grandbaby, talking 'bout 'what up gramps', ebonic talking fucking kid I don't think so. She better have a good reason why she was in his fucking car in the ghetto, if it was. I know it was," he kept saying to himself.

* * *

Jaia and 'em were all getting ready for their one and only dawg to step foot on their new empire from prison. They knew the shit is on once she is back on the scene. Vah, Labu and Jaia spoke of Aunya quite often to Seasonn. She could not wait to meet her. Although She'd seen pictures and thought Aunya to be very fine and handsome, as Uncle Muff is. She knew all these bitches are ride or die and was proud to be a part of it.

Vah said to Jaia, "Yo we gotta make sure all is secured for our welcome home bash for Aunya. You know nigga's gonna wanna get at us right? So let's be official and use the popo in our realm for some ole security shit, ya heard. Get Nubian, Damian, T.Dove and D. Them nigga's know the delio fo sho. We got a motherfucking banging crew."

Jaia replied. "Yo fuckin' ain't right."

Unc's like, "Yo who da fuck is holding our shit while we doing all this celebrating yo. Are we in the clear for a grandiose gala, ya feel me."

Vah spoke up, "Yo Unc everything is covered, trust and believe. We haven't come this far for years to let one night tear us down back to where we started. I do not think so bitch. Oh so you got it now Unc?"

They all started laughing. Jaia told Unc she's about to see them get their grind on when Aunya is aboard again.

"We all make a whole fucking extended family bitches. Hot, we are all no joke to be reckoned with. Labu I know ya ass is too hot in the pussy and running juices all over that vagina hoe."

"Shut up," Labu responded, "although you know that's right girl. I ain't frontin'. That's right my bitch is surfacing right here, all up in here and slap her hand all on her pussy, smiling like a damn cheesie kat. It's all good. Yes, I'ma get mines and ya'll bitches get to have her after she takes care of this here shit, a'ight bitches."

Labu laughed hard.

Seasonn told them about the strippers and how they need to be secured because when motherfuckers get their drink on shit goes haywire, even with the baller's. She told them how they're going to have some good clientele in the piece and they have to be on point.

"My shit is on fire and there is money to be made, ya heard bitches," Seasonn declared.

Vah's eyes captured Seasonn's and off they went telling Jaia and 'em they need to take care of personal business.

Unc said out loud, "Yo so if anything goes down, we're covered as far as cash, right ya'll? I just have this creepy feeling. Ya'll know how I get when we're on for the cause.

My mind starts racing and shit." As soon as everyone was in the strip joint enjoying themselves a big KABOOM went off...